Jinn

Written by Katica Howard

In loving memory of my grandfather, Howard Watts

Chapter One

Jinn City

Kesi

THE FIRST MOVEMENT of her Beginning Day was the slight fluttering of her eyelids before they opened wide, taking in the brilliant white light. It blinded her, causing her to squint her eyes as she struggled to adjust. As she did, her other senses started to come forth as her mind joined with her physical genie form. She felt the grass beneath her, prickling her skin. The hair that fell around her face was soft and tickled her ears. She extended her stiff, long limbs and gasped at the feel of them. Her sudden intake of breath caused a sweet smell to cascade over her. Intrigued, she took another deeper breath and found that her nose was filling with the lovely scent of wildflowers mixed with the smells of life.

Turning her head to the side, she found herself taking a glimpse of her own fingers and focused on them. They were pudgy, tan, and as she wiggled them playfully she noticed the way that her skin shimmered in the sun. Searching for more glittery surfaces, she moved her focus to the rest of her surroundings. An array of white flowers was just within her reach, petals spread wide open. She watched the way that the sunlight danced on the soft surface before she reached out and gently touched one of their elegantly curving stems.

"*Oh*," she whispered, surprised at the delicate texture underneath her fingers. The small utterance allowed her to hear her own voice for the first time, and, although it sounded small, she smiled at the sound.

Beyond the flowers was the soft baby-blue sky, and she watched in amazement as a tiny white splotch of cloud moved ever so slowly into her vision. As she turned her head to follow the cloud, a lock of her own hair fell into her eyes. *Blue*. Her hair was the same color as the sky above her. She decided she was pleased with that idea.

"Kesi," the voice was calming and feminine, "Kesi, child, can you hear me?"

She blinked, dazzled and confused by the voice. '*Is it talking to me?*' she thought. Was the voice talking to her? She wasn't sure what to say. She turned her head away from the cloud to find the figure of a woman looming over her. The woman's skin was just as tan and gold-dusted as her own, but her face was framed by fire-red hair. Gleaming orange eyes met hers as the woman stooped to help her up, and her bright red lips curved upwards into a smile as she continued to regard Kesi.

"Hello, young one," the woman said. "You will be called Kesi. Do you understand?"

Kesi furrowed her brow for a moment and glanced down at her tiny toes, "Yes." She looked up at the woman after testing the word in her throat and smiled.

The woman was wearing a red-and-gold array of clothing: a red cloth rimmed in gold draped around her chest and shoulder blades, and, bound in place by a gold band at her waist and ankles, a red cloth covered in a delicate, almost unnoticeable, flower pattern covered each of her legs separately. Half of her red hair was pulled into a bun at the top of her head while the rest flowed freely down her back. A band of gold holding a strange, round, color-changing jewel at its center rested around the woman's bun like a crown.

As she studied the captivating woman further, she found that some strands had tear drops of gold clinging to them, making them sparkle in the sunlight. The same teardrops were also attached to the bottom of the woman's top, decorating her bare stomach in a curtain of glimmering stone. Her entire appearance tugged at Kesi's imagination, '*She looks like golden rain. Melting golden rain.*'

"My name is Ena," the woman said. "In the same way that *your* name is Kesi."

"Why?" she asked, staring at the woman in amazement.

"We are in the Djinn fields, the birthplace of all genies. It chooses your name," Ena explained. "Hear the flowers whispering?"

She and the woman stood in silence for a long time while she listened. There it was, fainter than the wind: "*Kesi, Kesi…*"

"I'm a genie," Kesi replied, and Ena smiled.

"Yes, and there's a whole city full of other genies waiting to meet you," Ena said, taking the little girl's hand. "Come with me and I'll take you to them."

Kesi grinned, "Okay!"

Ena smiled again, "That's a good girl, Kesi. I just know you're meant for great things."

~Nine years later~

Kesi's bare feet slapped against the cool temple floor as she entered the marble space. Pillars of bright colors showing stories of The Great Jinn Heroes defeating horrendous Shaytan Villains spotted the room, sparkling almost as much as the water sprouting from Ena's Fountain on the very back wall. The marble fountain depicted Queen Ena looking down into her open palms as water rushed off her fingertips into the basin at her feet. It showed their immortal Queen's motherly, life-giving properties, and how she took care of all genies, Jinn and Shaytan.

There were only a few beings left in the hall, as the usual rush had already cleared out. Kesi knelt at the base of the fountain a few feet away from an older genie with a large, hooked nose and white-yellow hair that showed his elderliness. He was muttering inaudibly to himself, deep in a prayer to Queen Ena.

Kesi cupped her hands and placed them into the fountain, cleansing herself before beginning her own prayer to Queen Ena.

"Queen Ena, Mother of All," Kesi began in a whisper, "I thank you for giving me life, purpose, and love. Thank you, Great Mother, for being with me on my Beginning Day and for guiding me, and all my brothers and sisters that have come before and will come after me, from the Djinn Fields and into Jinn City." The beginning of the ritualistic prayer to Queen Ena was no stranger to Kesi. She had been speaking it aloud to herself almost every day since her first morning in Jinn City. She knew it like the back of her hand. "Your strength and courage are to be admired and aspired to by all. Thank you for battling evil, and for defeating and taming the Shaytan. Mother of all, help me be like you." Kesi steadied herself for the personal request required at the end of the prayer. It was a tradition that started long before Kesi, to try and make Queen Ena feel closer to the genies than she really was. The Queen spent so much time ruling Jinn City in the High Palace, that the only way she could connect with other genies was by answering their prayers. "And please, if you would... give me more purpose. Let me serve you. Let me do good... for you and my people."

"Youth," a voice said from behind her, making Kesi groan inwardly, "So dissatisfied, so restless."

Kesi cleaned her hands once more, closing the prayer, before turning to face the young green-haired Jinn woman. Pushing back her annoyance for the arrogant Jinn, Kesi managed to cough out, "Lady Divya."

Divya was a Councilmaiden on Queen Ena's personal Council. It was considered a very honorable job in the genie community, so honorable that once you tested into one of the 25 positions on the Council, you were no longer viewed as an average genie, but a pure-hearted, heroic Jinn. Of course, the testing itself wasn't so easy. There was a written exam, where hopeful genies showed their intelligence on matters of magic and history, and then there were the games, where genies were given an opportunity to show Jinn City how they would defend the people if the need ever arose. A new genie was recruited into the Council every year, and from then on they lived, slept, and worked in the High Palace.

Of course, there were some people that Kesi wasn't exactly so sure deserved the title, like Lady Divya.

"Kesi," Divya replied with little to no respect, "Be careful what you wish for."

"It's considered rude to eavesdrop on prayers," Kesi deadpanned, ignoring Divya's insult on her youth. She resisted the urge to note that Divya was only a few years older than her and was by no means free of a "dissatisfied" and "restless" attitude. "It's also rude to insti-gate sourness in the House of Ena."

"The Queen will forgive me," Divya replied sharply, referring to her closeness with the Queen. As a Councilmaiden she was one of the few who were able to see her regularly. "In the meantime…" Divya nodded her head in a way that signaled Kesi to follow before turning around swiftly and marching out of the temple. If Kesi hadn't been in the temple at that very moment, she would have rolled her eyes. Instead, Kesi trotted after the Councilmaiden some-what respectfully.

"Before I start," Divya said as they entered the sunlight shin-ing down on the dirt streets of Jinn City, "promise me you won't ask questions."

Kesi quirked an eyebrow. "Is this something I should be asking questions about?"

"There you go with the questions," Divya's frown deepened into a scowl. "It's bad enough that I was sent here to give *you* a message in the first place, much less one of high importance. So please do your best to keep your annoying curiosity out of the way, would you?"

Kesi crossed her arms and stared down the Jinn, prompting her to continue since it seemed that Divya wasn't going to be fond of her speaking today. Although Kesi shouldn't have been surprised. Divya and Kesi had never had a smooth relationship, full of childhood rivalries and battles of wits. Kesi always said that Divya was no fun. Divya, in turn, thought that Kesi was an irresponsible child. Kesi just wished that Divya wasn't so rude about it.

"It's a direct order from Queen Ena," Divya stated, dropping the information the way Kesi would expect one to drop a stone in a lake. That was often Divya's way of talking with Kesi. She never gave Kesi any details, which just created more questions.

Kesi blinked, "Queen Ena?" She hadn't seen her since she'd walked Kesi into Jinn City, then promptly disappeared into thin air. What could she be sending a direct order to her for? And why did it have to be through *Divya* of all Jinn?

"What did I say about questions?" Divya's yellow eyes narrowed. "She told me to tell you to be *here* when the sun sets. She wants to talk to you."

"Did I... did I do something wrong?" Kesi stammered, suddenly nervous. She hadn't heard of a genie being punished for stepping out of line for anything other than practicing black magic, and Kesi had strayed far from that. Still, she was fond of pranks and jokes. She hoped that no one had taken such offense that they had called upon Queen Ena.

Divya threw her hands up in the air, "Can you stop being so pestering for a second and just follow your Queen's orders?"

Kesi steadied her glare, Divya's childish temper inflaming her own. "I believe your orders as a Councilmaiden are to be kind to all genies, not irritating."

Divya's tan cheeks flushed red with anger. Kesi had to resist a grin. She always had a way of getting under Divya's skin. "Respect your elders, Kesi."

"You're only seven years older than me, Divya," Kesi shot back, abandoning the formal title that Divya was given. "You're hardly an *elder*. We grew up together."

"Then respect those serving your Queen on her Council," Divya corrected, rolling her eyes.

"Respect is earned, not bought," Kesi countered. "Just because you have a spot on Queen Ena's Council doesn't mean I should just fall at your feet."

"Well if you act like a Jann...," Divya replied angrily.

"I am far from a Jann!" Kesi tightened her hands into fists. *Jann* was an old term used for uncivilized or savage genies that didn't exactly practice black magic but weren't bent on keeping the peace in Jinn City either. Kesi was surprised that Divya had used it. There were plenty of modern insults that she could have said, although the type of word didn't matter. It still irked Kesi that, after nine years, Divya was still bent on picking on Kesi. And of course, she would use an old, important-sounding word to do it.

"Hey!" Kesi turned as a familiar male voice approached them. It was Ra'id, another Jinn on Ena's Council. He was nine years Kesi's senior and two years Divya's. He was like a big brother to most, caring for the little ones and befriending the older children. Kesi had yet to meet a person that said they didn't like Ra'id, and she would be appalled if she did. With his commanding yet gentle aura, there wasn't a genie in Jinn City that didn't care about and listen to him. Even Divya respected him, possibly because she was in love with him, and she wasn't the only one. Sure, Ra'id was handsome, with his slightly curled navy hair, gray eyes, and tall, broad-shouldered stature, but Kesi had grown up with him. She didn't see why so many girls claimed they were in love with him. She often wondered which one of Ra'id's many admirers would be his mate.

"What's going on here?" Ra'id asked, and Divya jumped at the chance to defend herself.

"I was simply delivering a message from our Queen to Kesi here when she decided to be *self-centered* and *disrespectful*. She bombarded me with questions that I'd already told her I had no answers to!" Divya stuck her nose up in the air before lowering it to look at Ra'id with wide, innocent eyes. Ra'id gave her a skeptical look that he slid over to Kesi.

"She called me a Jann," Kesi stated, causing Ra'id to cross his arms over his bare chest.

"Huh," was all he said, looking at the now-feverish Divya.

"I did not!" Divya pouted, mimicking Ra'id and crossing her arms over her own chest.

Ra'id paused for a moment, taking in her reaction. "You should go report to the Queen that you delivered her message successfully," he said, "and maybe refrain from using such insults in the presence of our Mother?"

Divya nodded solemnly and walked off in the direction of the shiny golden domes of the High Palace in the distance.

"Ugh! I can't stand her," Kesi huffed, turning away from Divya's receding figure.

"Don't let her get to you," Ra'id replied. "She's just jealous that Queen Ena likes you more than her."

Kesi blinked at him, surprised, "Queen Ena likes me? More than her own Councilmaiden?"

Ra'id shrugged, "She talks about your future seat on the Council often. And if she hears Divya's gossip she just laughs at your stubbornness and says something about needing your sort of fire on the Council. It drives Divya crazy."

"I'm not...," Kesi stopped herself, thoughtfully silent for a moment. She wasn't so sure if she should be more taken aback or overjoyed. "Well I'm... I'm pretty stubborn."

"You have a good heart," Ra'id replied. "That's what matters. Even if Divya can't see it."

Kesi paused for a moment, thinking over Ra'id's prior words, "She really wants me on the Council?"

"Once you come of age," Ra'id explained. "I don't know what she says to the Elders but...," he trailed off. "Can I ask you what the message was about?"

"Queen Ena wants to meet me here at sunset," Kesi explained, "Do you know what she wants to talk about?"

Ra'id shook his head, "No idea... but to kill time, the kids are going to play some game in the Ghul if you want to come."

"Sure," Kesi replied happily. Playing games, even with kids nine to three years her younger, always helped her relax and better her mood. It was something about the exercise she supposed. Kesi knew that Ra'id was aware of this and was most likely suggesting it so that she would be able to feel better about Queen Ena's request as well as Divya's rudeness. It seemed like something that Ra'id would do.

"Let's go," Ra'id said, starting off in the direction of the Ghul, which sat Northeast of Jinn City. There were five sacred landscapes surrounding the City: The Djinn Field, the Marid Waterfalls, the Ifrit Jungle, the Shaitan Mountains, and finally the Ghul. Each of the scared landscapes were unique in structure and purpose.

The Djinn Field was a wide stretch of land covered by lush, green grass and littered with beautiful green-stemmed white flowers. The sacred land of the Djinn Field forms the magic and body of each genie for six years until they are ready to be released into Queen Ena's care from beneath the surface. The flowers soak in the magical sunlight in order to form each genie with care, and the night before a genie is due to be born out of the earth, the petals glow white-hot for all to see. The Field is the first landscape that each genie witnesses, and it shows each newcomer the peace, tranquility, and beauty of the life that they would soon be absorbed into as they begin their long lifecycle.

The Marid Waterfalls are a large expanse of interweaving rivers, lakes, and waterfalls. The Falls were the birthplace of Queen Ena and housed her in her youth. The glowing, multicolored waters nurtured the young goddess with their life-giving qualities as she slowly grew into her destiny to become a ruler. Now, the Queen shares the magical gift the Falls gave her with her children.

The Ifrit Jungle was the smallest yet most dense of all the landscapes. Tall trees, shrubbery, and flowers were some of the various types of magical vegetation found there, each with their own medicinal properties. The animals that dwelled there were known to have their own unique magical powers as well.

The Shaitan Mountains served two different purposes. The South side of the mountain range faced Jinn City and acted as a barrier keeping the peaceful genies separated from the evil Shaytan. The Shaytan dwelled on the North side of the mountains, practicing black magic along with their wicked ways. Any genie often shuddered at the thought of them. In legends, they were known to be quite ugly creatures. The magic the Shaytans practiced went against the powers naturally given to them by Jinn City and slowly tore their bodies apart.

Long ago, the Ghul was a lava-ridden wasteland inhabited by the Shaytan king, Makalani. Makalani was born there just as Queen Ena was born in the Marid Waterfalls, but instead of using his magical powers for good, Makalani wreaked havoc on any living thing that came near him. After hearing of a prophecy predicting the birth of the first genie, Queen Ena realized that Makalani could no longer be allowed to destroy the world around him. The Queen intervened and saved the Ghul and, in turn, Jinn City and the entire realm from Makalani by trapping him in the lamp. In his absence, the Ghul came back to life, becoming a safari-like landscape with patches of thriving grass and plant life mixed with dry desert areas.

Jinn City wasn't very large. There weren't houses for each individual genie, because there was no need have a place for material possessions. What the city did not provide for them the genies could create with their powers, calling necessary items to them out of thin air. When a genie became old enough, they would choose a trade to go into in order to better serve their Queen and their people, as well as to help pass the time. Most of the trades involved setting up stands in the marketplace in the afternoon, so that Queen Ena did not need to create new buildings for each genie who entered a trade. A few of the buildings housed shops, but most trades that were indoors were eateries. However, Kesi did know a few people who used the buildings as a place to keep the fruits they had harvested from the Ifrit Jungle. Kesi liked to visit these places and stare at the magical plants growing up and down the sandstone walls.

The unused floors and roofs of the buildings were where the genies set up camp for the night. Some genies returned to one or two camps continuously, but most embraced the freedom of Jinn City and never tied themselves down to one place. The youngest children tended to stick together until they felt old enough to venture out on their own, but even so it was rare for one person to not share their sleeping spaces with friends at least every so often. Even Kesi, who often returned to the same camp every night, was not opposed to the idea of moving her camp if she wanted. The space wasn't hers alone. Everything in Jinn City belonged to everyone, so that no one person had more than the other.

It only took Kesi and Ra'id minutes to travel from the temple, across a small section of Jinn City, to the Ghul. Once they reached the boarder, they stopped to take in the sight before them.

The area was swarmed with carpets on the tall grass with various genies sitting on them, all laughing and watching the children prepare their game. As Kesi and Ra'id approached, they found the children on one of the various areas in the Ghul where the grass and plant life fell away to reveal dry, cracked earth. Several young genies sat on the ground there, wrapping their bare feet with bandages to protect them from the roughness of the ground. Two boys were kicking a tightly bundled ball of rags around on their feet and knees. Slowly, a sizable group of children gathered around and the two boys stopped playing by themselves. Kesi knew all these children by name and more.

"Boys against girls!" One of the older boys, Abubakar, yelled. The other boys cheered but stopped as Kesi joined the crowd.

"Well, that's not very fair," Kesi scolded, "There's only four girls and five- no, six-" she corrected herself as Ra'id placed himself among the children, "-boys."

"Please come play with us, Kesi!" one of the youngest girls, Selma, begged, her rose-colored eyes wide. Kesi looked over at Ra'id, who was grinning ear to ear. He shrugged as if to say, '*why not?*'

'*Like you thought I would say no,*' Kesi grinned back at him before turning back to Selma, "We still need one more girl."

The girls cheered for their newfound teammate as one of the older girls, Ni'mah, spoke up, "Where's Fatima?"

"I'm coming!" a small voice yelled over the excited chatter of the children, and everyone turned to see a little girl with orange hair hurling herself onto the makeshift field. She tumbled at the force of the movement and fell flat on her face.

"*Owww!*" she exclaimed, as Selma ran over to help her up. If Kesi admitted to picking favorites, Fatima would be one of them. Although her clumsiness and forgetful nature would most likely cause her trouble in the future, it made the little girl cute as a button now. Fatima had only been in Jinn City for little under a year now, meaning that her seventh birthday was coming up soon. For some reason, the young genie thought this would mean that she would have to make up her mind on what her trade would be in the future, but she couldn't settle on just one idea. According to what Kesi had heard so far, Fatima had entertained the idea of a carpet crafter, a silk weaver, a hat maker, a Councilmaiden, a baker, and an artist. Kesi would say that the girl's mind was just as wandering.

"I'm okay!" Fatima giggled as she bounced onto her feet. "Thank you, Selma."

"Reminds me of someone that I know," Ra'id said, smiling at Kesi knowingly. Kesi just rolled her eyes playfully.

"Okay, let's start!" Kesi announced, and the children cheered excitedly around her, "What game are we playing, Abubakar?"

Abubakar kicked the makeshift ball with his small, wrapped feet and declared, "The kicking game! The one that ends with ten points!"

Kesi smiled. She was rather fond of this game, "Alright, the tree at the far end of the field is where the girls are going to kick to, and Kefira is where the boys are going to kick to. Sorry, Kefira," Kesi said, throwing a wink at the older genie sitting on a carpet on one end of the field. Kefira had been a young woman by the time Kesi had come to Jinn City, and she made it her trade to help the new, young genies adjust to life in Jinn City. She'd helped Kesi learn how to control her magic, and often organized games in the Ghul to help the children bond. That didn't do much good when it came to Kesi and Divya, no matter how hard Kefira tried. Kesi was surprised that Kefira never tried to become a Councilmaiden with her love of peacekeeping and love.

"I don't think you'll let Ra'id score one goal, Kesi," Kefira mused, causing Kesi to grin.

"Very true," Kesi replied. "In fact, he better hurry up because I'm already in the lead!" Kesi laughed as she swung by young Borak, stole the ball from beneath his tiny feet, and began racing toward the tree at the other end of the makeshift field. The children yelped and followed her, eager to play.

CHAPTER TWO

JINN CITY

Kesi

THE GAME ENDED with Kesi's team winning due to her athletic ability, her gift of riling her team into a competitive spirit, and her determination to beat Ra'id. As Kesi was high-fiving and hugging the younger children, she felt Ra'id's hand on her shoulder.

She looked up at him, "Sore loser?"

He rolled his eyes at her and smiled. "No, but you're about to be late," he pointed a thumb over his shoulder, and Kesi turned to see the orange glow of the sun settling on the horizon of Jinn City. The sunset. Divya's message. Queen Ena…

"Oh crap!" Kesi exclaimed, and she bent down to hurriedly tear off the bandages she had put on mid-game. "I gotta go! Uh… Selma, Ni'mah, Bahiti, good job today! Taahira, don't let those boys get to you, you're a great player! And Fatima," she grinned at the little girl, who beamed back at her, "that was a great point you scored back there. Keep it up! Okay, bye guys!" Kesi waved and was met with a chorus of "*bye Kesi!*" as she ran across the cracking earth, through the tall grass, back to the cool, white-washed dirt streets of Jinn City.

'*I'm late, I'm late, I'm so, so late,*' Kesi thought, mentally scolding herself. How could she not have seen the sun setting sooner? By the time she made it to the temple steps she had given herself quite an internal beating, but was secretly proud that, through her powers of flotation, sprinting, and flight, she had made it to the temple while the sun still glowed orange. Queen Ena was nowhere in sight. Kesi smiled to herself, remembering Fatima's clumsy appearance at the Ghul a few hours ago. She shook her head, looking back in the direction of the Ghul. Ra'id was right, she and the little genie really were similar.

"Kesi," the familiar female voice was filled with gentleness as she spoke. Kesi spun around to see Queen Ena standing there, looking just as beautiful and gold covered as she had on Kesi's Beginning Day, not that Kesi had expected anything less. The power of Jinn City kept genies clean and healthy, meaning that there was no need to change clothing or worry about personal hygiene, because the city's magic-filled air took care of those things for them. Genies were always clean and never got sick, though, unlike with Queen Ena, the magic couldn't stop them from aging and eventually dying after a long life, which typically lasted about two hundred years. As Mother of All, Queen Ena was the exception and hadn't aged since her twentieth-year thousands of years ago. After nine years, the Queen looked the same to Kesi, further evidence that she was, in fact, immortal.

Kesi knelt before her, "Mother of All."

"Rise, my daughter," the Queen said. Kesi obeyed, butterflies crawling up her throat at the realization of what was happening. She was meeting with the all-powerful Jinn Goddess. The all-powerful Jinn Goddess wanted to talk to her.

Why?

The Queen chuckled, looking at Kesi's feet, "You've been playing at the Ghul I see."

Kesi looked down to see the dirt stuck to her feet and the lines that the bandages had made on her skin. She felt heat rise to her cheeks. "Oh, I…"

Queen Ena waved her off, "It's alright. No need to be formal with me. Believe me, if I didn't have so many duties as Queen and Mother, I would be playing games with the younger ones myself."

'*There's every reason to be formal with you*', Kesi thought, confused at Queen Ena's words, but she didn't say anything. After all, what did one say to such a statement?

"Walk with me," the Queen offered, turning to walk down the streets of Jinn City. Kesi nodded, hurrying to keep up.

Before silence could settle comfortably over them, the Queen spoke up, "Kesi, do you know about the human world?"

The question startled Kesi. '*What does this… do I… have to do with humans?*'

"I…I know some things, Mother, but I'm not so sure what's real and what's just a legend," Kesi replied carefully, unsure of where the conversation would go.

"Tell me what you know," Queen Ena commanded gently, and Kesi cleared her throat.

"Well they… they don't have magic there," Kesi began, and continued when she saw Queen Ena nod. "That's why we're able to go to their world but they're unable to do the same with ours. I know that humans have weird hair and eye colors, and that their skin differs from place to place. I know that we used to be very involved in their world, using magic to help them make their wishes come true or to better their world. Then they started abusing our power and even found a way to trap some of us in lamps to be their slaves. So, you… Am I getting this right, Mother?" Kesi paused and waited for the Queen to smile and nod at her again before she continued, "So you crossed the Barrier, freed all the genies from the lamps, and brought them back to Jinn City. In order to make sure that it could never happen again, you sealed the gates you created to their world, forever separating the two realms."

"Yes, that is all true," Queen Ena replied. "We call that the Great Division, but, like all things, once divided does not mean divided forever."

Kesi was confused. '*Not divided forever?*'

"What… what do you mean by this, Mother?" she asked.

Queen Ena's gaze flickered to the sky as the sun sank lower below the horizon. "There is a prophecy that tells of a human boy who is supposed to bring our two worlds together in perfect harmony for the rest of time. Now, I'm not particularly worried about the fulfillment prophecy, as fate will always be on the side of good, but the Shaytan have a very different point of view."

Kesi listened carefully, trying to take in all the information. '*A prophecy…to bring Jinn City at peace with the human world? A prophecy I've never heard about is being threatened in some way by the Shaytan?*' She still didn't see how this involved her. "The Shaytan? What is their… point of view?"

"They want to destroy the barrier between the worlds in such a way that will allow them to enter the human world, but to keep us from doing the same. If they achieve this, the humans will not have us, or magic of any kind, to protect them. They will be powerless to the Shaytan's destruction," Queen Ena explained calmly in a grave voice. "They want to take over the human realm for reasons we have yet to understand in full. Though it is my belief that they wish to have their own world to control."

Kesi was quiet for a long time, thinking. Of all the information given to her, only one question steamed on the tip of her tongue. "How…how do I fit into all of this, Mother?"

"The Shaytans don't know who the boy is yet, but we do," Queen Ena started. "However, it won't be long before the Shaytan follow. We have a head start, and we need to quickly deploy someone to protect this boy, even if he does not need it right now. We need someone kind, with a strong heart. Someone with fire and courage.

Someone with a sense of loyalty not just to her people, but to all kinds of people throughout the universe. Someone like you, Kesi."

Kesi gaped at her Queen, her mouth opening and closing rapidly, but unable to produce words. It took several moments for Kesi to gather her thoughts enough to say, "To... go to the human world?"

Queen Ena nodded. Kesi tried to slow her racing heart. *'Am I going to be sick? Yep. I'm definitely going to be sick. How is this happening? I can't do this! This is ridiculous!'*

"I...," she gulped. "How can I... I mean, there must be someone more suitable for the job, Mother," she stuttered. "Someone with much less...youth and...much more experience, someone with more...skill in magic. Ra'id, perhaps?"

"Ra'id's wisdom is needed here," Queen Ena replied calmly, as if she had been expecting this, "and someone much older than yourself would not be able to get close to the Chosen One with the plan the Elders and I have in mind."

Kesi thought for a moment. "What about Lady Karida?" she said, referring to the Queen's youngest Councilmaiden.

The Queen shook her head. "Her mind is constantly elsewhere. She would not be able to stay on task, especially not in the human world with its many distractions."

"Divya, then," Kesi desperately blurted, before realizing her rudeness in her sudden, yet short outburst. "I'm truly sorry, Mother, I just..."

Queen Ena held up a delicate hand, "I understand. You doubt yourself. But I assure you that you are fit to take the job. You have yet to realize it. If you change your mind come to the High Palace and request my presence by tomorrow night. The Elders and I will tell you the details of the situation. situation, but please try to hurry Kesi for we are running out of time."

Kesi just stared at Queen Ena. The Queen smiled in return.

"I have faith that you will think this through thoroughly, Kesi, and make the right decision. I do not believe I'll miss you tomorrow. Until then, goodnight, young one."

With that the Queen disappeared into thin air, leaving Kesi alone and confused with her thoughts. She stood there in total silence for a few moments, breathing in the warm Jinn City air, until the insanity of the situation broke through to her.

"What?!" she yelled in part panic and part bewilderment, startling an old shopkeeper down the street.

"Sorry!" Kesi called as she shuffled backwards a few steps before turning around and running in the direction she had come, trying to clear her mind. She didn't even know where she was going, she just kept turning and twisting through the semi-dark streets of the night-lit Jinn City that she knew so well.

She didn't care how many strange looks she got from genies she passed in the streets, not that there were many out. Once the sun set, most genies liked to take advantage of the cool night air, stargazing on the rooftops for a few hours. Others liked to take advantage of the climate change by starting their sleep early. The genies she did pass were too busy finding places to set up camp to pay much attention to her. As twilight dawned, genies climbed through the second-floor windows of shops and buildings in order to make camp for the night. Some settled in onto rooftops to sleep under the cloudless sky.

It wasn't long before the city fell away and Kesi found herself at the Marid Waterfalls, and their series of cliffs and caves housing glowing water that spread for miles. The scene before her was truly magical- dark, rocky cliffs hugged by lush green foliage, water pouring down from the tops and sides of each small mountain, caves tucked away inside the mountains were lit up from the inside by the magical water. As Kesi looked around she could see the glowing water running through the dark landscape like a network of veins, going up and down rocky cliffs and even pooling in places before starting out again.

She took a step forward, her bare feet taking notice as the soft white sand turned into damp moss-like grass. She followed the earth downhill to the base of the large lake where all the Marid Waterfalls' water started and ended and stuck her toes into the cool water. She sat down on the bank, hugging her knees, and watched the waterfalls carry water down, and sometimes up, through the beautiful system.

Kesi sighed and hung her head in between her legs. '*What was happening to my little world?*' One moment she was being told that she should stay in her place as a genie of no trade or title by Divya, and the next she was being asked to save the world by the most powerful Jinn the realm has ever seen. Kesi chuckled to herself. '*I'm going crazy, that's it, me and Queen Ena.*' Or perhaps she had just imagined the whole encounter in some fit of boredom.

Kesi shook the thoughts out of her head. No, the message from Divya, the fight with the same Councilmaiden, the conversation with the Queen, it was all very real. Only Shaytan, if plagued with black magic withdraw, hallucinated. Otherwise the magical air of Jinn City wouldn't allow for such illnesses.

'*I'm only fifteen for Jinn's sake. How can I be right for the enormous task of protecting the fate of a whole realm of humans, as well as my own people?*' She felt a tremendous weight come crashing down on her shoulders, like the colliding waters meeting at the lake from the cliffs all around her, and she hadn't even exactly taken on the burden yet. '*How can I accept the Queen's request? I know I'll mess it up somehow. There's no way I can do this. I'll get the boy killed.*'

The thought sent anxiety shivering through her. She could imagine it now- cockily taking up the offer, failing in the simplest of ways, humiliating herself by running back to Jinn City, and having to report to her Queen that she *broke* a prophecy and sealed the fate of billions of humans for good. No, she couldn't do it. She couldn't accept. She would just hide in her camp for the entirety of the next day. She wouldn't even allow herself to get up and contemplate the idea.

Still…if she was so sure that turning away was the best option, why did she feel like that very decision would lead to the downfall of her people? '*Yes*', Kesi agreed mentally, '*if this boy is truly who the Queen and the Elders think he is, he needs to be protected.*'

'*Just not by me. Not by me.*'

Making up her mind, Kesi stood. She bit her lip and looked over the waterfalls one last time, hoping that the magic in this place had helped her make the right decision. As she turned and started to walk back to her camp, she spotted a familiar-looking old genie sitting a little way off at the base of a tree, looking at her. His hooked nose was cast in shadow in the dim light, his whitening hair standing out in contrast. Even from a distance, Kesi caught his smile. She forced one back to him before turning away.

Kesi walked through the sleepy streets of Jinn City, hearing the occasional cries of joy from those who were still up somewhere in the maze of buildings. She walked past the buildings she knew the children liked to sleep in, already hearing a few snores. '*Probably Abubakar,*' Kesi smiled to herself as she looked up into the glassless window the noise was coming from. She felt a pang of guilt, remembering the children, Fatima most of all. They would have wanted her to take the Queen's offer, to be a hero.

Kesi shoved the thought away. She wouldn't be a hero if she got them all killed, or worse, enslaved by the Shaytan.

At night, Kesi usually liked to keep to herself. It was the reason she'd been sleeping on the second floor of a storehouse since she eight instead of with the others around her age for a few more years, which was the norm. She climbed up the sandstone walls of the storehouse and through the hole of a window that served as an entrance.

Most of the camps around the City looked the same, but Kesi's had a long sandstone slab in the back of the room that provided an elevated surface. She'd covered the slab with various colorful pillows and blankets, all of which provided a comfortable place to sleep at night. Scarves were tied to abandoned candleholders on the walls and hooks in the ceiling creating a blue and purple canopy around the makeshift bed. A small crate-like box rested in front and to the side of the canopy where a brush, a bowl of water, and a few white ribbons sat. Next to the box laid a square rug covering the floor, which gave her a spot to sit while she brushed her hair.

Facing the window, Kesi sat on her rug and began to brush through her hair, trying desperately to sooth her whirring thoughts. After a moment she gave up with a huff and put her brush back where she had found it. It was no use; her thoughts were too out of control to rein in.

Kesi sat by her window, laying her head in her hands as she looked out onto the city and the always clear sky. The stars twinkled mystically, matching the soft glow from the flowers of the Djinn Fields as their magic became alight with the water from the Marid Waterfalls running underneath the surface.

Kesi sighed exasperated with herself and buried her nose in the crook of her elbow. She glared at the city below her as if accusing it of making her life so confusing. She'd already made her decision. She had. There was no use thinking about it anymore…

Still, Queen Ena seemed convinced that she was the one. Even from birth, if Kesi remembered correctly, the Queen thought she was meant for "great things," and the Queen *was* the Jinn Goddess. '*Didn't that fact amount to anything? Shouldn't she know best? Shouldn't I trust my Queen, for more reasons than just loyalty and piety?*'

She looked up to face the city again, tears of frustration and anger in her eyes. Why couldn't she just make up her mind? Couldn't it be an easy decision for her? No, it had to be, "risk your own life and probably end up failing despite the *heroic* efforts," or "sit around and do nothing and probably doom two species because your Queen won't have anyone else."

'*I know I prayed for more responsibility and purpose earlier at the Temple. I wanted a chance to prove myself, to do good. But this is just too much,*' Kesi thought, and huffed a sigh. There was a difference between ability and wishful thinking, and the reality was that she wasn't so sure she *had* the ability to stand in the way of total destruction.

How could she leave Jinn City, her home and life? It was a silly question of course. Divya was right about one thing, she *was* curious. There was a whole other world out there, one that Queen Ena wanted to send her to. How could she not want to take Queen Ena's offer and use the opportunity to see it? When she was younger, she begged the older children to tell her stories of Queen Ena, of the Jinn Heroes, and even of the human realm repeatedly. The tales of adventure, of far off lands- Kesi loved it all.

'*How can I not want this?*' She thought, '*How can I not want to learn about the humans, to see their world? How can I not want to see what the humans are like, how and why they make boarders around pieces of land? How they expand them? How they make their camps, how they make more than one city? Don't I want to see the vastness of their population and the billions of different places in their world?*'

Kesi groaned, scolding herself again. It was just the child in her talking, she knew that, and she wasn't a child anymore, especially not now that she had to make a *very* adult decision. She couldn't go forward in this sort of adventure because of wanderlust.

'*I thought you'd made up your mind,*' Kesi groaned, hitting the edge of her palm against her forehead. '*Stupid brain.*'

Queen Ena was so convinced that this was what she was meant to do. '*Is she right? Could this be my trade? Helping people? Saving realms? Is that even a trade?* Queen Ena seemed to think so. Even if it was, it wasn't the trade for Kesi, she was sure of it.

Kesi buried her face in her arms, creating a warm and dark blanket for herself. All of this over thinking had exhausted her, making her eyelids heavy, dragging her down. In that moment it seemed all had become peaceful in Kesi's mind. The windowsill became a pillow. The lukewarm air became all the covers she needed, and before she knew it Jinn City had dragged Kesi deep into sleep.

CHAPTER THREE

JINN CITY

Kesi

GREEN EYES, DARK as the sky and as full of life as the Jinn City marketplace at midday. Long, night-black lashes. Cream-colored skin. Strong black eyebrows, serving as a frame.

The eyes blinked, showing they were alive.

"Kesi," a deep male voice spoke. It wasn't Ra'id's voice, or Abubakar's, or anyone else's voice that she had ever heard. It was rich and dark, tingling with feeling.

"Kesi," the voice said again. The eyes blinked once more, "I need you."

Kesi's mind was foggy, "You...need me?"

The eyelids drooped, the green color dulling, dying, "Help me. I need you."

"You're...you're the Chosen One that Ena was talking about," Kesi realized, unsure of what was happening.

"Help me," the eyes closed, the green disappearing.

"Help you how?" Kesi asked before the image before her started crumbling away into black dust.

"No! No wait!" Kesi turned frantic, confused and afraid, "Don't *go, I can help. I will help, I...," Kesi yelped as red flashed across her vision like lightning. Booms and screams sounded against the now-black backdrop, startling Kesi.*

Strange eyes emerged from the darkness, replacing the ones that Kesi had lost. The iris was black and purple, the colors put together like shattered pieces of glass. Veins of blood-red spread from the soulless pupil, moving and shifting like rivers of lava. Kesi shivered. They oozed darkness.

'Too late," a gruff, sinister voice laughed, sparking panic in Kesi. What is this thing?

"No, it's not!" Kesi yelled, "N-no. I swear to you, I don't know who you are but if you hurt the Chosen One I will... I will fix this! I will save him!"

"Too late," the evil voice laughed again. Kesi screamed, partly in frustration with the sinister creature, and partly in horror at the events taking place. How could this have happened?

"You should have tried," the voice answered her unspoken question before laughing for a third time.

"Stop doing that!" Kesi growled, "You don't have anything to laugh about!"

The voice didn't speak. The evil eyes burned.

"I will try," Kesi yelled at the eyes, "and you... whoever you are. You won't win. Queen Ena chose me. You're going to lose."

The eyes seemed to smile, "We'll see, Kesi."

"Kesi!" a voice yelled from down below her. Kesi jolted upright off the window ledge, shaking herself out of her nightmare. She frantically wiped drool off her face and considered slapping herself awake.

"Hey, Kesi!" She sighed breath of relief after recognizing Ra'id's voice. She peeked her head through the window to see the gray-clad Jinn grinning at her from the ground.

"Wake up, sleepyhead," he laughed cheerily. "You're going to miss the proper prayer time. Don't you know it's ghastly to...," he stopped when he realized that Kesi was simply gaping at him from above, her mind somewhere else. *Somewhere else,* was, of course, back in her nightmare, "Are you alright?"

'*Queen Ena chose me. You're going to lose.*'

Kesi closed her eyes and huffed. This wasn't a game. More lives than just the Chosen One were at stake here. Dream her was right, Queen Ena chose her, and it didn't seem like she was going to accept anyone else. She couldn't let her own doubts factor into the equation. There was no room for them. She had to go forward with Queen Ena's request, or she knew that something worse than her nightmare would be one step closer to coming true.

"Hello? Kesi? Are you listening?" Ra'id broke her trance. "You don't want to be caught in another fight with Divya just because you slept past normal praying hours, do you?"

'*Praying hours...prayers...Queen Ena... the Chosen One. The Chosen One,*' "Oh crap!" Kesi yelled, jumping to her feet, "I have to go!"

Ra'id rolled his eyes, "Yeah, I want to beat the afternoon rush too."

"No. Not to the temple," Kesi shook her head, disappearing into her camp and running her brush through her air at lightning speed. She quickly cleansed her hands in her small bowl of water and said a prayer to Queen Ena for strength, hoping it would make up for the traditional temple prayer she was about to miss. After she was done, she slid back over to the windowsill, finding the ability to smile at the confused-looking Ra'id standing on the ground below her. "We're going to the High Palace."

"The High Palace?" Ra'id questioned as Kesi climbed down the building, "Why are we going there?"

Kesi landed on her feet beside the older Jinn, "Oh no reason, just to help a human save the world," she grinned when Ra'id raised an eyebrow, clearly lost, "It's... complicated."

"Yeah, I bet it is," Ra'id replied sarcastically as Kesi used her magic to allow her to hover slightly in the air.

"Let's go! C'mon! C'mon!" Kesi motioned for him to get ready to fly too before she took off, winding through the streets of Jinn City, not looking to see if Ra'id was following her. All the while, she kept her gaze on the three golden domes of the High Palace, whizzing towards the center of the City. Even with all her speed, Kesi felt as though she couldn't get to the front gates fast enough and left her friend far behind.

Once there, she stood in awe, looking at the huge golden gates, which were swung open widely as if to invite her in. Kesi observed the High Palace's three circular domes and two spiraling pillars, each capped with glowing gold. The rest of the building was stark white and almost glowed.

The front lawn was decorated with flowers, trees, and a simple white dirt path that cut through the foliage and split around a marble fountain of Queen Ena. The fountain Ena had one hand in the air with water shooting out of her fingertips before falling back to her feet. The white path continued to the large, gold front doors behind the fountain, which were as wide open as the gates.

"Wow," Kesi breathed. She hadn't had a reason to come to the High Palace before.

A panting Ra'id came up behind her, landing on the ground. He hunched over and grabbed his knees for support, "P-pretty… pretty cool, huh?"

"Yeah," Kesi hesitated to take a step forward onto the path leading to the High Palace. *'Am I doing the right thing?'*

Kesi looked at the fountain, remembering what Queen Ena told her nine years ago. *'I just know that you're meant for great things.'* Maybe *this* wasn't exactly what Kesi had in mind when she heard those words, but it's what the Queen meant. What she wanted or feared didn't matter. The Queen had made it clear that she would only take her. *'The Queen herself believes in me,'* Kesi told herself, creating newfound determination she knew she needed. So, with a deep breath, Kesi began to march down the path.

Ra'id followed hurriedly, only just having caught his breath, "Wait! Wait, Kesi," he grabbed her arm, "What are we doing here?"

"I told you-"

"Yeah, I got your vague answer," Ra'id cut in, "I'm serious, Kesi."

"Look," Kesi glanced inside the High Palace before looking back at Ra'id, "I'm serious too, but I don't know if the Queen wants me to tell anyone yet. I promise that I'll tell you eventually."

Ra'id sighed, "I...fine. Fine. But you better tell me afterwards."

Kesi smiled at him. "I will," she said, before turning and walking through the open doors.

The main room that Kesi found herself in was large and expansive, covered in white, gold, and silver. It appeared to be one of the large golden domes that made up the High Palace. The ceiling lit itself with its magical stone. Huge white pillars held it upright, cracks filled with gold and silver. The floor was the same, marble themed in what seemed to be Queen Ena's favorite colors, at least in an interior design sense. Kesi's gaze turned to a gray stone desk that stood off to the side, outside the dome that created the bulk of the room as well as the circle of pillars. A short male genie with maroon hair sat at the desk, feverishly writing on a paper Kesi couldn't see. Marching up to him, Kesi tapped her fingers on the desk, waiting for him to notice her. When it became clear that the man didn't realize she was there, Kesi cleared her throat. Still, he didn't look up or pause his writing.

She looked over to Ra'id, who looked amused. Kesi rolled her eyes, frustrated.

"Um... excuse me?" Kesi glared when Ra'id started to chuckle. "Sir? ...sir?"

Kesi huffed, giving up and leaning over to tap the man on the shoulder. He recoiled, as if snapping out of a hypnotic trance, and almost spilled the ink in his inkwell as he scrambled to compose himself. He hurriedly pushed his round glasses up his little nose.

"Oh, I uh…I apologize for…," his cheeks were red, even against his tan skin. Kesi just blinked at the strange man. "Can I help you?"

"Yes, actually," Kesi twirled a piece of baby blue hair around her finger absent mindedly, averting her gaze from the genie behind the desk as she tried to find the words to say, "I…need to see Queen Ena. Or, well, she asked to see me," she smiled at the man, releasing her hair, "Do you know where she would be? It's kind of important."

"Ah, well you see-" the man paused as his glasses started to slip again and only continued after they were straightened, "no one can see the Queen without an appointment. Do you have a scheduled appointment?"

"Does the Queen requesting to see me by the end of today count?" Kesi laughed nervously as the man reached under the desk and look out a large, leather-bound book with a fat black ribbon pressed between some pages near the center. The man opened to where the ribbon was placed and began to read a long list of names off a grid that Kesi couldn't get a clear view of.

"What's your name?" he asked and glanced up at Kesi with narrowed eyes.

"Uh…Kesi," she answered. "But I don't think that I would be on the list, it was kind of sudden…um…," she trailed off when she realized that the man wasn't listening to her. Rather he had become engrossed with reading the list, his nose almost touching the papers as he leaned down to read. He clicked his tongue and closed the book quickly with a *bang!* Kesi jumped at the sound before meeting the man's glare.

"You don't seem to have an appointment, Miss Kesi," the man said, placing both of his hands on the book. "I can put you on a waiting list, and you may be able to meet with the Queen in a few months or so."

Kesi shook her head. "No, you don't understand. She *asked* to see me. I don't…please at least get her the message that I'm here," Kesi stuttered, trying not to lose her temper with the man.

The genie only shook his head, "Miss, as I've said before-," he started, only to be interrupted by the sound of bare feet slapping against the marble floor. They all turned to see Queen Ena coming towards them, her red-and-gold sash falling into the crook of her elbows as she walked regally with her hands clasped in front of her.

"Yahya, it's quite alright," she smiled at the genie, then at Kesi, "There's no need for Kesi to have an appointment. She was telling the truth- I asked to see her urgently. I'm overjoyed to see you here, Kesi."

The genie man sunk back into a kneel, a motion that Ra'id copied. Kesi started to sink to her knees herself, but the Queen held up a hand, stopping her.

"Please, no need to bother with such formalities," the Queen said, shocking all those gathered, Kesi most of all. "You're just as needed in this court as I. And now that you have accepted my offer as well as your own power, well…I'd say that there are quite a large number of people who need you more than they need me."

Ra'id craned his neck up to look at her, his body still locked in a respectful kneel in front of their Queen. Kesi saw many emotions cross his face: confusion, awe, bewilderment, but Kesi only gave him a fleeting glance before meeting Queen Ena's eyes.

"I… cannot tell you what great honor it is for you to see me in that light, my Queen," Kesi replied, confidence bubbling inside of her. The Jinn Goddess very nearly claimed that Kesi was even more powerful than herself. It must mean something. '*Maybe my ability isn't so different from my wishful thinking after all.*' "And I hope that I can align my actions with your beliefs in the future for the good of all those who need me."

The Queen smiled and clapped her hands together excitedly. "I knew you would come around. Come, follow me."

Kesi trotted past a still-confused Ra'id and followed Queen Ena out of the main room to a set of grand stairs around the corner of another large area. Another one of the three domes. A grand staircase bended away from it, up to bridge-like hallways far above her. Kesi followed Queen Ena up the staircase, passing fabulously done paintings on her way. Some were portraits of Elders from the present or past, but others showed stories that Kesi knew well. Kesi smiled when she saw one piece of art that showed the Queen leading a crowd of children into a sandy field between the five landscapes, buildings escaping the earth and growing like plants all around them. It was how Queen Ena made Jinn City after making the area safe from the Shaytan Makalani, who was threatening to destroy her and anything she created. Another showed Queen Ena being born out of the Marid Waterfalls, the water itself pushing her to the banks. One showed Queen Ena battling the evil Shaytan Makalani, who looked half-human, half… dragon?… mountain?… whatever he was, but that wasn't what struck Kesi. What struck her were the eyes of the creature.

Black. Purple. Laced in red.

The eyes from her dream.

Why had she had a nightmare about Makalani? Kesi bit her lip. She knew that, especially in Jinn City, dreams could mean an awful lot. And a dream about the eyes of an evil Shaytan that she had never seen before? It didn't sit right with Kesi, especially when she wasn't known to have such *meaningful* dreams.

Moving on quickly so as not to overthink it, Kesi reached the hallway that she had seen from the ground. It contained nothing except more artwork on its one solid wall, and a single tall doorway.

Kesi observed the only two paintings in the hall. The first had Queen Ena standing on what looked like cliffs made of misty, glowing clouds in the top left-hand corner. Scattered around the bottom was an array of strange-looking buildings and beings, all with their hands stretched upwards. Some were trying to grasp onto strings of glowing mist of all different colors as they flocked to Queen Ena's outstretched hand. Broken lamps scattered in pieces at the beings' feet, others were hunched over them in despair.

Kesi jumped when Queen Ena spoke. She didn't realize that she had stopped to observe the painting with her. "The Great Division. When Kahlil showed this painting to me, I didn't think it could ever happen. Hundreds of years later, he proved that he was always right, even in the most drastic circumstances."

Kesi turned to the Queen, "The prophet Kahlil? He foresaw this?"

Kesi knew the story of the prophet Kahlil. He was the very first genie born in the Djinn Fields, and Queen Ena's companion through all the trials she went through to make Jinn City safe for more people like Kahlil, which he prophesized would come. It was the first prophecy he ever made, although the swarm of children that he promised didn't come until after his death. According to the story, the two found that Kahlil wasn't the exact same being as Queen Ena when they both turned twenty and Kahlil continued to age and grow, though Queen Ena did not.

Kesi looked back towards the painting of Queen Ena and the making of Jinn City. Was that piece of paper, preserved by magic and kept under shining glass, Kahlil's first prophecy?

"Every piece of artwork is a prophecy, completed or not," the Queen motioned down the hall and to the staircase they left behind. "There's only one yet to be fulfilled. Come, look."

Kesi followed as Queen Ena showed her to the next painting, this one even more detailed than the last, as if Kahlil wanted to leave instructions, not a piece of artwork, behind.

The figure of Queen Ena was standing on the same clouds in the left-hand corner as she had been in the other painting, except this time she was quietly observing and not taking action. The buildings were in the same place as well, however, here they were taller, larger in number, and in different shapes and colors. The spaces between these buildings were cast in shadow, and Kesi could see Shaytan creeping out, mouths formed into snarls and showing teeth. Other glowing purple eyes hid deeper in the shadows, brooding. A glowing figure, colored blue, gold, and white, stood on the ground between the buildings and the rest of the picture, looking confident and powerful. In fact, it looked as if the Shaytan closest to it were shying away in fear or pain. Behind the figure stood a boy with dark hair that fell into his face, covering up most of his features. However, his dark green eyes showed through the gaps his hair created, reminding Kesi of two lanterns in a dark sea. His hands were gripping part of the multi-colored clouds that Queen Ena was standing on and appeared to be trying to tie them to the brown earth of his world as if they were fabric.

Kesi and the Queen stood there for many moments, as if the Queen were waiting for her to see something besides brush strokes. And she did. The green eyes, not just the color but also the shape, size, light, and life in them as well… those were in her dream too. The Chosen One. She was right! He *was* the boy with green eyes. Kesi shivered when she remembered the deepness of his voice. She couldn't believe that it actually belonged to a *person.*

Seeming satisfied, the Queen began to speak, "The real vision was much more complex than this painting," she said. "Kahlil explained it to me in great detail as he worked. The whole saga of the Great Division and the Convergence took him several nights to piece together through his dreams. For the last stretch of it he was in a coma for three days. I was so afraid; I didn't know what was happening." She paused, "It was the last vision he had before he died."

Kesi bowed her head, "I'm very sorry, Mother. The stories say that you were great friends."

Queen Ena chuckled. "Don't be sorry," she said, and reached out to touch the blue glowing figure from above the glass gingerly. "Kahlil used to see me like this, in his visions, except my color was as red as my hair. He said it was because my power was so great that sometimes even his gift couldn't allow him to see it. Imagine my surprise when he painted you this way."

"That's me?" Kesi squeaked, studying the picture again.

"Well, it is now," the Queen smiled at her. "He said I would know you when I saw you, and I'm certain that it's you, Kesi. You must believe that you can do this. You're meant to."

Kesi turned back to the painting, "Well, I don't suppose you'll take no for an answer anyway, will you... Mother?" she stuttered on the last bit, almost forgetting her manners.

Queen Ena laughed, "No," she paused, "Kahlil taught many things, and one of them is to trust my instincts. Now it's time for you to trust yours."

"I suppose you know that you've made a great friend when you start to pass on their wisdom," Kesi replied, grinning at her Queen. The Queen seemed amused.

"Just between the two of us, Kesi, the prophet and I weren't just friends," she laughed when Kesi's mouth hung agape.

"*Really?!*" Kesi exclaimed. The Jinn Goddess could have a love life? With a magical genie prophet? The notion was almost unbelievable to Kesi. She giggled for a moment before remembering who she was talking to. She coughed, "Mother."

Queen Ena waved her off, "What did I tell you about formalities, Kesi? I promise to tell you the story of Kahlil and I one day, perhaps when you've found someone of your own. Now, come, the Elders are waiting."

CHAPTER FOUR

JINN CITY

Kesi

QUEEN ENA LEAD Kesi through the doorway into a large, airy room with big, glassless windows. A round wooden table sat in the center, surrounded by seven chairs. One was especially large, draped in red cloth and as empty of an inhabitant as the Jinn City sky was of clouds. The other chairs were occupied, however, and draped in white cloth to symbolize that they were reserved for an Elder on Queen Ena's Council. The Elders ceased their chatting when the Queen and Kesi entered, casting them both smiles. Well, except for one. His mouth was sourly turned downwards at the sight of her, his green mustache so dark it was almost black. Kesi averted her gaze. What was with green-haired genies despising her?

"Welcome to the Elder's Table, Kesi," Queen Ena said as she filled the empty seat. Kesi observed the other, non-agitated-looking Elders in turn. The woman to the right of the Queen had to turn around to see her, her silver hair shinning in the sun coming through the window and her dark blue eyes reminding Kesi of Ra'id's hair.

Kesi had to suppress a wince when she thought of him, and how confused he must be right now.

The Elder next to Silver Hair had whitening blue hair, but even Kesi could tell that it used to be a bright, captivating shade of electric blue. He turned around too quickly for Kesi to notice the color of his darting eyes. The woman next to him had hair that was almost completely white, save for a tan tint that Kesi barely caught. She was easily one of the oldest on the Council. Kesi skipped over the green-haired Elder, who was still glaring at her, and observed the next Elder. She had dark, curly hair the color of plum. She sat next to an Elder with light yellow hair and twinkling dark gray eyes. His nose was large and hooked and his lips were the color of storm clouds. His mouth was framed by wrinkles. His eyes were too, showing that the man most likely had a good sense of humor. Kesi blinked at him, recognition surfacing, pushing through the clouds in her mind.

Kesi gasped. "You...you were at the Temple with me," she breathed, causing the Elder to grin. "And you... were you at the Marid Waterfalls too?" Kesi was confused by the Elder. Why wasn't he wearing his white Elder robes back then? She thought they never went anywhere without them on. Kesi paused, thinking it over, "Were you...*stalking* me?"

The Elder shrugged, "A little." His voice was rushed and quick, as if it were a race to push each word out.

Kesi turned to Queen Ena in bewilderment, causing the Queen to laugh.

"I see you've met Elder Ashraf," Queen Ena replied, still chuckling. "Ashraf has a very... peculiar power, much like the prophet Kahlil's, except Ashraf's is not as precise. He has the power of seeing possible paths in the future through dreams, as well as being able to send these dreams to others to show them a possible prophecy."

Kesi paused, taking in the information, before a realization hit her like a splash of cold water. "Wait! You sent me the nightmare I had last night, didn't you? ...Uh, Elder Ashraf... sir."

Elder Ashraf's smile grew from big ear to big ear. "Don't take it too harshly, it's nothing personal. I only reveal possible outcomes of a situation, nothing concrete. However, if you weren't standing here currently, I'd say that we'd be one step closer to your nightmare becoming the only path to follow," his words were rushed again. Was that normal for him? "I didn't know that my gift would be so useful for motivating a hero, though. The more you know, right?"

Kesi just blinked at him. '*What... just happened*,' was her only thought. All the Elders except for the sour, green-haired Jinn chuckled when her expression turned from confused to annoyed while she struggled to find the right words to say to the Elder.

"Wouldn't a... I... couldn't you have just *talked* to me?" Kesi questioned before hurriedly retracting her steps and adding, "Elder Ashraf."

"Aw, well that's not as fun," the Elder replied, confusing Kesi even more. Frustrated, she huffed and looked away from him, causing another uproar of laugher from the table. Clearly the Elders found her as amusing as Queen Ena did.

"Come here, child," the silver-haired Elder waved her over. "We promise that we don't bite. Well perhaps Farouk might. He's quite prickly."

The plum-haired woman with curly locks from across the table laughed, "Yes, we've been with him for years upon years now, and he still hasn't gotten any less critical. It's a miracle if he even smiles!"

More laughter. The green-haired Elder just stuck his nose in the air. Kesi concluded that the annoyed-looking Elder was named Farouk.

Kesi stepped forward as the silver-haired woman commanded, and she quickly grabbed Kesi's hands in her wrinkly ones. She smiled up at Kesi from her seat at the table, "My name is Iamar and I am delighted to meet you, Kesi."

"I...It's an honor to meet you too, Elder Iamar," Kesi stuttered before thinking of something, "Do you all have...special powers? Like Elder Ashraf?"

"Some of us do," Elder Iamar replied helpfully. "Others are here solely based on their wisdom. Some, like Elder Baha-" she nodded to the blue-haired Elder next to her, "-earned powers as gifts from Queen Ena for good deeds and heroic acts. I, personally, developed the gift of telepathy after I stumbled into the wrong part of the Ifrit jungle and was bitten by some type of snake or another."

"You mean... you can... read my mind?" Kesi stuttered, suddenly self-conscious.

Elder Iamar waved her hand in the air, releasing her hold on Kesi, "Oh don't worry, you have to give your consent for me to see anything. That was a gift from Queen Ena when my ability was providing some difficulties in my daily life. That was how we got acquainted and she convinced me to take the Council Exam."

"Oh," Kesi grinned sheepishly, "I'm glad... that it's a consensual thing, because... well, you know, um, Elder Iamar."

Elder Iamar chuckled, turning back to snotty Elder Farouk, "Never doubt our Queen's decisions, Farouk," she said. "This one has the fire the Jinn and the humans need."

"Too much fire can burn those who stand too close," Elder Farouk replied coolly, casting a glare at Kesi. She shrank away.

"Only if the fire is black and controlled by a dark heart," Queen Ena countered, seeming to silence the Elder as well as cut off his glare. Turning to look at Kesi, she continued, "And you, Kesi, have proved that your heart beats only for what's right."

"Proved that how, Mother?" Kesi asked. She briefly wondered if she would start talking in riddles as she got older. Or was that just reserved for Elders and immortal goddesses?

"By not ignoring the vison Ashraf sent you," Queen Ena explained, "You proved yourself simply by coming here."

Kesi grinned. "My Queen, I was expecting it to be more difficult," she said, causing more laughter.

"Speaking of difficulties," Queen Ena began, "Ashraf, would you like to explain the outline of our plan to Kesi?"

"I would love to, Mother," Ashraf said before turning to Kesi. "Now listen carefully, kid. We've been watching the human world for a while now, even after Queen Ena closed the gates to the human world. Although we can't go there personally, we can still look at it. Lately, the scene depicted in the prophecy was starting to resemble what's going on there- mainly the buildings, what people wear, what people look like, and other things like that. We started watching for sudden bursts of magic in an otherwise magic-less wasteland to signal where the Chosen One is and when his powers start developing. And as you can probably guess, we did find such a burst of magic coming from a boy that looks a lot like the guy in the prophet's painting. Coincidence? I don't think so. The seven of us came up with a genius plan and applied you for a program that brings people from far off lands to other far off lands. It's called a student exchange program. With a little help from the wonderful thing we call magic, we were able to manipulate the process so the Chosen One's family will be your host family. Ha! Aren't we geniuses?" He didn't wait for Kesi to reply. It wasn't like she could, half of the words he said didn't make sense.

'*What kind of powers does the Chosen One have? What's a student? What's a host family?*' Kesi wanted to ask, but Elder Ashraf was already back on his fast-pace speech, "Don't worry, we made you false papers and a fake backstory and all that. You'll live with the Chosen One, his father, and his mother. You do know how human families work, don't you?"

"Uh…," Kesi started, but Ashraf had already moved on.

"Good. You will play the part of a fifteen-year-old girl from Cairo, Egypt. Your mother is American, which is why you decided to participate in the program that would take you all the way to America, of course, and-"

"H-hold on," Kesi stopped him. "I don't understand half of the words you're saying. What's America?"

Queen Ena smiled. "You have much to learn. It may take a few weeks to teach you everything you need to know."

"We don't have a few weeks!" Elder Farouk insisted loudly. Queen Ena nodded, considering his words.

"Very true. We may only have hours, not weeks. We don't know if the Shaytan know as much as we do," Queen Ena replied, then paused as if thinking of something. "Iamar, can you translate information into Kesi's mind with your powers?"

"Whoa, wait-" Kesi started, but Elder Iamar was already answering.

"It's certainly possible, although she would have to be subconscious and give me her consent beforehand," Elder Iamar said, and all eyes turned to her.

"No w- I mean, with all due respect, Elder Iamar," Kesi turned to the silver-haired woman, "I don't know how I feel about having my mind read all the time."

Elder Iamar shook her head, "I won't be able to read it all the time, especially if you block me out after you wake up and my work is done. I promise that I won't rummage around in your thoughts, Kesi," the Elder said, "I'll be too busy processing information anyway. And after I'm done, you'll wake up in a few hours knowing everything you need to know."

Kesi thought it over. She didn't like the sound of someone implanting information in her mind and having access to all her private thoughts, but what else could she do? Queen Ena and Elder Farouk were right; they didn't know how much time they had. They couldn't waste it. She was just going to have to trust Elder Iamar.

"Okay," she said finally. "But don't…look around," she finished, and Elder Iamar gave her a grateful smile.

Kesi turned back to the Elders. "Okay, well, now that we have that settled…," Kesi suddenly thought back to the beginning of her nightmare the night before, "What even is his name, anyway? The Chosen One, I mean."

"Roman Lovett," Ashraf answered. "He's your age."

"Roman…," Kesi echoed, a zap of pleasure running through her. She liked the sound of that, "Right. Ok."

"Mother, we should probably hurry," Elder Farouk cut in, "With the telepathic transfer."

Queen Ena nodded, then looked over to Kesi, "Well, are you ready?"

Kesi sighed, "As ready as I'll ever be. Let's get unconscious."

CHAPTER FIVE

DANVILLE, VIRGINIA

Roman

"ROMAN, HONEY," HIS red-haired mother popped her head into his room, grinning, "I have some news!"

Roman looked up from his last-minute attempt at completing his over-the-summer homework at his mother. It wasn't odd to see Emma Lovett grinning like a teenage girl, although over the past year her smiles had become much less frequent and more forced. This, however, was the classic Emma grin that his mother would put on before the events of the year before occurred. Curious now, Roman spun his chair out from under his loft bed to face her in full. "What is it, Mom?"

She ducked under his loft to his desk area, pulling a file out from behind her back, squealing, and waving it around. Roman laughed at her before she started to speak excitedly. "I got this in a package from Students Abroad, and there was a letter in it that said we checked out!" Emma was ecstatic, waving the vanilla folder in his face. "We'll be hosting a girl from Egypt for the next year or so, depending on if her parents send enough money for the rest of the school year. Here, they sent this," she said, handing him the folder.

Roman took it with cautious hands, still chuckling at his mother. Emma was normally a cheerful woman and a great mother, with a rounded face framed by curly orange-red hair, and emerald green eyes. She looked almost girlish when she grinned, her sea of freckles making it worse. Very different from his cool-toned father, Emma was now the sole light-bringer to the house, although this was a little much for her. So, Roman gave her a reasonably questionable look.

Emma rolled her eyes. "She's your age, Roman!"

Roman's gaze turned annoyed, "*Mom*. Don't play matchmaker with our foreign exchange student, please."

Emma laughed, putting her hands up in the air defiantly. "I'm not! I'm not! I'm just saying!"

Roman turned away from his mother, looking over to the picture frame on his desk next to his open laptop. In it was an eight-grade version of Roman, laughing in the arms of an older teenage girl, who was hugging him from behind and grinning at the camera. Sophia, the girl in the photo, had the same red hair, green eyes, and freckle-filled face as his mother. But that girl, with all her likeness to Emma Lovett, wasn't his mother. She was Roman's wild and bright older sister who had gotten very sick a little under a year ago. Roman and his parents were told that there was nothing that they could do, and within a few months Sophia had passed away. The Lovett family hadn't been the same since, and they were still struggling every day to go on without her.

Emma sighed when she caught where his gaze had landed. "I miss her too, Roman, we all do."

Roman was silent for a moment. "Will she be staying in her room?" he said into his lap. Roman looked up slightly to meet his mother's gaze, who had crouched low to meet his eyes.

"Roman, you have to understand, there's nowhere else for her to sleep, not with the guest room in the basement being used as storage space," Emma answered and sighed when Roman broke eye contact. "I know it's hard. But maybe this will be good for us, for all of us. Roman...," she touched his arm lovingly, gaining his attention again.

Roman clenched his teeth as tears threatened to fall. He was so sick of crying, but he had done it so many times in front of Emma that he couldn't bring himself to care. "Don't try to replace her, Mom. Don't even try."

"No, sweetie, no," Emma grabbed his elbows and gave him a look full of such love and concern that Roman forced himself to turn away, afraid he would start bawling over this whole ordeal again. "I don't want to replace her. Never in a million years, you must understand that. It's just... we've been walking by her empty room at the end of the hall for a year now and it's...it's time to put some life back into this house. Or at least back into that room. We've drowned in this long enough, Roman. I'm afraid that if we don't do something, if we don't take steps to get better, then we'll never get past this," Emma's voice cracked, and Roman turned to see her quickly wiping away tears. "The fact is... the fact is Roman, that she would have wanted this. She would have wanted us to be happy. She said it herself, remember?"

Roman looked back towards the picture on his desk. "She said she wanted us to move on with our lives," he swallowed. "She was so selfless."

"That's something that she and her brother have in common," Emma smiled at Roman and cupped his cheek with her hand. "I love you, baby."

"I love you too, Mom," Roman replied, smiling sadly at her. Emma returned the favor before clearing her throat and standing up.

"Look at the folder," she pointed to the folder in question sitting abandoned on his desk before smiling and heading out of Roman's room.

"I will!" Roman called before Emma softly closed the door. He let the silence settle for a few moments before turning to look at the picture again. "I hope this is what you wanted, Soph," he mumbled, licking his lips nervously before he turned to the folder.

The first thing that Roman saw when he opened it was a crisp white page, the letters printed on it black and blocky. At the top, in big, bold letters, Roman read: *Kesi Haddad*.

Roman's eyes trailed down to the mesh of information scattered below, as if the girl was a criminal with a detailed profile report. *Age: 15. Home City: Cairo, Egypt. Ethnicity: 50% Egyptian, 25% German, 25% English. Date of Birth: July 16th, 2001. Location of Birth: Cairo General Hospital. Current school: Abd al Hakim's Secondary School. Relations: Father; Azeem Haddad (42 years of age), Mother; Bonnie Elizabeth Sparrow Haddad (41 years of age). Siblings: Panya Marie Haddad, (25 years of age) and Yasmeen Lily Haddad (9 years of age).*

Roman chuckled at the details and put the page aside, finding a yellow-toned, thin envelope that had clearly already been opened. Most likely by his mother and father, Roman guessed. He carefully peeked inside and found that the envelope housed a few pictures.

Roman pulled the first out gingerly, observing what was clearly a school picture. The girl in the photo, Kesi, had skin so tan that it almost reminded Roman of copper. Her platinum blonde air stood out in contrast against it, making her skin look golden. Kesi's eyes were sky blue and framed by dark lashes and equally dark eyebrows. She was smiling in a pristine school uniform, her back straight as she sat on the hidden stool that Roman was sure she was sitting on. After staring at the picture for a few more seconds, Roman placed it on top of the informational page he had set aside, and quickly revealed the second picture in the envelope, eager to see more pictures of this girl.

In this one Kesi was standing in the middle of a whole team of other girls, all in muddy soccer uniforms and cleats. Despite the mud crawling up her legs, Kesi was grinning wildly.

Roman picked up the last picture, showing the same girl

smiling like a lunatic while posing with a distracted-looking camel. Her blonde hair was tied up in a high ponytail and the fly-a-ways were sticking to her face. Her blue eyes shined so brightly that they seemed to reach out of the photograph and pierce straight into Roman, like two sapphire daggers. He sucked in a break and thought, '*She's pretty.*'

He moved to put the photo with the others when he noticed the loopy handwriting on the back. He turned the picture over to observe it, reading the words: *Kesi, 15, camel riding on her birthday!*

An Egyptian girl riding a camel for her 15th birthday, it didn't get any more stereotypical than that. Once it became clear to him that he was staring at her pictures a little too much, Roman finally put them back in the envelope. While placing the envelope back in the folder, he noticed a folded piece of paper attached to the inside of the back flap of the folder. Roman quickly grabbed it and unfolded it out of its three neatly creased sections. The paper was a typed letter, which Roman assumed, was written by Kesi Haddad.

Dear Host Family, whoever you are,

I'm overjoyed to learn that I've been accepted into this program so that I can have the opportunity that many do not, to study in the United States. I, personally, am perfectly content with waiting until we meet in person to get to know each other better, but apparently, I'm not allowed to do that. The adults at Students Abroad told me that I have to write a letter to you, even though I don't know who you are, and tell you all about myself before you see me in person (which seems ridiculous to me). What's completely unfair is that you will probably receive this letter before I receive your information, making you a complete stranger to me, whoever you are.

Anyway, this letter itself is a problem for me. I don't exactly know what to write. When Ms. Khour told me about this little project, I asked her what I should write about and she just stuck her nose in the air and said, "Don't you have favorite things?" which isn't very helpful but it was the best advice I got out of the woman.

I signed up for this program to visit the country that my mother is from, not to write about my favorite things, but as my mother always says, "if you push the boulder hard enough, it will budge," so I suppose this is just one annoying step that I have to work through. Just as a side note, because I am so unprepared, please excuse my scattered thoughts and my random order to the list I'm about to make.

Roman snorted at the girl's humor and attitude. He looked over to the picture of his sister again, "Soph, you would just *love* this girl." He chuckled to himself as he continued reading.

Anyway, to be a bit stereotypical, my favorite animal is a camel. I absolutely love camels. I asked my dad for a camel once, but he just laughed at me, so I don't think that childhood wish is coming true any time soon. I have ridden them on multiple occasions, though. Thanks Cairo tourism!

My favorite color is blue (I don't really know why). Maybe it's my eye color, maybe it's just a me thing, I don't know. I guess if you spend enough time under a clear blue sky, you might as well grow to like it.

Most of my teachers call me stubborn and headstrong, but Mr. Maalouf tells me that being stubborn and headstrong isn't a bad thing as long as I have a good heart. Mr. Maalouf is my favorite teacher. He also teaches one of my favorite subjects- English. He says I have a real talent for English. I love English, and science, and math. But not geography or art or music, oh no, please no.

I can't deal with any of those. Or Spanish. Try as I might, but I just can't speak it like the other kids can.

I can speak both Arabic and English, since I grew up with both Arabic and American parents, but I like Arabic better. We speak it more at home. Even my mom is partly fluent. Still, I think it's important to know both, especially since a lot of people speak English.

I also love to play sports, just like my dad and little sister. I play anything and everything. Cricket, rugby, horseback riding, camel riding, football, (soccer in America? Am I spelling it right?). I am willing to try pretty much any sport! My older sister is more like my mother (they can be real princesses sometimes). They like pretty things, I guess is what I'm trying to say. They don't like wrestling in the mud through a football match in the backyard after it rained all night long.

My mom met my dad when she was studying in Egypt for archeology. They went to the same college, although he was there to become a surgeon. They started dating, and, once they both started to follow their dreams, decided to settle in Cairo and start a family. My sister Panya is away at a university in England with some long name that I can't remember, and we're all very proud of her. She wants to be a doctor, like my father. She likes learning a lot and is close to my dad. My little sister Yasmeen either wants to be an actress or an athlete, she can't make up her mind. But just between you and me, I think she'll turn out to be a comedian. She's really funny.

I hope that you learned something about me that you hadn't expected, and I hope to see you soon in America!

Signed,

Kesi Haddad

Roman smiled. Kesi Haddad was certainly a character. Putting down the letter, Roman began to reassemble the folder to give back to his mother. Once finished, he turned back to his schoolwork, trying to complete the opinion essay on some book that he'd only half-read. The half-reading provided a problem in this case, seeing as the assignment was to write a two-page essay on who his favorite character was, and why they would be a good role model, and Roman only half-knew all the characters. School work was hard, but he supposed it was a small price to pay for being able to go to Waterford Academy, a very resourceful private school ten minutes down the road. He hoped that Kesi would like it.

Roman sighed to himself. Could he stop thinking about the girl for one second? He told himself that it was only because he was excited to host a foreign exchange student and have a new friend, but a small corner of his mind sat with the truth: He thought Kesi was kind of... cute. Not kind of, no one thinks in the terms of *kind of*. '*What an idiot, Roman*', his brain told him, embarrassing himself into a blush. Frustrated now, he pulled out his phone and searched for some music, as if outside noise would block out the thoughts brewing inside his mind.

It didn't.

Surely someone with as much spunk and stubbornness as his deceased sister would fit well in Sophia's old room, wouldn't they? He looked over to the picture of his sister again. He wished she was here to give him the answer.

"*Don't worry, Romey,*" he remembered her saying when she told him how sick she was, trying to soothe her crying 14-year-old brother, "*You'll be fine. It will all be fine. This won't be the end of you. There's still more for you out there.*"

"*You say that like you're sure you're going to die,*" Roman had choked as she hugged him.

"*Romey...,*" the memory was so vivid that Roman even

remembered his older sister biting her lip, uneasiness in her eyes. *"Romey, I am. There's no cure."*

"Please don't leave me, Soph." He closed his eyes as the lights in his bedroom flickered softly, although he was sure that it was just his overactive imagination. It was the same overactive imagination that allowed him to divulge into his memories of Sophia so completely.

"I won't. Not really," she had stroked his hair. *"I promise to look down on you, every day. I promise to send as many good things in your direction as possible, alright? You just have to believe in me."*

"Roman!" His father's deep voice resonated from downstairs, causing him to jump out of the memory. "It's time for dinner!"

"C-coming Dad!" Roman yelled back, glancing once more at the picture of his sister and the vanilla folder that contained a possible "good thing" coming his direction, before bolting downstairs.

CHAPTER SIX

JINN CITY

Kesi

"KESI," SHE RECOGNIZED Queen Ena's voice through her grogginess. "Kesi, are you alright?"

"Wha-?" Kesi questioned, coming out of sleep before releasing a sudden gasp. Her head thrummed softly, giving her a mild headache, but what captured Kesi's attention was the information buzzing around in her head.

"America is a country!" Kesi exclaimed. "That's what America is!"

Kesi focused her vision on the Queen as she heard her laugh, her mind returning to reality. She was sitting on the same little cot that she had fallen asleep on when Elder Iamar started her telepathic transfer. White silk scarves fashioned themselves into curtains, shielding her from the rest of what she now knew was the High Palace's infirmary. The small makeshift room held a small bedside table to Kesi's right, and a skinny, full-length mirror on the left wall.

"Here, drink this," the Queen said, handing her a cold glass of water. "Do you feel alright?"

Kesi took the cup gratefully, taking a sip from the cool liquid before answering, "I'm fine. I have a little headache, but I guess I slept most of it off."

The Queen hummed, "Another thing, Kesi. While you slept, I gave you the ability to change into a human with... well, you'll see. You're in your human form now, please don't be..."

Before the Queen could finish her statement, Kesi had jumped up made her way to the mirror hung on the wall by Queen Ena. In her haste, she lost her footing and stumbled over herself, almost onto the Queen. Kesi looked down, trying to find what make her slip. She normally wasn't clumsy unless she was moving at an unusual fast pace or she was somehow startled. Kesi widened her eyes when she saw that her normally bare feet were now covered by black-and-white tennis shoes, her legs covered in... jeans? '*Is that what these are called? Maybe they should call these shoes...*' her brain mumbled as she tried to get a grip on her new restrictions. The fabric on her legs felt tight on her skin and her toes felt pinched in the... '*... torture devices,*' her mind growled as she tried to wiggle her toes to find more room for them in vain.

The Queen chuckled. "Your human form seems a lot clumsier than your normal self," she said, but Kesi wasn't listening. She had caught sight of herself in the mirror and gasped at the half-foreign, half-familiar person staring back at her. Her hair was long and blonde, catching the light in a way that pleased Kesi. Her eyes had lost their gold flecks and now only held their sky-blue color. Her lips were also no longer gold, taking a hue of pink instead of the glittery color she was used to. Speaking of losing sparkle, her skin didn't simmer like a genies', neither did her eyelashes or hair. The loss of all these things made Kesi feel strangely naked in a way. '*But...,*' she thought as she twirled a lock of her new blonde hair between her fingers, '*I could get used to this.*'

She was wearing what she knew now were normal human clothes. In addition to the jeans and shoes, she also had on a teal-colored t-shirt and a gray zippered hoodie. Kesi touched a few fingers to a necklace at her collarbone. It was fairly simple: blue, teardrop-shaped pendant hung on a simple gold chain. Despite its simplicity, Kesi could feel the magic resonating off it, and a slight warmth on her skin, a warmth that usually came from the magic, running through her blood.

Her magic was gone. She felt like she had lost a limb or cut all her hair off. Magic had always been a part of her life; it had always been a part of everyone's lives. What would she do without it? The possibilities began to mount in her brain as her anxiety swirled into a sandstorm.

'*How will I be able to take care of myself without my magic? How will I be able to survive without being connected to Jinn City? I won't be able fast anymore. I won't be able to win games at the Ghul anymore. I won't be able to secretly throw balls of light at Divya when I see her in the marketplace. Oh Jinn... I won't be able to fly! How will I get around?*' Kesi's mind was racing with such horrible thoughts that she turned terror-filled eyes to meet Queen Ena's in the mirror.

"I don't have magic," Kesi whispered, her fingers still on the necklace. Queen Ena placed a comforting hand on her shoulder.

"You have a bit of magic, but much less than you're used to," the Queen explained. "That might be why it's difficult to sense. In time the feeling will come back to you, but even still, it will only be enough to do a few party tricks."

"How will I defend the Chosen One, then?" Kesi asked, panicking. She'd doubted herself before, but how could she do this without her magic? Human Kesi was still getting adjusted to shoes and socks.

"You can transform back," Queen Ena explained, and a sigh of relief escaped Kesi. "Just rub the pendant on your necklace and you will return to your genie form. Go on, give it a try."

Kesi obeyed, rubbing the smooth stone between her thumb and forefinger, and held back a shriek as blue mist erupted at her feet, swirled around her figure, and curled up her legs and torso before finally obscuring her vison entirely. Kesi tried to bat away the strange magic, but after a moment it all disappeared on its own, leaving Kesi standing in front of the mirror in her genie form again.

Kesi relaxed, feeling her magic return. Blue hair and all, she liked herself better this way, even if the new hairdo was kind of cool.

"Is she up?" Elder Ashraf's now-familiar voice said before he poked his head inside the fabric-walled, makeshift room. "Ah, finally. It's good to see you awake. Did you like your human form, Kesi?"

"I uh…," Kesi stuttered. "I did, actually. It was nice. I give my thanks to the Queen for making it for me," she nodded at Queen Ena, who only shook her head.

"I didn't make it for you. All genies have the power to transform into humans, I just locked it away after I closed the gates to the human world. You're the first genie who has had it reawakened." Kesi blinked in partial confusion at the Queen's words. "Your form is your own, it was not made by me, but by your magic."

"Oh," was all Kesi could think of to reply.

"Of course you will have to return to your human form sooner or later," Elder Ashraf put in, "and to do that all you need to do is think about your human form and the process of transformation, and that's exactly what will happen. But Kesi, you can't just walk around and transform in public, you must keep your identity a secret, to better hide the Chosen One. If you publicly proclaim yourself as both the exchange student by the boy's side, and the magical genie fighting off Shaytan, it won't take the Shaytan long to put two and two together. They're stupid, but not *that* stupid. Think of it like being like a superhero. Cool, right?"

"Having to lead two different lives at the same time?" Kesi questioned, not sharing the Elder's state of mind.

"Exactly. Your job is to protect the human realm from the Shaytan and to guard the Chosen One closely. To mend into both duties, you must lead two separate lives," Elder Ashraf answered unhelpfully. "You got that?"

"Yeah," Kesi replied before Elder Ashraf rushed to continue.

"Your fake forms should be arriving at the Lovett house today. In a week we'll be sending you into the human world. We'll place you in a busy airport, so you'll have to pretend that you'd just gotten off a plane from Egypt. You'll have a suitcase and a backpack with you, and it'll be filled with everything you need- clothes, school supplies, your phone, blah, blah, blah. The clothes and things should be enough to last you a few months until you can buy some more. The Lovetts will be waiting for you at the end of the hallway, so just walk forward until you see them."

"Ashraf," Queen Ena spoke up after his fast-paced speech was done, "have I ever told you that you talk more like a youth than Kesi does."

"I'm honored by such a compliment, Mother," Elder Ashraf bowed his head in respect, a grin spreading across his face.

The Queen smiled back before turning to Kesi, "Do you have any questions?"

Kesi shook her head. She had run out of questions after what Elder Iamar had done to her. It was an odd feeling, as if she were suspended in an ocean of midday Jinn City air, Elder Iamar's voice telling her all she needed to know as the information became her own. Some images were even transferred, some of Elder Iamar's memories from when she had seen glimpses of the human world. She felt as if she'd been sleeping for weeks, not one day.

"Kesi, pay attention," the Elder said, snapping Kesi out of her memories. "You need to know your fake backstory, remember?"

"Oh, right," Kesi replied, sitting down on the bed, hoping that would help her focus on Elder Ashraf's fast words.

"Your name is Kesi Ena Haddad," he started, and Kesi cast a glance over to her Queen quickly, who just smiled at Elder Ashraf knowingly. '*Was that her idea?*' Kesi thought and narrowed her eyes at Queen Ena's smile, '*Oh, it was definitely her idea.*'

"Your mother is American. Her name is Bonnie Elizabeth Sparrow Haddad. She met your father, Azeem Haddad, while studying to become an archeologist in Egypt. Your father is a surgeon, your mother is an archeologist. You, your family, and your two sisters live in a big apartment in Cairo. You can see the pyramids, faintly, from your bedroom window. One of your sisters' names is Panya Marie Haddad, she's twenty-five and in college studying medicine in England. Your younger sister is named Yasmeen Lily Haddad, and she's nine. She likes acting and sports, but she's also a sort of class clown. You went to Abd al Hakim's Secondary School and played on all the sports teams available at least once in your life, including the one year that they had an American football team. Abd al isn't a big school, so they appreciated your participation. All in all, you were a bit of a sheltered child, which you can use as an excuse if anyone notices how you're not exactly…*normal*," Ashraf waved his hands in the air at the last word, as if it didn't exactly matter. "You can speak both Arabic and English, and once you hear English, Iamar's own knowledge will start to kick in and you'll be able to speak it perfectly clearly. Arabic you know because that's what we speak here, but that shouldn't get confused with your English-speaking abilities. Or at least we hope so."

"Right," Kesi said after a few moments, starting to adjust to Ashraf's way of explaining things, "Sounds…good. I guess."

"If anyone asks, your two best friends in Cairo are Selma Koury and Abubakar Toma," Ashraf added, "But you are mostly friends with everyone. Oh! And your birthday is July 6th."

"July 6th… got it," Kesi repeated, nodding to confirm more to herself than anyone else that she had some sort of confidence.

Elder Ashraf smiled at her, "Apparently, Queen Ena has excellent taste in protectors of Chosen Ones."

Kesi felt heat rush up her neck at the compliment, but it was Queen Ena who replied.

"You admire me too greatly, Ashraf," the Queen chuckled. "Anyone can make a great decision if they listen to their heart. You should be praising Kesi for calling on mine." She turned to Kesi, "I think it's time you returned to the land of the living, no?"

Kesi smiled and nodded, "I think that's a good idea."

"Ashraf, will you take Kesi to the City?" Queen Ena asked, and Ashraf nodded.

"Come, Kesi," he said, turning away in such a quick manner that it left Kesi scrambling to follow. For such an old man, Elder Ashraf certainly walked as fast as he talked.

The Elder lead Kesi out of the makeshift room to the bulk of the Infirmary, which was full of cots closed off by white curtains just like the one she had slept on the night before. The Infirmary was on the first floor through a large doorway across from the grand staircase that Kesi climbed up yesterday, so it didn't take long for Ashraf to lead her out. The Elder made the most of it, though, chattering along the way.

"Return here in eleven days to prepare for your arrival in the human world. That is the when the portal will be the strongest and it will be the safest for you to cross into the human realm," Ashraf explained before taking one of his rare pauses. "Do you know how to kill a Shaytan?"

"Doesn't everyone?" Kesi answered almost immediately. The answer lay in one of the most popular stories of Queen Ena; one of the Queen in her youth.

In the days of the Kahlil the prophet, Queen Ena met the king of Shaytan, Makalani, in battle for the resurrection of the Ghul. On that fateful day, the Queen was able to injure the monster by shooting with an arrow she had summoned from her mind and then infused with her own magic. This action was so great, and Makalani's injury was so dire that, combined, they cursed all Shaytan beings to the same fate. They could now be destroyed by such a weapon- a blade, arrow, or sword of a Jinn's creation that was infused with that same Jinn's magic.

After wounding Makalani, Queen Ena was able to use her magic to trap him and his dark magic in a lamp that she pushed far beneath the Ghul's surface. In this sport, where good triumphed over evil for the first time in the history of Jinn City, the Ghul's first tree sprouted. The story was well known by all the beings in Jinn City and it was one of Kesi's personal favorites.

"Good, you'll need that information, hopefully later rather than sooner," Elder Ashraf replied. "Don't forget what I've told you, about your backstory. Or about coming back in eleven days. That might be important too."

Kesi giggled as they entered the main room, passing by Yahya the Receptionist, who was sitting behind his desk and writing just as feverishly as before. Reaching the open front doors, Kesi turned to him.

"Can I...tell people about this?" Kesi asked. "About the Chosen One, and the plan."

The Elder replied immediately, "Yes, I suppose, but only a few friends. It's not about secrecy, of course, the Queen doesn't like to keep things from her people. She just wants to tell them herself instead of having rumors flying around."

"I understand," Kesi said. She only planned on telling Ra'id anyway, and maybe Fatima, but Kesi feared that the little girl wouldn't fully understand. She didn't want to break her heart, "Thank you, Elder, for everything," Kesi said to him respectfully.

Elder Ashraf's eyes twinkled. "The honor was all mine, really, Kesi," he said, before turning and going back into the High Palace, leaving her alone.

Kesi turned on her heels as well, then ran down the front steps and onto the path that would lead her back to the City. She let her feet carry her as fast as she could, and while she ran the self-doubt, which had been threatening to seep back into her mind since she had left the Queen's presence, started to ebb away. None of it mattered anymore because the Queen had chosen her.

'*I can do it, I can do it*', Kesi thought to herself as she left the golden gates of the High Palace. '*Queen Ena chose me. I'm* her *Chosen One. Yeah, I got this. I can do it.*'

"I got this," Kesi said out loud as she walked through the dirt streets of the City. She needed to find Ra'id. If he was confused or worried before, he must be going mad after Kesi stayed the night in the High Palace.

Kesi decided to check in the marketplace, a huge square area clear of any buildings where many genies frequently set up stands to showcase and offer what they had made with their own magic. Ra'id, as a Councilman, didn't work there, of course, but it was busy most days except on hot afternoons. It was likely that he would be there. The marketplace was on the side of the City facing the Ifrit Jungle and wasn't too far off from the High Palace. It only took Kesi a few minutes to half-fly, half-walk there.

It wasn't quite midday yet, which meant that lots of genies packed the marketplace to grab some last-minute items. Kesi's stomach growled when she saw the various Ifrit fruits and vegetables displayed in brightly colored baskets at some of the stands, reminding her how long it had been since she ate last. Genies didn't have to eat often, mostly only once or twice a day, but Kesi now knew that she would be eating a lot more as a human.

Most stands were placed on the edges of the square, but a few of them made another, smaller, circle in the center of the area. The amount of people offering, talking, and wandering around was suffocating.

Kesi found a familiar face in the crowd, the genie Kefira, who often when to the children's games at the Ghul and was much older than Kesi. She trotted over to Kefira's stand, slipping in between people and trying not to push too much. Kefira sold magical herbs, fruits, and other edible and non-edible plants from the Ifrit jungle. The older genie smiled at Kesi and she approached, finally breaking through the bulk of the crowd.

"Hey, Kesi," Kefira said while handing her a ripe lion fruit.

Its shape was yellow, round and had dents fallen into the sides, making the fruit look like it had a lion's mane. Kesi took it gratefully, taking a big bite. There was no currency in Jinn City, and Trades were simply for pleasure, as the days could get quite boring if a genie didn't have something to pass the time. It didn't take much for genies, like Kefira, to use magic to create crops that grew on the walls of their camps to give out in the marketplace each day. Others made scarves out of their magic, or bowls that held water to use during private prayers. It was very different from the competitive world that Kesi knew the humans lived in. One thing was the same, though, children and teenagers weren't expected to have a Trade, as they were still getting a grip on their magic. Kesi always thought that she would be like Kefira, selling food or maybe fabric. She loved matching colors together to make a pleasant work of art on a piece of magical cloth she had conjured from her mind. Kesi was sure that if she ended up in a Trade involving food, she would eat half of it throughout the day. She almost giggled at the thought before returning to the conversation.

"Have you seen Ra'id here lately?" Kesi asked, leaning her elbows on the stand as she took another bite of the soft, sweet fruit. Kefira turned her attention to a passing genie, handing him the small bag of herbs that he'd pointed to.

"The two of you are really chasing one another around lately." Kefira's sunshine yellow eyes turned to her, "He was here earlier, asking for you. He seemed a bit frantic. Is everything alright?"

Kesi groaned, drooping her head for a moment, "Everything is fine, I just made him a promise I sorta forgot to keep, and he's probably... pissed."

Kefira passed off another fruit, "He seemed more worried than pissed. He said no one saw you come back to your camp last night?"

"Yeah, I...," Kesi waved her free hand in the air, "Was busy."

"With what?" Kefira's gaze turned mischievous as Kesi took another bite of lion fruit, "Or should I ask, with who?"

Kesi nearly choked on her food, "Wha- why would you- what?" Kesi shook the disbelief out of her head, "I *can't* believe you just said that."

Kefira just chuckled absentmindedly, "Well, you're nearly a grown girl, I wouldn't be surprised...," she trailed off when she met Kesi's glare. "Ra'id said he was going to check your camp. He only left a few minutes ago, you might still catch him."

"Thank you, Kefira!" Kesi grinned and took her last bite of the small fruit, "And thanks for the food!"

Kesi could hear Kefira's chuckles as she ran away, pushing herself off the ground to fly over the crowd, which cast a shadow over the other genies. If she lost Ra'id now, she didn't know when she would find him. Kesi wanted to keep her promise to him almost as much as she wanted to tell someone, *anyone*, what she was up against. What she was asked to do.

After all, this would be the last chance that anyone had to talk her out of it.

CHAPTER SEVEN

DANVILLE, VIRGINIA

Roman

ROMAN STOOD IN the doorway of his sister's empty bedroom, admiring a room he had once adored. He remembered sitting on Sophia's light green bed when he was around seven years old, pestering her about a boy he had seen her talking to in the school yard when he and Emma had come to pick her up. Roman remembered trying to find space on the covers between her backpack and books. Sophia was never very organized.

"*Romey I'm trying to focus!*" eleven-year-old Sophia had whined, trying to push him off the bed playfully and, scattering some books in the process

"*Who was that boy? Is he your booooooyfriend?*" Roman giggled and moved closer to her.

"*Okay, okay, I'll tell you, but you can't tell all your friends.*" Sophia couldn't keep a serious face for long before leaning in and whispering in his ear, "*His name is Max and he's the most popular boy in school, and he used to like…*"

"She said her favorite color was blue, right?" Emma's voice

interrupted his thoughts. Roman nodded, his world coming back into focus. After retiring from modeling when Roman was born, Emma had taken up a lot of hobbies, including painting. Thankfully she still had huge buckets of paint left over and abandoned in the basement, one the color of sky blue. Most of Sophia's things had been boxed and hidden away, making the room look bare. The only things that remained that were truly hers were a few sticky stars left on the ceiling.

Although both siblings had chosen green to decorate their rooms, Sophia had chosen a much lighter, pastel color for her walls and decorations. Most of her furniture, now covered with sheets, were white to match, along with the carpet. The room was prepped for painting with the dresser, bed, desk, and lounge chair pushed away from the walls. Roman's bare feet didn't like the feeling of paper on the floor, nor did he like the emptiness of the room before him. It used to be filled with the liveliest person he'd ever known.

Emma handed him a paint roller, "You ready, baby?"

"I guess," Roman said, taking the roller from her. Emma was fond of doing things as a family that would have been much easier with a hired professional, and that included redecorating rooms. Roman had helped his parents re-paint the walls of their room more than once, but this was the first time he'd painted without Sophia.

Emma and Roman started painting on opposite sides of the room, each with half of the bucket of sky-blue paint.

"I hope she likes this," Emma chatted absentmindedly. "Dad and I are going shopping for new sheets and things to match, if you want to come."

"No, thanks," Roman said. "I have school soon, remember? I still have to finish my essay."

"Ah, essays," Emma mused. "I remember those."

"Mom," Roman replied, "You graduated in sophomore year."

"I said I remembered, not that I did a lot of them," Roman heard her chuckle from across the room.

Roman couldn't find the words to reply, so he focused on rolling the light blue color over Sophia's mint green walls. He tried to imagine someone else living in this room, sleeping in her bed, but it was hard to think about. It had always been Sophia. Every inch of this room held too many memories.

Roman tried to push the thoughts away, falling into the rhythmic process of his work. In the same way that sports and schoolwork helped, doing any sort of activity that required some amount of concentration put Roman into an almost thoughtless state of mind, the only things present for him now were the roller, blue paint, and the wall.

"Roman?" Emma jerked Roman out of his trance, his hand jerking away from the small corner at the bottom of the wall.

"We should take a break for lunch," his mother said, observing Roman's work. "Good job, baby."

"Lunch? But it's only…" Roman looked around him to see that he had completely finished his wall, the blue paint shimmering as the afternoon sun burst through the windows. "…ten. Or not, maybe it's noon."

Emma laughed at him, "Time flies when you're having fun! Or maybe you were just concentrating."

"Yeah. Maybe," Roman replied, putting down his roller and looking around the room further. "How did you get two and a half walls done?"

"I'm a professional," Emma went to flip her red hair before realizing that it was still up in a bun on top of her head. Recovering quickly, she said, "C'mon, let's go downstairs."

Roman followed his mother to the kitchen, where she promptly pulled out some bread, sandwich meat, cheese, and lettuce for two.

"Are you excited for your first day of school tomorrow?" Emma asked as Roman pulled open a drawer full of cups.

"I guess," Roman replied. "They posted our schedules online today."

"Oh great!" Emma exclaimed while Roman went to the fridge to fill his cup with water. "What classes do you have?"

"I have Mrs. Pendergrass again for Algebra 2," Roman replied painfully, and Emma groaned.

"The crazy teacher?" Emma asked, and Roman nodded. Mrs. Pendergrass was known for her short temper, adoration for humiliating students, and giving unfair detentions. Of course, most of the students came back to class without a detention slip, because Principle Alves, having heard their ridiculous reasons for being sent to his office, would send them away without so much as a slap on the wrist. It was a wonder that the old woman hadn't gotten fired yet.

"But I have Mr. O'Connor for Humanities and everyone says that he's cool," Roman said as he sat down at the kitchen table. Emma placed a plate holding a sandwich in front of him before taking a seat beside him, her meal looking the same.

"Mr. O'Connor...," she hummed, "I think Sophia had him. She liked him." Silence reigned over the two at the mention of Sophia's name.

Roman chewed quietly, filing through memories. *'Yes... Sophia did say that she had Mr. O'Connor for Humanities sophomore year.'* Roman remembered her mentioning him frequently that year.

"Maybe you'll have him when you're a sophomore, Romey," she had said once. Roman's chest filled with melancholy at the thought of sharing something with Sophia now, especially since she was no longer around to see it. The lights in the kitchen flickered for a fraction of a second, but Roman was too submerged in his memories of Sophia to notice. She would have been so excited to learn that he had Mr. O'Connor this year, but it hurt Roman too much to think of that.

'If only you knew, Soph', Roman said to himself, losing his appetite. He put the sandwich down and stood, catching his mother's attention. She looked over to his plate.

"If you only wanted half, you could have just told me," Emma said, watching him leave the kitchen.

"It's not that it's just...we should finish the paint as soon as possible," Roman shifted on his feet as he turned to face his mother, "so that you and Dad won't have any trouble putting new sheets on the bed or whatever." Roman pointed to the stairs around the corner from the kitchen, "It's only half a wall. I can finish it, you keep eating, okay?"

"Okay...," Emma said, her voice dripping with concern. Roman jogged up the stairs before she could say another word, and down the hall to the bedroom he and his mother had been working on. Looking at it now with its baby blue walls and covered furniture, it looked even more alien than when they had started. It was easier to convince himself that nothing had ever happened in this room now that it was so different.

'*Sophomore year...*' Once it was over, Sophia said it might have been the worst year of her life. Roman sighed. If only it was the worst thing to ever happen to her.

February of sophomore year was the first time Sophia had ever locked him out of her room. She was crying, upset about something that Roman, Emma, and Daniel, their father, couldn't figure out. He remembered standing in front of her door, listening to her sob from inside.

"*Soph? What's wrong? Please tell me. Mom and Dad are worried,*" Roman had said cautiously, afraid he was just making it worse.

"*You don't understand,*" she cried. "*You wouldn't understand.*"

"*Well I... well you're my sister, and I care. So...,*" Roman stuttered. "*So, try me.*"

A pause, "*You mean that?*"

"*Of course, Soph.*"

Roman remembered hearing a *click* and being faced with his red-rimmed eyed sister, tears streaming down her face. Roman walked into her room silently, hugging her the best he could. Both Lovett siblings were pretty tall kids, although with Sophia's four-year jump on him meant she was always a full head or two taller. It made hugging a little awkward.

"*Justin cheated on me,*" Sophia said finally, "*With Liz. Of all people, why my best friend? Why my boyfriend...?*"

"*I never liked either of them,*" Roman commented, making his sister chuckle.

"*Remind me to take your advice next time, Romey…*"

Roman walked swiftly over to the last, unpainted wall and picked up the roller that he had left behind. There wasn't much left to paint, and it was over all too soon. As Roman observed his work for any spots he'd missed, he heard his mother clear her throat behind him. He turned to see her leaning against the doorframe, arms crossed over her chest, and her grin showing approval.

"Nice job, baby," Emma said. "You should be a painter."

Roman rolled his eyes, "Yeah, I'll think about it."

Emma looked around the room, "I think she'll like it. Kesi, I mean."

Roman followed her wandering eyes, "Me too."

"So… let me get this straight," Ra'id said as he walked with Kesi through the Ifrit Jungle. Well-worn, dirt paths scattered the Jungle, winding around the impossibly tall Ifrit trees and the various magical ferns and plants. Some genies said that if you climbed all the way to the top of the Ifrit trees, you could almost see the whatever-it-was that created Jinn City and Queen Ena. Others said that all you would be able to see are the faint outlines of Shaytan huts from the other side of the Shaitan Mountains.

As Ra'id and Kesi walked along their chosen path, the strange creatures that lived on the Jungle's floor and bushes scurried out of their way. Kesi caught glimpses of them, nasnas and shiqqs to be precise, peeking out from the shrubberies along the path. Nasnas were smallish critters with bat-like wings, lamb-like tails, and money-like faces. Shiqqs were smaller than nasnas and looked like the human equivalent of a money sliced down the middle. With only half a face and body, the shiqqs had to hobble around on one leg as if their feet were made of springs.

"You're going to have to go to the human realm… for an unknown amount of time… to protect a boy. A boy who's supposed to bring our realm and the human one together? Not just 'open the gates' but *together*," Ra'id made air quotes around "open the gates" before pausing to find the right words, "Like, bring peace to the universe together? *And…* you're supposed to protect him by *killing…* Kesi, *listen…* by *killing* the Shaytan that are trying to kill *him* because they… What? Want to take over their realm so they can control more land or something?"

"Pretty much," Kesi paused as they walked further into the Jungle, the sound of the Ifrit frogs' pretty songs echoing in the distance. The tune gave her an idea for what to say next, "I also have a lot of new information about the humans in my head. Like, for example, in their world birds sing like our frogs do."

Ra'id paused to listen to the music too. "Birds? Birds can't do anything but squawk. The human realm must be ridiculous."

"It is," Kesi agreed before coming to her next statement, "You're not… going to try and talk me out of it?"

"Talk you out of it?" Ra'id laughed, "Kesi, the Queen chose *you*, out of all the genies in Jinn City, she chose *you*. It's amazing! How could I talk you out of it? The Queen thinks you're the best for the job."

Kesi bit her lip and hopped over an Ifrit tree root to avoid stumbling, "But… what do *you* think?"

Ra'id took a moment to collect his words, "Kesi, I've known you all your life. You're the most adventurous, courageous, and intelligent person that I know. You can handle your magic better than anyone in Jinn City, you can beat a horde of genies older and younger than you in any Ghul game, you're quick on your feet and in your mind, and honestly, Kesi I…I don't think that there's anyone better for the job."

Kesi let out a sigh of relief. Surely if Queen Ena, the Elders, *and* Ra'id thought she could do this, it was at least possible, right?

Ra'id looked over to her, and as if reading her thoughts, he added, "Don't doubt yourself. I've known you long enough to know that's one of your habits. If you can't trust your own judgement or mine, at least trust Queen Ena's. She's had thousands of years to think about this, remember?"

"Right," Kesi nodded. "I just… hope you're right. That we're right. For Roman Lovett's sake," she finished, remembering the emerald green eyes from her nightmare begging for her help, and fading, fading, fading…

"What are you worried about?" Ra'id asked, breaking her out of her far-off thoughts.

"I guess…the actual protection part. You know, from the Shaytan," Kesi replied, "I know that genies are kind of built to fight them in some way and that I'll have instincts helping me but…I've never done it before. I've never even seen someone fight a Shaytan in person. How am I supposed to do it myself?"

Ra'id shrugged before ducking under a low-hanging branch. "As you said, instinct will take over when the time comes."

"What if I can't… fit in?" Kesi asked in a rush, all her insecurities about the whole affair pushing to the surface. "What if people can see right through me and be able to tell that I'm not… that I'm not *human*."

Ra'id laughed, "Do you know how many people are in the human realm? If you do act a little odd at first, they'll just blame it on you coming from a far-off place. That is who you're posing as, right? A girl from a far-off place."

"I guess." Kesi only felt a bit better, "But what if I…what if I fail?"

"The prophecy doesn't seem to think you will," Ra'id replied quickly. "You just need to set it in motion by getting there first."

Kesi relaxed, self-doubt releasing its hold at Ra'id's reason. "You're right. I can do this. I think. No," Kesi hit her temple with the edge of her palm, "I *know* I can do this. That's better."

Ra'id chuckled, "If humans are as weird as I think they are, I'm sure you'll fit in."

Kesi glared over at Ra'id, who was grinning in response. She playfully shoved him, and he returned the gesture. The two continued their playful pushing until they emerged out of the Jungle and back to the boarders of the City, where the happy shrieks of children could be heard in the distance.

"The kids are at the Ghul," Kesi concluded, picking up her pace, getting ready to fly across the city. "Come on!"

"Oh Jinn, not again," Ra'id groaned as Kesi vaulted herself into the air, laughing down at him. She only waited around long enough to see Ra'id start to hover before propelling herself above Jinn City, flying hard and fast until she saw the grassy land of the Ghul. She slowed down and lowered herself into the tall grass where the children were running around, playing a game of tag.

"Kesi!" Fatima ran out of the grass to hug her knees, giggling up at her. Kesi smiled back, embracing the little girl.

"You're playing chase again?" Kesi asked, crouching down to meet Fatima's jade green gaze.

"We ran out of game," Fatima pouted, "or, Abubakar did. He's not very good at making up games."

Kesi chuckled, her mind thinking on overdrive with what she knew about the humans and their games, their sports. She and the children had already played games that were very similar to the ones that the humans played, but there was one that was completely different from anything in Jinn City. It was a bit rough maybe, but Kesi knew that the children would love it.

"How about…we play a different game," Kesi said. "One that…I made up. We can call it…"

"The Kesi Game!" Fatima clapped her hands together and cheered, causing children to creep out of the grass to look at them. There were more of them tonight, and a couple of teenage genies near Kesi's age came out, too.

"Hey, we missed you guys last night," Kesi grinned at her childhood friends who hadn't been at the Ghul the night before.

Saalim and Mushtaree both fourteen years old, were the youngest of the teenage group of friends. They were inseparable and Kesi never saw one without the other.

Shakila was nineteen with a wonderfully kind face and teal-colored hair. Kesi didn't see much of her anymore because, being that she was merely a year away from being eligible to take The Council Exam, she had been spending most of her nights learning from other Councilmaidens about their duties and what she needed to know to pass the test. Kesi knew how badly Shakila wanted to be on the council and sincerely hoped that all her friend's hard work paid off.

Eighteen-year-old Idris had already found his Trade by selling magnificent, multi-colored carpets at a stand in the marketplace. Since Kesi often frequented the marketplace to grab a bite to each or to chat with friends, Idris, with his vivid pink hair and blazing eyes, would never become a stranger to Kesi.

Raihana was sixteen, with lovely white locks that curled and bounced with each move she made. and Kesi had often found herself envying Raihana's hair when they were younger, but now she had grown out of such childlike insecurities and preferred to enjoy Raihana's sparkly company instead.

Hussain was a year older than Raihana. He had mesmerizing periwinkle eyes that matched his vibrant purple-blue hair. Raihana and Hussain were struggling, in vain, to keep their romance a secret from the rest of the group, but they were so close that Kesi and the others could tell the exact moment when Hussain and Raihana's friendship crossed into something more. Still, no one said anything. Hussain and Raihana would tell them when they were ready, even if th3e waiting was terrible.

The seven of them weren't the only teenagers in the city, of course, but they were the only ones that liked to play in the Ghul with the younger genies. They had stuck together when they were younger and connected to each other in a way that surpassed similar interests. The seven of them were best friends. Kesi had grown up with them all, lived with them, slept beside them, played games with them, and shared everything with them for years. Their bond was too strong for any one of them to become distant from the group. They, like the genies who had helped raised Kesi when she was younger, would remain in her heart forever.

Shakila shrugged in response to Kesi's comment, "I was at the Library. I don't know where the rest of them were."

"I was with...um...," Hussain looked helplessly over to Raihana, who pretended not to notice him, and instead played with the fabric of her clothes. Kesi chuckled. Their long-time romance was painfully obvious to everyone a fact that was clearly lost on them. She wished that they would just realize that everyone *knew* about the two of them already.

"Oh, gross, you guys," Mushtaree spoke up, pretending to gag into the palm of her hand. Kesi laughed outright at her reaction.

"Gross, what?" Ra'id's voice startled the seven of them, leaving them stammering *nothing, nothing! -s* in response. Ra'id only gave them a skeptical look, especially Hussain and Raihana, who were blushing to their roots.

"Kesi, the *game*," Fatima whined at her feet, drawing her attention away from her friends.

"Right, ok," Kesi replied, standing up and looking around to see that all the younger children of Jinn City had gathered before her.

"Alright, this game is called...The Kesi Game," she smiled down at an excited Fatima. "What you do is... Well, there are two teams, each with their own side of the field. To score you must get all the way to the other team's side of the field. And... the two teams line up in two lines facing one another in the middle of the field. One team gets the ball first, but only one person can hold the ball at first and they have to stay in the middle," Kesi paused, trying to recall all the information Elder Iamar had shown her about American football. She knew all the proper terms for the game, but she wanted to make sure that those around her could understand, "To get the game started, the person with the ball has to lean over and throw it through their legs to one of their team members behind them."

"Then what do you do?" Saalim was clearly interested, moving forward to hear what she was saying.

"Then the one who caught the ball as to start running towards the end of the field in front of them," Kesi pointed to the horizon behind the children to demonstrate. "And…basically… if they get to the other side before someone tackles them, they get the point! If you know that you can't make it, you can always pass to your other teammates, but that means that the other team can steal it from the air!" Kesi clapped her hands around an imaginary American football, causing the other children to shriek in delight.

"We can tackle people?" Abubakar spoke up, clearly overjoyed by this insight.

"Yes, but not too rough," Kesi replied. "Or else you'll get in trouble."

As the boy pouted at her answer, Kesi summoned what she now knew an American football looked like into her hands, the surface glittering with its magical properties. The leather felt rough in her palms and she quickly adjusted her fingertips to the correct positions she knew they were supposed to be in. She grinned at the crowd of children in front her, all of them *ooh*ing and *aah*ing.

Kesi placed her free hand on her hip and widened her smile, "Boys verses girls?"

CHAPTER EIGHT

DANVILLE, VIRGINIA

Roman

*B*EEP, BEEP, BEEP, *beep.*

Roman groaned and slipped out of his loft bed, stumbling to reach the cell phone he had left charging on his desk the night before. After finally shutting his alarm off, Roman let his head fall onto his desk with a *thump* and groaned again.

He hated the first day of school.

Despite his grogginess and hatred, Roman managed to drag himself out of his desk chair, over to his dresser, where he grabbed the clothes he'd be wearing that day and made his way into his bathroom. After a nice, hot, and purposefully prolonged shower, Roman stood before his bathroom mirror, huffing at his partially put together appearance as he brushed his teeth. His reflection looked tired and sulky, but at least he had some decent clothes on and no longer smelled like he hadn't showered in a week, which somehow was the case whenever he skipped a shower. After wiping his mouth free of toothpaste Roman ran his free hand through his choppy black hair, glared once more at his reflection, and then stumbled out of the bathroom. He quickly grabbed his backpack off his bedroom floor before carrying himself downstairs, fully away that, this time and from now on, his sister would not be driving him to school.

'*Sophia…school…oh God no.*'

At Waterford Academy, Roman was seen by most of his classmates and teachers as somewhat of a broken boy. There were some people at Waterford that knew nothing about Roman other than the fact that he was the kid that lost his sister to cancer the year before and spend most of his rocky freshman year trying to get it together, and, more often than not, desperately, hopelessly failing. While he would never deny that he had struggled a lot with his sister's death, he couldn't help but feel as if the aftermath of the situation was less than justifiable. Mostly, his fellow classmates either avoided him, pitied him, or both. His teachers weren't much better. Those instructors that he was close to, in addition to random goody-two-shoe students, started to check up on him to make sure that he hadn't fallen into any "bad habits." If it weren't for his four best friends, Dimitri, Ben, Aasma, and Kharim, Roman wasn't sure he would have made it through the year.

Roman first met Dimitri Larin when they were both in kindergarten together, in some event that his teachers found adorable, but that neither boy could remember. Dimitri was a quiet guy, mostly because he was deaf in one ear and self-conscious about the way he spoke. No matter how many times Roman had assured him that he sounded just like any other person, Dimitri was still afraid to speak up too often. Dimitri's older sister, Yuliana, had been one of Sophia's best friends. The Larin's had been more than empathetic and kind since Sophia's passing.

In about second grade, Benita Perez moved to Virginia from California and befriended Dimitri and Roman. Mostly called "Ben," the girl dazzled the boys with her ability to speak both Spanish and English fluently, her outspoken nature, and her love for get-togethers and parties. Ben's parents and eldest sister were all immigrants from

Mexico, having come to American before she was born. She was the fourth eldest sibling out of six, and her brother, Ricardo, had been Sophia's age. Sophia and Ricardo had been good friends before she died, and Roman was pretty sure that Ricardo had had a crush on his sister.

Lastly, in their freshman year, the Seyegh twins started school at Waterford. Since they were from a Muslim family and practiced the religion themselves, most of the other kids in their year were rude or outright aggressive with them. Ben, Dimitri, and roman had accepted them into their small group of friends, helped them adjust to their new school, and, with lots of help from Ben, were able to shut up the biggest bullies in a matter of a few months. Aasma had the worst out of the two because her hijab made her stand out in a crowd. She didn't seem to heed any of it, though her brother, who was a bit overprotective of her, was easily angered by it all. In fact, Roman remembered Aasma trying to prevent Kharim from getting into a full-fledged fist-fight more than once, always chanting, "they're not worth it," in his ear. It seemed like the two of them were either busy protecting each other or fighting with one another. Sophia had bonded with Aasma over their shared love of art, and something called "fashion sense" which was something completely foreign to Roman.

Then Sophia died, and the five of them grew closer while growing farther away from the rest of the world. There was something special in the way that they bonded and stuck together, something that Roman couldn't explain, as if the five of them were just meant to be.

Roman was excited to see them, really, he just wasn't so excited about…pretty much everyone and everything else.

"Power through, babe," Emma chuckled as she watched Roman wander sleepily into the kitchen, preparing his breakfast.

"You should really have something more substantial than cereal," his mother mused, but Roman only found the energy to grunt in response.

Roman sat down at the kitchen table with his food, glaring at his mother's healthy plate of eggs, a bagel, fruit, and bacon. He knew that if he ate like her every morning, he would eventually become her, a night owl turned early bird, but he just couldn't do it, not when he could barely keep his eyes open.

"Did you stay up late finishing your essay?" Emma asked cheerily, taking a sip from her smoothie.

"*Mm-hmm.*"

"Maybe Kesi will be able to help you with your Humanities," Emma chuckled, wiggling her eyebrows at him. Roman just rolled his eyes as she continued, "Just imagine it…a study date… sort of… with your super-cute exchange student roomie."

Roman nearly spit out his cereal, "Wha-no. Don't you remember the last time you tried to set me up with a girl?"

"In my defense, I didn't know that Becky was that bad!" Emma replied hurriedly. "If I had known she was such a…witch, I wouldn't have told you to go talk to her. And you were in 7th grade, for God's sake!"

"She wouldn't stop telling everyone that I liked her for a month," Roman glared.

"I know, sorry baby," Emma looked sheepish, "but hey, at least it was only a month!"

Roman ignored her, lost in his own thoughts, "Who would *ever* like Becky Oakley?"

"Oh, I know, right," Emma rolled her eyes. "I can still hear her parents saying…" Emma stuck her nose up in the air and lowered her voice to resemble a man's, "'*Rebecca! Don't forget to tell your grandfather thank you for the pony and the 24-karate gold necklace, and the diamond bracelet, and the Ferrari that you can't even drive yet - oops, wait, no, that was a gift from us. Don't thank your grandparents for that,*'" Emma scoffed and Roman laughed. "Don't you forget that that family isn't any richer than us, baby. They just chose to spoil themselves and their kids and we don't," she finished, pointing her fork at him before diving back into her eggs. Roman just shook his head at her and returned to his cereal. He had only just finished when Emma jumped up from her own food, placing her plate in the sink.

"Come on, we're going to be late if we wait around any longer," she said, prompting Roman to grab his backpack and follow her out of the kitchen, dropping his bowl in the sink as he passed.

Car rides to school with Sophia mostly consisted of loudly played music and mini dance parties for the short twenty-minute ride, but of course he didn't share the same sort of thing with his mom. Instead, Roman sat in the passenger seat in silence as the radio played quietly in the background, reliving memories of this day a year ago.

"*Woo let's go! I gotta start off my senior year* right!" Sophia was ecstatic, turning up the radio loud to the sound of *Domino* by Jessie J.

"*You're really excited about this, aren't you?*" Roman remembered laughing.

"*Well of* course *I am, dear brother,*" Sophia cast him a cheeky grin as they left the driveway. "*One more year and I'm out of this hellhole! It's about time I started on my career. Or at least started studying it. I promise you, Romey, that I will be such a great fashion designer one day that our family will no longer be semi-famous, but super famous!*"

"*Wonderful,*" Roman deadpanned, dread creeping into his mind. Sophia had always loved the spotlight a thousand times more than Roman did.

"*Don't worry, Romey, it'll take a while.*" Sophia thought for a moment, "*Hey, maybe I could be an actress on the side, or a singer, or...*"

"*Please stop,*" Roman laughed, teasing. "*Please.*"

"*Or maybe you should be the singer,*" Sophia commented, before catching his distain-wrought face. "*Oh, come on, Romey, I can't believe that you haven't ever sang for anyone but me, Mom, and Dad before. Your voice is amazing. I dare you to be in the talent show at the end of the year. I just dare you.*"

"*Maybe you should be a professional annoying dare giver on the side instead of an actress or a singer,*" Roman groaned, and Sophia just laughed at his lame attempt at an insult. He should have known better. Nothing got to his sister.

"*You'll see, Romey*," she said, "*You'll see*."

He never found out what she meant by that, Roman realized. Maybe it was something about his singing, or the talent show? Roman chewed his lip absentmindedly, the thought bothering him more than it should, probably because Sophia was dead and gone forever. And forever was an awfully long time.

"Have a good day, baby," Emma mused as they pulled up to the front of the school, Roman ready and popping open the car door, "I love you."

"I love you too, Mom," Roman gave her a small smile before grabbing his book bag and hopping onto the pavement. He was all too aware of his mother watching him with concern form the car as he slid through the front door of the school.

There were quite a few students in the airy foyer of Waterford Academy, and they all did a double take when they saw him. Roman ducked his head, looking away, not wanting to even contemplate what they were thinking about him.

Roman hadn't made it that far into the school before a small body collided with his, nearly sending him tumbling to the ground. The figure wrapped around him in a tight embrace.

"Ben!" Roman whined as the brunette ruffled his hair with her hands.

"Hey, dork, that's what you get for not coming to our going back to school party," Ben grinned.

"I was busy painting the room for our exchange student!" Roman defended, noticing Dimitri quietly approaching the two of them.

"Right, right, chico," Ben replied, rolling her eyes. She placed her hands on her hips as Aasma and Kharim appeared at her sides, Dimitri slowly bringing up the rear.

"Sophomore year!" Kharim cheered. "We're not loser freshman anymore!"

Roman looked around at the other Waterford Academy students giving the five of them weird looks, "I think we're still losers."

"I think you're too pessimistic," Aasma answered, wiping imaginary dust from her jeans. "New year, new start! Or whatever."

"Yeah, *whatever*," Kharim imitated, causing Aasma to turn on him furiously. "Hey, chill. Take a joke."

"It wasn't a *joke* Khar, you meant to be *mean*," Aasma retorted, "and annoying, too, apparently."

"Ladies, ladies," Ben chuckled. "Calm down. Don't spoil the first day of school!"

"As if it could be spoiled more," Roman responded. "It spoils itself by existing."

Kharim shook his head at Roman, "Man, maybe you'll be the one to ruin the first day. At least try to make the most of it, Rom."

"We should probably get to the auditorium," Aasma said, pointing towards the double doors behind them. A sea of students was slowly making its way through the auditorium doors for the first school meeting of the year. Every Monday, the whole school had to congregate in the auditorium in order to receive the weekly announcement from the school staff. Being that they were on block scheduling, these meetings cut their breaks after the first and third classes from forty-five minutes to thirty minutes, which many students didn't appreciate. Roman, however, found that the meetings were a good way to find out what was going on at school, since he often forgot to check his school email and the school website. If it weren't for the meetings, Roman wouldn't have a clue what was going on that week.

Roman and his friends filed into the auditorium and picked seats in the near-middle area of the space that was designated for sophomores. Roman nestled into his seat as other students washed in, filling the other empty seats. A couple of people sent glances his way before turning to their friends and whispering. The most prominent member of this whispering group was Becky Oakley, a girl known for her popularity, her promiscuous attitude with boys, and her vexing nature with almost everyone she came across. That was, of course, the nice way to put it. Ben preferred to use words that Roman wouldn't dare repeat in front of his mother.

Becky's long, mousy brown hair fell in loopy curls that ended near her stomach. When she looked over towards Roman and his friends, her jade green eyes flashed mischievously. Turning to her friends, Becky held up a freshly manicured hand adored with a hoard of small rings in front of her mouth to try and hide the fact that she was whispering about them. The girl she was whispering to, Karoline Blanchard, had hair the color of hay cut to the middle of her neck, and large hazel eyes that always adoring and fearful when resting on Becky. Karoline was normally quiet and submissive when it came to Becky, but completely different with everyone else.

Becky, Karoline, and all eight of their gossip-fueled friends sat in one row, behind a large group of boys who Becky giggled at fondly. Much like Becky and her friends, these boys seemed to have no social compasses and only cared about a girl's body and how willing she was to be with them.

"Don't you ever become like them, Romey," Sophia's voice echoed in her head, *"There's a group of them in each grade, in every school, but Romey I swear to you, if I ever hear of you acting like them I will beat your ass, you understand?"*

'*I understand*,' Roman thought in response, looking over to the senior area where Justin Mikals and his friends used to sit the year before. Justin, Sophia's cheating ex-boyfriend, was another of those boys, especially after he cheated on Roman's sister. He turned his head to where Elizabeth Brown, the girl Justin cheated on Sophia with, used to sit. She reminded him of Becky, or at the very least, of one of her friends. There were so many people connected to his sister that had sat in those senior seats every day, even after her death.

But none of them were here now, only their younger siblings or underclassmen friends. Roman looked over to the group of boys by Becky, focusing on the curly-haired Nico Romano. His older sister,

Elene, had been one of Sophia and Liz's friends in junior year, but when it became clear to her that she had to choose a side, she didn't choose Sophia. Karoline's older brother, Brice, had also been a mutual friend between the two girls and had made a choice similar to Elene. Roman wondered if either of them regretted that decision now.

'*Maybe Soph was right*', Roman thought to himself, '*Maybe she really never left after all.*'

The sound of fingers tapping a microphone quieted all the chatting students, and Roman looked to the stage to see Mr. Murray up there, smiling. Roman wasn't exactly sure what Mr. Murray taught, but he was the face of all the school meetings and always gave the important teacher announcements and introduced the students who had signed up to explain fundraisers, games, or school projects or achievements. Never mind the fact that he was Roman's football coach.

"Hey, hey everyone! Welcome to the first school meeting of the year!" Mr. Murray began before mumbling into the microphone, "Just kidding. We all hate this place. And we know it- yeah," he paused as a couple of students cheered. Mr. Murray grinned again at the attention. His love of being in the spotlight was what made him so good at these morning meetings. Roman was sure that he would fall asleep more often than not if Mr. Murray wasn't the one giving the announcements.

"Anyway, today is an A day, and for those of you newbies or freshman who have no idea what that means, it means that you have blocks A, B, C, and D today, in that order," Mr. Murray explained. Roman could tell that he had rehearsed this speech many times before, but he still took it slow so that everyone could understand. Roman sat back and closed his eyes. He was sure that no one would blame him if he zoned out for a few seconds. "… club sign ups and sports sign-ups are happening next week, but we'll remind you about that next Monday…

"Let's see, what else did Mr. Alves ask me to tell you guys? Oh right! Ha-ha, don't worry about being late to classes today, the teachers will excuse you for being late if you got lost or couldn't figure out what class you were going to. Ask some upperclassmen or fellow classmates for help. It's a big building, we get it. Just generally, if you have science, you're in the Science Wing at the other end of the building. If you have math, you're in the Math Wing above us, etc. etc.," Mr. Murray continued, pointing in the direction of each section of the building. "If worse comes to worse, you can always ask Mrs. Fenton at the front desk for help. I'm sure she knows…something. I actually have no idea, that's just what I've been told to say," Mr. Murray chuckled at himself almost as much as the students did. "Anyway, here is our very own Principle Alves with his annual back to school speech!"

Mr. Murray moved to the stairwell by the edge of the stage as the white-haired Principle Alves took over the microphone, nodding and smiling at Mr. Murray.

"Thank you, Dave, for that lovely introduction. I'm sure you've been looking forward to this day and to giving that speech for part of your summer break," the principle began before addressing the students. "It's nice to see that auditorium full again, and to see the many new and old faces in the crowd," he continued, smiling out at the freshman section of the auditorium, and then the remaining sections. "The new faces here probably are not aware of the tragic event that took place last fall," Roman cringed in his seat as what seemed like the whole school turned to gawk at him. He felt like a zoo animal, and thought to thought to himself, '*Presenting, the boy who lost his sister to cancer! Look and marvel at how this creature acts in its natural habitat!*' "Our very own Sophia Lovett lost her battle with cancer, but I assure you that we will be putting the past behind us in order to move forward, just like Sophia would have wanted."

"What do you know what she would have wanted?" Roman mumbled, causing Aasma to place a reassuring hand on his arm.

"Here's to a new year and new beginnings. Happy first day!"

Mr. Alves finished, walking off the stage while people clapped. Mr. Murray jumped onto the stage, taking his place in the spotlight once again. Roman simply didn't know how he did it every Monday.

"Thank you, Mr. Alves," Mr. Murray said before looking at the watch attached to his wrist. "We have a few minutes, do we have any announcements from the floor?" he asked, prompting students or teachers to raise their hands to give their own, unplanned announcements. When the crowd before him made it clear that no hands were going to be raised, Mr. Murray continued, "Well, I'll just let you go a few minutes early, then. Have a good day, and remember, it's A block!" Students stood up to leave before he had even finished his sentence.

Roman hurried out of the auditorium, his friends following close behind. He was sure that he would explode if someone stopped him to ask him how he was *doing* for the millionth time since Sophia died. *How was he doing?* Why did people who didn't even know him or Sophia before all this cancer crap happened keep asking him that? Why couldn't they just stop pretending like they cared or understood what he was going through? The people who knew him best and cared about him the most knew not to ask *that* question. They knew that asking him that wouldn't help. Sometimes though, if he admitted it to himself, he wished they would ask. That way he would be able to unload all his horrible thoughts and overwhelming emotions onto someone who wouldn't judge him for them; someone who loved him as much as they loved Sophia.

"Roman!"

He groaned as he recognized the voice that was calling him. It was Ruby Willow, a self-declared Democrat and feminist, who clearly had no idea what either of those words meant. She had short-cropped, raven-black hair styled into two pigtails on the sides of her head, with bangs running in a straight line across her forehead. Her dark blue eyes were hidden behind square, black-framed glasses that made her eyes look bug-like, which Roman had heard were there just for show. Ruby enjoyed preying on people's differences, using them to bolster her various imaginary campaigns against inequality and the like. She and her equally as enthusiastic friend, Alexis Folley, liked to bombard people with differences as small as crooked teeth to as big as religion or race with tons of questions and then plaster their responses, made up or otherwise, all over the Waterford School Newspaper each month. Alexis had cut almost all her hair off and dyed the rest neon green, leaving it in a short, badly dyed pixie cut. The color made Roman cringe. *'Out of all the colors in the world...'*

The two of them had been harassing Roman for an interview every chance they got after he talked with them for a few moments at the end of freshman year about his sister for the school newspaper. They enjoyed cornering him and asking him loud, private questions about Sophia ever since she had died. Roman thought that they must secretly love watching him squirm under their scrutiny and cringe with pain at the mention of his sister. He had done his best to dodge them at every turn. He didn't understand why they wouldn't just leave him alone. In his mind, he had given them more than enough. The two of them just couldn't drop the subject.

'It's been a year for God's sake. Can't they take a hint?' Roman's mind grumbled angrily. *'I don't want to talk about her.'*

Roman ignored their voices and kept moving, but soon the two girls were blocking his path, a favorite tactic of theirs. Neither of them was tall, so Roman towered over them. Despite his physical advantage, Roman shrunk back. Nothing good ever came from these two.

Ruby had short-cropped raven-black hair that she kept in two messy pigtails and in bangs that ran straight across her forehead, square, black-framed glasses on her face. Roman had heard that Ruby didn't even need the glasses- she wore them just for show. Personally, Ben had told him on more than one occasion that it was better if she ditched them, since it made her dark blue eyes look all too bug-ish.

"We would like to talk to you about your sister," Ruby began, taking out her notepad and pen from her notorious hidden inside jacket pocket. "What were her views on the pay gap? Were there any stereotypes for girls that she felt strongly about breaking?"

"I gave you an interview last year. I really don't want to talk about it again," Roman huffed. He felt as if he had been reciting the same speech for a year to a garden of brick walls. "Because, you know, she *died* and she was my *sister*. Please have some respect for me and my family. I just really, really don't want to talk about it. Please."

"It'll only take a few minutes," Alexis put in, still not allowing him to pass through the doorway. Roman watched his friends pass behind the two girls helplessly. Aasma held back Ben from attacking the girls while Dimitri watched with a worried look on his face.

"Yeah, I know it would," Roman replied swiftly, talking in the harshest tone that he had taken with them yet. They seemed a bit taken aback, not used to Roman using a dark tone with anyone. "But I don't want to talk about it. Can't you just use what I gave you last year? I don't understand why you *still* need to write an article about her."

"It's important to document her ideals so we have good material for our next article." Ruby talked to him as if he were a child. "People, like Alexis and myself, want to work to make Waterford a better place in her honor."

Roman clenched his jaw. "I'm not talking to you right now."

"God! Who do you think you are?" Alexis blurted angrily, causing Roman to spin on her just as he was slipping by them. Judging by her jerky hand movements, and the tightness in her features, Roman guessed she was about to go on one of her infamous nonsense rants. Roman tensed. When Alexis was angry, she didn't hold back. "You must think you have it all. You have no idea how hard life is!"

Roman snapped, raising his voice the most he had in years. "My sister. Is dead. Don't tell me that I don't know what pain is."

Ben came to his side, fury clear on her features. "Listen, you have no right to say anything about Roman, Aasma, Kharim, or Sophia, because you don't know crap about them. And for the record, Sophia wasn't *eso*…like you," she shot as she guided Roman and their other friends away. When they first met, Roman though that Ben's frequent angry slips into Spanish were involuntary. Now Roman knew that it was a habit she'd formed when she felt herself about to cuss and didn't want to get caught by teachers. "She was a better one than *you*."

Roman swallowed his own anger in shame, catching the looks he and his friends were receiving as they moved through the lazy bundle of students crowding the halls.

"I'll show them, those b-" Ben stopped when she noticed Roman's downcast look, "Rom?"

"I'm sorry, I shouldn't have gotten angry like that, it wasn't…" He couldn't find the right words to say. It wasn't what Sophia would have wanted? It wasn't what Ruby and Alexis deserved? Nothing seemed to fit what he was feeling.

"Don't apologize, Roman," Dimitri said quietly.

"D is right," Kharim added. "They were asking for it. I mean, what did they think would happen? You have nothing to be sorry for, man."

Roman sighed deeply, looking at each of his friends with tired eyes. "This is going to be a long year."

CHAPTER NINE

JINN CITY

Kesi

KESI WOKE UP the next morning with a start, the same way she had been ever since she'd came home from the High Palace. '*Was it really only three days ago?*' Kesi thought to herself, '*It feels like it was only yesterday.*'

This morning was different, though. Instead of being jolted awake at the flood of terrifying yet exciting memories and information breeching her subconscious mind, Kesi awoke at the sound of trumpets and horns, a signal that all genies knew well. Queen Ena was about to give one of her rare public announcements.

Kesi vaulted herself to her feet as another thought struck her. '*What if the announcement is about me?*' That thought fresh in her mind, Kesi sprang out of her camp's window, and made her way down the building to the soft ground, collecting her thoughts before starting to fly. '*When was the last time Queen Ena gave an announcement? It had to have been years ago... Where are the announcements again?*' Kesi hardly remembered it. All she remembered was gripping teenage Kefira's shoulders with her legs and looking over the crowd of people gathered in the clear square as the Queen hovered in the air to see all her people. '*The clear square…the only place in Jinn City large enough to hold all the genies…*'

"Kesi, you idiot," Kesi felt the urge to hit herself upside the head. "Of course, she would be in the marketplace," she said to herself before pushing herself into the air and soaring towards the marketplace.

When Kesi arrived, a large crowd had already gathered, larger even than the copious amounts of people that usually showed up at the marketplace during the day. Kesi had to remain hovering to see any of what was going on, the constant shifting of the people and sheer number of genies making it impossible to see anything.

The makeshift stands that were put up each day were tucked away in some hidden corner of the streets around them, creating more space. A circle of white-clad men and women stood at the center of the square, all surrounding the glowing Queen Ena. One of them, Elder Iamar, looked up and smiled at Kesi. Kesi blinked before smiling back at her. Did the Elders accompany the Queen to the last announcement she had given?

Kesi looked at the crowd and found several genies mimicking her actions, floating above the rest to get a better view. She spotted the children sitting on the edge of a nearby rooftop, and looking down on the scene below, their legs dangling. Many other young genies were with them, including Saalim, Shakila, Raihana, Hussain, and… Divya. She was brushing up against a very uncomfortable-looking Ra'id while Idris and Mushtaree just laughed at them.

Kesi sighed, considering turning away and finding her own place in the crowd, far, far away from the green-haired Councilmaiden. She was about do just that when Ra'id waved her over, his eyes pleading for help. Kesi huffed at him. Sometimes Ra'id was just too nice. He wouldn't let Divya down, even if he was the only one who could do it as gently as possible. Kesi didn't want to have to save him from himself, especially when it involved Divya, but she knew that he

wasn't going to do anything on his own. Besides, she would have
who knew how long before she had to interact with Divya again after
she was sent to the human realm, so she supposed that she couldn't
complain now. After all, shouldn't she at least try to mend whatever
fences were broken before she left?

'*Fine*,' the snarky part of her submitted before she carried herself
over to the rooftop, landing gently beside Ra'id and the other genies.
For once Divya remained quiet towards her, completely focused on
Ra'id.

"This makes me want to vomit," Kesi mumbled into Mushtaree's
ear as she moved past, making the girl giggle.

"Hey…Ra'id," Kesi rocked back on her heels as she approached
the two, causing making Ra'id to pause in his kind attempts to peel
Divya off his arm.

"Hey! Kesi!" Ra'id gave her a forced, uncomfortable smile, causing Divya to shoot her a glare.

"Can't you see we're *busy*?" Divya hissed. "Go play with genies
closer to your age."

"Oh yes, so busy. I can see that," Kesi replied. "Unfortunately, I
do need to borrow Ra'id for a second to…um…"

"To make plans for the Ghul game tonight," Ra'id finished, and
Kesi gave him a grateful look.

"Yeah, to do that," Kesi said before grabbing Ra'id's free arm.
"So, if you wouldn't mind…"

Divya tugged Ra'id's arm back to her side, jerking him away from
Kesi, "Why can't you do that right here?"

"Because you're cutting off Ra'id's circulation with the physical
declaration of your undying love," Kesi gestured to Ra'id's arm. Ra'id
closed his eyes and grimaced, his face etched in embarrassment. He
never liked the blunt approach that Kesi often took. "And if you cut
off his circulation, he can't think straight."

Divya looked up at Ra'id and seemed to read from his features
that he was a boy in pain, because she quickly let go of his arm but

stayed glued to his side. Kesi took the opportunity to grab Ra'id's other arm and drag him away from Divya. "Thanks, I'll return him I promise. Bye!"

"Thank you," Ra'id breathed once they were a sizeable distance away and safety hidden behind Raihana and Hussain, who were busy talking amongst themselves.

"Anytime, princess," Kesi laughed at him and he glared. "You really need to tell her that she's not you knight in shining armor."

"She doesn't *like* me she just…," Ra'id paused while searching for the right words, "Admires me, I guess. Looks up to me?"

Kesi snorted. "That is not the look of a girl who thinks of you as a brother, Ra'id. That's the look of a girl who's in love with you."

Ra'id shook his head, "She's not in love with me. She doesn't know what love is."

"Well, she knows what infatuation is," Kesi replied. "Clearly."

Ra'id cringed, "Clearly."

Kesi looked over to the children, who were all sitting on the edge of the building's roof, chatting amongst themselves, "I'm going to go talk to the kids. Want to join?"

"Do I have anywhere else to go?" Ra'id replied, casting a glance over to Divya who was talking to Shakila and looking at Ra'id longingly.

"Jinn, I hope I never fall in love," Kesi laughed as they walked to the roof's edge. "It looks like it makes you into a blundering idiot."

Ra'id shook his head, "You say that now, but you'll be the blundering idiot soon enough."

"Sure," Kesi rolled her eyes as she took a seat next to Fatima, causing the little girl to look over at her with wide eyes.

"Kesi!" Fatima cheered, embracing her from the side.

"Hey, kid," Kesi laughed, hugging her back. "How did you sleep last night?"

Fatima scrunched up her nose, "Abubakar *snored.*"

Kesi smirked. "Doesn't he do that every night?"

"He was *especially* loud last night," Fatima explained. "Selma and I thought about throwing him out the window."

Kesi threw her head back and laughed at the thought of the two small girls dragging the bigger boy to the window and pushing him out, only to find that it didn't stop his snoring nor his sleep. The magic of Jinn City wouldn't let its creatures get hurt.

"You know, we had a kid that did that too, when I was younger," Kesi leaned in so that others couldn't hear.

Fatima's face brightened. "Really?! Who?" She giggled when Kesi pointed a sly finger over at Divya, who's attention was split between Queen Ena in the marketplace and Ra'id sitting next to Kesi.

The story wasn't an untrue one. When they were younger and Kesi still slept in the camp that the kids had made together, Divya often kept quite a number of them up with her notorious snoring. Kesi often wondered if she still did it back at the High Palace where the Councilmen and maidens made their camps, and if anyone nearby could hear it. Kesi giggled at the thought, attracting the attention of Ra'id.

"What?" he asked, and both Fatima and Kesi quickly replied with a series of "*nothing, nothing! -s.*"

The trumpets and horns sounded again, and Kesi turned quickly to find the Elders blowing into the metal-and-stone instruments. She adjusted herself into a comfortable position on the roof, eager to hear the announcement. The marketplace hushed once the music was over, and Queen Ena smiled down at all the genies in the square, spinning slowly to see them all from her position in the air.

"My dear people," she began, her voice cascading through the people, streets, and buildings, touching every ear. "I have gathered you here today to share the most glorious news," she paused, either for dramatic effect or to better present the information, Kesi wasn't sure, before continuing, "our world will be reunited with the human realm once again."

The marketplace became filled with whispers and mumbles, each genie buzzing with questions and confusion. Ra'id gently nudged her shoulder with his and said in a whisper, "I'm glad it's you."

"I'm glad you think so," Kesi whispered back before Fatima pulled on her arm, averting her attention from Ra'id.

"What is she talking about?" Fatima squeaked. "I thought humans weren't really real."

Kesi rubbed the girl's head. "You'll see," was all she could offer her.

"My people… my children," the Queen said calmly, silencing the genies gathered before her. "Let me explain. There are two players in this game, the Chosen One and the Jinn Savior."

"Wait-" Kesi jolted, panicked. The *Jinn Savior*? *The* Jinn Savior? '*That's my title in the prophecy? The Jinn Savior? What does that even mean? Am I a Jinn?*'

"Calm down," Ra'id reassured as Queen Ena continued her speech.

"The Chosen One is a human boy chosen by Fate to bring our two worlds together," the Queen said. "The Jinn Savior is a genie of my own choosing who will venture to the human realm and protect this boy from the Shaytan, and any other corruptions. The Elders and I have been training the Jinn Savior and preparing for the journey in secret, but as the departure date now in nine days' time, the Elders and I have decided that now is the time to announce our plan and introduce the Jinn Savior."

Kesi gulped nervously. '*Sure, Ra'id might think I'm the perfect… Jinn Savior, or whatever… but will everyone else?* Kesi stole a glance over at Divya. '*How will genies like her react?*'

"The Jinn Savior that I have chosen is bold, brave, brilliant, and powerful. She has a soul of fire and a heart full of love. You must not doubt my decision or hers to comply with my request, as we all have to give our full support and faith sin order for her to succeed," Queen Ena stressed the last statement, looking at everyone seriously. Her gaze softened as she lifted it to Kesi, smiling at her, "May I introduce our Jinn Savior, Kesi."

All eyes turned to her, and Kesi felt heat rush to her face in part embarrassment, nervousness, and pride. She swallowed her fear and sat up a little straighter, reminding herself that the Queen *chose* her. An immortal goddess with millions of years of experience knew, without a shadow of a doubt, that she was the right one to be the Jinn Savior. She had to take a page out of her Queen's book and trust in herself, no matter what anyone else said.

Silence settled for a few moments before a voice sounded from behind Kesi, surprising her. "Savior Kesi!" it cried, and Kesi turned to find the genie who belonged to voice. Divya had one fist in the air, her mouth open and wide, forming a smile. Cheers erupted from all around her, bubbling and raising through the crowd.

"What…just happened," Kesi mumbled to Ra'id, who was smiling.

"What else was she supposed to do?" Ra'id chuckled, "The Queen chose you, and she's trying to get the Queen to notice her."

Kesi shook her head, smiling. "Your knight in shining armor is devious."

Ra'id huffed, about to say more, before Kesi felt another tug on her arm. She turned to see big-eyed Fatima, her face one part excided and one part sad.

"You're leaving?" She asked, her voice wavering and her eyes filling with tears. Kesi hugged her close, kissing the top of her head.

"I'm sorry," she said to the little girl, who shook her head vigorously and pulled away.

"Don't be sorry, Kesi!" Fatima gave her a big smile, "You're going to save the whole world! And don't worry, I'll take care of the Ghul games while you're gone!"

Kesi laughed and hugged her again, "Aw, thanks kid. You're the best."

"I know!" Fatima giggled as the other children gathered near.

"You met Queen Ena?" Selma squeaked, jumping up and down. "That's so cool! Did you go to the High Palace?"

"Is that how you knew about that new game?" Abubakar asked, clearly curious.

"Can you teach us other human games?" Borak shoved his way past Abubakar.

"Do you know a lot about humans now?" Ni'mah looked star-struck, "What are they like?"

"What do they do without magic?"

"How are there so many of them?"

"Why do they all look weird?"

Ra'id chuckled. "Now then, give the Jinn Savior some space," he said, pulling Kesi to her feet as the children swarmed around them, swamping her with questions. Kesi shuffled through them slowly, trying not to step on any little feet, and answered as many questions as she could. Eventually the children disbanded, flying, climbing, and running away, giggling and whispering about the new information they had just received. Kesi found her way over to Divya slowly.

"Let's not," Ra'id gulped before they came into earshot. "I can still feel her fingernails digging into my arm."

"You can leave," Kesi chuckled, "But just know that lover girl here will start chasing after you."

"Not if you buy me some time," Ra'id smiled at her gratefully before flying off. Kesi moved closer to Divya.

"Hey," she said. "Thanks for...you know."

Divya shrugged, "Everyone was just confused and startled, I think."

Kesi paused, "Are you confused?"

Divya thought for a moment, "I...don't question the Queen. But just know that I'll always have wanted it to be me." She looked at her for a moment, "I guess you'll do, though."

Kesi rolled her eyes, "Hardy har har. Very funny."

Divya huffed, "Yeah, I know, I'm hilarious." She crossed her arms over her chest, "Or at least funnier than you."

As she turned to fly away, Kesi called after her, "Hey! Since I'm a Jinn now I guess we're equals! Or maybe I'm higher than you, because, you know, *Savior*."

Divya turned to her and glared, "You wish, Kesi."

Kesi chuckled as she flew off, leaving her with the genies she had grown up with. Seeing Divya leave, they took it as time to attack her with hugs and playful shoves.

"Hey! There's my girl, Kesi!" Idris rubbed his knuckles against her scalp, holding her shoulders tightly.

"*Idris!*" Kesi complained, shoving him off as Shakila hugged her.

"Always knew you were meant for something, Kes," she said lovingly. Kesi grinned at her.

"You say that now, but when we were kids, I remember you saying that I was going to be nothing but trouble," Kesi's grin turned to a smirk as Shakila playfully rolled her eyes.

"I wasn't wrong, was I?" she laughed before Mushtaree slammed into her with a suffocating hug, ecstatic.

"Kesi! Oh, my Jinn! You're going to be *amazing* I just know it," she giggled, showing off pearly white teeth.

"Thanks, I sure hope so," Kesi replied. Hussain put a hand on her shoulder, smiling down at her. Raihana grabbed her hand.

"So," Raihana began, "I'm thinking, when you come back from the human world, which I know you will, you can bring me a little something back? Like a souvenir, preferably a shiny one?"

Kesi laughed at her, "Sure, Raihana. I'll try my best."

"Kesi!" a voice yelled from below them. All seven teenagers ran over to the edge of the building to see many genies on the ground, smiling and cheering up at Kesi.

"Kesi!" the voice said again, and she turned to see Kefira waving at her. Kesi waved back.

"How does it feel, Kesi?" Kefira teased. "Look at all your adoring fans!"

Kesi glanced down at the crowd below. "Uh, it feels great! Totally...awesome," she giggled as the genies started asking her more questions. Kesi recognized a lot of them, most of them being Councilmembers that she knew by sight or that Kesi had spent a few years within a camp as a child. Kesi saw Lady Karida, Lord Haytham, Lady Nweh, and old Lord Ziyaad, all looking at her hopefully.

Kesi turned to her friends, "I don't feel much like a hero."

"You will, once you actually start being heroic," Shakila mused, rubbing her arm reassuringly.

"Just try not to burn the human realm down in the process," Idris winked, causing Kesi to roll her eyes.

"Gee, thanks, 'Ris," Kesi droned, causing him to laugh.

"Jinn Savior!" a few genies in the crowd chanted, drawing her attention again.

"I...could get used to this," Kesi chuckled, sparking grins on her friends' faces.

"That's more like it, Kesi," Saalim punched her arm softly. Kesi climbed down the building with ease, landing on her two feet amid the crowd. People pressed around her, asking an abundance of questions that Kesi tried to answer. Shakila gripped her hand, making sure that Kesi didn't lose her friends in the middle of all the excited chaos. Most of the faces before her were pleasant, although a few had worried or doubtful looks on their faces, whispering to each other quietly. Kesi looked away from these faces, smiling brightly, determined to keep self-doubt out of her mind.

"You're just a girl," a gruff voice rose above the rest, making others stop to listen. Kesi turned to see a tall, middle-aged genie. She knew he was on the Council; she'd seen him walking towards the High Palace often enough, but she didn't know him by name.

"And the Chosen One is just a boy," She replied.

"The world needs an adult to rely on for these matters," the Jinn countered, his expression stubborn.

"The world needs us both right *now*, regardless of our age." Kesi continued, "At the very least give me a bit of your trust, for our Queen, if not for yourself."

Kesi moved on without waiting for an answer, knowing that the Jinn would come to the same conclusion she had, eventually. She hoped. At the very least, turning away and not listening to the Jinn will show that others should believe in her confidence. She could do this. She had to.

Kesi turned back to her friends and said, "Ifrit Jungle, five minutes?" then smiled when they nodded, and took to the sky, flying away from the pestering people. She should probably leave the explaining to Queen Ena or at least someone who knew the human realm, the plan, and the Chosen One better than she did.

When she caught sight of the jungle, Kesi slowly lowered herself to the ground and slipped past the few buildings remaining between her and her destination. Knowing that her friends didn't have as steady a control over their magic as she did and couldn't fly as fast as her, Kesi decided to walk the rest of the way. Crossing from the white, sandy streets of the City and onto a soft dirt path of the jungle, Kesi walked farther into the foliage. The shade of the trees cascaded down her figure, allowing her to escape from the heat of the sun. She found a nice sized boulder to sit on white she waited for her friends and picked invisible dirt out from underneath her golden fingernails.

"*Chirp.*" Kesi turned as a small Ifrit frog jumped out of the bushes beside her, its orange stripes flashing in the spots of sunshine the gaps in the Ifrit trees provided. The frog looked up at her with big eyes, changing the iris from their black color to Kesi's blue, signaling that it wasn't hostile. Kesi laughed and picked up the small creature, chuckling at the thought of the small frogs ever being dangerous.

"*Chirp, chirp,*" the frog squeaked, bouncing around to face Kesi in her palms.

"Hi," Kesi laughed at it, which the creature responded with more chirping. "You're cute."

"*Chirp, chirp, chirp-chirp.*"

Kesi sighed, staring at the frog, "What about you? Do you think I can do this?"

"*Chirp,*" the frog replied.

Kesi placed the frog on the ground at her feet, "Me too, buddy, me too."

"Man, how are you so fast?" a voice drew Kesi's attention. Kesi smiled at Idris as he led their friends into the forest, each taking spots on the ground, rocks, and logs around her.

"Don't listen to Lord Qaabil," Shakila offered. "He doesn't know you or the Queen at all. He has no idea what the human realm needs."

"I know," Kesi replied. "I've had three days to work through everything, and... and well, Queen Ena won't really take no for an answer, so I have to dive in headfirst, there's no other choice."

"You have to believe in yourself too," Hussain said. "Remember what Queen Ena said? Uh..."

"'*We all have to give her our full support and faith so she can succeed,*'" Raihana quoted, receiving a grateful smile from Hussain. "Or something like that."

"Yeah." Hussain continued, "That means that you have to have some self-faith too."

"I do," Kesi replied. "A little, I think. The more people that think I can do it...I don't know. The more people that say that I'm perfect for the job the more I believe it, I guess."

"Well, we all think that you're perfect for the job!" Mushtaree smiled, "And so many other people in Jinn City do too. That Councilman was one of few, don't worry."

"Besides, you shouldn't listen to them anyway," Saalim said. "If they don't trust their Queen, how can you trust them?"

Kesi sighed happily, grateful for her supportive friends. She only wished that she could see what they so easily saw in her. "I... you're right. Thanks, guys."

"Aww, don't mention it," Shakila leaned over and rubbed Kesi's head. Kesi shoved her hand away before she could do too much damage to her hair.

"I think we should celebrate, or something," Mushtaree mused.

"Maybe… we could go to the marketplace later during the day and see if Aban will be there to play us some music to dance to."

Saalim crinkled his nose at her, "You just want to go because you think he's *hot.*"

"I do not!" Mushtaree defended, glaring at him, "I just think he's very nice and… plays good music on his instrument thing."

"I think it's called an oud," Kesi replied. "Or at least that's what the humans call it."

"An *oud,*" Mushtaree said to Saalim, who only rolled his eyes at her.

"Saalim is only jealous," Idris chuckled. This time it was Saalim who turned defensive.

"Wha- why would I be jealous? That's stupid," he crossed his arms over his chest, and Kesi laughed at him.

"How old is Aban?" Shakila asked.

"I think he was brought in the same year as Divya," Kesi replied. "So around twenty-two if he hasn't had his birthday yet."

Shakila hummed, "I think I remember him from our camp when we were younger. He was thirteen or fourteen when I was ten. I don't remember playing with him in the Ghul, though."

"I think he always went to the marketplace to play his instrument," Idris said. "I kind of remember him. He was a quiet kid."

"Maybe we should go talk to him then!" Mushtaree squealed. "You know, introduce ourselves?"

"Mushtaree, he already knows who you are," Saalim commented, "Remember? He caught you stalking him that one time you dragged me along."

"You *stalked* him?" Kesi shook her head as the girl giggled sheepishly, "'Taree… you gotta get your head checked out."

"We should go now, then," Raihana said. "Don't want to miss out on meeting Mushtaree's boyfriend."

"He only plays right before sunset," Mushtaree answered

immediately, before thinking back to Raihana's words. "Wait! He isn't my *boyfriend*, just…eye candy."

"I'll believe it when I see it," Shakila laughed.

"We should do something to pass the time," Hussain replied. "Maybe… swim in the Marid Waterfalls?"

"Good idea," Raihana agreed, fanning herself. "It's hot today."

"It's hot every day," Kesi chuckled. "Let's go." She stood and started walking down the path towards the Djinn Fields, the landscape that stood in between the Jungle and the Waterfalls.

"Wouldn't it be faster if we cut through the city?" Mushtaree questioned as she jogged to keep up with Kesi. She had always been an unusually fast walker.

"The scenic route, 'Taree," Kesi explained. "Always take the scenic route."

"It's easier for you!" Idris called from behind her. "You never get tired!"

"That's not true," Raihana countered. "Kesi sleeps like a camel! Drools a little, too."

"Be quiet," Kesi huffed, rolling her eyes.

"Hey, what's up with Divya and Ra'id?" Shakila mentioned, in a tone that Kesi knew meant she had been waiting to talk about it all day.

"The usual. Divya fawning over Ra'id, Ra'id feeling uncomfortable yet not believing that she's in love with him, etc., etc.," Kesi turned and started walking backwards a few steps to face her, bounding over roots that stuck up from the ground in her wake, "Why?"

"She's just gotten clingier, physically, I noticed, I just wondered if he's leading her on…?" Shakila left her statement unfinished, thinking it over for a moment. "Unintentionally, of course. I know that Ra'id would never do that."

"He just doesn't know how to tell her no," Kesi explained. "He waited too long, now it's going to be nearly impossible for him. He's too nice."

"Maybe Divya can make him meaner," Mushtaree giggled. "They could be cute together."

"Yeah, if Divya fixes her attitude," Kesi rolled her eyes, facing forward again.

"*Ooh*, are you jealous, Kesi?" Saalim teased, coming up on her other side and struggling to keep pace.

"Ra'id is like a brother to me," Kesi replied, then cringed as she thought of the two of them being anything more. "Uh, *ew*. Don't even mention that again."

"Man, Kesi, you're never going to find a Mate," Idris laughed, and Kesi shot him a glare from over her shoulder. The magic of Jinn City had power over things that genies, even Jinn like Queen Ena, did not, and that included things like happiness, death, life, and love. In this way, the City itself kept its own peace by helping its genies keep a healthy lifestyle, both mentally and physically. It's because of this that magic genies live up to be two hundred years old, and why Queen Ena never died, and how genies find Mates.

Each genie falls in love only once or twice in their lives, in order to limit the despair of an unrequited love scenario. Once a genies' feelings are returned, though, the other person is their Mate. Most genies find their Mate at a fairly young age, like Raihana and Hussain, although Mates aren't easy to spot. Genies must learn to love, but once they start to fall together, that's how they know that they've found their Mate. Of course, genies can't have children, but love and relationships are very possible. The Mate system was just another way that the City kept its own peace and prosperity between its beings.

It was so different from how the humans did it. All the things that they had- girlfriends, boyfriends, husbands, wives, cheating, affairs, breakups- simply didn't exist in Kesi's world. Love seemed so fickle in the human world. She supposed that was what happened when their realm didn't protect the human one.

"Yeah, ok, sure," Kesi shook her head. "You know that's not possible."

Idris chuckled, "You could be the first."

Kesi turned to him to say, "Well, the Jinn Savior don't need no man," before turning back around and pushing through the last stretch of trees to the Djinn Fields.

The Djinn Fields' white flowers almost glowed in the afternoon sun, reflecting the light into Kesi's eyes.

"I swear, Kesi, if you're about to suggest a race-" Raihana groaned before Kesi interrupted her, grinning.

"Let's race! Ready, set, go!" Kesi yelled before turning and running across the Field, admiring the way that the wildflowers felt under her feet. She loved the way the wind rushed through her long hair as she expanded her bounds, using her powers of flight and hovering to propel herself faster. Her friends cried out in anguish and annoyance as they followed behind her. Kesi could feel the looks they were getting from genies standing near the border of the Fields and the City and could almost hear their chuckles. Everyone who knew her would be able to recognize her even from afar, Kesi was sure. No one moved as fast and as ecstatically as she did.

"Heads up!" Kesi yelled as she approached the Waterfalls' bank, not hesitating to stop before she jumped into the air and used her magic to propel her far enough out that she landed in the deeper water. Kesi dove under the fresh, glowing water, the light of which was slightly dimmed by the morning sun. When she emerged, her face, clothes, and skin were all completely soaked, and she wiped the water out of her eyes as she turned around to see Idris running full speed towards her.

"'Ris, don't you dare!" Kesi laughed as Idris cannonballed into the water, splashing her further from head to toe. When he surfaced from beneath, Kesi glared at him, her face soaking.

"I hate you," she deadpanned, before breaking into a smirk and shoving water into his face.

"Love you too, Kesi," Idris grinned and dove into the water, leaving Kesi confused and alone.

"Idris?" Kesi waited, "Where are- Agh!" Kesi yelped as Idris emerged from the water underneath her, forcing her to sit on his shoulders.

"Idris, put me down!" Kesi laughed as the others joined them, each cascading Kesi and Idris in water as they jumped in. Eventually, Idris let go of Kesi's legs to wipe his eyes, and she let herself fall backwards into the water, laughing.

Kesi had laughed more today than she had since meeting with the Elder Council and Queen Ena. She knew that as the date of her departure drew nearer, she would be laughing less and less, but until then she was going to enjoy herself. Melancholy was another feeling that the city's magic wouldn't allow the genies to feel.

It was sundown when the seven of them decided to abandon the water, stumbling out onto the bank. Kesi gripped Hussain's arm to keep herself upright, as she was doubled over with laughter. Hussain didn't provide much support, though, because he was laughing as well.

"We have to...do this more often," he huffed between laughter. Kesi nodded.

"It's been too long," she agreed. Kesi sighed and touched the ends of her hair, which were already beginning to dry in the magic air and straightened herself to look around at her friends.

"I'm going to miss you guys," she said seriously, her smile turning bittersweet.

"We'll miss you too, Kesi," Shakila replied, placing a warm hand on her shoulder, "Think of us often, alright?"

"I will," Kesi nodded before Idris butted in.

"Why are we acting like she's leaving today? We still have nine more days!" he said before glancing back to the City. "We should probably go see Mushtaree's boyfriend now."

"He's not my boyfriend!"

"Sure," Kesi and Idris replied at the same time, causing more laughter.

Their laughter didn't lessen as they approached the marketplace, even the boys' giggles turned high-pitched as Raihana's jokes turned more ridiculous.

"I can't believe- oh hush!" Mushtaree blurted, ducking around a building that sat in the mouth of the marketplace. "There he is!"

Kesi peeked around the corner to see a young genie sitting on a box in the middle of the near-empty marketplace, playing a pear-shaped instrument with a long neck and four strings attached to it. He plucked the strings playfully, creating a cheery tune in the dimming sunlight. His hair was a rusty red and his face was hand-some, Kesi supposed, but he was clearly closer to Shalika's age than Mushtaree's.

"Don't make it so obvious," Mushtaree hissed, yanking Kesi back around the corner. "We don't want him to see us!"

"Why?" Kesi asked, "Didn't we come here to listen to his music?"

"Oh," Mushtaree paused, "Right."

Shakila chuckled, "You do really need to get your head checked, 'Taree. Are you sure you don't want me to take you to someone?"

Mushtaree pouted, "I think I'm perfectly fine."

Kesi just shook her head before grabbing Mushtaree's hands, "Come on, let's dance!"

"Dance? Oh, I don't know how to-" Mushtaree started before Kesi dragged her into the marketplace and over to the space before the young genie who Kesi assumed was Aban. Kesi spun the flustered girl around in circles, laughing and prancing to the beat that Aban created. The others joined Kesi and Mushtaree joyfully, mimicking her movements and spinning in the marketplace. Kesi heard Aban chuckle and turned to see him staring at Shakila with deep eyes. Kesi watched in amazement as Shakila caught sight of him and blushed before continuing her dance with Idris and Saalim. Kesi almost laughed out loud. There was no way, in all of Jinn existence, that she had just witnessed one of her best friends find a Mate in the marketplace after sundown, dancing to music from an oud. She spun Mushtaree around quickly so she could catch more glimpses of the two, and she found that Aban had efficiently enchanted his instrument to keep playing without. He walked over to Shakila and took her from a rather stunned-looking Saalim and Idris. Kesi simply shook her head and twirled Mushtaree once more, pushing her over to Saalim.

It wasn't long before other genies joined the festivities, even those who had been working at their stands. Kefira took Mushtaree's place and laughed over at Shakila and Aban before taking Kesi's hands and spinning her in circles.

"You seem like you're having fun," Kefira said as she touched her toes to the ground, grinning like a little girl.

"Genie's gotta live," Kesi replied, before Kefira corrected her.

"Jinn. Jinn's gotta live," Kefira smiled as the two circled each other.

"I'm not a Jinn yet," Kesi countered. "I want to earn it first."

Kefira chuckled and shook her head at Kesi, "That's the thing that we love about you, Kesi. You have a strong heart."

Kesi just smiled in response, getting lost in the music and the dancing as the stars pulled themselves up high in the sky. The entire City seemed to breathe for this moment.

CHAPTER TEN

DANVILLE, VIRGINIA

Roman

ROMAN FLOPPED DOWN in his desk chair, exhausted from another day at school, and tossed his book bag aside. '*I barely made it through the first little short week of school. How am I going to get through this full one?*' School was utterly draining, especially since pre-season football practice had started. Sophia used to be a cheerleader and would always wave to him from across the field during practice which, at the time, Roman had found embarrassing. But now that the far side of the field was empty of her orange-red hair Roman wished that he could see her wave her green and white pom-pom frantically at him one more time. Roman cross his arms on his desk and laid his head on top of them, burying himself.

"Roman?" Emma's voice sounded from around the corner. Roman just groaned in response. His mother took it as her que to enter, chuckling at Roman's position.

"Tough day?" she asked, leaning against his loft bed.

"Becky Oakley," Roman stated, "is trying to kill me."

"What'd she do?" Emma asked, tilting her head to the side.

"Decided to remind me that she took Sophia's spot on the cheer-leading squad," Roman replied, sinking his hands into his dark hair.

"Oh, babe," Emma sighed. "She's just jealous."

"Of what?" Roman turned to look at her seriously, "She has *everything*."

"She doesn't have pride," Emma explained, "because she has to pick on others to feel secure in her life. And she doesn't have a sibling."

"Neither do I," Roman replied bitterly.

"But you did," Emma said softly, "and that's something that she'll never have."

Roman shook his head, "You're telling me that she picks on me because she's jealous that I have a dead sibling?"

"She's jealous because now, after Soph is gone, she can see how close you two were," Emma replied. "She's… probably lonely, and sad. That doesn't make it right, but that's the reason." His mother offered him a sad smile. "Now, hurry up and take a shower. Dad's going to be home soon, and I'm almost done fixing dinner. Plus, we're going to pick up Kesi from the airport tomorrow night, and you don't want to be smelling like a…boy…do you?" she fanned a hand in front of her nose, making a disgusted face. Roman laughed at her.

"Okay, okay, fine. I'll be down in a second," he replied as his mother took her leave. Roman looked over at the picture of Sophia on his desk, smiling at her. For the last time, he hoped that he was going right by her, especially where Kesi was concerned. '*What would she want me to do? Probably open up to Kesi, and not let her know that she'll be sleeping in my dead sister's room on my dead sister's bed. She would want me to be Kesi's friend, maybe even more, knowing Soph.*' Roman nearly rolled his eyes at the thought. Sophia always held grand romantic and adventurous notions.

Roman sighed and turned away, heading towards the bathroom. It was the least he could do for Sophia, much less Kesi Haddad.

"Danville isn't an insanely small town, but it isn't a city either," Elder Ashraf explained as Kesi stood before the Elders' table, shifting nervously on her feet since the day of departure had come. Kesi had hardly made it through the thick crowd stationed in front of the High Palace, full of all the genies in Jinn City waiting to see her off. There were so many eager citizens there that Queen Ena was forced to close the huge doors to prevent anyone following Kesi inside the High Palace, leaving the people in the garden.

"If it's so small… won't people recognize me in my genie form?" Kesi asked, turning to the yellow-haired Elder. Ashraf shook his head in response.

"We put a thin barrier spell in your charm, so that when you transform, only someone with magic will be able to see you for who you are," he replied quickly. "It's not a very strong spell, but since the human realm doesn't have magic, no one should be able to find out unless you tell them."

"But the Chosen One has magic," Kesi said, "so, he'll be able to figure it out."

"His magic is still forming," Queen Ena assured. "It's not strong enough to form into something powerful yet. You will have, at the very least, a few months in secrecy before his magic starts to break through your spell. At that point, we hope he will be ready to save our worlds."

"How is… how is he supposed to do that, anyway?" Kesi asked hesitantly, unsure if it was proper to ask such a question as it might show mistrust in the Queen.

Neither the Queen nor the Elders seemed to notice. Perhaps she was overthinking the etiquette required with the Queen, since they all seemed to think of Kesi as an equal. Kesi chuckled inwardly. *'How can I ever measure up to these powerful Jinn? What am I saying...'* Kesi thought, *'Measure up to Queen Ena? There's no way! No matter how many heroic things I do, I'll never come close to the immortal Jinn goddess.'*

"We're not so sure," the Queen answered. "The prophet's vision didn't give us much information on the actual process. We're hoping that the path will become clearer the closer we get to that day."

"So, we're...just trusting Fate here?" Kesi asked, cocking an eyebrow. The Elders and the Queen nodded in response. "Alright. Fate it is, I guess."

"Kesi," the Queen began slowly, "if you are...having second thoughts...please be sure to push them aside. We can't afford to have doubts in the way."

"I've been pushing them aside for the past eleven days, Mother," Kesi gave her a grin and a cheesy thumbs up. "It's habit now."

Queen Ena laughed, clearly humored by Kesi, "I'm glad. Are you ready, Kesi?"

Kesi took a deep breath. *'Am I ready? Absolutely not. I'll never be ready to leave this place.'*

But she was ready to serve her Queen, to save another world, and to protect a human boy. In a sense, she supposed, she was ready, at least for what Queen Ena asked. *'I can do this. I can.'*

With that thought, Kesi nodded, and the Elders, along with the Queen, stood up. It is custom for the lesser genies to stand respectfully of to one side in order to allow the Queen and her Elders to pass, so Kesi stepped aside as they approached her. To her surprise, however, Queen Ena grabbed her by the hand to walk side-by-side with her in front of the Elders. The Queen guided their procession down the stairs, and through the main room. Yahya, the receptionist, was startled out of his writing at the sight of the group, and quickly moved to his knees in a bow. He was muttering something to himself that Kesi couldn't hear. As they passed him, Queen Ena waved her free hand at the huge front doors, and they began to open slowly open, letting the dimming light of day to flood the room. When the warmth of the sun's rays cascaded over her face, Kesi straightened her back a bit more, held her head high, and squinted her eyes trying to see the genies that were waiting from them in the High Palace garden.

"Remember," Queen Ena mumbled into her ear, "you're the Jinn Savior. You're more powerful than you or anyone else here knows."

Kesi nodded, the doors opening in full as they approached, the cheers of genies reaching her ears. Kesi spotted those who she loved- Kefira, Ra'id, Saalim, Mushtaree, Raihana, Hussain, Idris, Shakila, even little Fatima- frantically waving and calling her name. Kesi tossed smiles their way then turned back to the scene ahead of her. The crowd parted like the Red Sea for the Queen and her.

'*You're the Jinn Savior*', Queen Ena's words echoed in her head, causing her to lift her chin, '*I'm the Jinn Savior.*'

Queen Ena, Kesi, and the Elders walked all the way through the City to the Djinn Fields, people trailing in their wake. After a while their cries ceased and they returned to an excited silence, nervousness and giddiness brimming in the air. Once Kesi's feet touched the soft grass of the Fields and the wildflowers started to tickle her ankles, the Queen leaned over and whispered into her ear again.

"Don't forget, you'll arrive with your bags in the busy airport. The Lovetts are at the end of the hall," she said.

"Right. Busy airport. Bags. End of the hall, got it," Kesi nodded in understanding as they stopped in the Field, all the genies of Jinn City standing around them. The Queen let go of Kesi's hand and used both arms to address her people. As the Elders lined up behind Kesi, their white robes turned orange in the rapidly setting sun. The genies fathered around in a semi-circle, and Kesi saw a few pushing and shoving each other to try and get a better view of the scene. She saw Idris was one of these genies, and he gave her a sly grin as their eyes met. Having all these eyes on her, especially knowing what she was about to do, was a bit nerve-racking. '*On another day,*' Kesi thought to herself, '*I might have enjoyed all this attention. Maybe even loved it.*'

"My children," Queen Ena said, smiling. "Today is the start of a new era, not just for you and me, but for a whole realm of people we haven't seen in thousands of years!" She paused to let the cheers die down before continuing. "After this day, we are one step closer to being united to our sister realm. One step closer to defeating all evil. One step closer to bringing magic and light to all!"

The genies of Jinn City rose into cheers once again, and Queen Ena turned to her, "It's time, Jinn Savior."

Kesi nodded seriously as the Queen passed her, mumbling, "It's time to say your goodbyes."

Kesi moved forward and scanned the crowd for her friends before feeling a small, warm body latch itself onto her leg. Kesi looked down at a giggling Fatima hugging her leg. Kesi laughed and bent down to hug her, squeezing her tight.

"Man, am I going to miss you, kid," Kesi mumbled before pulling away from the girl, smiling. "You be good okay? No throwing Abubakar out any windows, alright?" She chuckled as Fatima giggled again, still holding her shoulders, "And if anyone new comes while I'm gone, you take good care of them, okay? I'll be back before you know it."

Fatima jumped up and down excitedly, "You're going to be a hero!"

"I hope so," Kesi smiled, and Fatima gripped her big hands in her tiny ones.

"You'll always be *my* hero, Kesi," she said half-seriously, a lop-sided grin on her face. "Even if you're not here!"

Kesi chuckled, blinking away tears. Who knew how long it'd be before she'd be able to see Fatima again? "I'll try to be your hero in the human world too, kid."

Fatima giggled and placed a kiss on Kesi's cheek before running to join the other excided children in the crowd. Kesi's childhood friends were the next ones to attack her with hugs. Rather than fighting for a turn, all six teenagers decided to give her one big group bear hug. Kesi sighed sadly.

"Hey, don't be upset," Shakila cupped Kesi's chin in her hands. "You're going to be great. You're going to become a human, make some human friends, defeat some evil Shaytan, you know, the usual." Both girls chuckled. "You're going to be…you're going to be better than anyone ever thought you could possibly be. You have to believe that."

"I… I do," Kesi said, and for the first time she really meant it. She could do this, and she would.

"I'll write you letters!" Mushtaree jumped in. "Even though I doubt I'll be able to get them to you even with my magic. At least you'll have something to read about our lives when you get back."

"Thanks, 'Taree," Kesi giggled.

"Kick some Shaytan ass for me, will you?" Idris held out a fist, which Kesi promptly bumped with hers.

"Try to remember *everything*," Raihana put in. "I want to hear all about the human realm when you come home, and I mean every last detail!"

Kesi smiled, "I'll try, I promise."

"And maybe have a little fun?" Hussain suggested. "I don't think you'll be killing evil genies all the time. Will you?" He seemed to be rethinking his previous statement. Kesi laughed outright.

"I doubt I will, Hussain, and I'll take your advice," Kesi shook her head at him before Saalim engulfed her in another hug.

"I'll miss you, Kesi," he said as the others mimicked his movements.

"I'll miss you guys too," Kesi replied, trying to laugh as she choked back tears.

"Lady Divya," Shakila muttered as they pulled away, returning to the crowd as Divya approached her.

"Divya-" Kesi began, but the young Councilmaiden sank to her knees before Kesi could finish.

"What are you…," Kesi started, but stopped as she realized what Divya was doing. She was bowing, showing her respect to Kesi. The sight was unnerving and unsettling, although Kesi had to admit that seeing her childhood enemy showing her such respect was a bit satisfying. "Divya… I…Divya, rise."

Divya obeyed, coming to her feet as Kesi continued, "Don't bow to me."

"The Queen walked *hand in hand* with you," Divya explained. "You're her equal. Why shouldn't I bow to you?"

"Because I haven't earned it yet," Kesi replied before slipping into a grin. "I still have to help save the world."

Then Divya did a very rare thing in the presence of Kesi. She smiled back. "I suppose so," Divya paused, clearly trying to find the right words, "Good luck, Kesi."

"Thanks," Kesi nodded to her respectfully as she moved back, revealing Ra'id standing behind her. Kesi saw tears in his eyes.

"Ra'id…," Kesi sighed and hugged him tighter than she had hugged anyone else. Ra'id held her just as closely. They stayed like that for several moments before Ra'id pulled away.

"I'm sorry, I just…," Ra'id laughed, blinking away the wetness in his eyes. "It's just…I watched you grow up, Kesi. I was your age when you came to Jinn City and…and now…I mean, you're my little sister. Nothing can change that."

"Even if we're a whole realm away," Kesi added, giving him a smile. "I promise to bring you something back."

Ra'id chuckled, shaking his head. "You cocky idiot, I'm going to miss you," he said, and pulled her into another hug.

"I'm going to miss you too," Kesi said into his shoulder, embracing him more tentatively this time, knowing that she had to leave.

"Kesi," a calm voice said from behind her, and Kesi pulled away from Ra'id to see Queen Ena standing only a few feet away, the Elders making a wide circle around her. "It's time."

Kesi gave Ra'id one last look, not willing to say the word *goodbye* directly, afraid that then she would start to really cry. She stepped away from him and turned to face Queen Ena.

"I'm ready," she said, and received a nod of confirmation from the Queen. In one swift movement, Queen Ena dragged an elegant hand through the air in a straight line from the sky to the ground. The sound of clanking metal could be heard as a gold chain and padlock appeared out of thin air. They quickly broke into pieces and dimmed into nothingness, revealing a doorway or pure white light in the middle of the field. The light from the doorway shined so bright that it cast a glow over everyone standing before it. The Queen stretched a handout to Kesi, silently asking her to take next step. Cheers erupted from the crowd once more as Kesi stepped forward and clasped her hand. As the Queen guided her towards the portal, Kesi turned to take one last look at all her friends. Each one had an identical sad yet excited, afraid yet happy look on their faces. She gave them a reassuring smile, and waved at her people once more, knowing that this would be the last time she would see them in a long time.

Cheers erupted from the crowd again as Kesi took the Queen's outstretched hand as was guided to the bright portal. Kesi turned one last time to look at her friends, who all looked excited yet sad, happy yet afraid, as they looked at her face. Kesi gave them a reassuring smile and waved at her people, knowing that this would be the last time she saw them in a long time.

Kesi looked over to Jinn City now, the buildings of the City and the towering structure of the distant High Palace ingrained in her mind forever. One last time, Kesi admired the way that the white dirt streets merged into Djinn Field grass, the glowing flowers popping all around her like stars.

"I'll miss you," Kesi said to the City, to her people, her friends, and her Queen. She sighed heavily and turned back to Queen Ena, who looked at her knowingly.

"Good luck, Jinn Savior," the Queen smiled at her before letting go of her hand.

"Thank you, Mother," Kesi said before turning to the door of light in front of her, and without a second thought, stepped inside.

Slowly, everything faded away. The cheers and joyous cries of the people dimmed into nothingness. The creaks of the Djinn Field crickets fell away from her senses, the sound of the Ifrit frogs disintegrated, leaving her only with the strange whispers of the Djinn Field flowers. They were saying one word, one name, over and over again.

Kesi... Kesi.... Kesi...

It wasn't long before that faded too.

CHAPTER ELEVEN

DANVILLE, VIRGINIA

Roman

ROMAN'S FAMILY STOOD at the end of a long hallway where various baggage claim stations were sprawled out. It was busy, which Roman found a bit odd for seven thirty at night, but perhaps he just didn't fly enough at the end of the day. He was put in charge of holding a large sign that read *Kesi Haddad* in big, bold letters while his father and mother stood side by side, patiently waiting for the girl in the pictures to come walking down the hall.

Roman could see people looking at his family sideways, and instinctively sunk back and held the sign slightly in front of his face, as if trying to hide himself from them. He could only imagine what they were thinking.

'*Hey, isn't that the one model from... something? Victoria's Secret? Forever 21? No... some fashion line. Wasn't she married to that rich businessman? What a match made in heaven. Didn't she retire a couple years ago?*

Didn't her daughter die?'

Roman shook the thoughts out of his head. Sophia always told him not to let the negative voices in the back of his head get to him so much.

"*More than half of the things you're thinking are the farthest thing from the truth, Romey,*" she always said, tapping the side of his head persistently. "*Trust me, I've already been through... anxiety,*" she'd always shudder dramatically. And Roman would always laugh.

"Where could she be?" Emma asked quietly, obviously a bit nervous. She had been frantically adjusting and cleaning things throughout the house all day.

"They have customs before the baggage claim here," Daniel reassured her. "There's probably just a long line since…you know."

"Since she's from the Middle East?" Roman pipped in, and his father gave him a sad glance. "She's…just a kid."

"People are just scared," Daniel offered, looking into the crowd of people again. His face slipped into a quiet smile before he elbowed Roman gently, "Look."

Roman obeyed, trailing his eyes to where his father was looking. He blinked at the sight before him, his brain not fully registering what he was seeing.

The crowd had almost shifted to let her pass, creating a little bubble of space to move through and control. She wore jeans, a teal-colored t-shirt, a gray hoodie, and white-and-black tennis shoes. A necklace at her collarbone reflected the florescent light on its blue pendant. Her blonde hair cascaded down her shoulders and back, almost glowing against her tan skin. Her blue eyes looked around her in wonderment, flashing with excitement at everything she saw. She walked with ultimate confidence, one hand on her dark blue suitcase that trailed behind her and the other on the pale blue strap of her backpack. Roman admired the curve of her face and felt heat rush to his cheeks.

'*She's even prettier in person,*' he thought, hiding more of his face behind the makeshift sign to cover his blush. *'Honestly, can I keep it together for one second?'*

He was considering ducking his head away completely, when her gaze fell on him. There was an odd look in her eyes, one that Roman couldn't place, something that was lost in the sky-blue color of her eyes. They lowered, focusing on the sign that Roman held in his hands, and her lips formed a smile into.

"Kesi!" His mother yelled, jolting him out of his thoughts. The girl's attention snapped to Emma. "Over here!"

Roman watched as Kesi trotted over to Emma, catching herself from a near-stumble as she tried to slip through the crowd. He shoved down a chuckle, ducking his head away for a moment to compose himself before returning his gaze to her.

"Hello," she said, and his eyes widened at the sound of her voice. She wasn't addressing him individually, but their gazes locked for a moment, sending another rush of heat up his neck. The girl, *'Kesi. Kesi Haddad,'* moved her eyes away from him to study his mother and father. "Tell me if I'm wrong," she said, a goofy grin slipping onto her features, "but I'm guessing that you're Mrs. Lovett," she looked at Emma, "and you're Mr. Lovett," she motioned to Daniel, before turning to him, "and you're Roman."

'Roman.' She put a bit of stress on the *o* that wasn't necessary, showing her foreignness. Still, the small quirk made a smile creep onto his face. He nodded shyly and ran a hand through his dark hair nervously, before dropping his smile to the ground. A sort of... giddiness, if that's what he could call it... filled him suddenly.

"Please, call us Emma and Daniel," his mother stepped in. "I can't tell you how excited we are to be hosting you! How was your flight?"

"It was...ah...," Kesi bit her lip and tried to contain her smile. It was no use, Roman could see even now that her grins and smiles were uncontainable. "Shorter than I expected, actually. I must have... slept during most of it. Or something."

"Danny likes to sleep on planes too," Emma giggled. "He snores a lot, so the rest of us can't sleep a wink."

"I do not," Daniel rolled his eyes, but Roman could see the playfulness in his eyes towards his wife. "Roman, would you take Kesi's suitcase?"

"Uh, yeah. Sure," Roman stuttered, moving closer to Kesi.

"It's really no- oh, uh, thank you," Kesi smiled at him sheepishly as he reached for the handle of her suitcase. Their fingers brushed briefly, causing both teens to blink in surprise, and Roman to start blushing again. Recovering from the awkwardness of the situation, he quickly grabbed her bag and moved to a more respectful distance away from her.

"It's... it's late. We should be heading home now, or soon," he looked to his mother. "School."

Emma nodded before turning her eyes to Kesi, smiling, "I'm sorry that you had to come on a school night, but at least it's Friday tomorrow so you'll have an incredibly short week."

"I'll go get the car," Daniel flashed Kesi one of his rare, teeth-showing smiles before walking away.

Emma turned back to Kesi, clearly excited. "In your letter you said that you like sports. Waterford Academy offers a ton of those, and I think that the sign-ups are still open. But you...probably already knew that, since Students Abroad probably told you," Emma bit her lip, "I could reach out to some of the coaches for you, if you want."

Kesi's face lit up like a campfire, "Oh, yes, of course! Thank you... Emma." Kesi thought for a moment, "Do you think they'll allow girls on the American football- erm, football team?"

Roman laughed. Kesi spun on him, a questioning, almost daring look in her eyes. Roman quickly cleared his throat, straightening, "I mean, you play football?"

"I...," Kesi paused, "They introduced the game last year to my school to try and get more people interested in sports. But not enough boys signed up, so they let girls on the team."

"I play football," Roman replied quietly, looking away from her intense blue gaze. "I've...I don't think there's ever been a girl on the team, but I could ask."

Kesi gave him a cheeky grin, "That'd be awesome."

"If... if not, field hockey is pretty much the girls' equivalent to football," Roman rambled on nervously, wanting to keep the conversation going. "It's really competitive."

Kesi's grin widened, "Perfect."

Emma laughed, reminding Roman that they weren't alone. "Great. Now we have two athletes in the house."

Roman licked his lips and looked away from them both. Emma knew very well that the only reason he started doing sports after his sister's death was to keep himself busy. Even now, having too much free time to think was just... too much. He always ended up thinking about Sophia. He filled his time with sports, music, school, reading, video games, and, if he ran out of those, extra schoolwork and more exercise.

The house was too lonely, too empty, without Sophia. Too much time to think just ended up making Roman depressed.

When he turned back to Kesi, she was looking at him quizzically, making his face heat up when he realized she was trying to read him. Trying to make sense of the emotions he was sure were written clear as day across his face.

Emma's phone *dinged* and she reached into her pocket to glance at the screen. "Dan is ready with the car. Let's go," she motioned for the two teens to follow before¹ she addressed Kesi again, "Tell me about Cairo! I've been to so many places in Europe, but I've never stepped foot in the Middle East. It's on my bucket list, though."

Roman perked up at the change in subject while pulling Kesi's luggage behind him. Sophia and himself had shared a dream of traveling around the world in one summer before Sophia went to college. She'd plastered various pictures of almost every major city on her walls and mapped out a detailed route by the time she was fourteen years old. Even when she was sick and dying, she never lost sight of their dream.

Now Roman had all her pictures and plans in a small box tucked away under his desk. All he wanted to do was go to each of the cities they dreamed of going to and find a piece of Sophia in them.

"It's…," Kesi seemed to be searching for the right words. "It's big," she chuckled, "And hot. It's always crowded with tourists and there are old buildings right on top of new ones." Kesi thought some more, "You should visit it sometime."

Emma grinned, the three of them approaching the doors leading outside. They opened when the group approached, and Roman heard Kesi gasp slightly and looked over to see her feverishly trying to school a shocked expression. Roman chuckled at her. *'Scared of automatic doors, I see,'* he thought to himself.

When they stepped outside, Kesi gasped again, louder this time, "Oh! It's… kind of cold." Roman watched as she wrapped her hoodie around herself tightly.

Emma turned to her this time, "Sorry, it does get a little cold here now and then. Here he is, in the black SUV!"

Roman caught Kesi's distasteful look at the word *cold* and smiled at her before running to put her suitcase in the trunk of his family's car. He then yanked open the door and collapsed into the seat beside Kesi, flashing her a grin until he noticed how she was shivering. *'Has she ever been cold before? I guess not…'*

Roman leaded forward and pressed the button for the seat warmer in front of them before smiling at her again. This time Kesi smiled back.

"Do you have warmer clothes?" Emma asked as the family and Kesi got situated, picking the conversation up where it left off. "If not, we can always go shopping."

"Uh...yes, I think we'll need to do that...eventually," Kesi grinned. "I don't think I own any warm clothes to be honest."

"Well, that will change," Daniel looked at her through the rear-view mirror, his dark blue eyes looking almost black in the dim light. "Probably not for a little while. We still have a few more warm days left."

Kesi nodded, smiling at his reflection in the mirror.

Most of the drive was spent in silence, the exhaustion of the day hitting them all, even Roman's excited mother. He looked over at Kesi, who was gazing out the window peacefully. She looked over at him suddenly, but, as embarrassed as Roman was, he couldn't bring himself to look away. She blinked at him for a moment, then gave him what he now understood was her trademark grin. Roman smiled back before ducking his head, blushing into his lap. *'Maybe Kesi is a good thing coming my way after all.'*

'Well, this is certainly an interesting night.' She wasn't so sure what she was expecting from the human realm or the Lovett family, but she was certain that it wasn't... Roman. *'Maybe it's the magic in his blood that's making him seem more... attractive. Or something.'* At least that's what she convinced herself it was.

'Roman Lovett. The Chosen One.' She was still grappling with the idea. She'd heard and learned so much about him, but seeing him in person now, meeting him in this moment, it was so... different. His hair, his eyes- it all correlated with the prophecy in the High Palace that she had seen, but there was so much more depth to the Chosen One than that. His hair was choppy and a bit unkempt, his eyes were just as vibrant as they were in her nightmare over a week ago. His skin was a lot paler than hers, almost cream-colored, and he had a tall, broad structure that he filled nicely. He seemed shy and reserved, having a habit of conjuring pink dust on his cheekbones.

'*Which are, by the way, pretty nice cheekbones. Or at least it's a nice facial structure overall,*' Kesi noted as she cast another glance over at him. '*Why do I keep doing that?*' She wanted to mentally slap herself. She was here to protect the boy, not... '*Turn into Divya when she's around Ra'id.*' Kesi briefly wondered how he would deal with her now that she wasn't there and smiled at the thought of the two of them being Mates. That would be an ironic turn of events.

Kesi watched the streetlights and cars flicker by as Daniel continued to drive, allowing her to see the human world up close for the first time. Much like Roman, she'd heard about all these things but seeing them in person... it was almost mystifying. All the lights that weren't from the stars or magical waters, all the cars that moved as fast as Kesi could fly, it was like nothing she had ever seen before. Gigantic buildings stood like tall, silent shadows in the distance and continued to grow smaller the farther they drove. Pinpricks of light dotted the buildings, like tiny, all-too-bright stars.

Kesi nearly jumped out of her skin when Roman started to speak, "That's Rosdale, it's the city that we're a township of, I guess. If that's what you call it."

"I think that's what you call it," Kesi replied, still looking out on the city. '*Rosdale,*' "But don't ask me. English isn't my first language."

"Right," Roman chuckled and Kesi bit her lip.

'*What?!*' her brain screamed, confused. She thought she knew what she was doing, but now that she was here... well, there weren't exactly any Shaytan to protect the Chosen One from, were there? Her nervousness wasn't making fitting in and relaxing easy.

The car soon pulled off the highway, dragging the image of Rosdale away from them. Kesi watched curiously as Daniel took them down smaller streets, some lined with stout buildings, some with trees. They soon turned into a neighborhood with a long entrance road. A large stone sign surrounded by florescent lights, reading *Mountain Falls*, stuck out like a sore thumb as they passed, drawing

Kesi's attention. Roman must have either seen her head follow the sign or read her mind, because he spoke up once again.

"That's what our neighborhood is called," he answered her unasked question. "Mountain Falls, if you were wondering."

"Oh," Kesi replied, pausing. "I don't really live in a neighborhood, back at home, I mean."

"Right," Roman said awkwardly as the car found its way down the winding road, passing other streets that branched from it like a spider's web. Eventually the car veered off onto its own path, climbing up a small hill and rolling up a neatly paved driveway.

Kesi arched her neck to see the large house that she was sure was going to be her new home as the car came to a stop. It was far bigger than the building she had used for her camp back in Jinn City, but it wasn't nearly as huge as the High Palace or Library. However, the light-colored stone that it was made of did remind her of home. The thought sent a pang of homesickness to Kesi's heart, but she pushed it aside. She had a job to do, and she couldn't let pesky feelings of regret and cold feet get in the way.

Mimicking the others, Kesi slowly unbuckled her seatbelt and opened the car door, barely remembering to grab her backpack from the floorboards before turning to face her new home. Closing the door behind her, Kesi looked up at the tall walls of the house, the roof slanting in ways that she wasn't used to. The air was chilly, much colder than it ever got in Jinn City, even at night. Despite the shivering threatening to break her in two, Kesi continued to observe the Lovett's house.

"It's... I hope you like it," Roman said, startling her less this time. She was becoming used to his quiet nature. She turned to see him looking at her with wide eyes, two hands on the handle of the suitcase in front of him. Kesi could feel heat threatening to reach her cheeks and tore her gaze back to the building before her.

"I do," Kesi replied softly, turning her gaze back to his once more. She almost giggled when she found red dusting his cheeks as he nodded, shuffling past her to the side door. It was tucked away against the wall of the house by the garage and guarded by a few steps. Kesi followed him, and the rest of the Lovetts, through the door, stepping into a small, marble-floored room with black coat hangers on one wall and a window on the other. Kesi watched all three Lovetts kick of their shoes and push them over to lay on top of black mats in a semi-orderly fashion before deciding to mimic them. She followed the family further into a black-and-white themed living room attached to a similar-looking kitchen. Kesi moved through the space curiously, observing the gray couch and white cabinets, trailing her fingers over the cool black granite countertop in the kitchen.

"Roman, will you show Kesi to her room?" Emma said to the boy before turning to her. The woman's green eyes were absolutely electric, buzzing with even more energy than her sons'. "School starts at eight and it takes ten minutes to get there. When would you like me to wake you up, Kesi?"

"I...," Kesi thought for a moment, considering all the activities she knew she would have to perform in order to take care of her body, and to seem presentable to human society. "Maybe... seven fifteen? I'll need to shower and everything."

Emma nodded. "Seven fifteen sounds good," she paused, hesitating to turn away. "And Kesi, if you need any help getting situated tonight, just let me know," she smiled in s motherly way. "I promise that we'll have plenty of time to decorate and reorient things tomorrow after school."

Kesi smiled and nodded, exhaustion hitting her in waves.

"C'mon," Roman nodded his head to motion for her to follow. She trotted alongside him as he guided her through the marble-floored foyer and up the staircase, gripping her suitcase with both hands. The stairs emptied into a hallway that wrapped around the space in a sort of square shape. Roman pointed to the open door on Kesi's left before speaking.

"That's my parents' room," he said before turning to the right and passing yet another door, this one closed. "This is my room."

Roman lead her to the very end of the right side of the half-square, where a door stood by itself, barely cracked open. "And this is your room," Roman finished, placing the suitcase down. He couldn't seem to bring himself to look at the door, which Kesi found odd and slightly unsettling. *'What's wrong with this room?'*

Kesi grabbed her suitcase and peeked into the dark room. It was filled with things she had recently learned about. A dresser sat on the far-right side, a bed and a nightstand in the middle of the room between two windows, a desk against the same wall as the door, and an empty bookcase on the left wall. Every piece of furniture was as white as a cloud and the walls were painted as blue as the sky, matching the blue sheets on the bed. Kesi felt the softness of the gray carpet through her socks as she dragged her suitcase inside.

Two doors stood on the same side of the dresser, one leading into a tile-floored bathroom, and the other to a darkened closet. Kesi left her suitcase by her bed and walked over to one of the windows, placing her fingertips on the cool glass. She wasn't used to cities, houses, families, cars, windows with glass. Seeing all these new things really made Kesi realize how far from home she was. *'I really* am *in a different realm.'*

She looked into the distance, the bright lights from the other houses nearby and below the hill in addition to the twinkling stars above her faintly reminding her of home. Wasn't it only last night that she had looked onto a view similar to this in Jinn City? Of course, if it was, all those street and house lights would be magical lanterns from the marketplace or the soft glow of the Djinn Field flowers in the distance, not to mention the thousands of more stars she would be able to see. It wasn't home, but still, it was sort of beautiful, in its own way.

She looked at her reflection in the glass, her human form still so strange and alien to her. Her gaze flickered to Roman's figure behind her, leaning against the doorway casually, watching. His dark eyes held a sort of understanding for her predicament that Kesi couldn't quite understand.

'*What does he miss?*' Kesi's mind mused to itself. '*Or who?*'

Kesi blinked, returning to the present. "We could make this a lot less awkward if you stopped staring at me like that," she whispered, smiling as he ducked his head away, red spotting his face again.

"S-sorry," Roman stammered, shoving his hands into his jean pockets. Kesi tapped her fingers nervously on the windowsill before turning to look at him.

"I...," Kesi struggled to find what she wanted to say. "I know it's late but... I um...Could you tell me a little about your school? I uh... I just don't know what to expect."

Roman gave her a goofy grin, "Yeah, of course. I mean... what do you want to know?"

"Everything," Kesi said hurriedly, excitement and curiosity taking her over, "The teachers, the classes, the people, the everything."

He laughed at her, his whole face lighting up in a way that made Kesi's chest warm. She liked making him laugh. She supposed she was afraid that she wasn't going to be able to do that to humans, as if genie humor didn't transfer over into his world.

"I... God, I don't know where to start," he shook his head, amused. Kesi placed her backpack down on the floor and rocked back onto her bed, looking at him eagerly. He chuckled before taking a seat beside her.

"I guess... my favorite class is Humanities, which is like English and Social Studies combined, because I really like that subject," Roman began. "I have Mr. O'Connor, he's pretty cool, but he gives a lot of homework."

"Homework," Kesi repeated, her head searching for the definition. "Oh, I know. That sucks."

Roman stared at her quizzically. Kesi rushed to correct herself.

"Uh... sometimes Arabic and English get messed up in my

head," Kesi stated. "Especially since English isn't my first language… sometimes it takes me a little bit. I'll get better though, probably. Anyway, what were you saying?"

Roman seemed to accept her lie. "Well, I like Humanities. I think you'd like Mr. O'Connor too, a lot of people do," he paused. "I also like Dr. Denney, she's my Chemistry teacher. She's cool. But… Mrs. Pendergrass," Roman rolled his eyes and huffed loudly, making Kesi laugh, "She teaches Algebra 2, my class, and she's a witch," he paused when he noticed Kesi's confused expression. '*She does magic?*' her brain stupidly thought. "She's mean. And she hates me."

"Oh!" Kesi replied, putting two and two together. '*That's two slip-ups in one day, Kesi. Get yourself together.*' "Well, I doubt she hates you," Kesi said, adding in a playful roll of her eyes.

Roman shook his head, "You should hear half of the stuff she does."

Becoming interested, Kesi cocked her head to the side and stared at him, causing him to smile again.

Roman ran a hand through his black hair. "Man, I don't even know how to explain her… She likes to give out detentions like crazy. At our school, the teacher sends you to the principal's office to get a detention slip to cause students more shame or whatever," Roman rolled his eyes, "but mostly it's just to make sure that the teacher isn't giving out unfair detentions, which Mrs. Pendergrass always does. Sometimes Principal Alves just sends students back without any sort of slip because her reasons are so ridiculous."

"What do you mean?" Kesi prompted, a question which Roman seemed happy to answer.

"I mean, yesterday my friend Dimitri sneezed after she had finished yelling at our class about being too loud, so she sent him to the office," he offered, "It was the weirdest thing. I would love to have seen Mr. Alves' face when Dimitri told him what happened," he smiled at Kesi, who quickly smiled back.

"That *is* ridiculous," Kesi agreed. "Remind me to kick her ass."

"Believe me, people have tried," Roman chuckled. "Nothing seems to be enough to get her fired."

Kesi leaned back on her palms, "Well, she hasn't met me yet."

Roman laughed, shaking his head at her, "You really are something, Kesi."

Kesi blinked. It was the first time he'd ever said her name.

'*What*?!' Her brain started screaming again.

"What classes do you have tomorrow?" Roman asked her, snapping her out of her trance.

"I uh...I should probably check that," Kesi giggled before biting her lip. Where would Queen Ena have put her school information?

Kesi decided on her backpack, opening the largest back pocket to reveal a thin, black laptop. Roman leaned over to observe the contents of her bag as well.

"Hey, you already got your tablet," he said, prompting Kesi to pull the device out.

"I... haven't really used it yet," Kesi stumbled. "Kind of scared."

Roman chuckled, "Bad luck with technology?"

"Something like that," Kesi chuckled as she opened the lid. A small piece of paper was taped to the dark screen, having the printed image of a grid on it. Kesi held the paper closer to the window light to better see what it said. "I think this is my schedule," Kesi concluded, reading the grid by columns. "A block... Algebra... B block... Chemistry... C block... Free... D block... Spanish 2 Honors... there's only four classes per day?"

"The program didn't tell you?" Roman questioned, and Kesi blinked at him for a few moments before understanding.

"Oh, I must have forgotten," Kesi replied, making Roman laugh.

"What are the rest of your classes?" Roman asked, and Kesi complied by reading the rest of the block correlations.

"Uh... E block is Health or PE, F block is Humanities, and G block is art," Kesi finished, turning to face a slightly confused-looking Roman. "What?"

"We have all the same classes." He thought for a moment, "Maybe that's part of the program?"

"Or maybe I just got lucky," Kesi replied before rushing to explain herself, "I mean, I don't know anyone else at Waterford, other than you."

"Right," Roman ducked his head for a moment before continuing, "I um… well, you'll meet Mrs. Pendergrass, I guess." He looked up and grinned at her. Kesi grinned back.

"I promise you, I'm going to kick her ass," Kesi said, and Roman just laugh.

"I'll believe it when I see it," he replied, before pausing. "You know, I… You won't be alone at Waterford. I'll introduce you to my friends and everything. If you want, that is."

Kesi smiled at him softly, "I would like that very much." She turned back to her schedule. "Health or PE… how do I know which one it is?" she said, pointing her finger at the little box. The piece of paper didn't offer much information.

"We have an assigned PE day," Roman said, moving closer to explain. "See, every day we just move through the alphabet by blocks A through G, and once we get back to A again, we call that a rotation. So, "A" days are your A, B, C, and D classes and "E" days are your E, F, G, and A classes and so forth. When I first had E block they gathered us all in the gym and told us that C days would be the day that we have PE, and all the other days we have Health instead," he glanced up to meet Kesi's eyes, as if trying to make sure that she understood. "Don't worry, you'll have me. I'll help you out."

"Thanks," Kesi sighed, her eyelids becoming heavy as she closed the lid of her computer… or tablet, whatever Roman called it, sealing her schedule inside. She would definitely need that later. "I should… I should probably get to bed," she said, looking at him shyly.

Roman stood abruptly and cleared his throat, "Right. Uh… I'll see you tomorrow?"

Kesi smiled, "Do I have a choice?"

Roman shook his head and chuckled, "Not really. School is school, and we... live together, I guess."

Kesi flopped down on her bed, "Night, Roomie."

Roman paused for a long moment. Kesi almost thought he had left without saying a word before he replied, "Night, Roomie."

Once Kesi heard him close the door softly, she sprang into an upright position. She knew that humans slept in special sleeping clothes. '*Pajamas? Pjs? Honestly, who even knows,*' and that she should do that too, since she was, well, she was mostly human. '*But where will I find some?*'

Kesi's gaze landed on the suitcase she had left at the foot of the bed, Ashraf's words from eleven-or-so days before coming back to her.

"*You'll have a suitcase and a backpack with you, and it'll be filled with everything you need- clothes, school supplies, your phone, blah, blah, blah.*"

She guessed that sleeping clothes were part of the *blah, blah, blah* the Elder had mentioned. Kesi quickly flopped the suitcase on its side and opened it carefully, peeking inside. She blinked when she saw exactly what she was looking for on top- a soft, thin tank top and long pants, both in the color blue. There was an orange sticky note attached to them, one that Kesi quickly removed and held up to the dim light cascading from the window.

I knew you would be looking for these first. Makeup and toiletries are in the clear bag underneath.

-Ena

P.S. Isn't he cute?

Kesi almost laughed out loud at the note from her Queen, partly because of her cleverness and party because of her girlish nature.

"Sort of cute," Kesi said to no one, answering the Queen's question before placing the pajamas to the side. Again, the Queen was true to her word. A clear plastic bag containing a toothbrush, toothpaste, and other necessities as well as bulging black bag with the word *makeup* sewn stylishly in pink on the side were sitting in the suitcase amongst clothes and shoes. Kesi carried the bags to her bathroom, flicking on the light and blinking at the brightness. She dumped the contents of the one bag onto the counter and shoved them off into various corners as a sort of organization, then rummaged through the black makeup bag. Kesi held up various things such as blue eyeliner and black eyeshadow before settling on a few items that she thought were enough- basic concealer, mascara, black eyeliner, and a neutral brown eyeshadow. Everything else she simply tucked into a bottom drawer, unsure why Queen Ena thought she would ever use half of those things.

Kesi then washed her face, knowing that it was something that humans did, with the small bottle of facewash that the Queen and Elders had provided. She accidently got some in her mouth and she spent quite a few minutes trying to spit the taste out.

Next, she brushed her teeth, which proved to be awkward and difficult. The toothpaste kept falling off the edge of the bristles of the toothbrush and into the sink. She couldn't control the toothbrush and often poked her cheeks with it harshly, making her wince. After she spit the toothpaste down the drain, she decided to tackle the hardship of getting dressed for the first time.

As a genie, the fashion wasn't very covering, but Kesi still rarely saw her body without any clothes on. In fact, Kesi wasn't so sure that she'd ever seen herself anywhere close to completely naked. Even though she wasn't really in the same body, Kesi blushed throughout the entire ordeal and made sure to keep her eyes on the clothes in her hands and not on herself.

Finally, after what seemed like years, Kesi turned off the bathroom light and returned to the main area of her bedroom. She walked over to her suitcase again and found that the piles of clothes inside created individual outfits, so Kesi didn't exactly have to worry about creating any herself yet. Silently thanking Queen Ena for thinking ahead, Kesi grabbed one of the small piles of clothes and placed it on the floor, ready for the next day. She also placed the shoes that were pressed up against the outfit she chose on the floor as well, creating a small mountain on the carpet. Exhausted from the day's events, Kesi crawled under the covers of her new bed, the warmth more than welcoming. She'd thought that she wouldn't be able to get a lick of sleep during her fist night in the human world, but as soon as her eyelids slammed shut, there wasn't a thing that could stop her from being pulled into complete human tiredness.

CHAPTER TWELVE

DANVILLE, VIRGINIA

Kesi

ESI SAT UP groggily as a soft knock sounded on her door, a sort of heaviness clinging to her limbs and face. She propped herself up on the headboard, rubbing her half-closed eyes as the image of Emma Lovett's orange-red hair peeked through the bedroom door. Kesi looked over to the window, seeing not a speck of light breeching through the window shade. '*What time is it?*' Kesi thought slowly, '*I've never ever woken up this early in my entire life.*'

"Hey," she cooed. "Time to get up for school."

"Oh," Kesi blinked sleepily, causing Emma to giggle.

"Not a morning person?" she questioned, her tone light.

"Eh…," Kesi's head bobbed to the side as her eyelids slammed shut again. Her reflexes wouldn't quite let her fall back asleep as she jerked awake before her body could tumble sideways off the bed.

Emma just shook her head at her. "Your food will be on the table when you come down, I'll fix you something to get you through your first day of school."

"Thanks," Kesi offered sleepily as Emma left the room, disappearing into the hall. It took several seconds for Kesi to find the strength to haul herself out of bed. The air in the room felt cold compared to the covers she had just been hiding under, making Kesi shiver momentarily. Still half-asleep, she stumbled over to the light switch by the door. Kesi blinked at the sudden bright light, squealing in surprise at the sharp pain behind her eyes before slamming her palm against the light switch and returning her room to darkness.

"If this isn't black magic, I don't know what is," Kesi mumbled before dragging herself in the direction of the bathroom. She didn't even get close to the door before she caught her foot on her still-open suitcase and plummeted to the floor. Kesi groaned, the bottom half of her body being poked by the suitcase. She picked herself up slowly before losing her balance again and stumbling into the bathroom.

Kesi picked out the bottles of shampoo, body wash, conditioner, and other necessities she knew humans used in the shower from the pile she had made on the counter the night before. After placing these inside the tile-floored shower, Kesi observed the silver pieces of metal that controlled it. Gingerly, she reached forward and gripped the handle of one of the controls, pulling it forward carefully. Kesi furrowed her brow when it refused to budge, yanking it harshly. Cold water sprayed out of the shower head, hitting her face and hair with such force that she leapt out of the shower, no longer sleepy.

"Jinn!" she yelled. "Why does this world hate me?!"

Showering proved to be just as awkward and foreign as changing clothes, and it didn't help that Kesi had forgotten to lay a towel within arm's reach when she was done. Something she realized only after she had turned the shower off. She scrambled to find some in the cabinets under the bathroom sink, shivering and dripping water. Kesi felt much more awake after her shower, as if the water had scrubbed the tiredness from her skin. The wetness of her blonde hair reminded her of the day that she and her friends went swimming in the Marid Waterfalls after she was announced as the Jinn Savior.

The thought made her melancholy, like a different kind of heaviness pulling her down. Kesi sighed and adjusted the towel around herself, determined to focus on what she came here to do.

When she was finally dry, she dragged herself over to the pile of clothes she had created the night before. She had gotten better at changing, she noted with delight, as she walked her fully clothed self into the bathroom once again to begin what she assumed would be, her normal human morning routine.

'*Points for Kesi*,' Kesi grinned after spitting toothpaste out of her mouth, happy that she didn't completely murder the insides of her mouth this time. She turned almost giddy when she managed to not swallow the face wash or even get it in her mouth. Kesi found hair-brushing to be quite difficult, mostly because of the thickness and length of her blonde hair. She was also startled by the fact that it didn't dry immediately before remembering that the human realm didn't take care of its inhabitants like Jinn City.

Huffing, Kesi pulled a lock of her hair out from her body and pressed two fingers along it harshly. She jumped when she felt her fingers warm with a familiar feeling, and, as she moved her fingers, found that they left a trail of dry blonde hair in their wake.

Kesi grinned down at her fingers. "Man, how I've missed you," she said, before casting both hands over her head of wet hair, using the little magic she had to dry it. When she was done, Kesi picked up the makeup she had set aside last night and applied it the best she could, using her magic or a wet rag to fix her mistakes when something didn't look quite right.

Admiring her work, Kesi stood back to see herself in the mirror. She was wearing an off-the-shoulder olive green top with quarter sleeves and dark-colored skinny jeans. The tan wedges that she had put on barely lifted her off the ground, but it felt like a standing on top of a mountain to Kesi. As Kesi moved back, she found the wonderful *click*, *clack* sound that they made on the hard floor of the bathroom and grinned in delight. Checking herself once more in the mirror, Kesi nodded to her reflection.

She was ready. '*Jinn, how do humans do this every day? Getting ready takes* forever.'

Kesi walked out of the bathroom and switched off the light, alarmed at the darkness that surrounded her. She blinked furiously, but it didn't improve her vision.

"Not this again," Kesi groaned and carefully picked her way over to the main light switch, hating the feeling of not being able to see for the second time that morning.

Once the light was on, Kesi turned to her backpack. She knelt carefully and opened the largest pocket, taking out her tablet. She then opened the second biggest section, finding a folded-up messenger bag inside.

Kesi took it out, admiring its blue color. Queen Ena definitely liked color-coordination, not that Kesi minded. The baby blue shade was spectacular to Kesi.

She opened the bag and found space enough for her tablet inside, which she quickly filled. Kesi's eye caught onto another shiny screen in one of the inside pockets, and pulled out a smartphone from the bag, smiling as she turned on the screen.

Kesi paused, her smile dropping slightly. The image on the lock screen was that of her smiling next to another blonde-haired woman, both of their eyes warm and blue. The hair and eyes were nothing like hers, but Kesi could tell that the woman was unmistakably Queen Ena.

Kesi pocketed the phone in her jeans and searched the rest of the bag. A few pencils were found in another side pocket, as well as a long, black charger cord and another, shorter one that was as white as snow. The small one was wrapped around another white box- a charger. The two parts together were a phone charger. Kesi almost hit herself upside the head. '*Why did it take me so long to figure this out?*'

Leaving her messenger bag open on the floor, Kesi searched the second pocket of her backpack further for anything else she might need. Kesi found a book with thin pages and a yellow cover, the words *Spanish 2* printed on the front. Kesi put that next to her tablet as well, sure that she was going to use it sooner or later.

Finally, Kesi grabbed her bag and stood to her feet, wobbling a little on her heels. Gathering her confidence, she walked out of her bedroom and down the wood-floored hallway, almost giggling when her shoes started to *click-clack* again.

Kesi walked down the stairs carefully, fearing she would fall. Once her feet hit the floor, she almost sighed in relief before turning to face the kitchen to her right.

The kitchen was empty except for Roman, who looked up from his bowl of cereal to blink at her from the counter. He shoved a spoonful of cereal into his mouth and pointed to the seat next to him, which held a plate full of food that Kesi couldn't see, sending steam into the air.

Kesi approached it slowly at first, but upon hearing her stomach growl she started to pick up the pace, hunger gnawing her from the inside out. She'd never been this hungry before.

Kesi sat down next to Roman with a slight sigh, staring at the sunshine-yellow eggs, brown-and-red bacon, and cloud-white yogurt before her. She leaned forward to see what was inside the red cup set before her, finding it to be water.

Kesi settled back into her chair. Water. She was used to that.

Kesi picked up the fork next to her plate and gripped it with her fingertips tightly, aiming it towards the delicious-looking eggs. The fork tumbled out of her hands before she could even get anything on it, falling into the rest of her food. She glared at the fork, causing a laugh to erupt from Roman.

"What?" Kesi spun on him as he continued to laugh, "It's not funny! I bet you... I bet you drop stuff all the time!" Kesi huffed, which only made Roman laugh harder. With newfound determination, Kesi grabbed the fork and plunged it into the eggs, sticking a huge bite into her mouth while looking Roman right in the eye, glaring. He stared back at her amusingly.

The eggs melted into her mouth, the warmth and softness taking over Kesi's senses. She'd never tasted anything like it before, although now she wished she had. With a slight sharp twinge of salt and a bright flavor, eggs were easily the most wonderful thing she had eaten before.

"Twhis iws gwood," Kesi mumbled, pointing to the eggs and shoving another bite into her mouth before picking up a piece of bacon. It felt greasy and oily, giving off a sort of burnt scent.

"Why are you looking at it like that?" Roman asked, startling Kesi from her thoughts.

"I'm not," Kesi replied quickly before shoving the food into her mouth. At her tongue's first taste her eyes went wide.

'*I take it back*,' she thought, 'this *is the best thing I've ever eaten. The best. Thing. Ever.*'

Roman laughed, clearly reading her expression, "Have you never had bacon before?"

"*Mm,*" Kesi replied, placing another piece in her mouth before taking a sip of water. "I'm a sheltered child."

"Please tell me you've had yogurt before," Roman smirked, nodding his head over to the white pile of yogurt left untouched on the plate.

"Of course," Kesi replied curtly, moving to grab the spoon that was left on the other side of the plate. She was grateful for Elder Iamar's spell then, saving her from looking like a *complete* fool. At least she knew *how* to eat yogurt.

Kesi put a spoonful of the cold yogurt in her mouth, marveling at it's smooth, not-quite-liquidly texture. After Kesi licked the spoon, she turned to Roman.

"Not... yogurt like that," she said, feeling the sugary flavor roaming around her tongue.

The two fell into silence as they ate, Kesi trying and failing to mimic Roman's actions of eating more slowly. She was too engrossed with hunger to really care that much, just happy that she didn't end up having food splattered all over her face.

Kesi pointed down to her empty paper plate, "Where should I...?"

Roman jumped up from his seat then, abandoning his almost-finished cereal and grabbed her plate and silverware from the counter, dumping it into the nearby sink.

Kesi giggled, "You read my mind. Next time, try to do it without the spoon still in your mouth?"

Roman rolled his eyes at her, moving his bowl over to the sink as well before finally pulling the spoon out from between his lips and placing it in the shiny sink. "Did you sleep okay?" he asked finally, looking up at her shyly from behind his shaggy hair.

Kesi bit her lip. "You know, I thought that I wouldn't because of, well, everything, but I guess I'm a nervous sleeper," Kesi shrugged then grinned.

Roman snorted, shaking his head at her.

"You think I'm crazy," Kesi noted, leaning forward to observe him with her chin in her palm.

"Crazy is relative," Roman grinned, sparking a smile in Kesi.

"Wow, someone's a poet," she chuckled, causing red to sprout on Roman's cheeks.

"I uh...yeah, I guess," Roman rocked back on his heels, awkward silence settling over the two before it was interrupted by a pajama-clad Emma bursting into the scene. She slid by the counter to grab a pair of car keys sitting by the edge before turning to Roman and Kesi.

"Alright, are we ready?" Emma waited for Kesi to nod before continuing. "Okay, let's go!" she grinned, walking through the kitchen and back past the stairs, prompting Kesi and Roman to follow.

Kesi grabbed her messenger bag while Roman grabbed his

backpack, both hurrying to follow the red-haired woman. Emma lead them down a thin hallway and through a door that lead to another marble-floored room with black hooks, this one much more populated with shoes and coats. She pushed through another door to reveal a large room, floored with cement and filled with bikes, folding chairs, and two large areas clearly left for cars.

One of these areas was occupied by the same black SUV that Kesi had ridden in the night before. She watched as Emma climbed into the driver's seat, still in her pajamas and slippers, then jumped as the car shuttered to life. Roman moved past her and slipped into the car as well, to the same spot he had been in last night. Kesi quickly followed him, crawling inside carefully. Copying the movements she'd done before, Kesi put the metal end of the seatbelt strap into the small, red-and-black box on her other side.

Kesi looked up to see Emma's green eyes staring at her through the rearview mirror, "You look cute," she remarked, making Kesi smile.

"Thanks, Emma," Kesi replied before Emma turned a nob up by the screen to her right, causing music to flow into the car.

The music was much different than what Kesi was used to. There was a whole synthesis of sounds that didn't seem natural, that didn't seem to come from any instruments at all. The lyrics stopped and started and held out in long notes before starting all over again, going against and with the background music at the same time. The rhythm and words soothed Kesi, making the hair on her arms stand up and warmth to buzz beneath her skin. It wasn't the same sort of warmth that magic gave her, it was something... different. Different but still something powerful and mystical.

"Oh!" Kesi mused. "What is this?"

"Bruno Mars," Roman answered. "You like it?"

Kesi grinned, "Yeah. It's... Yeah. I like it a lot."

"Turn it up, Mom," Roman said, a smile overtaking his face as Emma turned the knob again, making the music louder.

"This is so cool," Kesi laughed as Emma started to sing along to the song, exaggerating her facial expressions to make Roman and Kesi chuckle.

"Have you never heard this song before?" Roman asked, and Kesi shook her head, "It's called 'That's What I Like,'" he paused as the music played on. "I like Bruno Mars."

"I do too," Kesi replied. "Well, now I do."

Roman chuckled, "I'll have to show you more of his stuff. Señora Z really likes him, so she always plays his music when she gives us time to do our homework at the end of class."

"Sen-who?" Kesi questioned, cocking her head to the side.

"Señora Zarate, or just Z, since Zarate is kind of... hard to remember," Roman explained, "She's my- well, she's our Spanish teacher. She's nice."

"Right, Spanish," Kesi said, remembering the workbook she had put in her bag. She hoped that Queen Ena had remembered to magically teach her some Spanish, "I'm... not too good at that."

"I'll help you," Roman replied. "I'm pretty decent."

"Thanks, Roman," Kesi smiled at him gratefully. He smiled shyly before ducking his head away from her. *Why does he keep doing that? What does that mean?*

"M-most of our teachers are nice," he continued. "Except for Mrs. Pendergrass. She's the worst. I mean, even Coach Ridley, our PE and Health teacher, is really nice as long as you don't backtalk or be mean to other students. If you do that, she makes you do laps," Roman smiled slyly.

"I'm guessing you've never had to run laps," Kesi replied, "because you seem pretty amused with the idea of running laps."

Roman shrugged, "I just make sure never to piss her off."

"Fair enough," Kesi grinned. "I'll take your advice," she paused, "What does Coach Ridley coach?"

"Girls' volleyball and basketball," Roman answered before reading her curiosity, "Mr. Murray coaches football."

"Mr. Murray?" Kesi asked, turning to him.

"Yeah, he's cool," Roman replied. "He teaches something or other for upperclassmen too, but I haven't figured out what it is yet. I'm sure he'd let you on the football team if you asked. It's the other teachers on the board or whatever that we have to worry about."

"Is it really a problem if I'm on the football team?" Kesi asked, still confused on the notion. Roman had said that he'd never heard of a girl being on the team, but why was that so? '*Why is football only for boys?*' Kesi would never understand humans, she was sure of it.

Roman opened his mouth to reply before closing it, trying to find the right words to say. "Not to me," he decided, causing heat to crawl its way to Kesi's cheeks. "I mean, probably not to a lot of other people, too, but it's just that some adults think that you'll hurt yourself or something."

"I could hurt myself in any sport," Kesi replied, "and so could you."

"I know, but," Roman shifted uncomfortably, "some people just think that girls are more delicate or something and shouldn't play rough sports like football."

"Oh," Kesi thought it over. She knew what stereotypes were by definition and a few that the humans referred to often, but she hadn't thought that they would be quite so… everywhere. She thought it would be on more big-scale things, adult things. Not in things like sports teams or schools. If she were in Jinn City there would be no question about her on a sports team. The whole ordeal just didn't make sense. '*How can* all *human girls be delicate when there's so many of them?*' The idea made her want to furrow her brow. "I'll just have to prove them wrong, then," Kesi decided, making Roman chuckle.

"I'm sure you of all people will be able to," Roman replied. "I…I hope to see you on the team, Kesi."

"Me too," Kesi replied before she felt the car slow. She looked out the window to see the car turning onto another road, pulling up beside a grassy field with a huge building in the distance.

"Whoa," Kesi breathed, admiring the building made of glass and steel, looking like a house with its many slanted roofs. Cars lined up to the left side of the building, making a long line of shiny metal that looked almost like a slimy bug in the sunrise. Kesi saw tiny figures jump out of those cars and walk under a rounded white-stone awning and into the building. The cars rounded a small garden area that was spotted with cement to make the space more sidewalk than foliage.

Emma turned onto another road, this one bringing them closer to the building. As they approached, Kesi spotted a second building across the small street, shrouded by trees, flowers, and other kinds of plants with a small courtyard facing the road. Many teenagers rambled about there, sitting on the various benches with backpacks on their backs.

"No way," Kesi gasped. "*This* is Waterford? This is amazing!"

Emma laughed from the driver's seat, "I'm glad you think so. Roman sure doesn't."

"*Mom*," Roman groaned.

"Is that a *tower*?" Kesi gasped as they came closer to the school and she spotted the small, cone-shaped roof of the courtyard-bearing, smaller building. Unlike the main building, this one didn't look like it had a second floor, except for the small tower jutting out from the side.

"Yeah," Roman replied. "It's the Reading Room. We have two libraries, one in there that we call the Kasper House, and one in the main building. The one in the Kasper House is pretty small, so they made that little tower as an additional place to hold books and read. A lot of people use it to meet with teachers or whatever."

"That's *so cool*," Kesi said, knowing for a fact that most schools in the human world did *not* have reading rooms. Kesi turned to the larger building across the street, "What's that one called?"

"That's Fiore Hall," Roman explained. "It's where all of our classes are. In the Kasper House we eat and kind of hang out. In

Fiore Hall there's five wings for all the different types of classes… I'll tell you about them later."

Finally, Emma's car pulled up to the front. Roman quickly unbuckled and grabbed his backpack from the floorboards. Kesi copied his actions, still marveling at the sight of the two buildings. She'd never seen so much metal and glass in her life. The sheer size of Fiore Hall challenged that of even the High Palace in Jinn City. *'If humans can build this, what else can they build?'*

"Alright, kids, here we are!" Emma chatted excitedly. "Have a good day you two! I hope you have a great time, Kesi!" The woman tossed her a charming smile, one that Kesi easily returned.

"Thank you, Emma!" Kesi replied before jumping out of the car after Roman, wobbling a little in her wedges. She walked around the back of the car to meet Roman on the sidewalk, who waited for her patiently. Kesi looked past him and gawked at the rounded white awning, the stone reminding her of the High Palace, except with the words *Waterford Academy* plastered on it in silver steel.

"Nervous?" he asked, snapping her attention back to him.

"A little," Kesi admitted. *'For more reasons than you know, Roman,'* Kesi thought before taking a deep breath and moving forward.

He held the door open for Kesi as she walked through, watching her as closely as she was observing the space around her. Kesi could feel his eyes on her and briefly wondered who was more nervous- Roman or herself?

The tall ceiling and open spaces were the first thing that Kesi noticed when she walked into Waterford Academy. The floor was marble, or granite, or some other stone that Kesi couldn't quite put her finger on. Comfortable-looking chairs dotted the area, four surrounding a black grand piano which held two joyous students happily playing and laughing along with one another. There was a small set of stairs to Kesi's left that led to a long hallway Kesi couldn't see the end of. To the right was a wall of clear shelves holding various trophies that stood between doors leading to glass-walled classrooms.

Roman approached her carefully, pointing down the hallway to her left, "That's the main part of the Humanities Wing. That's where all the language and Humanities classes are."

"You said five wings," Kesi noted, making Roman nod.

"There's also the Arts Wing, Science Wing, Math Wing, and Health and Fitness Wing," Roman replied. "We'll get to all of them eventually, don't worry."

"A block… Algebra 2," Kesi thought aloud. "That's in the Math Wing. Where's that?"

Roman chuckled, "Come on, let's go."

Kesi followed him as he started walking down the hall straight ahead. They passed a desk holding a cheery-looking woman who was talking to a few older students and a small station with the word *Café* embedded in the stone above it in silver letters. The Café had bustling women hurrying to and fro behind the counter and a large line of eager students, all with green dollar bills or shiny metal change in hand. The two of them passed all of those and rounded the corner to face a large and wide set of stairs, busy with its own crowd of students sitting on the sides or running up and down the steps. A hallway aligned itself onto the staircase's left side, and Kesi could see that it turned to the Humanities Wing, or whatever Roman called it. Kesi turned to her right and saw another area full of the same comfortable-looking chairs as before and a large doorway to an even larger space full of white tables and chairs.

Roman must have seen her looking, because he leaned in and said over the commotion, "That's the Arts Wing. The main area of that is the Qualls, which is another hang out place, I guess. The Arts department uses it to hang up all of our work."

"That's cool," Kesi replied before following Roman up the steps. "Where are we going?"

"The Math Wing is above the Arts Wing," Roman explained, and Kesi nodded in understanding.

At the top of the stairs, there was another little area of chairs in front of a long glass bridge extending to another part of the building.

"What's *that*?" Kesi stopped and pointed. Roman joined her.

"It's one of the sky bridges," Roman replied. "There's three: One connecting the Health Wing to the main part of Fiore Hall, another connecting the Math Wing to the Science Wing, and a third one connecting the two parts of the Math Wing together." Roman paused before adding, "This one goes to the Health Wing."

"How did you make all of this?" Kesi asked, awe struck and shaking her head.

"Lots of money," Roman replied. "Some guy with the last name Waterford founded this place, with the help of his rich friends Fiore and Kasper. It's a fairly new school, it's only been around for like fifty years. The building is even newer."

"Wow," was all Kesi could say before shaking herself out of her trance. "We have to get to class."

"Right," Roman chuckled. He seemed to have been off in his own world too, "Come on, the Math Wing is close."

Kesi followed Roman as he turned right and walked down the small hall that opened up to another chair-and-table adorned space. This one had high tabletops and a sort of bar pressed up against one wall. Kesi and Roman turned right again soon after, finding themselves in a short, wood-floored hallway with only three doors. Roman moved to open the first one before stopping.

"What?" Kesi asked as the boy turned to face her.

"I sit with my friend Dimitri in this class," Roman explained, "and normally by friend Ben, Benita, sits by herself. I think she would like you."

Kesi blinked, "So…I should sit with her?"

Roman shrugged, "I mean, if you want."

"Just open the door," Kesi rolled her eyes playfully at him. Roman complied, letting out a rush of student chatter. While Roman slipped in with some level of confidence, Kesi strayed behind, inching through the doorway as she observed the room.

There were no white or chalk boards, however all the walls gleamed with a shine that suggested they were painted with white board paint. Three rows of two white tables were set up before one of the walls, a box-like projector hung above the area in the middle of the wall. The ceiling was tall and slanted and the huge windows on the far side of the room had screens pulled over them, giving the room a grayish glow.

Kesi watched as Roman slid into a seat beside a short blonde boy by the window, giving her a reassuring smile. Kesi looked around at the other tables in the room. Most were full, except for one. A girl sat in the seat in front of Roman, her face buried in her phone. She had deep, dark brown hair and tan skin that wasn't as tan as Kesi's but suggested that she spent a lot of time in the sun. She wore a blood red tank top covered by a black leather jacket, and jeans of the same black color. With her red lipstick and black eyeliner, she looked almost daring in a way, as if she knew that even if she asked for trouble no one would be brave enough to give it to her. 'But will she be kind?' She assumed that this was Roman's friend, but she couldn't tell if the girl was someone who would be open to other people.

Gulping, Kesi willed herself to march across the room and take the window seat beside the girl. Biting her lip nervously, Kesi spoke up, "Hi, I'm Kesi Haddad." She continued when the girl's dark brown eyes met hers, "I'm… I'm an exchange student…?"

The girl cut her off, "I know who you are." Kesi froze at her words. 'Oh Jinn, did I do something wrong? Are there different rules for communicating with humans? Is this how you make friends? Did I offend her? She looks offended. Crap, crap, crap.'

Suddenly the girl gave her a devilish grin, her face lighting up warmly. Kesi had to hold back a sigh of relief. 'Seems like she's nice after all.'

"You're all Roman could talk about since Wednesday of last week," the girl said before sticking out a hand to shake. "I'm Benita Perez, but most people just call me Ben. I'm friends with Roman, if that helps."

Kesi shook the girl's hand gratefully, "Wow, *Benita*, that's very…"

"Latina, I know," Ben rolled her eyes. "Hey, don't be ashamed to say it. My parents are from Mexico."

"Well, I wasn't going to say *that*," Kesi chuckled at her. "I was just going to say that it's a very pretty name. We don't have those kinds of names in… Egypt. But I guess it's what you said, too."

Ben nudged her. "That's right! The much-anticipated mystery girl from the Middle East!" She paused and Kesi laughed warily. "People will give you crap about that."

Now Kesi was confused. "Why?"

Ben opened her mouth to respond, but then closed it before nodding her head to the table across from them. "See those two girls? That's Becky Oakley and Karoline Blanchard. Karoline, the blonde, is okay, when she's alone, but once she's with Becky…," Ben rolled her eyes, which seemed to be a habit of hers.

Kesi moved to see the two girls that Ben was talking about. One had long, curly brown hair that was a few shades lighter than Ben's. Her eyes were a light green color, much lighter than the dark green skirt and top she was wearing. She picked at invisible dirt from under her long, French manicured nails, her light pink lipstick forming into a sort of scowl on her face. Kesi concluded that she wasn't the most pleasant person.

Her gaze moved to the girl sitting next the brunette. The girl's hair was cropped to about her shoulders and was a sort of toned-down blonde color. Her eyes were large and hazel, and when she saw Kesi she quickly tapped the other girl on the shoulder and began whispering in her ear. Kesi averted her gaze back to Ben, not wanting to see what happened next.

"Becky has the brown hair?" Kesi guessed, and Ben nodded before leaning close.

"Don't look now, but the two boys sitting behind them are kind of like Becky and Karoline, except with, you know, guy parts," Kesi giggled as Ben grinned. "The curly-haired Italian-looking guy is Nico, and the dude sitting next to him is Taylor. Taylor likes to try and get all the girls, so if you make eye contact with him, he'll think that you're wanting to be his prey."

Kesi flicked her gaze over Ben's shoulder, where she caught sight of the boys that Ben was talking about. Curly-haired Nico sat behind Karoline and appeared to be playing some intense video game on his computer. Taylor was dark-skinned and towered over the other boy, egging him on. Luckily Taylor was too engrossed in whatever Nico was doing to notice her. Before Kesi could observe any further, however, she felt a light slap on her arm and returned her attention to Ben.

"I said don't look!" she said, grinning, before they both broke out in laughter as the door to the classroom opened and closed in one single moment.

"Miss Perez!" a gruff yet feminine voice yelled, sucking the laughter and chatter out of the air. They both turned to see a big-nosed woman standing at the front of the room. Her skin was oily and covered in wrinkles, and her sunken gray-blue eyes were framed by messy brown hair. She had a tall, thin, wiry figure, and the tips of her big ears burned red with fury as she glared at Kesi's new-found friend.

"What did you find," the woman spat, "so *funny*."

Ben squirmed, "Nothing, Mrs. Pendergrass."

"Mrs. Pendergrass," Kesi repeated, starting to grin. When she noticed the teacher's stormy gaze on her, she widened her smile further. "I assure you it was nothing, Mrs. Pendergrass."

"This is not happening," Kesi heard Roman mutter from behind her.

"*Mm,*" the teacher replied. "Nothing? Miss...?"

"Kesi Haddad," Kesi replied, propping her chin up with her palm. It was clear that Mrs. Pendergrass was used to conducting power over her students, but Kesi wasn't afraid of her. She was just another person, after all. It didn't matter how nasty she was to others. "I was just telling my good friend Ben here a story about my younger sister, who currently resides back at my home in Egypt. I can repeat it for you if you would like."

"That will not be necessary, Miss Haddad," Mrs. Pendergrass snapped. Kesi pouted.

"Are you sure? It's quite a funny story, actually," Kesi replied, almost daring Mrs. Pendergrass to make a move against her.

The woman seemed to be almost startled. "Well!" she huffed upon noticing Kesi's never-fading grin. "I... Miss Haddad, would you like to introduce yourself to the class so we can get on with our day?"

"I would *love* to," Kesi replied, smirking as she stood to face the awe-struck students sitting in the rows around her. Her initial nervousness about being accepted were fading. These were just people, and Kesi knew how to deal with people. It didn't matter that they didn't have magic or glittery skin. "I'm Kesi Haddad. I'm from Cairo, Egypt. I'm currently acting as an exchange student here and I... hope to make the most of it."

Mrs. Pendergrass huffed as Kesi sat down. "We've wasted enough class time on this... nonsense... business," the teacher waved her hands in the air. "I'm afraid that we now have no time to review names and Miss Haddad," she pointed her big nose in Kesi's direction, "will have to trudge through on her own."

"No problem, Mrs. P," Kesi replied quickly, grinning and giving her a small salute.

"Right," Mrs. Pendergrass glowered. Kesi hoped that she honestly didn't think that was *intimidating.*

'*Humans, humans, humans,*' Kesi thought, mentally shaking her head in amusement. She was sent to another realm to fight creatures of pure evil magic; how could she possibly be afraid of one magic-less human who obviously thought she was better than everyone else? '*I can't*,' Kesi thought, answering her own question. '*If I'm afraid of her, then I'll be terrified of the Shaytan. And I'm a Jinn now. I can't be afraid of people like her.*'

"Does anyone remember where we left off?" Mrs. Pendergrass spun on the class. "Taylor?"

The whole class turned to look at the tall, dark-skinned boy as he immediately became flustered and started stuttering, failing to produce an answer.

"Detention. Out," Mrs. Pendergrass pointed a long, bony finger at the door, and Taylor quickly gathered his things and sulked out the door, clearly embarrassed. Kesi bit her lip. She supposed the only way to escape detention was to keep talking over the notorious teacher, not giving her time to reel her anger into a weapon composed of thin finger bones and a craggily voice.

It was going to be a long class.

CHAPTER THIRTEEN

DANVILLE, VIRGINIA

Roman

"THAT WAS AMAZING!" Ben yelled, her voice brimming with pure excitement once they were released from the classroom, putting a hand on Kesi's shoulder. Roman was astounded at how close the two girls got within only minutes. Maybe it was a girl thing.

Roman, Ben, Dimitri, and Kesi all crowded out of the classroom together, eager to start their morning break and trying to avoid the other students. Becky was thankfully far ahead of them, sashaying next to Nico and Taylor as Karoline strayed behind.

Kesi waved Ben off, "It was nothing. You just kind of have to keep talking so she doesn't have a chance to reply."

"Don't kid yourself, girlfriend, *no one* has survived standing up to Mrs. Pendergrass for one whole minute much less a whole class! You're practically a legend now."

Kesi threw her head back and laughed at Ben's enthusiasm, making Roman turn away to hide his blush when he realized that he was observing her too closely. Roman caught Dimitri's eye, and the blonde boy raised a quiet eyebrow at him. Roman shot him a glare, only making his friend smile. Although he was quiet, Dimitri could read people inside and out, especially someone he'd known as long as he'd known Roman.

The whole exchange seemed to make Kesi notice Dimitri, and she turned to him, smiling, "Hi, I'm Kesi. You must be Dimitri?"

Dimitri nodded and offered a little wave, making Kesi giggle.

"Sorry if Dimitri is awkward," Ben said. "He thinks he talks weird."

Kesi seemed amused with the idea, "Why?"

"I can't... hear out of my left ear," Dimitri offered. "I've only heard half of the English language my wh-whole life."

"Oh," Kesi replied, clearly puzzled by Dimitri's analogy. "I think you sound fine, by the way," she paused. "I see where you're coming from, though. English is my second language and sometimes I don't even know what I'm saying."

Dimitri smiled again, showing his gratitude, as Ben spoke up next, "What's your first language?"

"Arabic," Kesi answered, making Ben turn to Roman.

"We have to introduce her to the twins!" she declared, tugging Kesi forward.

"Who are the twins?" she questioned as Dimitri and Roman struggled to keep up with the two girls.

"Our friends Kharim and Aasma," Roman replied. "We have a forty-five-minute break now in between classes, so we can all hang out. They'll probably be in the library, Ben," Roman told the dark-haired girl, who threw him a solid thumbs-up.

"Which library?" Kesi giggled, and Roman beamed at the fact that she'd remembered.

"This one," Ben told her as she dragged her around the corner, passing the grand staircase.

The Fiore Hall Library wasn't extremely large, just four rows of waist-high bookshelves and lots of room for couches, chairs, and tables behind and to the left of them. Three glass-walled rooms covered one wall, holding students crowded around tables and in swivel chairs. To the right of the bookshelves sat the rounded librarian's desk, where Mr. Brown sat behind his computer. To the left of the desk, Roman could see the edges of the Criswell Center, where students often went to receive help on writing assignments. To the right of the desk lay a wall of magazines and newspapers which Roman noticed were updated regularly despite never being looked at. Behind the desk was a hallway with a sort of bar-like, white structure on the side, commonly called Seifert's Bar. It was already crowded with students getting a head start on their night's assignments.

Ben laughed, pointing a finger to a table in the back of the library behind the bookshelves. Aasma and Kharim stood there, arguing furiously in a language that Roman and his friends had known to recognize as Arabic.

Kesi must have recognized it too, because she soon cried out in excitement and ran over to the twins, chattering in the same tongue as the two of them. The twins seemed startled at first, but both relaxed after Kesi introduced herself. After a few minutes of the three of them talking cheerily while the rest of Roman and his friends stood awkwardly to the side, Aasma turned to him.

"You didn't tell me she was coming today!" Aasma said, her white teeth standing out against her dark skin as she grinned.

Kharim rolled his eyes, "Yes, he did, stupid."

Aasma whirled on him again, ready to shout a retort when Kesi started to giggle at them. As if remembering that Kesi was there, Aasma joined in sheepishly.

"You didn't tell me that you have friends that speak Arabic," Kesi said to Roman before turning to Kharim, "and that is a fact, I promise."

Roman shrugged, "Surprise."

"Rom, you're lame," Ben laughed at him, playfully hitting him on the shoulder. Roman rolled his eyes at her.

"Yeah, yeah," he mumbled, sneaking a half-apologetic glance at Kesi. She smiled in return.

"Hey! New girl!" Roman cringed when he heard the voice boom from behind them before turning to see Nico and Taylor approach them from a nearby table, leaving their snickering group of friends. Roman groaned inwardly when he saw their grins. '*This isn't good...*'

All eyes in the library were on them now as the two boys came closer. Roman instinctively inched towards Kesi. She didn't know the kind of trouble Taylor and Nico often brought, making the stupidest things turn into a whole ordeal that always ended up with someone getting hurt.

"Go away," Ben spat at them, crossing her arms over her chest. "No one wants you here."

"Relax, señorita," Nico smirked. "We're not talking to you," he pointed a finger at Kesi, "We're talking to her."

Kesi put her hands on her hips, her face showing that she was clearly not amused, "*Her* has a name, you know, and I know that you've heard it because you were in my last class."

"Yeah, it's *exotic*," Roman glowered when he noticed the way that Taylor was looking at Kesi, deciding that he didn't like it one bit. "You're from the Middle East, right?"

Kesi looked at them as if they were the dumbest people she had ever laid eyes on, "I believe I said that, too. What, do you have short term memory loss or something?"

"Why's your hair blonde?" Nico questioned, reaching out to try and tug on a lock of her hair. After hitting his hand away with a loud *slap!* Kesi answered him.

"My mother is American," Kesi huffed, rolling her eyes, concurring with Roman's earlier theory that Kesi thought the two boys were beyond stupid. "I'm assuming you know how sex and genetics work, but if you don't, I'm going to have some serious worries about the education they give here," Kesi gave a wide-eyed glance over to Roman that said '*really? Who are these guys?*' If Roman didn't know that there was worse to come, he would have laughed.

"Where's your scarf thing?" Nico sneered, causing Kesi's fiery gaze to snap back to him.

It was as if the entire world had stopped moving to hold their breath, staring at Nico and Kesi as they leveled glares at one another. Roman swore he could cut the tension in the air with a knife. He didn't know what to do or how to defend her and judging by the looks on the faces of all those around him, no one else knew what to do either. Roman considered whirling around and punching Nico before he felt someone grab his arm. He looked over to see Ben looking at the two boys with a twitching jaw, fury etched into her features. Although she wasn't looking at him, Roman could read the emotions in her gesture. '*Don't be rash, you know what could happen if you start a fight. See if she can take care of herself.*'

"Excuse me?" Kesi chuckled angrily, shaking her head at him as if she couldn't believe what he had just said.

"Your scarf thing, like hers," Nico pointed to Aasma, which made Kharim surge forward, lunging towards Nico. Aasma quickly stood in his path, speaking to him softly.

"He's not worth it," Aasma said, making him relax ever so slightly while guiding him away from the infuriating boys.

"Where is it?" Nico continued, turning back to Kesi after it was clear that Kharim wasn't going to start throwing punches.

"Up your ass," Kesi growled, making Taylor and Nico chuckle.

"Oh wow, look at you," Taylor smiled at her. "You know, they say that the meaner girls are the best at... well, *you know*. Should we test that?"

Ben dug her fingernails into Roman's arm as he tensed, grinding his teeth. '*Leave her alone, leave her alone, leave her alone,*' Roman wanted to scream, but Kesi beat him to it.

"Ooo, *wow*," Kesi retorted. "How very kind of you to offer, but…," Kesi pretended to ponder Taylor's words. "It's never gonna happen, especially not with…well, *you*." Kesi looked him up and down, "Partly because you and your little friend here tried, emphasis on *tried*, to marginalize me on something that I don't even have. And partly because the thought of doing… well, *you know*," Kesi deepened her voice in a crude imitation of Taylor's, "makes me sick." Kesi walked forward, getting in the two boys' faces, "And that scarf thing? It's called a hijab. Next time at least try to know what you're talking about when you're being an asshole," Roman was amazed as Taylor and Nico's faces turned uncomfortable. "Nice try, though, I'll give you some credit," Kesi smiled at them, which seemed to surprise the two boys, giving her the opening she needed to push them both backwards in one single movement. "You can go."

Taylor and Nico looked at each other, contemplating what to do, shock and embarrassment clear on their faces.

"Well?" Kesi waited. "I said you can go."

The two boys moved to do just that, although they didn't get farther than one step before falling over each other, tangling their limbs. The library roared with laughter as the two struggled to their feet, only to fall on top of each other again.

"Hey!" Taylor grumbled. "Who tied our shoes together?" He tried to send a glare through the crowd, but everyone was too busy laughing. Taylor looked at his friend beside him.

"It wasn't me!" Nico defended, his face beat red. Embarrassed, the two dived to untie their shoelaces from each other's, but were too eager and couldn't seem to slow down enough get anywhere. Finally, clearly desperate to get out of the mortifying situation, the boys decided to take off their shoes entirely and bolt out of the library in their socks, slipping on the hard wood in their haste to escape.

It took several minutes for the hysterical laughter to die down in the library, much less between Roman and his friends. Almost teary-eyed, Roman turned to Ben, who had been standing almost directly behind Taylor and Nico. "That was... that was genius, how did you do that?"

Ben shook her head, doubled over in laughter, "Wasn't me, buddy."

Roman ceased his laughter, looking around at his friends, "Wait... who... who tied their shoelaces together?"

Kesi grinned, "Must have been magic."

"Or *karma*," Kharim blurted, and they all laughed again. This time, Roman kept his gaze on Kesi. He was glad to see such unbridled joy on her face, proving that she hadn't taken what Nico and Taylor had said too seriously, and that she was fitting in well. Roman silently promised himself not to let things like that happen ever again. If he couldn't do that, he could try to be a little more like Kesi and stand up for himself more often. That would certainly impress her.

"Kesi, you're my hero," Ben chuckled, walking over to sling her arms around Kesi's shoulders. Aasma hugged Kesi at the waist.

"And mine too," Aasma added. "I could never have done that. I mean, I could, but not as well."

Kesi shrugged. "What did you expect me to do? If someone doesn't tell them that they're actually not cool, who will?" she said, making them all laugh again.

Aasma reached into her jeans pocket and pulled out her phone. "We still have a lot of time," she noted before Ben took over.

"Roman, please tell me that you've given the girl some sort of tour of the school?" she said, pulling Kesi closer.

Roman winced, "Ah...well..."

"Roman!" Aasma shook her head at him.

"I think we got here a little late," Kesi offered. "He did explain about all the wings and buildings and stuff."

"I guess it's up to us to do your job, Roman," Kharim sighed dramatically. "As always."

"*Hey*," Roman glared. "Rude."

Aasma took Kesi's hands in hers, "What would you like to see first, Kesi?"

Kesi grinned, "The Reading Room!"

Aasma turned to her brother, "Maybe Roman didn't do such a bad job after all. She knows what the Reading Room is."

"Yeah cause it's a giant tower on the side of the Kasper House," Kharim rolled his eyes at his sister, making her glare.

"Alright, kids, the Reading Room it is!" Ben said hurriedly, tossing Kesi a look that said *disaster averted*, which made both Kesi and Roman laugh.

Roman and his friends guided Kesi through the crowds of students in the library and to the grand staircase as Aasma explained more about the building.

"It's a bit confusing at first," she was saying, "But once you know what classes you have and what rooms you're in, it'll be as easy as pie. The only bad thing is that we have to walk outside to get to lunch in the winter." Aasma shivered. "It gets cold here."

"I've heard," Kesi groaned, "and I'm not looking forward to it."

"First years are always hard, it doesn't matter where you come from," Aasma laughed. "Luckily…erm, maybe not so luckily, I've had my brother in all of my classes, per my parents' request," Aasma tossed her brother a sheepish smile after noticing his glare. "They thought it would be better if we stuck together."

"Roman and I have all the same classes," Kesi replied before pausing. "Maybe my parents did that too."

"That means you're in our Chem class!" Ben said excitedly. "Oh God, with all six of us in there, we're going to burn the place to the ground."

"You all have Chemistry at the same time?" Kesi seemed just as excited as Ben.

"Yup," Kharim interjected. "It's a real party, I assure you."

"Oh no," Kesi groaned, faking dismay. "I wonder why I don't believe you."

"We're not that bad," Roman corrected. "If anyone else besides Dr. Denney were teaching the class, though, we would probably all hate it."

"What do you mean?" Kesi asked, and Roman just laughed in response.

"You'll see," he answered, causing confusion to wash over Kesi's face.

"Roman's right," Aasma put in. "It's hard to explain Dr. Denney."

"Try me," Kesi replied as they ended their climb down the grand staircase.

"She's very... energetic," Kharim tried, "and... clearly has too much coffee."

They all laughed when it was clear that Kesi's curiosity for the teacher only grew, her face scrunching into a scowl when she realized that they really didn't have an answer for her.

As they passed the Café, Roman spotted Becky and a few of her friends standing in line for some drink or scone. The brown-haired girl quickly turned to look at Kesi due to a whisper from one of her friends. He stole a glance at Kesi, who didn't seem oblivious to Becky's glare. Tossing her a blue-eyed wink, Kesi continued on her path with Roman and his friends, not giving Becky a second look. Roman chuckled at the sound of gasps from the girls behind them as they passed, laced with angry whispers.

'*You really are something, Kesi Haddad,*' Roman thought, shaking his head in amazement. Things were already changing around Waterford, and she hadn't even been there a full day. It made Roman wonder what would happen in a year. '*Will Mrs. Pendergrass show an ounce of kindness? Will Taylor and Nico give up bullying? Better yet... will Becky Oakley turn into a decent human being?*' Roman almost laughed out loud at the thought.

Roman held the door open for Kesi as they exited Fiore Hall and entered the warm pre-autumn air. Many students followed in their wake, walking back and forth across the empty street that divided

Fiore Hall from the Kasper House. Roman could tell that Kesi was relishing in the sunlight, her face brightening.

"I hope it gets warm here too," Kesi said as they hurried across the street to the Kasper House.

"It does," Ben reassured her. "In Danville, you get the full glory of all four seasons!"

Roman chuckled at her response, "It'll get really warm soon, I promise. And you might grow to like the snow."

"The *snow*," Kesi gaped at him. "Oh no, no, no. I can't do snow."

"What?" Roman replied, "It's kind of pretty, and when it's not cloudy it's sort of sparkles in the sun…"

"Okay, Edward," Ben laughed. "We all know that it's cold as hell here, don't try to sugarcoat it."

"Why… why did you call him Edward?" Kesi stuttered, confused. Ben gasped.

"Have you… never seen Twilight?" Her brown eyes were wide as Kesi shook her head. "What about the books? You've never read the books?"

"So, you have never eaten eggs before," Roman started. "Never listened to Bruno Mars before, and have never seen Twilight?" Roman waited for her to nod before going on. "The last part I get, not a lot of people like the movies or the books, but…"

"*Chica*, we need to get you to live a little," Ben shook her head, disappointed. "That's too many firsts. How many more do we still need to check off?"

Kesi thought for a moment, "A lot."

Roman turned to Ben seriously, "She's a sheltered child."

"Not so different from you, Rom," Kharim said. "Oh wait… except… you shelter yourself."

"Hardy har har," Roman glared, "*So* funny."

The teens made their way through the courtyard of the Kasper House, passing benches holding students who started whispering to one another once they caught sight of Kesi. Roman knew that she noticed but didn't pay them any mind. In fact, she didn't even seem to be bothered by it.

Roman sighed inwardly and looked away. '*I wish I could do that… care a little less.*'

Kharim pushed open the glass doors leading into the Kasper House, leading them into the carpeted foyer housing a few tables and vending machines on one wall. The hall ahead opened into the dining hall where Roman could hear the kitchen staff preparing the food stands and lunch tables for the first wave of students. Roman and his friends turned before meeting this doorway, guiding Kesi to a thinner hall that lead them to two sturdy wooden doors propped open.

The Kasper House library was much bigger than the Fiore Hall library, but since it consisted of tall bookshelves and not as many tables, not a lot of students came there unless they really needed to study. Due to the earliness in the school year and the lack of upcoming exams, Roman wasn't surprised to find the library almost empty.

The library was in an arched shape, creating the bottom of the tower that held the Reading Room. There were two levels, one that only had two or three wooden tables, and another that was connected to the main part of the library by a short set of stairs on either side of it. That level was full of rows upon rows of tall, full bookcases that were pushed away from the walls to provide room for a set of spiraling metal stairs, which disappeared underneath the wooden ceiling above them.

"That's the staircase you were talking about?" Kesi mumbled to him as they let the rest of their friends lead the way to the second floor.

"Yeah," Roman answered, before adding, "I think you'll like the Reading Room. It has this cool stained-glass window, but all the books up there are kind of weird."

"Weird?" Kesi questioned, curiosity clear on her face.

"It's stuff from that old guy Waterford's personal collection that he donated to the school before he died," Roman explained, going off what his sister had told him. "They're just really old, really long, and really confusing"

Kesi hummed, "Waterford had weird taste."

"I think so too," Roman agreed. "I don't know how he had time to read all of them while running a school at the same time."

Sophia had read a few herself, Roman knew, which was how he knew so much about the books in the Reading Room. Roman remembered her telling him how she was sure that something in that room held an adventure for her when she first started high school at Waterford's upper campus, awed by the idea of a room full of dusty old books.

"*You have no sense of adventure,*" she would always say.

"*You're crazy,*" Roman told her once she had explained one of her many theories- about a hidden code in one of the books.

"*Crazy is relative, Romey.*"

After dragging herself through a few long books, Sophia realized that "Old Waterford," as she liked to call him, somehow found reading history books with hundreds of pages interesting and didn't have any secrets to hide. Roman remembered it as the beginning of Sophia growing up, although she had always been so much more level-headed than he was.

Roman paused in front of the stairs that led to the second level, overcome with the bitter pain that always came after he remembered his sister. He saw the lights flicker out of the corner of his eye, causing him to blink his world back into focus. For a moment, Roman could have sworn that he saw a flash of red-orange hair before the lights started to flicker more violently. Roman looked up in concern.

"Earth to Roman?" Kesi's voice snapped him out of his memories. She was standing on the first flight of steps up to the second floor, waiting for him. She was smiling, but Roman could tell that she had been looking up at the lights, too. She opened her mouth to say more but seemed to decide against it. She waved at him to come along.

"Sorry I'm…. I'm coming," Roman offered, hurrying to catch up. The rest of the walk was silent, Kesi jogging ahead of him on the metal stairs the best she could in her wedges. '*Man, how do girls walk in those?*' he cringed as he followed her. '*Those can't be fun to wear. They should be illegal or something.*'

"Oh, *wow*," Roman heard Kesi say as the stairs emptied her out into the Reading Room. Roman walked in behind her, observing his friends sitting in the leather armchairs stationed around one of the few coffee tables dotting the space. The floor was dark, hardwood, and covered by a soft Persian rug colored black, red, and tan. A good-sized round stained-glass window was placed on the wall overlooking the woods that lay to the right of the building. The mismatched colorful pieces of glass depicted a white flower on a lily pad in the middle of a blue, water-colored circle, the Waterford crest. The walls were made of stone, though it was hardly seen in any spot except around the window, because of all the bookcases surrounding the space. The ceiling wasn't very tall but was pointed as it came into a cone shape, topping off the tower.

"How nice of you to join us!" Kharim grinned at Kesi while Dimitri gave Roman a soft smile, "What were you two doing down there, *hm*?"

Kesi rolled her eyes. "God, Kharim, get your mind out of the gutter," she said, before placing herself in the empty armchair beside him. Roman sat next to Dimitri on the small couch between Kharim, and Ben and Aasma. The two girls were sharing one chair, clearly having saved the last one for Kesi.

"So, what do you think?" Aasma asked, leaning forward to look at Kesi, who was still observing the room.

"This is so cool," Kesi answered. "I wonder why more people don't come up here."

"Probably because it's so far away from everything else," Ben said, checking her phone. "If people didn't leave for class early, they would probably be late. Like we will be, if we don't leave now."

"To Chemistry!" Kharim yelled, jumping up from his seat and causing the rest of them to laugh.

Kesi whined, "But we just got here."

"I know, and I love Dr. Denney and all, but she does not tolerate lateness," Aasma said before standing up to join her brother, adjusting the hijab on her head slightly. "So, we should really go."

Groaning, Kesi stood, making Roman chuckle. The six of them jogged back down the stairs and out of the library, rushing across the street to Fiore Hall.

"The Science Wing is behind the Math Wing," Ben explained to Kesi as they continued to walk outside along the sidewalk that ran alongside Fiore Hall. "It's faster if we walk around everything else."

"Oh, okay," Kesi replied as Roman and his friends guided her around the main bulk of the hall. They traveled through the school and the Qualls, going through a glass door that lead them outside. They hopped down the short staircase to cross a thin street to approach another building. Once their direction became clear, Kesi pointed to the rectangular-shaped building ahead of them.

"Is that the Science Wing?" she asked, looking around at the others who mostly seemed out of breath from all the jogging and running. "Wow, you guys are really out of shape."

Roman laughed, "They don't do sports all year like I do." He paused, "You know, you'll probably have to stay late after school, because I have practice."

"That's okay," Kesi answered as they came closer to the glass double doors, "as long as you promise to talk to your coach for me."

Roman chuckled, "Fair enough, Kesi Haddad."

"Better be, Roman Lovett," Kesi grinned at him as they emerged into the small foyer of the Science Wing, with its set of classic Waterford chairs dotting the area.

"Aww, you guys are so cute!" Aasma mused. "Hundred bucks says you'll get married."

"Get *married*?" Kesi seemed flabbergasted by the idea while Roman felt his cheeks warm at Aasma's comment. Roman felt Dimitri elbow his side, smiling like a schoolboy.

"Don't say a word," Roman mumbled so only he could hear.

"Do I ever?" Dimitri shook his head. "Don't think I would betray you *now* Roman." He paused, "I like her."

Roman looked over to Kesi, who was happily laughing with the twins and Ben ahead of them, Kharim directing her to the door of their Chemistry classroom.

"I think Soph would tell you to go for it," Dimitri said after a while. Roman turned to him in surprise. He normally didn't mention Sophia, the little times that he did talk, "But I know that you won't let yourself."

"I shouldn't be thinking about girls," Roman said quietly. "I shouldn't be… she *died*, D."

"Almost a full year ago," Dimitri replied. "And she wouldn't want you holding back your whole life for her. Even before she got sick, she was always telling you that you need to live a little."

Roman stayed silent for a long time as they entered the classroom, "I will… just not now. Not yet."

Dimitri shook his head, not willing to say more now that they were in a more public setting.

All the science classrooms were relatively the same. Black countertop tables formed a U-shape around the boarders of the room, the walls glowed with white board paint, and the windows were covered in mathematical equations, the markers laying on the countertops nearby. The floors were made of tiles, and the ceilings were tall. Dr. Denney stood behind the podium with the Waterford crest on its wooden surface.

Roman and his friends always sat at the table by the windowsill, away from the other in the people in the class that they all agreed were either annoying or despicable. Every class was the same- a bit of Becky's friends, a bit of Nico and Taylor's, and a bit of others who were tolerable, if not friends. In Chemistry specifically, the dynamic was seemed like this: Karoline Blanchard and Samantha Carlton sat at the table opposite of Roman's, and a group of Taylor and Nico's friends sat next to them. In between Roman's table and the others sat the people Roman deemed tolerable. There was Savanah Reed, Thora Rivers, and Logan Hager, to name a few.

Roman pulled up a chair for Kesi from one of the empty countertops, placing her beside him at the very end of the table. The sound of the chair scrapping the tile floor drew the attention of Dr. Denney, who looked up and smiled at Kesi through dark bangs.

"Hey there!" she chirped, grinning. Dr. Denney was one of the youngest, brightest teachers at Waterford. She was only twenty-six and was one of the best teachers that Roman had ever had. She made the classroom fun and extravagant, and reminded Roman of his mother, and in the same way of Sophia.

Kesi smiled back at the woman, "Hi."

"You're the exchange student," Dr. Denney stated, before observing Kesi more closely. "Ah, I *love* that top."

"Really?" Kesi looked down at her outfit, "I do, too... My mom bought it for me... before I left."

"Your mom has good taste," Dr. Denney laughed. "Anyway, welcome to Waterford. I'm Dr. Denney. Some people call me Dr. D, Miss Denney, even Rose, I don't really care. Whatever you want."

"I'm Kesi Haddad," Kesi replied, the expression on her face showing that she was taking a liking to the young teacher.

"Well?" Dr. Denney turned to the class. "Aren't you guys going to say hello? Wow, how rude are you."

The class laughed in response, before droning a "Hello, Kesi Haddad," with Dr. Denney.

"There we go!" Dr. Denney smiled at the class, "*Much* better."

Kesi giggled while Dr. Denney continued talking, "Why don't

we go around and introduce ourselves, yeah? Alright, Karoline, you start. Say your name and your…," Dr. Denney threw her hands up in the air, "I don't know, your favorite dessert. Go."

Karoline cleared her throat nervously, "I'm Karoline and my favorite dessert is…probably ice cream?" She looked over to Samantha sitting beside her.

Dr. Denney had a comment for every student, whether she was agreeing with their choice of dessert or scolding them for not looking up from their phones. Roman wasn't sure if she was doing this to try and make Kesi more comfortable or to waste time. In any case, Roman got so wrapped up in laughing along with the class that he only snapped to focus when it was Dimitri's time to introduce himself.

"I'm… D-Dimitri," Roman's friend said quietly, "And I guess I like anything."

"I'm Roman," Roman said, picking up where Dimitri left off, "And my favorite dessert is ice cream."

"Oh!" Kesi said when Dr. Denney turned to her. "I'm Kesi Haddad, hi, and my favorite dessert is probably…," Kesi thought for a moment. "You know what? You've probably never heard of it."

"Fair enough," Dr. Denney shrugged. "Alright, now, let's get this class started."

CHAPTER FOURTEEN

DANVILLE, VIRGINIA

Kesi

FREE BLOCK AND lunch moved smoothly, just like the rest of Chemistry class. Kesi was still astounded by the feeling of hunger emerging more than once a day. She'd completely devoured the sandwich she had gotten for lunch, which was stationed in the middle of second block for underclassmen to shorten the lines. Or at least that's what Kharim said.

Kesi really liked the twins, for more reasons than just sharing a language. Aasma had a button nose with a small gold hoop in her left nostril and dark eyes that looked almost black. She was much better at makeup than Kesi, everything was blended and used perfectly. It was clear that Kharim was related to her. They had the same facial structure. Kharim was funny, but a bit impulsive, it seemed, especially when it came to his sister. Aasma was clearly his anchor, reminding him to think about the consequences of his actions.

Dimitri was even shyer than Roman, but Kesi could tell that he was constantly thinking and participating in each conversation silently. He and Roman seemed especially close, and Dimitri's gray eyes always seemed to hold when looking at him. It was the same with the others. When Roman wasn't looking, they took care to observe him, as if checking that he had all his limbs and fingers. It only made Kesi more curious about the Chosen One and all the mysteries that surrounded him. There were sometimes, in the library at the Kasper House, for instance, where he seemed to be somewhere else, somewhere distant. *'Where does his mind go?'* It was a question that Kesi couldn't stand to leave unanswered.

Ben had to teach her how to use her tablet in the beginning of math class, which was more than a little embarrassing. Looking back on it now, Kesi wanted to slap herself for being so amazed at the fact that the computer could fold over so only the screen was showing. Honestly, it was a wonder that anyone actually *believed* she was human. Who got so excited over a touch-screen computer with a hidden stylus to write with? Kesi hoped there were more humans that had never seen that sort of thing than just her.

Kesi spent her free block with Roman and Aasma as the others were away at different classes, the two of them helping her with Algebra and Chemistry homework. She was still trying to get a feel for how to use her tablet, writing on the screen to complete the worksheets and book pages that her teachers had posted online for homework.

"You're not allowed to help," Roman said to Aasma at one point, as Kesi and Roman finished up on their last piece of Algebra homework. "You're too smart, it'd be like cheating."

"Too smart?" Kesi laughed. "Is there such a thing?"

"He just means that I'm in a higher math class," Aasma offered. "Which would be all the more reason to have my help!"

"Well I… don't understand Chemistry at all," Kesi replied, as she scrolled through the worksheet that they had completed earlier in the free block. "Can your super-special math powers help me with that? I don't feel like I got any of these right."

Aasma shook her head. "Sorry Kesi, Chemistry is impossible."

Kesi groaned. "I've figured that much out."

"Dr. D doesn't give too much homework," Roman mumbled. "I heard that the other teachers swamp students with homework. Like, two or three assignments per night, on a good day."

"Yikes," Kesi cringed. "Isn't that Mrs. Pendergrass' job though?"

Roman laughed. "Oh yeah, her too. Right now, it's ok, though, just a lot of formulas to remember."

"I know what you mean," Aasma added. "For my final last year I considered writing all the formulas on the insides of my fingers because they were so confusing. I decided not to, because I was so sure that I was going to get caught. Cheaters never win."

"Why can't your brother listen to you?" Roman chuckled. "I always had to talk him out of cheating in Physics last year."

"Physics was the worst!" Aasma declared before turning to Kesi. "Physics is awful. Did you have to take it freshman year?"

"Uh...," Kesi stuttered, trying to find the right words to use. "Yeah. Stupid... forces."

Aasma laughed. "Yeah, that's about all I remember too."

"Hey, guys," Ben said as she approached, flopping down on the couch next to them. "One more class, and we're done. God bless."

"Was Dance really that hard?" Aasma giggled as Ben leaned her head all the way back and propped her legs up on the small table in front of them.

"I caught Taylor staring at my ass," Ben groaned. "Why does he take Dance? He hates dancing."

"Taylor takes Dance?" Kesi asked, surprised. From what she knew about Taylor, he seemed like the kind of boy who didn't have enough pride to dance.

"Probably as a joke," Roman replied. "Or a dare or something. That's kind of something that Taylor and his friends do often. They turn everything into a joke."

"They're jokes," Kesi scoffed, rolling her eyes. From what Ben told her this morning and the rude comments from both Taylor and

Nico during break, it was safe to say that Kesi didn't have the best first impression of them. She could tell once the boys started talking that they weren't used to having to walk away, so Kesi decided to teach them. She wasn't exactly offended or angry, she just knew that it wasn't worth yelling about. '*Better to just shut it down and make them turn the other way,*' Kesi thought to herself, remembering the whole ordeal, '*but tying their shoelaces together with magic was kind of fun.*'

Kesi smiled at the memory. She did find it odd how easily her newfound friends dismissed the mystery of Taylor and Nico's shoes. She supposed if you grew up in a world without magic, you couldn't really fathom magic actually existing, much less inside the girl standing nearby.

"I feel you, girl," Ben looked at her with wide eyes. "On a deep, deep spiritual level."

Kesi laughed at her before Ben sat up, continuing. "Besides the butt-staring thing, it was kind of funny because Taylor kept checking his shoes, like he was afraid that his shoelaces would be tied together or something."

"Man, karma got him good," Kesi giggled as Kharim and Dimitri approached.

"Hola, amigos," Kharim said to them as he sat beside Ben. "I just came from Spanish."

"We have that next," Kesi grinned, elbowing Roman softly. "Right?"

Roman nodded. "Yup."

"I just heard the craziest thing," Kharim continued, settling into the couch. "Miss Rebecca Oakley hates you. Who knew!"

Kesi shook her head, not believing what she was hearing. "How does she hate me? She doesn't even know me."

"Becky likes attention," Aasma explained. "So, when someone... a new girl from a far-off place, for example... steals the show, even if just for a few days, she gets rather... jealous."

Kesi looked over Aasma's shoulder as Becky swaggered down

the hall, coming closer to the hallway. Her short green skirt swished dangerously around her legs, exposing skin that Kesi was sure wasn't allowed. Becky tossed a subtle glare in Kesi's direction.

She crinkled her nose. "Green is *so* not her color."

"Metaphorically or literally?" Roman replied, catching her eye.

"Both," Kesi rolled her eyes, making her friends laugh. She smiled at her own joke. Roman was right, she wasn't going to be alone here. She already had five friends- and possibly a few enemies.

"Please tell me that you're going to put her in her place, like you did with Taylor and Nico," Ben asked excitedly. Kesi opened her mouth to reply before Roman turned to her sharply.

"Kesi, no," he said, his green eyes wide.

"Kesi, yes!" Kesi cheered, before laughing at Roman's frustrated blush. "Don't worry, I'll only say something if she can't shut up."

"How do you *do* that?" Aasma asked in wonderment. "Whenever I try to fight back against people like Becky, it just turns into a big mess."

"Because you *fight*," Kesi explained. "There's a difference between biting back and wanting someone to walk away. I was just trying to make them walk away and shut up. I wasn't trying to argue with them or even change their minds about what's right and wrong. Arguing doesn't help anyone."

Aasma turned to her brother. "Listen to *her*!"

Kharim glared back. "You're picking a fight right now!"

"Alright," Kesi giggled, finding the twins absolutely hilarious. "Calm down, you two."

"You both argue a fair amount," Ben added, also laughing. "Thanks for the life advice, Kesi."

"No problem," Kesi grinned.

Aasma turned to Roman. "Look at that smile! How can you not fall in love and get married to that smile?"

Roman's cheeks turned pink and he glared at Aasma. "You really want that hundred bucks, don't you?"

"Desperately," Aasma answered. "I'm broke and I want a new art set."

"A new one?" Kharim seemed taken aback. "But you have like… twenty!"

"I have one," Aasma corrected, "and it's only for colored pencils and charcoal. I want a paint set."

"You like art?" Kesi questioned, curious to know more about her new friends.

Aasma nodded, her face lighting up. "I *love* art. I'm kind of trying everything from makeup to fashion designing, but I can't figure out what I like best," she thought for a moment. "If I do anything with art as a career, I think I'll do fashion designing, though. You can get a lot of money out of that."

Kesi nodded slowly, trying to understand all of her words. "Right."

Ben turned to Kesi, smiling wide. "Aasma is really good, her designs are amazing! You should really see them sometime," she gasped. "I know! We should have a party!"

Roman groaned. "No, Ben-"

"Relax, *chico*," Ben rolled her eyes playfully at him. "It'll only be the six of us. And we have to celebrate Kesi somehow!"

"Celebrate me?" Kesi chuckled. "What is it, my birthday?"

Ben punched her arm softly. "Nah, we have to celebrate you coming to the U.S.! Or at least your first day of school."

"I don't know if-" Roman tried again, but this time Kesi cut him off.

"Sounds awesome!" she said, excited. Her first party! And it would be all for her! Kesi felt almost giddy. "When should we have it?"

Ben thought for a moment. "Everyone free Saturday? We can show up to Roman's at like… Five? Have dinner and then leave by nine or ten."

"I give up," Roman sighed. "Sure. I think my mom will be fine with that."

Roman's mother... that reminded Kesi of something. "Oh! Emma is taking me shopping on Saturday, or maybe today, I can't remember."

"You'll probably be back by five," Roman reassured her before turning back to the group. "Does that sound good?"

"Our parents should be fine with it," Kharim said, his sister nodding beside him. "Dimitri?"

"Saturday, five, that's good," Dimitri replied, giving a small smile. It was the third time that Kesi had heard him talk that day.

Kesi's gaze flickered to Roman as he checked his phone. "We should get to class. You ready, Kesi?"

Kesi grinned at him. "Ready as I'll ever be," she answered before turned back to her friends and grabbing her messenger bag. "See you guys later!"

"Have fun in Spanish!" Aasma cheered as the two left, Roman guiding Kesi through the library. They passed a dark-haired man sitting at a round white desk, his nose buried in the computer screen. Kesi almost giggled. He looked so much like the genie at the front desk in the High Palace. She tried not to let homesickness take ahold of her as they walked past offices and took a small staircase back to the first floor. They passed a bar-like area before avoiding a mess of glass-walled offices at the end of the hall, taking the small staircase to their right instead. Roman lead her to a classroom door and opened it slowly.

This classroom had the same white tables as the math classroom and were arranged in another arc shape. The chatter in the room quieted when Kesi and Roman entered, many noticing Becky Oakley's ice-cold stare at Kesi from her table near the back. Kesi smiled at her, wondering if Becky would cause her any trouble. She didn't know if the brunette was as bold as Taylor and Nico.

The room was spotted with students, the side with Becky's table being the most crowded. A group of girls sat around Becky, and a bundle of boys sat at the table next to hers, a few of them Kesi recognized from Chemistry class. Two older kids sat at the table against the far wall, leaving the whole right side of the room empty. Roman chose a table near the back, and Kesi was quick to sit beside him, ignoring Becky's ever-present glare.

"Kesi Haddad, right?" a clipped voice reached Kesi's ears, making her cringe. Kesi turned to see Becky looking at her with pursed lips, waiting for Kesi to answer. Roman tensed beside her, not going unnoticed by Kesi.

"So foreign," Becky continued. "How… *mysterious.*"

'*Why does everyone keep saying that?*' Kesi wondered, '*do humans not get visitors often or something?*' "You like it? I do too. It was my dad's idea."

Becky just scoffed at her, making Kesi bite the inside of her cheek. It didn't seem like she was planning on being nice, but Kesi was determined to stay true to her word to Roman and not throw the first punch.

"Look," Becky said, slowing her speech as if she found Kesi too stupid to comprehend her words. "Waterford is a modern, civil place, if you haven't noticed."

"I have," Kesi raised her eyebrows, as if asking her what her point was. Becky glared at her for interrupting before continuing.

"We don't need any… *girls like you* stirring up trouble," Becky replied curtly. "So why don't you just hop on your magic carpet and fly back home, hm?"

A few chuckles rippled through the class, especially from Becky's friends and the boys sitting around them. Kesi laughed along with them, causing confusion to crease Becky's features.

"What do you mean by *girls like me?*" Kesi asked, all eyes turning to her as the class quieted once more. Honestly, was the notion of standing up to bullies so rare around here?

"Oh, you know…," Becky waved her hands in the air. "Where you're from… people are so *old fashioned.* I mean, we're moving on from the Medieval Ages, don't you think? Get with the times."

Kesi stared at Becky for a moment, trying to understand Becky's statement. *'Don't humans think* anything *nice about one another? First Taylor and Nico, and now Becky?'* With all this hate going around in a simple high school, Kesi briefly wondered how the humans had managed to not kill each other until they faded into extinction.

"Really?" Kesi started, leaning forward onto her elbows and letting her words drop into the silent air. "Because I seemed to recall that being a witch is *really* out of fashion. *So* 1600s, if you ask me. Hey- here's a thought: Maybe you're the outdated one, not me," Kesi smiled at Becky's glare. "So why don't you hop on your broomstick and fly away, hm?" She finished, marveling at the way she was able to give the girl a taste of her own medicine by using her own words against her. Becky's face turned bright red with anger as the class roared in laughter.

"You'll regret that," Becky hissed as she turned to her friends, who began to coddle her as if she were a wounded puppy.

Kesi turned back to Roman, who was staring at her with his mouth as wide open as the High Palace's front gates. He looked at her for a few moments more in awe before he started to laugh.

"What?" Kesi questioned, his deep laughter becoming contagious. "Does no one stand up for themselves around here?"

"Not like you do, Kesi Haddad. Not like you do," Roman shook his head, his emerald green eyes sparkling.

Kesi opened her mouth to reply but she couldn't. Instead she just chuckled into her lap, heat brimming on her face.

'At least Roman has something nice to say,' Kesi thought, stealing another glance over at him. The human world couldn't be so vicious if there were people like Roman in it, could it?

CHAPTER FIFTEEN

DANVILLE, VIRGINIA

Roman

"LET'S GO, LOVETT!" Mr. Murray yelled from across the field as Roman successfully caught the ball that Logan had thrown to him. He plowed his way through his other teammates, who were acting as the opposite team and ran into the end zone.

The brown-haired teacher jogged over to him, yelling to the other boys. "That's good for today! See you on Monday, boys!"

"Bye Coach!" several boys called before making their way towards Fiore Hall in the distance, eager to get to the locker rooms and change.

"Good job today," Mr. Murray said to him as Roman handed him the ball. "You were really on your game."

Roman pulled his helmet off his head, wiping sweat off his forehead. "Been feeling good, I guess."

"Whoever's making you feel good, I hope she stays around," Mr. Murray chuckled.

'*Speaking of which...*' "Actually, Coach, I do need to ask you a question," Roman started as they made their way across the field.

"Do you need girl advice?" Mr. Murray questioned, "because I'm still a single bachelor, so I don't think I could help you there."

Roman laughed, "No, not exactly. My family is hosting a girl from Egypt for a year, and she said that her old school let her play football last year. I was thinking… maybe we could let her on the team? Maybe even just for practices. She really wants to play."

Roman looked to his coach hopefully as he thought it over. "She still here?"

"Probably," Roman replied. "No one could pick her up any earlier."

"Can your mom wait to pick you guys up?" Mr. Murray asked. "I want to see what she's got."

"Really?" Roman gaped, excitement thrumming through his veins. He could imagine Kesi's face, lighting up like a fire when he told her that Mr. Murray wanted to talk to her about football.

"Sure," Mr. Murray said. "If she got on the team she must have some sort of skill. If I think she's good enough for the team I'll talk to the higher ups."

"Thank you, thank you," Roman replied, his face cracking into a grin. "I'll be right back with her, I promise. You'll love her."

Mr. Murray just smiled. "I'll be right here, don't worry."

Roman was sure that he'd never run as fast as he did then, not even during practices or games for any of the sports he played. He ran under the sky bridge connecting the Health Wing to the main part of Fiore Hall before throwing open a door that lead him to the edge of the Humanities Wing where it collided with the grand staircase. Roman hobbled up the stairs in his cleats, not caring if he left any mud or dirt on the floor. He'd left Kesi in the library to do her homework, in one of the glass-walled study rooms. When he flew through the door Kesi looked up at him, startled.

"Mr. M... Mr. Murray wants to talk to you," he panted. "Football."

"*Really*?!" Kesi squealed, jumping up from her seat. "Oh no, I'm not prepared! I don't have good shoes or…"

"Text… Ben…," Roman breathed, typing in his password and throwing her his phone that he had been keeping with his water bottle that day. "Ask her… for her shoes."

"Right," Kesi fumbled with the phone, biting her lip as she searched the screen. "Okay… Ben… Okay, sent!" Kesi looked at Roman with a bright grin. "I'm so ex… Oh, ok," she looked back down at the screen again. "She replied. Ok. Locker 17. Password, 6-16-2. I got this," she handed Roman back his phone as they left the study room. "Thank you, by the way."

"No problem," Roman replied. "You shouldn't keep Mr. Murray waiting."

"Aren't you coming?" Kesi asked, her face falling slightly.

"I just sprinted all the way here," Roman argued. "You gotta give me a second. I'll be there in a minute."

Kesi giggled. "Fair enough! Thanks again Roomie!" She waved before starting to run off, not even making it past the bookshelves before giving up and yanking off her wedges. Roman chuckled as she continued running, shoes in hand.

"Sky bridge!" Roman yelled, and she gave him a thumbs-up before she took off down the sky bridge at the top of the stairs.

Roman watched her go for a few more moments before turning back to his phone and quickly texting Emma.

Sorry, we're going to be a little late. Kesi is trying out for football, he sent before tucking his phone in his back pocket and walking in the same direction that Kesi had gone.

The second floor of the Health Wing was for Health classrooms, the nurse's office, and storage spaces, while the first floor was decorated with locker rooms, two gyms, a wrestling room, a swimming pool, and the school weight room. The second floor also had extra locker rooms that most sports teams used during home games, so the other team could use the main locker rooms if needed.

Roman found his way to the second-floor boys' locker room, which was mostly empty now since most boys had already packed up and changed. Roman could hear a few of the showers running, signaling that there were still a few kids left. He never used the school showers, since they seemed to be the only thing that Waterford didn't update or check up on often. Plus, he was also just too exhausted at the end of practice to go through the effort of showering. He would rather relax and almost fall asleep in the car with his mother first, to gain some sort of energy.

"Hey Roman," Roman turned as he approached his locker, one of the senior boys waving to him. Ian Burrows was the captain of the team, and Roman had known him for a full year now. He was much taller than Roman, much stronger too, making him one of the best players Roman had ever seen.

"Hey, Ian," Roman replied.

"Nice playing today," Ian complimented. "Maybe you'll be team captain when you're a senior."

Roman laughed. "Thanks, Ian."

"Don't mention it," Ian called as he exited the locker room, bag in hand.

Roman quickly grabbed his book bag, which he left in his locker, and slung it over his shoulders, deciding to carry his sports bag by the handles. He made his way over to the football field, hearing yelps of joy and excitement even from afar. Roman smiled to himself, hoping it was a sign that things were going well.

As he approached the field's fence, Roman noticed a silver car that he didn't recognize pulled up to the side of the field, watching. He was about to turn away and ignore it when a familiar voice called to him from the driver's window.

"Hey, Roman!" Ian called, waving a hand. Roman jogged over to the car, placing his bags down by the fence. When he got to the window, Ian leaned his elbow on the side and poked his head out, sunglasses already placed on his nose. "Who's that girl playing with Mr. Murray?"

Roman turned to see Kesi running across the field in Ben's black tennis shoes, jumping up to catch the football that Mr. Murray had thrown to her. Less than a second after she caught it she sent the ball back, spiraling through the air.

"She's good," Ian continued. "I haven't seen her before."

"She's... my exchange student," Roman answered. "I mean, we're hosting her. She said she could play."

"Damn right she can play," Ian chuckled, "or at least catch and throw." Roman watched as Mr. Murray yelled at Kesi to do something as she caught the ball again and she took off running towards the other end of the field. "And run, too apparently. Look at her go." Ian snorted.

Roman grinned at the senior. "She'd kick your ass."

"We'll see about that!" Ian smiled at him. "See you on Monday, Roman."

"Yeah, see you," Roman stepped back as Ian drove away, leaving only him to watch Kesi play. Roman propped himself on the edge of the fence, leaning forward to get a full view of the field. Kesi had already made it to the end zone by now, spiking the ball before tripping over it, falling into the grass. Roman laughed loudly, causing Kesi to sit up and look at him. She laughed too, picking up the football and chucking it at Mr. Murray.

"Lovett!" Mr. Murray smiled at him. "How nice of you to join us!"

"Need someone to tackle Kesi?" Roman called back as Kesi got to her feet.

"Hey!" she yelled at him.

"Go easy on her," Mr. Murray said, lowering his voice as he approached Roman.

"I think she'd kill me if I did," Roman chuckled, opening the gate and allowing himself in.

"Not you!" Kesi yelled at him from across the field. "Coach Murray, kick him out!"

Mr. Murray grinned at Roman. "I see you've already grown close."

"She's crazy," Roman said, widening his eyes, only half-serious. He did truly believe crazy was relative, after all.

"Roman is just gonna push you over a few times!" Mr. Murray called over to Kesi, who's response was putting her hands on her hips.

"He can try!" Kesi cheered, still holding the football with one hand.

"I don't know if I can push her," Roman looked at Mr. Murray as they started walking closer to Kesi.

"Just pretend she's one of those annoying freshmen on the team," Mr. Murray offered. "Oh! Pretend she's Jay. He's *especially* annoying."

Roman laughed. "Alright."

"You know what," Mr. Murray said to Kesi once they got close enough. "I changed my mind. I want to see if you can push Roman over."

"What?" Roman spun to Mr. Murray.

"*Yes*," Kesi grinned, tossing Mr. Murray the ball. "Let's go, Roomie."

"Uh... I don't know-" Roman started but was cut off as the air was sucked out of his lungs and his back collided with the ground. Roman groaned and looked up to see Mr. Murray chucking and shaking his head.

"She didn't even tackle you," the teacher said. "That's sad."

Roman arched his neck to look behind him, where Kesi was whooping and thrusting her fists in the air. For a second, he could have sworn that her hair was shimmering blue in the sunshine, but before he could get a proper look, the moment passed and Kesi was back to normal.

"Ha-ha!" she cheered. "That's what you get for hesitating."

"And you could use that to your advantage," Mr. Murray told her. "If the other team figures out you're a girl."

"Does that mean I'm on the team?" Kesi bit her lip, trying to contain a smile.

"Not yet," Mr. Murray said. "You still have to hit Roman a few more times."

"Not cool," Roman mumbled, getting to his feet.

"I love this game," Kesi countered.

The rest of the mini practice continued like that. Every time Roman lunged to tackle Kesi, she slipped away from him and continued prancing down the field as if she'd just won a glorious battle. Every time she tackled him, she'd always catch him by surprise and Roman would end up on the ground somehow. Roman did have a couple of things to his advantage, though, his size and frustration with the blonde, for example.

Mr. Murray tossed Kesi the ball, which was Roman's cue to try and tackle her to the ground. Before Kesi even had her hands on the ball, which was something that Roman normally waited for, he lunged for her waist while her eyes were still on the ball.

"Agh!" she yelled, and Roman could tell that the ball had fallen far out of her grasp.

Both teens collided with the ground, Kesi huffing particularly loud because of Roman's weight on top of her. She didn't say anything, though, which caused Roman to mentally slap himself as he saw her wincing features when he pulled away.

"God, I'm so sorry Kesi, I-" Roman felt heat creep up onto his face as she took a few deep breaths.

"No, it's ok, it's… part of the game," she replied, almost wheezing. "If I want to play… I'll have to live with it."

"Are you okay?" Roman asked, searching her face as she took a few more deep breaths.

"This is suggestive," Kesi groaned, placing hand over her eyes. Roman was confused for a moment before realizing that she was talking about the fact that he was still hovering over her, their bodies tangled on the ground.

"Oh!" Roman yelped, jumping to his feet. "S-sorry," he stuttered, before holding out a hand for Kesi to grab, feeling his face redden even more.

"Man, you're heavy," Kesi gripped onto his hand as he hauled her to her feet, laughing nervously at her comment.

"Y-yeah," Roman ran a hand through his hair, "I um…yeah."

Mr. Murray approached them, laughing loudly. "Uh… Kesi," he shook his head. "I'll talk to Principle Alves to see if you can join the team. Anyone with that good of an attitude about taking a hit is good enough for me."

"Thanks Coach Murray!" Kesi said cheerily, grinning.

"You kids should probably go," Mr. Murray continued. "You've kept your mom waiting twenty minutes."

Roman winced. He'd forgotten all about his mother. He turned to Kesi, "I'll go back to the library and grab your bag and stuff, you just worry about putting Ben's shoes back."

"Right, ok," Kesi nodded. "Thanks again Coach Murray!" Kesi waved to the teacher as the two jogged across the field. Kesi grabbed Roman's sports bag as she ran down the road, lightening Roman's load. She even took it with her to the girl's locker room on the first floor while Roman dashed to the library and stuffed Kesi's tablet in her blue messenger bag. The girl wasn't kidding when she said that she loved blue, Roman noticed, as everything that he'd seen of hers had all been the same color.

"Kesi's coming," Roman panted as he crashed into the backseat of the car behind his mother, tossing both his and Kesi's bags into the passenger seat.

"Did Coach Murray like her?" Emma asked eagerly before they both spotted Kesi half-running towards them, the wedges back on her feet and Roman's bag in her hand.

"She's so *fast*," Roman panted, still tired from having run across the school yet again.

"Hi Emma!" Kesi chirped as she filled the seat beside Roman. "Sorry to keep you waiting!"

"It's no problem, Kesi," Emma laughed, "How did you like football?"

"It was great!" Kesi beamed before adding proudly. "I didn't even stain my clothes or anything!"

"Because I couldn't tackle you, that's why," Roman added, turning to his mother. "She's slippery."

Emma laughed at them both, driving the car away. "I take it you had a good day then?"

"Yeah," Kesi answered, almost immediately. Roman turned to her, almost surprised. He thought that things with Taylor, Nico, and Becky may have spoiled things a bit for her, but she didn't seem to really be bothered. He found himself smiling before she had even finished her statement. "It was great."

Emma's smile could be seen even with just the view of her green eyes in the rear-view mirror. She quickly cast a wink at Roman. "I'm glad."

'*Me too*', Roman thought, pulling his gaze away from Kesi, '*me too.*'

CHAPTER SIXTEEN

DANVILLE, VIRGINIA

Roman

ROMAN HAD BEEN lazily sitting in front of the TV, watching a show but not really paying attention, when Kesi flopped down on the couch after a long day of shopping with Emma. Her arms were laced with bags from various stores that Roman knew were stationed at the Danville Mall and some that were from shops around the area. Emma walked through the living room, smiling, not looking nearly as tired as Kesi.

"Don't forget to take those upstairs, Kesi!" Emma grinned before walking into the kitchen, her own, smaller, bundle of bags on her arm.

"I won't, thanks Emma," Kesi sighed and sank deeper into the couch.

Roman laughed at her. "Rough day?"

"I haven't shopped... in a while," Kesi answered. "It was fun until I had to try on a bunch of clothes."

"I don't get how shopping is fun," Roman said. "Too much walking."

"I like shopping, I think," Kesi replied, "but my legs don't."

"Do you think you'll be too tired for the party tonight?" Roman teased, making Kesi grin.

"Don't count on it," she replied, pulling out her phone. Roman guessed that Kesi must have had some other brand of phone back in Egypt, because she still seemed to be trying to figure out how it worked. He found it amusing how she fumbled with it and sometimes even had to ask him for help on how to work it. She smirked mischievously, filling Roman with dread. He'd come to know that smile meant trouble.

"I bet I could get more people to come," Kesi said, making Roman groan.

"Please don't," he replied, looking over at her seriously. "I hate people."

Kesi shook her head at him, "Introvert much?" Roman glared at her comment before she continued, "Fine, fine, it can just be the six of us." She looked down at the horde of bags she had placed at her feet, "I don't know what to do with all of this."

"This, what?" Roman questioned, propping himself up on the couch.

"Clothes, mostly, for winter," Kesi scowled as she said the last word, "but also some decorations for my room."

Roman thought for a moment. "I could...help you? Decorate, I mean."

Kesi's head snapped upwards to look at him. After observing his face and finding that he was serious, she snorted.

Roman put a hand on his heart, feigning offense. "How dare you laugh at me?" he laughed along with Kesi before continuing. "At the very least I could just do whatever you tell me to do."

Kesi waved him off, "I was just laughing because...I'm pretty sure I would fail at decorating. You and me together," she shook her head, grinning. "Oh well, we can try."

Before Roman knew it, Kesi had shoved four bags into his hands and took three of her own. He wobbled through the kitchen and up the stairs with the bundle, wondering again why anyone would want to go shopping for as many things as this.

Roman nearly dropped all the bags on the floor once they got the Kesi's room, the handles of the bags digging into his arms. Kesi took his bags carefully while Roman sent her a grateful smile, placing them on the ground next to her bed with the rest of her things.

"Okay, so," Kesi started, dragging three bags away from the rest. "These are decorations, and the rest are clothes. You… go through these," Kesi pointed to the three bags at her feet, "and… I don't know. Put them in piles- stuff for the bathroom, stuff for the main area, and stuff for my closet, I guess."

"Okay," Roman replied, sitting on the floor to do just that as Kesi carried the other four bags to the wall holding her dresser and closet. They worked mostly in silence, except for Kesi humming a Bruno Mars song that Roman recognized. He almost laughed out loud when he realized what it was.

"You really like that song, don't you?" Roman smiled, looking up at her. She closed one of the drawers on her dresser and turned to grin at him.

"Of course," Kesi replied before turning back to the bags before her. Roman did the same, sorting through things like lamps, fake seashells, and boxes to hold things like toothbrushes or pencils.

"Hey, what's this?" Roman asked, holding up a book that was tucked at the very bottom of one bag before laughing. "*Twilight*? Seriously?"

"I need to know what Ben's joke was about!" Kesi defended, running over to grab the book from his hands and stopping at her empty bookcase. "This is the start of my collection! I plan to read a lot of h- American books while I'm here," Kesi grinned over at him before placing the book on one of the shelves. Just as she was about to turn away, she stopped, something catching her eye.

"What is it?" Roman asked, standing up to see what she was

staring at. He gulped when he realized what it was. A small edge of the wall blazed light green, standing out against the baby blue paint that Roman and Emma had painted over it. He must have forgotten to do that one spot when he was painting.

"That's a pretty color," Kesi noted, and Roman nodded, not knowing what to say. He mentally hit himself upside the head, scolding, '*stupid, stupid, stupid.*'

"What was this room before I came here?" Kesi asked, turning to look at Roman. He couldn't meet her eyes. He was afraid that she would be able to see right through him.

"Just a guest room," Roman lied. "We painted it over when we got your letter and you said you liked blue."

Kesi was quiet for a long time. "Okay," she replied finally, in a tone that told Roman that she wasn't fooled. She didn't say anything for a while. "Should I put that shaded lamp on my desk or on by bedside table?"

"Bedside table," Roman answered, and Kesi nodded.

"I was thinking that too," she said, before walking over and grabbing the shaded lamp from the floor and placing it on her bedside table. "Where's the outlet thing?"

Roman laughed and found his way over to her, taking the cord from her hands and wiggling it in the outlet hidden behind the nightstand.

"Thanks," Kesi giggled. "Is it the same for the desk?"

"Yeah," Roman replied. "I'll set that up for you. You worry about your clothes."

"Alright," Kesi smiled and bounced back over to her dresser. Roman watched her go, trying to calm down his fast-beating heart from the near disaster that just occurred. Roman didn't want Kesi to know that she was staying in Sophia's room. He was sure that it would make her look at him differently. Roman didn't know if it was because Kesi was just a new person in his life, a friend, or something else, but one thing was for sure, he couldn't have Kesi seeing him as the broken boy that everyone else did.

Kesi fingered the ends of her blonde hair in the bathroom mirror, observing the outfit she had put on for the party that was about to commence downstairs. It was a simple t-shirt and jean shorts, nothing too fancy or extravagant. She didn't suppose that her new friends really cared about her appearance that much, especially when it was just clothes.

She was nervous. Even if it was just six people, it was still a party. And she had never been to a party before. She didn't even know what parties with her friends were like. She didn't know how to act, what to do… *'I'll just hope that I'll be able to pick it up along the way, just like everything else.'*

Ring…ring…

Kesi stood, dumbstruck, as the phone she had placed on her bathroom counter started to ring and vibrate on the granite. After a few moments, Kesi said, "Oh!" out loud and rushed to answer it. It was the first time it had rung since she'd found it in her messenger bag when she first arrived two nights ago. The screen read: *Mom*, and it took Kesi a few minutes to figure out what the contact name was alluding to. Chuckling, Kesi swiped to answer the call, something she was getting better at. She'd often had to ask Roman for help on how to work the device, not to mention the amount of concentration it took to not let the phone slip out of her clumsy fingers.

"I'm so sorry that I wasn't able to call sooner," Queen Ena's voice tinkled clearly from the phone. "We have been keeping a close eye on the Shaytan to make sure that they didn't follow you through the portal."

"That's alright, Mother," Kesi replied. "The safety of the human world is more important than mine. Although I didn't know that there was cell service in Jinn City?"

The Queen laughed. "My, what cleverness! I trust that you're having a good time?"

Kesi glanced towards her bedroom door. "I am, Mother. The humans have made all of these tall structures out of metal and glass, and there's so many buildings…," Kesi trailed off. How could she start to explain the human world? "But they don't seem to like each other very much. The humans, not the buildings."

Queen Ena hummed. "Yes, that's the sad side effect of having such a populated world that doesn't care for their wellbeing. How are you getting along with the other humans?"

"I think I'm fitting in okay," Kesi answered. "I've made friends, and Roman- the Chosen One…"

The Queen giggled. "He's quite handsome, isn't he? I knew you would like him!"

"I didn't- I never-!" Kesi huffed. "I believe that it would be improper to encourage feelings between the two of us, especially since I'm supposed to focus on protecting him."

"That's exactly why I should encourage feelings between the two of you," Queen Ena countered. "It will establish a link that will give you the motivation you need."

Kesi sighed. "If you say so, Mother," she replied, not entirely convinced of the Queen's words. "Did Shaytan escape through the portal?"

"Not yet," Queen Ena replied, "but with you on the other side, I can't close it to ensure that it won't happen. The City won't let me. It's only a matter of time before they realize that we've taken action, and crawl through the portal themselves."

"Can't you stop them?" Kesi asked. "The Shaitan Mountains are all the way across the city from the Djinn Fields. How could they even break through the Barrier?"

Thousands of years ago, after Queen Ena had defeated Makalani and trapped him in a lamp, she was unaware that other genies had the same capacity for evil as he did. She buried his lamp in the ground beneath the land that is now the Ghul, believing that it would keep them all safe. However, the Shaytan King, though trapped, was able to use his magic to telepathically reach out to the minds of genies who wandered too close to the area he was buried in. Some of the genies enjoyed the darkness Makalani spoke about and began to practice magic under his instruction. The dark magic corrupted these genies from the inside out, turning them into creatures that were similar in appearance to Makalani. Desperate to keep the peace, and because she loved all her children no matter if they were good or bad, Queen Ena divided the realm in half. The City to the north of the High Palace was for black magic users, while the south side was for light magic users.

This division only worked for a time. Soon the corruption of the black magic turned the Shaytan violent and dangerous to all light magic users. A large portion of the population was wiped out because of the rampage of blood that followed, so Queen Ena decided to act against them. After pushing back the Shaytan in a bloody campaign, Queen Ena locked all the Shaytan and their black magic behind the Shaitan Mountains with a barrier spell, which prevented them from leaving their new part of the realm. The black magic the Shaytan were using not only made them immortal, but it also gave them the ability to create more creatures like them out of clay and other earthly materials. The rumor was that the Shaytan spent their time making clones of themselves for one reason or another. Since they were all locked away, Kesi had never seen a Shaytan in person, but much of the artwork in the Temple depicted Queen Ena and her Jinn heroes fighting and banishing the Shaytan, so she had some idea.

"The portals aren't stationary," Queen Ena explained. "It moves around as the City breathes and lives, only appearing in one spot when it is summoned, concentrating its power. All the Shaytan must do is summon it over the Barrier and slide through into the human world. Although the Barrier does weaken the portal," the Queen continued. "It won't be strong enough to send an army through, not without an enormous amount of magic."

"Could they have that kind of magic?" Kesi asked, becoming increasingly worried. She wasn't prepared to fight a whole *army* of Shaytans.

"Not without Makalani," the Queen answered before going silent. "I'm glad you're enjoying yourself."

"I'm not so sure that's a good thing," Kesi replied, the seriousness of her mission setting in once more. "I don't want to be distracted."

"When the times comes, you won't be, believe me," the Queen reassured her. "After all, Shaytan aren't easy to miss. They don't have human forms."

Both were silent for a long time before Queen Ena continued, "Continue to have some fun, Kesi, you may only have limited time to do so."

"I'll try, Mother," Kesi replied.

"Goodbye, Savior."

"Goodbye, Mother," Kesi felt a sort of emptiness envelop her when the line went dead. She hadn't exactly let herself feel any homesickness since she left, partly in excitement and party because of her mission. But now she craved her Queen's guidance or Ra'id's reassuring words, maybe even a bit of Divya's bitterness. She missed Jinn City's warm nights and the yelps of children from the Ghul. She missed dancing in the marketplace and all her friends that she had grown up with. She missed her camp, and the High Palace, and all the sandstone buildings. '*I just miss my* home.'

Kesi turned back to the main part of her bedroom, moving herself to sit on the edge of her bed. This was her home now, whether she liked it or not. Anyway, it was only temporary, and it might not even be a full year before Roman fulfilled his destiny.

Her bedroom door shot open. Instinctively, Kesi jumped up and reached for the necklace around her throat, thinking that perhaps the Queen and the Elders hadn't been watching the Shaytan and the portal closely enough. She relaxed quickly, however, when she saw Ben and Aasma in the doorway, Ben with two hands in the air as if celebrating some grand feat.

"Welcome to America, *chica*!" she cheered as Aasma squeezed her way past her and into Kesi's room. Kesi giggled at them both.

"Emma just told us to come up," Aasma explained, pointing a thumb at the door behind her. "The boys are downstairs, eating all the food," she finished by rolling her eyes and smiling.

"C'mon!" Ben laughed, running over and grabbing both of Kesi's hands. "It's a party, it's a party, it's a party!"

"Ben!" Kesi chuckled as Aasma started to push her forward from behind, dragging her from the room.

"How long have you guys been here?" Kesi asked as the two girls guided her through the hall and down the stairs.

"Eh, only ten to twenty minutes," Ben replied. "We had Roman sitting at the foot of the stairs making sure you didn't come down to the kitchen before we finished decorating."

"Decorating?" Kesi questioned. "How come I didn't know any of this was going on?"

"Because that's what happens when Ben throws a party for someone," Aasma giggled, pushing Kesi down the last step.

"Ta-dah!" Ben gave her jazz hands as they approached the kitchen, which was decorated with colorful streamers hanging from the tops of the windows, confetti on the kitchen table, and several colorful bowls chips, pretzels, and other assortments. There was also a large box of pizza on the counter, open wide and steaming. Kesi's stomach growled. Being a human meant a lot more hunger than she was used to, and even though she had never eaten pizza before, it did look appetizing.

Kharim, Dimitri, and Roman were all sitting at the kitchen table, and when Roman noticed her, he held up his own piece of pizza. "Look," he told her, bug-eyed.

Kesi folded her arms over her chest and pointed a finger at Roman. "Pizza?"

"The best kind!" Aasma nudged her before noticing Kesi's confused expression at all the excitement. *'Are they okay? What's so good about pizza?'* "You've never had pizza, have you?" Aasma looked almost offended.

"Uh...," Kesi started, but Ben cut her off with a gasp.

"*Kesi!*" she put a hand on her hear. "Who are you and what kind of life have you been living? Roman, get the girl some pizza!"

"That's ok, I can get some my-oh!" Kesi yelped as Ben shoved her into a chair at the kitchen table. Roman jumped up and ran over to the pizza box before running back and placing a paper plate with a slice of pizza on it in front of her.

Kesi observed the piece of food before her. Warmth floated up to her senses, cascading her nose with the smell of melting cheese and tomato sauce. The cheese made little pockets of the sauce pop out, giving the surface a sort of patter. She looked up at her friends with a cocked eyebrow that only crawled higher when it was met with their expectant grins.

Slowly, Kesi slid a hand under the pizza, her finger scraping the rough and slightly greasy bottom. Kesi kept eye contact with all the teenagers crowded around her as she placed the edge of the slice into her mouth before clamping her mouth over it. Her eyes went wide as the warm gooiness of the cheese spread onto her tongue along with the sharpness of the tomato sauce.

It was like heaven.

"Owh mwy- hwow iws twhis *rweal*!" Kesi moaned, her mouth full of food. Her eyelids fluttered closed as she took another bite. At her third, she heard Roman chuckle.

"It's good, huh?" she could hear the smugness in his voice.

She ignored it. "*Mmm.*"

The whole room burst out into laughter, expect Kesi who was, of course, busy eating.

"Someone get her another slice!" Ben called as Kesi garbled down her pizza. Kesi licked her fingers as she finished, making wide eyes as Aasma placed another piece in front of her. Kesi looked up at her gratefully, noticing that the girl had grabbed one for herself too.

"You eat like a pig," Roman laughed, and Kesi glared at him.

"Yeah, well… I don't care," Kesi replied, "You…are a pig. *So*," she shot him a glare as she started on her second slice.

"Let her eat in peace," Kharim laughed, and Kesi paused a moment to point at him.

"Twhank ywou!" She swallowed the pizza in her mouth. "Thank you!" She thought for a moment. "Not just for *defending me,* Kharim," she pouted playfully at Roman. "You guys are the best."

"Aww," Aasma hugged Kesi from behind with one arm, her other hand still holding a slice of pizza. "We love you too, Kesi."

"Besides, friends who eat together, stay together," Ben used her own pizza as a way of pointing at Kesi. Kesi laughed at her.

'*Maybe I can enjoy myself after all,*' Kesi mused to herself, finishing her pizza.

"You want another?" Kharim joked, making Kesi roll her eyes.

"Uh… no," Kesi replied, slamming a fist against her chest. "I think… I'm good."

She wasn't lying- the warmth of the pizza had filled her up fast. Kesi couldn't imagine eating any more, or at least she wished she could without being sure she was going to explode.

"We'll save the ice cream for later, then," Ben decided, chuckling. "I think we should play…"

"Don't say it Ben," Roman groaned.

"Please," Aasma whined.

"Truth or dare!" Ben waved her hands in the air again. "We have to show Kesi what Ben's Truth or Dare is all about!"

"Ben's Truth or Dare?" Kesi questioned before being hauled to her feet by Ben.

"To the basement!" she declared, running out of the kitchen.

"Ben's Truth or Dare?" Kesi repeated, turning to the others.

"Don't chose dare," Roman warned before following Ben out of the room. Kesi shrugged to no one in particular before doing the same.

Roman and the others took Kesi down the hallway that led to the garage, but instead of stopping halfway through, they opened a door a little farther down the hall. Kesi trotted down several white-carpeted stairs before finding herself in a large white-walled, dark-floored space with a large couch, TV, and even a counter with several bar stools. Ben placed herself on the floor by the couch, and the others helped her form a sort of circle. Kesi mimicked their movements, sitting between Aasma and Roman.

"Why do we have to be down here to do this?" Kesi questioned, her brain racked with cloudy confusion.

"Because it's a tradition!" Ben answered. "We always do truth or dare down here."

"Oh…?" Kesi was still bewildered. She knew what truth or dare was, a game that humans played, daring each other to do strange thing and asking for truthful, honest answers to random questions. What she didn't understand was why the others looked so annoyed.

"I think Kesi should go first," Ben announced, but Aasma was quick to protest.

"No, Ben, don't do that to her," Aasma said. "I'll go first."

"Okay," Ben replied, "Truth or dare."

"Truth," Aasma answered, rolling her eyes when Ben commented, "You're boring!"

"Okay, truth…," Ben thought for a long while. "If you had to get rid of one, who would you keep- your little sister or Kharim?"

"Aasma, I swear," Kharim glared over at Aasma as she smiled.

"No interfering," Dimitri mumbled.

"Sorry, Kharim, but Zaida is just so much cuter than you," Aasma shrugged and giggled. Kesi laughed too after seeing Kharim's dramatically hurt expression. This game was fun.

"Okay, *now* Kesi," Aasma turned to her. "Truth or dare?"

"Um...," Kesi poked her fingertips together. "Truth?"

"I got a good one for this!" Ben yelled before leaning over to whisper in Aasma's ear. Aasma laughed and nodded in response.

"Okay, okay," Aasma said, pushing Ben away playfully. "Out of all three boys in this room, who would you like to kiss the most?"

"What?" Kesi replied, startled. She felt heat start to climb up her neck, but she swallowed it down. "I don't... I don't even... I mean, I uh..."

"You have to answer," Ben giggled. Kesi glared at her. Now she understood the annoyance.

"I guess... um... I guess Roman," Kesi stuttered. "Only because I know him the best," Kesi ducked her head into her lap, not daring to look at Roman beside her. She did finally look up to meet Ben's mischievous eyes. "I can see why *no one* likes this game."

Ben only laughed. "Now you have to ask someone, Kesi."

"Okay," Kesi turned to Kharim. "Truth or dare."

The night continued that way, passing the phrase around the circle formed on the floor of Roman's basement. Kesi made Kharim sing his favorite song, then learned later that Dimitri's favorite color was orange. Kharim dared Ben to carry Dimitri on her back for a full ten minutes, which caused her to collapse on the ground, nearly dropping the blonde boy.

"Agh, I need some ice cream," she complained, and they all laughed before going upstairs and back to the kitchen. Ice cream was another wonderful thing that Kesi learned to love, although the coldness of the treat gave her a headache.

"Ow!" she exclaimed, dropping her spoon on her bowl and grasping her head.

"Poor girl," Aasma cooed, patting her shoulder. "It's just a brain freeze, give it a second."

"I'm never eating ice cream again," Kesi groaned. "Food isn't supposed to be this cruel."

"Roman, we need music," Kharim turned to Roman. "Get your guitar."

"Get your guitar *please*," Roman corrected, making Kharim laugh.

"You play guitar?" Kesi questioned, blinking at him with wide eyes.

"I uh… a little," Roman ducked his head, but Kharim gladly picked up where he left off.

"And drums, and piano, and the… clarinet? Right?" he looked at Roman.

"A little," Roman repeated.

"Why don't you take Kesi upstairs to show her?" Aasma suggested, nudging Kesi playfully. "I'm sure that she'd like to see all your instruments."

"In my room?" Roman stared at Aasma bewildered, who only nodded vigorously.

"That's where you still keep them, right?" she asked innocently.

"Right. Right," Roman licked his lips nervously. "Okay then," he met Kesi's eyes. "Let's go."

CHAPTER SEVENTEEN

DANVILLE, VIRGINIA

Roman

H E REALLY DIDN'T want Kesi in his bedroom, and not for any rude reasons. She lived with him, it wasn't like he had any right to keep her out, but he didn't want her to see the pieces of Sophia he kept hidden in every nook and cranny of his room. He didn't want her to know that he'd had a sister. He didn't want her to know that she was sleeping in a dead girl's room, and that dead girl was Roman's best friend.

"Wow," Kesi said as he guided her through his bedroom door. He tried to look at his room through her eyes. His dark green walls looked almost velvety in the dark. Windows stood on the far gray wall, covered in shades. His bed and his black couch stood across from each other. His dresser was plastered onto the wall of his loft, and the carpet was black. Under the window sat most of the instruments that Kharim had mentioned, their shiny surfaces glinting in the streetlight peeking through the shades. The doors to his closet and bathroom stood on either side of the couch, framing it like a picture.

Kesi walked ahead of him in the direction of the instruments, and Roman was careful to step in front of his desk, hiding the picture of Sophia.

"These are so cool," Kesi continued softly, crouching down to observe his acoustic guitar. "I've never... it's so different."

"Different from what?" Roman asked, thankful that she hadn't turned around yet.

"From home," Kesi stared at the instruments before her for a few moments before continuing. "Everything is so different from home."

Roman was surprised at the edge in her voice. An edge that he had heard in his own voice so many times, especially after Sophia's death. It was the sound of loneliness creeping through the cracks of the everyday routine, or in Kesi's case, the excitement of new things.

She felt alone.

Roman moved to crouch beside her, not daring to touch her, in case that would make it worse. Instead he followed her gaze to the guitar and the dim light sprinkled on it. "Do you miss it?"

"Very much," Kesi replied. "People aren't... well, people can be mean, but not about how someone looked or where they were from... Everything was a judgement of character, not of looks."

"That's how it should be, I think," Roman mused. "What else do you miss?"

Kesi chuckled sadly, looking down at the floor as she collapsed from her crouching position. Roman followed.

"Why do you care?" she asked, her voice breaking as she looked away from him.

"Cause we're roomies," Roman offered, making Kesi snort. She was silent again for a long time before she began to speak.

"It's warm," she started, "Insanely warm, sometimes, you know? But I'm used to it. The marketplace...marketplaces are always really crowded and there's fountains... and all the buildings are light-colored and there's these huge mosques and... and at night the whole city is lit up like a wildfire. It's beautiful."

"It sounds beautiful," Roman commented, relaxing a bit as he saw the calmness in her expression. She didn't seem so sad anymore. Then she looked over to his shadow-covered desk. Roman gulped, turning with her, his heart in his throat.

"That's cool," she commented, rising to her feet. Roman copied her hurriedly.

"N-not really, it's just a…," Roman watched helplessly as she ducked under his loft, plopped into his swivel chair and turned the lamp on. "…desk."

Roman panicked when he saw Kesi's eyes latch onto the picture of him and Sophia, his feet glued in place as his mind spun.

'*Of course, the* one thing *I didn't want to happen, happens,*' Roman's head cried as he watched Kesi stare at the picture.

"Is this your mom?" Kesi asked, before thinking it over. "No, she's…young…an aunt? But…Roman, who is this?"

"My sister," Roman answered quietly, although the words broke out from his lips like water from a broken dam.

"Is she at college?" Kesi asked, turning to look at him. Roman quickly looked away.

"No," he offered, unable to finish his thought. '*She's dead. She's dead. She's dead.*'

Kesi was still for a long time. The silence was killing Roman. The sound of rain started to resonate from his windows, darkening the room further. All he could hear was his own terrified heartbeat and Kesi's thoughtful breathing, so much calmer than his. '*Say something,*' his brain screamed, although he wasn't so sure if he was trying to send a message to Kesi or to himself.

"What took her?" Kesi asked softly, so softly that Roman was afraid that her tone was going to shatter him into a million pieces.

"Cancer," he choked out. "Brain tumor."

Roman clenched his jaw, determined not to cry in front of Kesi, when he felt a warmth envelop him, the feeling both suffocating and reassuring. Slowly, Roman wrapped his arms around Kesi's small frame as she hugged him tightly in a way that Sophia would have. Roman gasped when she pulled him closer, certain that her kindness was eating away at his insides now.

Kesi didn't offer him any words. No, '*I'm sorry*,' or '*It's ok*' or anything close to words. She only held him as his breathing faltered and calmed and then faltered again. After a few moments he realized that she wasn't going to say anything. Roman buried his face into her neck, closing his eyes and trying to hide from the rest of the world.

Roman felt Kesi prop her chin up on his shoulder as she sighed sadly. Still, she didn't say a word.

"Thank you," Roman mumbled into her neck, making her shiver.

"No problem, Roomie," Kesi replied, her tone still quiet. "What else am I here for?"

She pulled away then, leaving Roman feeling cold. Kesi's face was filled up with a genuine grin, not one of the fake smiles that sometimes even his friends put on to try and make him feel better. Roman sighed in relief and confusion. However grateful he was, he couldn't understand how she could not look at him any different after everything she'd just learned.

Kesi poked him in the chest, saying, "Don't think I'd let you off the hook that easy, Roomie. You still gotta play me a song on the guitar thing."

Roman smiled sheepishly and rubbed the back of his neck, "Ha, ha. Okay, what song?"

Kesi thought for a moment, then shrugged, "I don't know. I don't know many songs. You can choose."

Roman paused, trying to think of a song to play for her. Finally, he made up his mind and walked over to his guitar, sitting back on the ground. Kesi did the same, looking at him with wide, eager eyes. Roman shook his head at her, his smile returning, gratitude for the strange and captivating girl in front of him warming his chest. That gratitude pushed words out of his throat that were already building deeper in his being.

"Thank you," he blurted again, heat rushing to his cheeks as her eyes met his. "Thank you."

Kesi threw him a playful wink. "Don't worry about it, you don't have anything to thank me for."

Roman opened his mouth to reply but decided to slam it shut instead. It wasn't like he wanted to continue to talk about this topic anyway. He turned to his guitar, picking it up and placing it in his lap. After tuning the strings quickly, he began to play, singing along to a song that Sophia had taught him.

"*When the world gets too heavy, put it on my back. I'll be your levy. You are taking me apart like bad glue on a get-well card. It was always you falling for me. Now there's always time calling for me. I'm the light blinking at the end of the road. Blink back to let me know...,*" Roman blushed when he noticed the wonderment in Kesi's eyes as he sang. She had no idea that she was bringing new and wonderful memories to the song while bringing up old ones. When Roman had first started to learn guitar, he'd insisted Sophia teach him instead of finding a professional instructor. Sophia was thirteen at the time and Roman had been nine.

He remembered clearly the day that he had played this song through fully for the first time, receiving cheers from his sister.

"*Ahhh! Romey I'm so proud of you!*" she giggled, "*I love that song, it's my favorite! Maybe we can start a band and I'll sing, and you'll play guitar...*"

"*...I'm a fly that's trapped in a web, but I'm thinking that my spider's dead. Lonely, lonely little life, I could kid myself in thinking that I'm fine. It was always you falling for me...*" Roman quickly glanced up at Kesi and smiled when he realized she was still watching him. He dropped his eyes back to his guitar blushing, trying not to think of the way her eyes lit up, "*...That I'm skin and bone, just a king on a rusty throne. Oh, the castle's under siege, but the sign outside says 'Leave me alone.'*"

"*... And I'll teach you hundreds of songs, I promise!*" Sophia said, beaming at him, *"And you could show off to all your friends and we can perform at the school talent show…"*

Kesi watched Roman; thinking over the lyrics while the rain softly fell against the windowsill. She smiled when Roman glanced at her again, and Roman could tell she noticed how his cheeks were turning pink. When he looked back down at his guitar, he was only mildly aware that his desk lamp flickered for a moment and tiny sparks seemed to shoot out of his fingers. It happened so fast that Roman shook it off as a trick of the light, but Kesi had her brow furrowed. Then, she flashed a grin. Roman wished he knew what she was thinking.

"It was always you falling for me, now there's always time calling for me. I'm the light blinking at the end of the road, blink back to let me know. Blink back to let me know." Roman strummed the final cord and, without looking up at Kesi and with pink tingeing his cheeks again, set the guitar back in its spot carefully.

"Wow," she gasped, causing him to face her. "That was amazing! Where did you learn how to do all that? Where did you learn to *sing* like that? That was… *wow*."

Roman chuckled. "Glad you liked it."

"See, I have no musical talent whatsoever," Kesi said. "Sports, school, I can do that. But not music. That's a whole other realm of…" She waved her hands in the air. "Mystery and magic for me. You're so cool."

Roman bit his lip and hid his blush at the compliment. "Thanks."

"Can I ask you a personal question?" Kesi asked, leaning back on her palms. Roman looked up at her expectantly, a sign that she took to mean for her to continue, "Why do you think the lyrics to that song are so sad, but the music isn't?"

Roman thought for a moment. "I think it's because he's not really sad. He knows that some things are just meant to happen and meeting this girl somehow helped him or would help him as a person, so he doesn't regret meeting her or being with her. He's only sad that he didn't get to be with her for longer or be with her at all because of his own mistakes. He doesn't blame her at all. I think he's kind of glad that she's not with him because he knows that maybe he couldn't have loved her like he should have," Roman's eyes met Kesi's again, "Or something like that."

"*Or something like that*," Kesi mimicked, laughing. "You know, for someone so reserved, you sure have a lot to say, or at least a lot you *should* say."

Roman tilted his head to the side, confused. "What do you mean?"

Kesi leaned back further, looking towards the ceiling to find the words that she wanted to say. "I mean, you're not shallow, you're not superficial, you're not... you're *smart*, and not just academically. You think and feel things deeply, and I think that means you deserve to be heard," she looked to him. "You're the kind of person who could save the world if you really wanted to."

Roman snorted. "Okay, now you're just being overdramatic."

Kesi laughed, reaching for his arm. "No, I'm serious!" She paused. "There's this... poem book, I guess, that... my mom used to read to me. A... prince-and-princess sort of story, expect- spoiler alert- the princess kind of ended up saving herself. Or the queen, rather," Kesi stuttered, "But when they describe the prince, they... I think it goes like... *He is like the sky; he only feels things in their depth. When he is sad, floods grow. When he is worried, clouds reign. When he hates, lightning strikes*" Kesi recited, and Roman found himself lost in the poetry and rhythm of her words. "*But when he loves, when he loves the whole sky is lit with twinkling stars and magnificent grace, and no one in this world would ever see something as beautiful as his sky.*"

"That's beautiful," Roman noted after she had finished, and Kesi nodded.

"What I'm saying is, if you can feel things the way that you do, you can do anything, because you and feel and think about anything.

It all starts with a thought. Imagination is the limit, and all that," Kesi explained, and that time Roman almost believed her.

"I'm coming up here so if you're doing stuff or whatever be prepared to be walked in on," Ben's voice wafted up the stairs into Roman's bedroom, startling both teens.

"You're fine," Roman laughed. "We weren't even doing anything."

"Sure," Ben's head appeared in the doorway as she studied them both closely. "Sure."

Kesi laughed at Ben as she entered the room warily.

"I heard you playing from downstairs," Ben said to Roman, making him look away from Kesi. "And sing, too. You haven't done that in a while."

Roman hung his head. Even before Sophia's death Roman rarely sang, and when he did it was only with his sister. Still, sometimes he would sing wispy snippets of songs stuck in his head under his breath before Sophia got sick, which was the only hint that his friends had ever gotten of his singing voice.

Ben turned to Kesi, "I can't believe he sang for you. He doesn't sing for anyone, not even us. That's the first time that I've actually heard his voice."

Roman looked over to see Kesi grinning like a madman, "Isn't he great?"

Ben nodded. "He is." She leaned in to whisper into Kesi's ear, loud enough for Roman to hear. "Whatever you're doing, keeping doing it. It's making him come out of his lame boy shell."

Roman rolled his eyes at his friend. "Hardy har har, very funny Ben."

"I know, aren't I hilarious," Ben grinned. "Any chance you would come down and play us a song?"

"No way," Roman retorted, causing both Ben and Kesi to laugh.

"Well, we still have to finish our game," Ben informed. "Let's go! Come on!"

Kesi and Roman groaned as they stood and followed Ben

downstairs, Roman stealing glances at Kesi, realizing how Ben was right. Kesi had brought something to the table that wasn't there before, and now he was feeling things and doing things that he had never done before. He just didn't exactly know what that meant to him yet.

CHAPTER EIGHTEEN

DANVILLE, VIRGINIA

Kesi

IT WAS MONDAY, which meant it was Kesi's first day of real football practice, and the first day of her first full week of school. Monday held a lot of firsts, and Kesi was excited about all of them. Although she was sure that she would never get used to waking up early, her daily routine did help to wake her up. It was just another thing that she was going to have to force herself to get in the habit of. She'd barely been able to contain herself during her first morning meeting in the auditorium, Ben having to physically hold her to keep her still.

"Our first class is Health," Roman explained as he guided her through Fiore Hall, and across the sky bridge. "Which means that we can put our sports stuff in the locker rooms before we get to class."

"What did you do on Friday?" Kesi asked. "We only got here a few minutes before class started."

"My mom told me to pack an extra set of gear and stuff and leave it in my locker on Thursday," Roman explained. "She knew we might be late because you were still getting adjusted. Are you ready for practice today?"

Kesi held up the red sports bag that Emma had bought her on Sunday, holding all the football gear and clothing she could ever need. Luckily that shopping trip required much less time and trying on clothes than the first. If it had, Kesi was sure that she would have died from exhaustion. "Ready as I'll ever be!" she cheered, the heaviness of the bag pulling her arm back down.

"If anyone gives you crap just…," Roman seemed to be struggling to find the right words. "You know what? Just tackle them. Or punch them. Or beat them in a race. It should be enough to shut them up."

"And you know how much I love shutting people up," Kesi grinned at Roman as he pointed her to a doorway down the hall.

"That's the girls' locker room. The boys' is farther down. I'll wait for you outside, so you don't get lost," Roman smiled at her kindly. Kesi returned the favor.

Something had changed Saturday night after Roman had told her about his sister and sang for her. They'd both taken down walls and somehow gotten closer, even if Kesi's "secret" was really a secret nestled in another. She felt awful that she couldn't be as honest with him as he was with her. Everything she told him wasn't a full truth. He didn't know that the city she missed so much wasn't Cairo. He didn't know that the poem that she recited to him wasn't a story book, it was one of the Epics of the Jinn, one of the long poems that depicted stories of Jinn heroes that defended and bettered Jinn City. The poem was about Kahlil the prophet, although it was written many years after his death.

She promised herself that, once Roman was ready, she wouldn't wait for his magic to break through her spell completely. She would tell him who she was herself. Of course, she had to be sure that he had some sort of useable magic so that he could learn to protect himself as well. Perhaps she could teach him how to use his magic, if it was anything like her own. She didn't see him as just the Chosen One who she had to protect anymore. He was a real boy with real baggage, and there was so much more depth to him than his role in the prophecy.

Kesi walked through the doorway into a thin hall that placed the locker room far from prying eyes. There were two doorways on either end of the hall, each muffling their own chatter from the girls within. Kesi chose the doorway to her left, finding herself in a room full of rows upon rows of gray-green lockers that stretched towards the ceiling. There was another doorway to Kesi's right that opened into a small space housing two bathroom stalls, with sinks stationed on the tile wall. Kesi walked to the section of lockers at the very end of the room, passing girls talking to each other as they changed into shorts and t-shirts for PE. Finding an empty locker, Kesi quickly took the small lock that Roman had given her out of her messenger bag.

"It comes with the code 0-0-0 to unlock it, and I just leave it like that," Roman had told her the night before. "It doesn't happen often, but some kids like to take other people's stuff from their lockers if they don't have PE clothes or whatever. If you have a lock on it, no one will touch your locker. This way you don't have to put your code in every time you change, but you still don't have to worry about your stuff being taken."

'*Thanks Roman*,' Kesi thought to herself as she ran her thumb over the little numbers. *0-0-0*. Kesi carefully placed her bag into the locker and closed the lock around the handle, securing it in place. She was about to turn around and leave when she heard a half-familiar voice.

"Kesi Haddad," Becky Oakley said. "How nice to see you again."

Kesi turned around to see Becky standing there, hands on her hips, which were covered by short athletic shorts.

"I was just heading to the weight room to work out for

cheerleading," Becky continued, "and now I've run into you! What a day I'm having."

"The best kind, I'm sure," Kesi deadpanned. "But as you can see, I have to get to class. Rain check, maybe?" Kesi smiled at the brunette who only glowered at her. Without another word, Kesi squirmed past her and made her way out of the locker room, adjusting her messenger bag on her shoulder. Roman was waiting for her outside, leaning against the far wall, his nose buried in his phone.

"Hey," Kesi said, making him look up.

"Hey," he smiled before peeling himself off the wall. "Let's go, yeah?"

Kesi nodded, which prompted Roman to start walking further down the hall. He soon turned to the right and walked a little farther, ending up at another one of Waterford's glass doors.

Roman held it open for Kesi, letting her inside. The Health room was the same as the rest- white walls, white tables, and blue chairs. Students huddled in groups around the tables, abandoning their bags and books in their chosen chairs.

"I sit over here," Roman started, moving to a corner of the room, but when Kesi moved to follow him, two girls blocked her path.

One girl had a brightly dyed pixie cut colored lime green in the most horrendous fashion. Her face was scrunched and large, her eyes dark. The other, taller, girl had a cleanly cut dark bob with bangs, her gray-blue eyes shielded by square-framed glasses.

"Hi...?" Kesi stated, the seriousness on the girls' faces making her uncomfortable.

"You're Kesi Haddad, right?" the dark-haired girl asked, taking a notepad and pen out of her jacket.

"Uh, yeah," Kesi laughed nervously. What were these girls doing? "I guess there's not many new kids around here, huh?"

The girls seemed to ignore her comment, their eyes just as serious as before. This time the green-haired girl spoke.

"I'm Alexis Folley, and this is Ruby Willow," she explained. "We write for the Waterford School Newspaper." Her tone implied that she was very proud of that fact. "And we would like to interview you for our first addition of this year."

"Um…," Kesi was confused. Interview? What for? Were new students really such a surprise here? "Maybe… maybe later… Class…?"

"Coach Ridley won't stand in the way of social justice!" Ruby seemed appalled by such an idea. "If she does, I'm sure that Alexis and I can go to Principal Alves and have her fired."

Kesi just blinked at the two girls, the feeling of trouble creeping up in her gut. Whatever was about to happen between the three of them, Kesi was sure that it wasn't going to be good. She looked over to where Roman was standing nervously, glancing between Ruby, Alexis, and Kesi before back to Ruby again. They clearly didn't sit well with Roman either. When he caught her gaze, he winced apologetically before mouthing, *sorry* over to her. Kesi huffed and looked away. '*Some good he is.*'

Returned to the present, Kesi turned back to Ruby and Alexis, "Social justice?"

"Yes, your voice *must* be heard," Alexis answered confidently. "Don't worry, Kesi, we're feminists and Democrats. You can trust us."

Kesi mulled over Alexis' words for a moment before finding the definitions to the things she didn't know. Those answers only left her with more questions. "I don't think… You don't seem to be acting like a… Um, well, I don't see how you being a feminist or a Democrat means I should just *trust* you." She laughed, thinking it was surely some kind of joke. Humans couldn't be that naïve, could they? "I don't know either of you at all."

"Don't panic, Kesi," Ruby chuckled, her tone suggesting that she hadn't listened to Kesi's words at all. "We just want to ask you a few questions." She clicked her pen, preparing to write down Kesi's words as she read from her notepad. "How do you feel being labeled as 'other' because of your ethnicity?"

"Labeled as other?" Kesi laughed outright. She couldn't believe that these two were *serious*. "This is literally my second day of school."

Ruby and Alexis both shook their heads. Alexis spoke to her friend sadly. "Kids can be so quick to be cruel."

Kesi gaped at them for a few moments before speaking. "No, you're not listening to me. I meant-"

"We'll start with a lighter question," Ruby cut her off. Kesi bit her lip as her temper started to boil. "What sort of behaviors have students exhibited due to the stereotypes about the Middle East and how has that effected your school life?"

"I don't understand why I have to answer all of these questions," Kesi growled, her body tensing in anger. Even Becky, Nico, and Taylor hadn't acted... like *this*. It was clear to Kesi that Ruby and Alexis both thought of themselves as righteous when they were causing more harm than good. She knew from the Elder's spell that the groups that Alexis and Ruby were aligning themselves with weren't supposed to act this way. What did they think they were doing? She needed to shut this down fast, before she *really* got angry. "I'm going to sit down for class," she moved to walk past the two girls, but Alexis jumped in her way.

"If we spread the word of your suffering and your ideas, we will be able to rally an army to support you for the good of the feminist and Democratic movements-" the green-haired girl started, and with that one comment Kesi proceeded to snap.

She laughed harshly, making the two girls jump. "That's right," Kesi shook her head at them, "For the good of *your movements*." She paused, trying to find the right words to say when they started pouring out of her like water. "Not for the good of me, or anyone else here." Kesi felt her voice rise, but there was no way to stop it now. "Look, I'm not your charity case. I feel bad for everyone who you've turned into some sort of poster figure for whatever the hell you're trying to do here. And I don't think that what you're doing is really helping anyway. You shouldn't be involved in social justice to make yourselves look like heroes. That's not what it's about."

"No-?" Ruby tried, but this time Kesi cut her off instead of the other way around. Kesi couldn't stand being talked over, especially not by people who didn't know how to listen.

"No, *you* shut up." Kesi pointed a finger at her. "You want to victimize me. I'm not a damn victim. When I want to use my voice, I will. You can't force me to do anything. Let me through." Kesi shoved past the two girls angrily, plopping into the seat beside Roman.

"'*I'm not a damn victim*,'" Alexis repeated to Ruby. "That's a good quote, write that down."

"We still have time before class," Kesi heard Ruby reply. "Let's go find Charlotte! She'll be *sooo* jealous that we got an interview with Kesi Haddad!"

With that, Kesi watched the two girls hurry out of the room. Kesi was quick to release a string of curses in Arabic under her breath as the door closed behind them.

"That was so cool," a voice said from the other side of Roman, and Kesi leaned forward to see a fairly short boy with brown hair and dark eyes sitting on Roman's right. He had a small nose and wide eyes with a sort of delicateness to his face that made him seem softer. "I could have never done that. They're always trying to interview me for the Waterford School Newspaper, and I can't ever shake them off."

"Why?" Kesi asked. "Why do they want to interview you, I mean."

The brown-haired boy blushed and looked away from Kesi, "Cause I'm... gay, I guess."

Kesi huffed. "They think they're such heroes, don't they?"

"Seems so," Roman replied before pausing. "Sorry that I didn't come over to help you. It's just every time I try to communicate, they kind of... freak out."

"I know the feeling," Kesi groaned.

"It's probably their conspiracy theory that people with light skin can't have hard lives and can't be redeemed," the brown-haired boy added. "I'm… Asher, by the way."

Kesi smiled at him. "Hi Asher, I'm Kesi."

Asher laughed at her for a moment before saying. "I'm sorry that Ruby and Alexis are so… difficult. I have an interview about being gay in high school my freshman year, and now they keep asking for other interviews about things I know nothing about. I mean, I stand for all the things they say they stand for- equality, justice, all that. But the way they go about it is just…"

"Embarrassing," Roman offered.

"Destructive," Kesi replied.

Asher nodded at both of them. He paused before asking, "Are there a lot of gay people from where you're from?"

Kesi paused at the question, thinking. She didn't know much about the people in Egypt, but she did know that back in Jinn City it wasn't uncommon for genies to find Mates of the same sex, although they didn't have a word for it like the humans did. It just didn't matter who your Mate was enough to label it as a different kind of love. "I don't really know, why?"

Asher shrugged. "I just… just when I told you that I'm gay, you didn't seem to really care."

Kesi chuckled. "Am I supposed to?" She really couldn't understand these humans. They cared about every little thing too much. '*It must make living really difficult*,' Kesi thought to herself.

Asher stared at her for a few moments. "I guess not."

Roman turned to Kesi then, trying to save the conversation, and explained. "Asher is cool. He hangs out with good people, not with Alexis or Becky or anyone like that."

"I think my friend Thora said something about being in your Chemistry class, Kesi?" Asher questioned, and Kesi shrugged.

"I… think I remember her?" she replied, knowing it wasn't much of an answer. "The introductions were kind of quick."

Asher laughed. "At least Dr. D let people introduce themselves. I heard about what happened with Mrs. Pendergrass."

"Man, news travels fast around here," Kesi shook her head as a tall, long-faced woman with dark brown hair entered the room.

"Coach Ridley!" a student from the back cheered affectionately, and the woman smiled at her.

"Alright," the woman started. "First things first…," she stared at the clipboard in her hands, "We have a-"

"Did we make it?" Alexis' voice filled the doorway, her green hair popping into the room.

"No," Coach Ridley answered. "Take your seats, girls."

Kesi had to resist a giggle as the two girls slumped into their seats, and Coach Ridley continued, "As I was saying, we have a new student with us. Kesi Haddad?"

"Hi!" Kesi waved at the teacher, who waved back at her in a way of greeting.

"Hi, Kesi," the woman responded. "I'm Coach Ridley, and this is Health 2. We're learning about CPR and things like that," she explained. "It's required by a lot of schools now, but don't worry, we haven't started much."

"That's good," Kesi replied. "I was afraid that I wouldn't be able to catch up."

Coach Ridley shook her head. "No, you're fine. On C days we have PE, and we meet in the hallway outside the Green Gym. I'm sure that someone can show you when the time comes."

"I'll show her," Roman announced, then sank back as all eyes turned to him. "She's living with me, it's the least I could do."

Coach Ridley smiled at Roman. "That's nice of you, Roman," she turned to Kesi again, "You're in very good hands, Kesi," Coach Ridley paused as Kesi smiled back at her. "And… let me see, what am I forgetting? I'm sure that Roman can get you up to speed on the schedule and material. We play a lot of games in PE, but they're fairly easy to pick up so I think that you'll be fine."

"Thank you, Coach Ridley," Kesi said gratefully, glad that Health wasn't as information heavy as her other classes. Even though she had hardly missed more than over a week, she still felt left behind. She didn't know what she would do without her friends' help with home and schoolwork.

Coach Ridley was right. Health wasn't very intellectually inducing, and soon it was over and Roman lead Kesi back through the Health Wing to the library where the others were waiting.

"How was Health?" Aasma asked, giving her a warm smile.

"It was fine," Kesi paused. "Except for Ruby and Alexis."

Ben groaned. "What did they do? I swear, I will-"

"It's fine," Kesi laughed at her anger. "I took care of it."

"Of course you did," Kharim replied, laughing. "How could we expect anything less of our own Kesi Haddad?"

Morning break didn't seem to last as long now that Kesi was actually enjoying her free time, and soon Roman announced that it was time to go to Humanities.

"In the Humanities Wing?" Kesi asked excitedly, and Roman laughed.

"Where else?" he grinned before standing up from his place on the couch. Kesi followed him down the discrete set of stairs that he had led her down the day before to get to Spanish class. This time, however, he guided her down the long hallway she had spotted on Friday.

"Mr. O'Connor is really cool," Roman explained as they continued to walk. "He's funny."

"All the teachers here are funny." Kesi laughed. "Even Mrs. Pendergrass, even though she doesn't mean to be."

Roman shook his head at her in disbelief. "You're really not afraid of anything, are you?"

'*Not anything from* this *world*,' Kesi thought before answering him, "Well, if it can't kill me, why would I be afraid of it?"

Roman just shook his head again before opening one of the

many doors on the left side of the hall, the right plastered with glass showing the offices within. "Here, this is our class."

The Humanities room was themed the same as the others, this one in particular with a podium in the front and all the tables stationed in a horseshoe. Roman hurried over to the seats of a table at the far end, facing away from the window. Kesi slipped past the other students and followed him. She noticed distastefully that Taylor was sitting at the table across from them, laughing until he made eye contact with Kesi. She smiled at him, making Taylor turn away quickly. Kesi almost chuckled to herself at his reaction.

Soon after Kesi sat down and got settled, a tall man with a short brown beard entered the room. He had black, square-framed glasses and a professional-looking sweater. He made eye contact with Kesi first, and his dark eyes seemed almost surprised.

"Oh!" he said, walking further into the room.

"Hello," Kesi offered. "I'm new."

The man searched the surface of the podium for a moment before retrieving a black Expo marker. "Well... I'm Mr. O'Connor, and welcome to Waterford...?"

"Kesi Haddad," Kesi chuckled as she finished his sentence. "I'm an exchange student from Egypt. I'm staying with Roman."

Mr. O'Connor looked over to Roman briefly before looking at Kesi again. "I'm glad you could join us, Kesi, and I'm actually really, *really* horrible with names so if I ever call you by the wrong name or mispronounce it, tell me," Mr. O'Connor said as he started to write on the white-board walls. "I had a student once who'd I'd been pronouncing her name wrong the entire first semester and she didn't tell me. I only found out when I heard her friends say her name and I was like-" Mr. O'Connor paused in his writing to let out a stream of nonsense mumbling and stuttering before saying finally. "'Why didn't you tell me? I was pronouncing your name wrong the entire first half of school and you didn't tell me?'"

Kesi giggled at his dramatic storytelling. "I promise to tell you if you ever do mispronounce my name, don't worry."

"Good," Mr. O'Connor pointed his marker at her before finishing writing on the wall. When he pulled away, Kesi marveled at how neat and nice his handwriting was, and mentally scolded herself for not writing more in Jinn City, although the action was as near to natural to her in her human form.

Humanities 10, the board said, and under it listed several items ordered with bullet points, *Ancient Chinese philosophy... Warring States Period...Confucianism... HW: Confucianism Reading.*

"He's spoiling the class," Kesi mumbled over to Roman. "Dang, I was really hoping for a surprise."

Roman laughed at her. "You don't even know what the things on the board *are* though."

"Sure, I do," Kesi bragged, Elder Iamar's knowledge coming into play. "The Warring States Period was a two-hundred-year war and Confucianism a philosophy."

Mr. O'Connor must have heard her, because he spoke up to say. "Kesi, you've learned about China before?"

"I-" Kesi stuttered, caught a bit off guard by the question. Recovering quickly, Kesi answered. "Yeah, last year. It was the very last thing we studied in... Freshman year."

Mr. O'Connor sighed dramatically, seeming exasperated for her. "Ah, well, you'll just have to study it again."

"That's okay," Kesi replied. "I'll probably learn something new." Racking the parts of her brain that weren't exactly hers, Kesi added cleverly, "As Confucius said, 'If you study but do not reflect, you will be lost. If you reflect but don't study, you will get into trouble.'"

Mr. O'Connor snapped his fingers at her in praise and hummed happily. The other students cheered and laughed for Kesi.

"Alright, alright, enough of that," Mr. O'Connor held two big hands up in the air. "Let's start with the lesson so you can try and catch up to Kesi. And I say *try* for a reason," he finished, making the class laugh.

After such a rough start to her day and dealing with the incredibly obnoxious duo, Ruby and Alexis, Kesi practically beamed at Mr. O'Connor. He was kind and smart, and she was overjoyed to find there were more people at Waterford Academy that were like Roman and her other friends. She hoped to find more of them.

CHAPTER NINETEEN

DANVILLE, VIRGINIA

Roman

"HOLD STILL," ROMAN laughed as he adjusted Kesi's football helmet on her head. He'd waited for her outside of the girls' locker room to make sure that she would be able to find her way to the field. When Kesi stormed over to him with her helmet in one frustrated hand, declaring that the clip that was supposed to attach under her chin hated her, Roman found it too adorable and hilarious not to help.

"How are *you* able to do this and not *me*?" Kesi huffed. "This is impossible; I swear it is."

Roman unclipped the helmet and handed it back to her. "Here, at least you'll know that it's possible next time."

"Is that our new recruit?" Ian's voice sounded from down the hall as he approached them, dressed in full football gear.

"Yeah," Roman replied. "Kesi, meet Ian, our team captain."

"Oh!" Kesi turned to him hurriedly, fumbling under the helmet to get a better look at him, "Hi, I'm Kesi," she stuck out her hand to shake.

Ian chuckled as he shook it. "It's nice to have you on the team, Kesi."

"I'm glad to be here," Roman could see Kesi's grin flash, even from under the helmet. "Roman thought I couldn't do it."

"I did not!" Roman defended, turning to Ian. "I just didn't know if they would let her play."

Ian shook his head at them both. "Sorry to say that I might be hard on you, Kesi, especially after seeing what you could do after school on Friday."

"You saw that?" Kesi's voice was overflowing with excitement. "That was awesome, right?!"

"You're fast," Ian noted. "We need that. All we have is bumbling fools like Roman who only know how to use their own weight to push people over."

"Hey!" Roman crossed his arms over his chest. "You... you do that too, you know."

"Then maybe Kesi can teach me a thing or two," Ian smiled at Kesi and placed a hand on her shoulder before walking to the stairs that would lead to the first floor.

"Well," Kesi said, turning to Roman, "I think that went well."

"Ian's a good person," Roman told her. "We should go. We don't want to be late."

"Right!" Kesi jumped up and down happily. "Let's go!"

Kesi then proceeded to grab Roman by the hand and drag him down the same path that Ian had taken, nearly making him trip on the steps as they took them two-by-two all the way down.

"I'm so excited!" Kesi yelped as they emerged out of the back door of the Health and Fitness Wing. "How many people are on the team? Do you think I'll get to tackle people? What do we even do in football practices here?"

"Kesi, you're pulling my arm out of its socket," Roman groaned and Kesi quickly let go of his hand, giggling sheepishly.

"There are fifteen people on the team- sixteen including you,"

Roman explained as they walked along the paved road to the football field. "And you'll… most likely get to tackle. Probably because the other guys won't want to tackle you."

"I don't understand that," Kesi stated, and Roman felt a twinge of guilt. The more she didn't understand about things like girls not wanting to be allowed on football teams, the more messed up he felt his world was being revealed as.

"We're just taught not to hit girls, that's all," Roman told her. "Part of being a gentleman, I guess."

"Well, you're obviously not a gentleman," Kesi poked his arm. "You tackled me."

Roman's face burned at the mention of the memory. "Sorry about that."

"No, it's fine," Kesi's tone was cheery. "It's not going to be the last time it happens, and it was kind of fun… in a… wind-literally-being-knocked-out-of-you sort of way."

Roman laughed at her humor before she pointed to the fence lining the football field.

"There it is! Let's go! C'mon, hurry!" Kesi's joy prompted Roman to run alongside her, though she was too fast for him and beat him to the field, pouncing onto the grass. Roman joined her shortly, Mr. Murray catching both of their eyes.

"Kesi! I'm glad you could make it!" he said, smiling.

"I wouldn't miss this for anything," Kesi replied before more boys crowded around the coach.

"Listen up!" Mr. Murray said to the football-decked students in front of him. "I can't call you all 'boys' now because, for the first time ever, Waterford has a girl on our football team!"

Kesi waved to the group of boys who all stared at her in disbelief from behind their helmets. "Hi, I'm Kesi."

Mr. Murray turned to the blonde, "I yell at them enough for you to get to know their names. Now, put your helmets and water bottles down and do one lap around the field, let's go!"

Normally Ian was the fastest runner in the pack for warm-ups, but today it was Kesi who was leading the rest around the field, seeming almost bored as she ran. No matter how hard Ian and even Roman tried, they just couldn't match her speed. Roman swore it was inhuman.

Kesi high-fived Mr. Murray as she finished her lap, panting with a smile on her face. She kept that smile all through stretches and all through their water break, not once caring to listen to the mumbles of the boys around her, questioning her reason and ability to be there with them.

"This is so cool," Kesi said to Roman.

"I'm glad you think so," Roman laughed at her as Mr. Murray told them that their water break was over, and they had to start practicing plays. The other boys didn't really seem to pay much attention to Kesi until the very end, when Ian let them split into two teams to play a game of football until practice was over. Ian was choosing players for one team, while another senior named Peter was choosing for another.

"I want Kesi," Ian said first, causing one of the freshman boys, Jay, to grumble.

"Come on Ian," he half-laughed, clearly irritated. "She's a girl."

"And she's better at passing than you," Ian shot back. "Peter, your turn."

Thankfully, Roman and Kesi ended up being on the same team, so Roman didn't have to worry about hurting her in any way. The fear of causing her any harm had more to do with the fact that Kesi was his friend, not because she was a girl. After how many times she had made him fall flat on his back on Friday, Roman didn't have any doubts about Kesi's skill or talent.

Ian started with the ball once it was tossed to him, and almost as soon as he turned in Kesi's direction, another boy tackled her to the ground without notice, startling everyone around them. Roman heard Kesi yelp as she hit the ground, completely swallowed up by the large body of her attacker.

"Kesi!" Roman yelled as Kesi disappeared from his sight. Ian got to her first, though, and peeled Owen Green, one of Taylor's friends, of course, off Kesi and pushing him away from her.

"That was uncalled for, man," Ian barked. "Get yourself together. Take a walk." He pushed Owen again, sending him backwards as he did what Ian commanded. Mr. Murray appeared by Kesi's side as he helped her stand to her feet, along with Logan Hager and Roman who practically leapt to her side.

"Are you okay?" he mumbled in her ear. Owen was a big kid, much bigger than Roman. She couldn't be feeling spectacular after that body-slam which she hadn't been prepared for. Owen had done that to Roman on more than one occasion, and even with Roman's height rivaling Owen's, it still took him a few seconds to get himself together.

Kesi didn't reply to his question, but Roman could hear her gasping for breath, trying to regain the wind that was knocked out of her. He could see her blue eyes darting rapidly as she tried to get her bearings on shaky knees. Once she was on her feet, she stumbled into Roman's arms and said quietly, "He said that I should know not to try a guy's sport."

"He's wrong," Roman assured her as she steadied herself. He would hate it if some stupid boy like Owen caused Kesi to want to leave the team.

"I know, but that's the reason he did it," Kesi told him, composing herself. "He was trying to scare me."

"Don't let him scare you," Roman replied. "He's stupid."

Kesi grinned at him from under the helmet. "Well, he can't kill me, can he?"

Roman chuckled and shook his head at her. '*How is she not freaking out right now? She doesn't even look mad.*'

"Why was he so angry anyway?" Kesi asked. "No one else said anything to me."

Roman looked over to where Owen had gone before replying, "He's... not a very good player. Mr. Murray benches him often, and since you're already better than him, he's probably scared that he won't ever get to play in games."

Kesi was silent for a long time. "Maybe fear is more powerful than hate."

"Maybe it is," Roman agreed before Mr. Murray put a hand on Kesi's shoulder.

"I'll talk to Owen," the coach told her. "He shouldn't have done that."

"It's alright," Kesi reassured. "He just wants to be able to play."

Mr. Murray looked as if he wanted to say more, but he only nodded before walking away and addressing the rest of the boys. "Alright! What are you standing around for? Get back to it!"

The rest of practice was fairly quiet, even after Owen returned. Roman could see him glaring at Kesi from a mile away, but the girl didn't pay him any mind. She even blocked a pass that was directed towards the bigger boy before slipping down the field with her unusual speed.

"That's all the time we have for today!" Mr. Murray declared, checking his watch as Kesi made it to the end zone. "Ian's team wins! Good job, Kesi!"

"Thanks, Coach!" Kesi replied cheerily, tossing him the football with one hand, using the other to fiddle with her helmet. Roman stayed behind to wait for her as the others filed off the field, watching her as she flung her helmet off. Roman could see the anger in her eyes that he didn't notice earlier, making him worry. '*Why did she hide that from me, and why was it just coming out now?*'

"You okay?" Roman asked as she passed him, grabbing her water bottle from the grass. "You look pissed."

"Of course, I'm pissed," Kesi replied. "I'm either a victim or someone to victimize here, there's no in between."

Roman sighed before racing to keep up with her. "You can't think like that. You decide who you are." He paused. "Why did you just blow it off earlier like it was nothing?"

"Because, Roman, there's… a lot of worse people in this world than that kid, I shouldn't be mad," Kesi grumbled, not looking directly at him.

"Yeah, but those people aren't here now," Roman couldn't understand her. '*What do you mean by* worse people, *Kesi?*' "You're allowed to be angry, Kesi."

Kesi ducked her head. She didn't say it, but Roman knew that she thought he was right. After a while she said, "I wish there was a way to get back at him."

"There is," Roman offered. "You beat his ass at football and get him benched every game."

Slowly, Kesi smiled and turned to Roman. "Sounds as good of a plan as any."

"Sorry he ruined your first practice," Roman said meekly, making Kesi scoff.

"You think I would let some guy like that ruin my day?" Kesi's grin returned as she took a sip from her water bottle. "He's not worth it."

"You sound like Aasma," Roman chuckled, and Kesi poked his chest with her water bottle.

"Hey! That girl has some good advice," she noted, making Roman laugh more. "And a good music taste. She gave me some new Bruno Mars songs to listen to. And some band that she likes? One Direction? But they broke up or something, apparently."

Roman groaned. "Oh no. Not you too."

"Relax," Kesi laughed. "It was only one song. I mean, I forgot it already! But it was actually a good song. I don't know why you're complaining."

"When it's all you hear from Aasma, you will be," Roman explained. "Did Ben get you into Michael Jackson yet?"

"Yes!" Kesi yelped, throwing her water bottle hand into the air. "*You need some lovin', tender lovin' care. And Iiii-'ll take you there!*" she yell-sang between laughs, her voice as rough as sandpaper.

"Ow," Roman covered his ears. "You're right, music is *not* your talent."

"Rude," Kesi glared at him. "That was *so* rude."

Roman laughed at her, throwing his head back as they approached the back of the Health and Fitness Wing.

"I'll see you at the car," Kesi said to him as they jogged to the second floor. Well, Kesi jogged, Roman was at more of a fast walk.

"I could just wait for you outside the locker room again," Roman blurted, feeling his face grow hot. '*Why did I say that? What's wrong with me?*' He thought, cringing. '*I need to get my act together as much as Owen does.*' "S-so, you know, you don't get lost."

Kesi smiled at him as they approached the doorway leading to the girls' locker room. "I'll probably need that, actually, thanks."

It was a lie. Roman knew that. She had run all the way to the front of Fiore Hall just fine on Friday after playing with Mr. Murray. Roman felt more heat crawl up his neck at the thought of Kesi *wanting* him to wait for her. It was a stupid thing to get flustered about, he told himself, she probably just didn't like walking around the big building all alone.

Roman stayed true to his word, though, and, after grabbing his bags from the locker room, he waited outside the girls' locker room for Kesi, staying as far away from the entrance as possible. Still, it didn't stop the girls' who entered and exited from giving him weird looks.

"Waiting for your girlfriend?" a snarky voice asked, and Roman looked up to see Becky standing in the doorway, smirking with mischievous eyes.

"Y- n- s-she's not my girlfriend," Roman stuttered, shifting uncomfortably on his feet. Becky hadn't addressed him directly since she'd announced loudly that she was occupying Sophia's spot on the cheerleading squad the other day. Honestly, Roman was surprised that she even looked sideways at him since she liked to ignore those who she thought were lower than herself. "She's just my friend."

Roman began to panic as one of Becky's friends, the dark-skinned Amber Spring, appeared at her side in a green-and-white volleyball uniform. Things always turned messy when Becky had one of her friends glued to her side.

"Do you think they've done *it* yet, Amber?" Becky said to her friend, not tearing her eyes away from Roman. Roman felt disgust and embarrassment bubble up within him at Becky's words. '*How can she even suggest that?*' "I mean, it's only been a few days, but they do live together…"

"Seems suspicious," Amber giggled.

"We… we don't have… we never had…," Roman fumbled with his words as Becky laughed.

"Can't even find the right lie to cover up your tracks?" Becky crossed her arms over her chest, "You're just trying to fill the hole in your heart shaped like…" She placed a long fingernail on her chin, humming as she pretended to think. "What was her name again? Stephanie? Sasha?"

Roman just stared at Becky with dread and anger, feeling himself about to snap into either sadness or fury, he couldn't tell yet.

"Ah, *Sophia*," Becky continued to smirk at Roman. "And Kesi… well, I don't know what she's doing. Probably just being a-"

Clunk. A familiar water bottle bounced off Becky's head from inside the locker room and onto the floor, causing a shriek to escape Becky.

"Ow! What the hell was that?" Becky grasped her head, spinning on the figure standing behind them, which gave Roman just enough room to see who it was as well.

Kesi stood behind them, hands on her hips and her two bags at her feet, looking eerily calm.

"Oops," Kesi deadpanned. "I guess I didn't hit you hard enough. I wanted to see if you had any brains in that shallow skull of yours." She glared at the brunette. "Guess you're more thick-headed than I thought."

Becky hissed at the blonde. "*You.*"

"Me," Kesi rolled her eyes. "Really, don't you have something better to do with your time than picking on others to fill the hole in your heart shaped like a…" Kesi waved her hands in the air. "What's it called? Oh yeah, a *life.*" Kesi smiled as Becky glowered. "Maybe when you get that you can come up with better insults that are harder to copy." Kesi grabbed both of her bags and swooped up her water bottle from the floor before rushing over to Roman.

"Let's go," Kesi shoved her water bottle into her sports bag and grabbed his arm, dragging him away.

"You can't just insult me like that and then walk away!" Becky shrieked, seemingly unwilling to chase after the two of them.

"Watch me," Kesi called back, and Roman looked over his shoulder to catch the complete anger etched into Becky's usually composed features, making Roman grin. When Becky caught his smile, she grew even angrier, yelling in exasperation and dragging Amber back inside the locker room.

"That was so cool," Roman turned back to Kesi as she released his arm. "How do you *do* that?"

"I'm just not scared of her," Kesi answered. "She's not so terrifying when you remember that she's just a teenage girl who obviously has a lot of insecurities."

"And that she can't kill you," Roman added, echoing Kesi's philosophy. Kesi turned and grinned at him.

"Right. She can't kill you," Kesi repeated, looking proud. "I think you're almost ready to fight some bullies on your own."

Roman shook his head. "No, I don't think I could do it as well as you can."

Kesi only chuckled and waited until they were walking down the grand staircase before asking softly. "Her name was Sophia?"

"Yeah," Roman ducked his head away, not wanting to look Kesi in the eye. Even after Saturday night, he didn't exactly want to even come close to bawling in front of her.

"Man, I can't believe that she even said that she thought that we've had... you know." Kesi changed topics swiftly, making Roman sigh in relief.

"Yeah, she just likes to think that there's more Sophomores getting it on than there really are," Roman told her, "so she doesn't feel like the odd one left out, I guess."

"She's...," Kesi turned to Roman as he nodded. "Oh, *gross*! With who?"

Roman shrugged, "First I heard it was with Taylor last year."

"*Ewww*!" Kesi scrunched up her nose in disgust. "Don't put that image in my mind."

Roman laughed. "Already did."

Kesi cringed. "That's true. And now it's burned there forever. There's Emma."

Roman held the door open for Kesi as she exited Fiore Hall and walked with Roman across the sidewalk to his mother's car. Roman could feel her smile even from several yards away.

"How was practice?" Emma sounded ecstatic as both Kesi and Roman got settled in the car.

"It was awesome!" Kesi smiled at Emma. "I think I'm going to start taking my showers at night, though."

Emma laughed. "Good idea. How was school?"

"It was good," Kesi replied again, glancing over at Roman as he placed his head against the window tiredly. "I met a lot of people. Mr. O'Connor is cool."

"I told you," Roman mumbled as he closed his eyes, exhausted.

"Yeah, yeah," Kesi replied. "You told me so… are you going to fall asleep over there?"

"Yes," Roman replied, turning farther away from her. "Goodnight."

"He's always tired after practice," Roman heard Emma explain from his sleepy state. "Anyway, Ben called me while you guys were playing football and asked if you could have another get-together on Friday to celebrate your first full week in the United States. What do you want to do?"

"That sounds amazing!" Kesi exclaimed. "Will there be pizza?"

Roman chuckled with his eyes still closed at her comment before Emma answered, "I'm not so sure. She said that she was planning on taking everyone downtown to have ice cream and just hang out. It's supposed to be nice Friday night, too, a clear sky and everything."

"Oh!" Kesi replied. "Ice cream! I like that too." She paused. "Is downtown the place with all the tall buildings? Do you mean Rosdale?"

Emma laughed. "Oh no, we mean *Danville's* downtown. It's just a small square with a bunch of cute little shops and restaurants around it. I think you'll like it."

"They set up a huge Christmas tree in the middle during the holidays," Roman mumbled sleepily.

"Christmas…," Kesi said softly to herself before coming to some sort of a conclusion. "I can't wait to see it."

"That means snow," Roman added, making Kesi groan.

"Never mind, the Christmas tree can wait," she said, and Roman snorted at her but couldn't offer any words. The chatter of Kesi and his mother droned out the farther that Emma drove, Roman's own head swirling with thoughts- mostly of Kesi and Sophia.

For some reason, the way that Kesi had stood up to Becky seemed to be more for Roman's dead sister than for him. She seemed to genuinely care about what had happened to Sophia without letting it define her opinion of Roman at the same time. Something that hadn't been done for him before. Even his parents were constantly worrying about how he was taking it, and who he was becoming because of the loss that he had endured. Roman had to admit, it was nice to have someone care more about him than what might happen to him because of Sophia's death. Kesi hadn't known him for long, but it was clear that she was confident in him. She wasn't afraid that he would turn bad or crumble at her feet. He had someone who believed in him again.

CHAPTER TWENTY

DANVILLE, VIRGINIA

Roman

"TODAY IS OUR best day," Roman told Kesi as they walked through the front doors.

"Why?" she questioned, curiosity clear on her face as she turned to him.

"Because we have two free blocks," Roman answered. "Our Health block is last, so we get an extra free."

Kesi pumped one hand in the air and cheered, startling several students walking around them. "Homework free night!"

Roman laughed at her. "It's the little things that get us through."

"Amen!" Kesi giggled. "You know, this is starting to feel almost normal."

"What is feeling almost normal?" Roman asked as she smiled at him, making heat threaten to rush to his face.

"This. Waterford. School. *Life*," Kesi clarified. "Your life."

"There's a lot more to my life than just this," Roman replied. "Waterford. School."

"It's a piece of your life," Kesi explained. "Isn't that what exchange programs are all about? Living part of someone else's life?"

Roman chuckled. "Now you're being the poetic one."

Kesi shook her head, "Nah, I'm more of a poem. I don't have any control over any of this. My story is already written." She replied cryptically. "You're the poet. It all depends on you"

"I'm the poet?" He found her witty and wordy games both alluring and amusing.

"You shape your own life," Kesi said. "I'm just living a part of it."

Roman thought her words over. "I guess that makes sense."

"Of course it does, I said it," Kesi tossed him a wink as they walked through the Qualls, and for once Roman didn't care about any of the other students around him, or what they might be thinking. The two exited the Qualls and moved into the Science Wing.

"You seem to be in control of your little piece, though," Roman commented as they entered the Science Wing.

"Gotta live with what you got, Roomie," Kesi grinned again, trotting over to their classroom door, making Roman laugh as she slipped inside. Roman followed her, joining the rest of his friends at their table on the far side. Ben saw them first and immediately waved.

"You guys!" she said as they approached. "Did Emma tell you about my genius plan?"

"Yes!" Kesi replied excitedly. "And Roman and I will be there!"

"We will?" Roman looked over at Kesi as they sat down. *'Did I miss the memo that we were actually going?'*

"Yup!" Kesi giggled before turning to Ben. "He fell asleep on the way home yesterday."

"I did not," Roman glared. "I just... rested my eyes for a few minutes."

"Hey guys!" Dr. Denney's voice sounded off the Chemistry room's walls, "How's it goin'?"

"Good!" Savanah Reed replied happily to Dr. Denney. The teacher smiled at her.

"That's good! It's always nice to know that you guys aren't totally dead at this point of the year yet," she replied, making the class chuckle. "Alright, shall we get this class started or what?"

It seemed to Roman that the school days were passing by a lot faster now that he had Kesi with him. He spent half of his time laughing at her and the other half with her. Kesi made school more bearable, and it was getting him to come out of his shell more. So far there hadn't been any more incidents with Becky, Owen, or anyone else that would normally be causing them trouble. He felt content just sitting with Kesi in a study room in the library, chatting and finishing homework at the end of the day.

"I have a question," Kesi said as she put down her stylus. "What happened yesterday… does that happen often? With Becky, I mean."

Roman thought for a moment. "She's never… called me out like that before, unless I talked to her directly. Which I try not to do for obvious reasons." He rolled his eyes. "But she does things, like make up rumors, if you piss her off enough."

"Oh, well, I pissed her off pretty bad," Kesi chewed on her bottom lip to try and tame her grin. "I can't wait to hear the crap she tries to spread."

Roman chuckled. "You're actually excited about that?"

"Uh-huh," Kesi replied. "I want to see how low she'll sink. She thinks that she can hurt me by using things that I don't care about. Like, I don't care what she says or thinks about me, but she seems to care an awful lot about me. Which, I guess, works to her disadvantage, because that means that whatever war she's trying to start, she won't win." Kesi looked at Roman. "Is this how kids always are? Trying to take each other out?"

Roman leaned back in his chair. "Not everyone. Did you not have people like Becky at your old school?"

"I, uh...," Kesi thought for a moment. "I guess, but they never used things that people can't control against them. They never teased someone for losing a loved one." She looked at him seriously, her gaze full of kindness, not pity, as if trying to tell him that she would be there for him even if she didn't understand what he was going through. Roman looked away then, not sure what to say. They sat in silence for a long time before Roman found the courage to speak.

"She was a cheerleader," he said finally. "Sophia. She was a cheer-leader. Becky got her position in the lineup or something."

"She doesn't deserve it," Kesi replied quickly, leaning forward and placing a hand on his arm. Roman looked down at her fingers on his forearm, feeling the buzz of her energy on his own skin. The last time she had touched him like this was when she had pulled him into a hug after learning about Sophia.

Kesi quickly pulled away when she noticed him looking at her hand, and it was clear from the expression on her face that she thought his moments signaled that he was uncomfortable. Roman opened his mouth to tell her that it was fine when the door to their study room flew open, making both teens jump. Roman's panic didn't dissipate when he saw who was standing in the doorway.

"Oh, I'm so glad we found you!" Ruby smiled at Kesi, who had been startled to her feet.

"I'm not," Kesi growled, crossing her arms over her chest.

"We're um...," Roman started, eager to act as he was sure that Kesi wanted him to. After all, it would probably take an army to get these two girls to leave them alone. "We're actually studying for... a Spanish quiz right now, if you wouldn't mind....?"

Alexis' face furrowed in fury upon noticing Roman. "Kesi, you need to get out of here. You know that *boys* only think about one thing. Look at the way he's trying to get you alone!" She turned back to Roman and said, "God, you're *disgusting*."

"What?" Kesi looked at Alexis in confusion. "You... you're

not making any sense. Don't call Roman disgusting, please. Cause he's not."

"Come on, Kesi," Ruby reached forward to grab her arm. Kesi reacted by pulling away. "It's time for a proper interview, don't you think?"

"No," Kesi replied, making both Ruby and Alexis' faces contort in confusion.

"What do you mean?" Alexis asked, chuckling. "It's a perfect time for an interview! It's free block!"

"I mean," Kesi rolled her sky-blue eyes. "I don't want to be interviewed."

"Of course you do," Ruby laughed and took out her notepad and pen. "Don't worry, these questions will be about other issues at Waterford and won't exactly concern you directly."

"Then why am I needed for this?" Kesi was clearly becoming irritated.

"Question One: Do you feel that Waterford should have safe spaces for people of the LGBTQ community?"

"Oh my... I don't know!" Kesi laughed at Ruby. "Seriously? I don't know. I've only been here a few days, and I have no idea what it feels to be in that group."

"We need a more specific opinion than that," Alexis told her, and Kesi rolled her eyes.

"That *is* my opinion," Kesi replied, before pausing. "I really don't know how to answer that." She thought about it some more. "Why would you *need* them?"

"To make those of that community more comfortable and feel as if their needs are met," Ruby replied, scribbling on her notepad.

Kesi took a deep breath. "Okay, but...I still don't think I'm exactly qualified to talk about that."

"Maybe you can ask Asher or some of his friends," Roman added. "Kesi can't speak from that perspective."

"*Well*," Alexis spun on Roman. "You don't get to talk."

"That wasn't very nice," Kesi's tone dropped, threatening that another spin of anger was about to occur. "I think we've entertained you long enough, you can leave now."

"Don't you want your voice to be heard?" Ruby's bewilderment and shock was clear on her features. Roman sank into his seat, trying to avoid Alexis as her glare began to settle comfortably on him.

"If I wanted my voice to be heard, believe me, you would hear it," Kesi huffed. "But I don't, because honestly I just want to be *left alone*. Thanks."

"But you're...you're *Middle Eastern*, there are so many stereotypes... You *need* to battle them!" Alexis seemed to be on the verge of a nervous breakdown.

Kesi sat back down in her chair cautiously, observing the two girls that still stood in the doorway. "Okay, then that's my job, not yours. I don't need you to help me talk about my own life."

"How can you... how can you just not *care*?" Ruby was flabbergasted. Kesi leaned forward to address them. Roman could tell that she was trying not to lose her temper.

"I do care," Kesi explained. "I do care, but that doesn't mean that I'm going to talk about issues on things that I don't understand. Unlike you, I don't see people just as the traits that make them a minority. It's a part of them, yeah, but it's just a part of who they are. I judge people based on their character, not on things they can't control." She leaned back in her chair. "You say that things like gender and race don't matter to you, but you can't see past those labels. Why can't you ever just interview someone because they're a *person*, because they're *smart*, because they're more than just a person of color or a gay boy? There's more to people than that. If you really cared about people you would see that, but you don't. You just want to seem like a good guy."

"We just...," Ruby answered almost immediately. "We just care about..."

"Yeah, okay." Kesi cut her off. "Time to leave. Goodbye."

Roman watched in amazement as Alexis and Ruby actually did as she asked, looking embarrassed and feverish as they closed the door behind them. Roman turned to Kesi after they had left, grinning ear to ear.

"You didn't even have to yell at them this time!" he said excitedly before noticing Kesi's expression. She was chewing her bottom lip softly, her face concentrated and deep in thought. "What's wrong?"

"It's just… where I come from, this doesn't matter at all," Kesi answered, turning to him. "But here it does."

"Welcome to America," Roman groaned. "People can't find a balance between harming and helping people over here."

"That's horrible," Kesi looked distraught before saying. "You never harm anyone."

"Yeah, because I have a brain," Roman rolled his eyes. "I stay out of everybody's way and help when someone is in trouble, but I don't pick fights. Like what you said on Friday about arguing, it never gets anyone anywhere. You can't fight fire with fire."

"You fight fire with water," Kesi added, making Roman nod in agreement. "Too bad no one else realizes that."

Roman snorted. "Believe me, I know. Most adults don't know that."

"Then, how do we?" Kesi turned to him expectantly. Roman stumbled over an answer, not exactly sure what to say.

"I guess because we grew up in the fire," he decided. "We've always known how to push it back."

Kesi smiled then, seemingly satisfied with his answer. "You know, you have to give yourself some credit. You're smarter than you know."

Roman ducked his head, trying to school his blush and scolding himself for not being able to take a compliment like a normal person. "Thanks, Kesi." He paused for a moment. "I think she would have liked you."

"Who?" Kesi asked before answering her own question. "Oh! Sophia."

Roman smiled at her sheepishly. He didn't know why he told her that, but then again he didn't seem to have much control over his words lately. "Yeah. You would have gotten along."

"I'm sure we would have," Kesi replied softly before taking the silence that Roman emitted as a sign to change the subject. "Well, school is almost over, so do you want to head over to the locker rooms early?" she asked, and Roman nodded in response.

As Kesi was gathering her things, she asked, "Will you wait for me? You know, I might still get lost."

Roman laughed, "Sure, anytime, Kesi."

Kesi grinned and swung her messenger bag over her shoulder. "That's great, because I'm... prone to getting lost, of course." She grinned at him. "Okay, let's go, Roomie."

CHAPTER TWENTY-ONE

DANVILLE, VIRGINIA

Kesi

K ESI WAS SURE that she was about to fall asleep in art class. She never had much artistic talent, and with the gloomy overcast to the sky and her stomach full of food from lunch earlier that block, Kesi couldn't help but feel sleepy. Aasma and Roman, however, were more than engaged, sketching almost picture-perfect drawings of the flowerpot placed in front of them. Their teacher, Mr. Bratton, had called this unit "Still Life's," and Kesi was no closer to making her drawing anywhere near A-range material, than Aasma was to making hers near F-range material.

"How do you do that?" Kesi mumbled to Aasma quietly as Mr. Bratton had requested complete silence as they worked, a rule that most students ignored.

Aasma shrugged. "I don't know. I just kind of zone out."

Kesi observed Aasma's drawing in wonderment. The flowers curved elegantly and Kesi could almost see the textures in the petals. The reflection of the lamp light on the glass vase was described with detail and grace. Kesi leaned forward to catch a better glance at Roman's drawing, looking like a photograph. Kesi's, however, resembled more of a hairy Easter egg. Even Kharim's drawing, made of mostly dark lines and cartoonish shapes, was far better than hers. She huffed. *Art is impossible. How do Roman and Aasma make it look so easy?*

Aasma giggled at her. "Don't worry, Kesi, you'll get there."

"I'll be right back," Kesi heard Roman grumble as he stood and walked out of the room, leaving the others behind.

Watching him go worriedly, Aasma said to Kesi, "Did he tell you about his sister?"

Kesi nodded solemnly. Whenever she or anyone else mentioned his sister, his eyes would become duller and his smile would disappear. Kesi wished she could help him in those moments, but the best she could do was change the subject.

"Good," Aasma sighed. "He needs someone to talk to. Someone who wasn't involved with her."

"Were they close?" Kesi asked, switching to Arabic for more privacy before guilt crawled to the surface. She should have enough courage to ask Roman these questions, but she was just too afraid to push for details in fear of hurting him. Kesi knew that he should be allowed to keep some things to himself from a girl he had met just under a week ago.

"Very close," Aasma looked downcast. "Everyone who met Sophia just fell in love with her. She didn't deserve to die."

"No one does," Kesi added, glancing away before thinking of something else. "You think that he'll talk to me about it?"

"When he's ready," Aasma explained. "You've been here less than a week and he's already opened so much of himself up to you. You have a special relationship, and I'm not just saying that because I think you'd be cute together as a couple."

Kesi chuckled along with Aasma. "Thanks, I guess?" She paused. "I wish I knew how to help him."

"He'll tell you how if he wants your help," Aasma assured Kesi.

"Believe me, I know him, he will. That's just how he is. He gets it from his sister."

"He said that we would have gotten along," Kesi said, recalling their conversation the day before.

Aasma seemed to think this over. "He's right. You would have loved each other like sisters."

Kesi felt a wave of sadness crash into her at Aasma's comment. If Aasma could recall Sophia in such detail, then Kesi couldn't imagine what Roman was feeling while still trying to deal with her death.

"How long ago was it?" Kesi asked, "Her death, I mean."

"They found out that she had cancer around this time last year, only a few weeks after school started," Kharim answered her from her left. "She died a few weeks later. There was nothing that anyone could do."

"How old was she?" Kesi questioned, turning between Kharim and his sister.

"Eighteen," Aasma replied sadly. "She didn't even get to graduate high school, and she was so excited about going to college too."

Kesi sat in silence for a long time, going over the twins' words. She could feel the sadness radiating off the two of them and she could almost hear their brains going through memories. Kesi felt guilty in a way that she couldn't describe- she wanted to be able to relate to them, to be able to console them, but no one that she had ever been close with had ever died. Even if they did, funerals in Jinn City were an extravagant affair, celebrating the fact that a genies' soul would return to the magic of Jinn City to help more genies come into being, give Fate its power, and help take care of all the loved ones that they left behind. For humans, it was different. There was no magic for the souls to return to. No one knew where people went when they died.

Kesi observed Roman as he came back into the room. He seemed to be doing alright, and even if it was just acting, Kesi respected that. Remembering Aasma's words, Kesi turned back to her drawing, telling herself that Roman would ask for her help if he needed it. Until then, she needed to give him his space. They were still just getting to know each other, after all.

By the end of Art, her drawing looked no better. Mr. Bratton collected their papers as they filed out of the class, emptying out into the hallway.

"Math!" Kesi said excitedly as they gathered their bags from where they left them leaning against the wall.

Roman laughed. "You're really excited about showing Mrs. Pendergrass up again, aren't you?"

Kesi grinned at him. "Of *course,* Roomie, why not?"

"You have to tell me what happens," Kharim said to Kesi as they came closer to the grand staircase.

"What do you have?" Kesi asked the two of them before Aasma pointed in the direction of the Health and Fitness Wing.

"We have Becky in our class," Aasma rolled her eyes. "It sucks."

"Ooo, have fun!" Kesi waved at them as they approached the top of the stairs.

"Alright, lovebirds," Kharim laughed as he and his sister started to walk down the sky bridge. "We'll see you in Chemistry."

Kesi turned to smile even wider at Roman, who had pink dusted on his cheeks. "Lovebirds? Who, us?"

Roman chuckled nervously at Kesi as he watched Aasma and Kharim leave. He didn't really seem to be *seeing* the twins, though, his mind looked as if it were somewhere else. He was so out of focus that he didn't even notice the light flickering overhead. Kesi jumped into action.

"What are you thinking about?" She asked as she watched him. He jerked his head back around to look at Kesi.

"Wha- oh," Roman ran a hand through his hair. The flickering of the lights stopped. "Just... nothing."

"Mm-hmm," Kesi smiled, seeing through his lie, but didn't press the matter further. She knew better than to try and get into someone's head like Ruby and Alexis did. Kesi had to resist cringing at the thought of them. The situation that had occurred yesterday hadn't been pretty, and she especially didn't like the way that Alexis talked to Roman.

'*Some heroes*,' Kesi thought bitterly, pushing the notion aside and heading to math class. She couldn't let the two girls ruin her mood the day after the fact.

Algebra class ran smoothly for the most part, except when Taylor entered the class late and Mrs. Pendergrass sent him straight to the principal's office. Kesi was starting to realize that he was the one who missed class the most.

When afternoon break came, Ben dragged Kesi and Roman over to where the twins and Dimitri were waiting in the library, clearly excited.

"Okay, *chicos* and *chicas*!" Ben began, dropping her book bag on a nearby table. "While going through my contacts and *trying* to make a group chat for our little party in two days, I realized that we are all missing one component from our phones." She pointed a finger at Kesi. "Kesi's number!"

"Oh!" Aasma exclaimed. "That's right! We never got your number or anything. How could we have forgotten that?"

"I know, babe, I know," Ben shook her head. "Exchanging numbers is a huge milestone in any friendship, and we almost completely forgot about it. Kesi… where's that phone of yours?"

"Um…," Kesi offered as she scrambled through her bag for her phone. "Here," she said, holding out the light-blue cased phone to her friend. It almost slipped through her clumsy fingers before Ben took it, letting herself into Kesi's phone and clucking her tongue.

"Girl, you really need to get a passcode on this thing," she said disapprovingly before typing on the screen then handing it to Aasma standing next to her.

"I love this case," Aasma commented before typing herself. "I'll put you in, Kharim."

"I can do it myself," Kharim grumbled before Aasma handed the phone to Dimitri and turned to grin at her brother, saying, "Too late."

Roman was the last person to put in his contact, and once he handed her phone back to her, Kesi quickly slipped it into her bag. "So... I'll... make a group chat... or something... later."

"Probably with my help," Roman laughed. "Seriously, have you never had a phone before?"

Kesi gulped and felt heat rise to her cheeks. "Uh... not... this kind of phone?"

"That's what I thought," Roman replied, not noticing her awkwardness. "Do you want me to help you put a passcode on your phone?"

Kesi pouted. "No, I can do it myself, thank you very much."

"You've still gotta tell me your password so I can get into your phone," Ben said to her, confusing Kesi.

"Then what's the point of having one?" Kesi asked her.

"To keep everyone else out, obviously," Ben flashed her a grin. "But I'm fine."

"I wouldn't trust her with your phone," Kharim commented, making Ben glare and everyone else laugh.

"I think I'll have to take Kharim's advice on this one," Kesi giggled. "I don't want to know what you would do with my phone."

As if on cue, Kesi felt her phone vibrating from inside her bag, and Kesi placed it on the table closest to them and took it out again. Seeing that it was Queen Ena calling, Kesi became worried. *'Is something wrong in Jinn City?'*

"Who is it?" Ben asked, leaning over to see the contact name on the screen. "Oh, why is your mom calling you?"

"Uh... it's about six thirty there," Kesi explained. "She might have just gotten home from work. I'll be right back." Kesi tossed them a smile before walking away, swiping to answer the call.

"Mother," Kesi said into the phone, switching to the soft rhythm of Arabic as she slipped through the crowd of students stationed in the library.

"Kesi," Queen Ena replied, her voice as calm as always. Kesi let herself relax a bit. Perhaps her home was safe after all.

Kesi passed the librarian's desk and stationed herself by the bar-like area, which housed only a few students.

"I wish that I was calling to bring good news," the Queen's statement made Kesi stand on high alert. Although the urgency of her mission was always in the forefront of her mind, now that Queen Ena was on the phone, calling about "bad news," Kesi couldn't help but forget about everything else except her duty to the Chosen One.

"What's wrong?" Kesi asked, knowing that she wouldn't like the answer. She stole a glance over to Roman. Pleasantries and friendliness aside, she still had to protect him.

"The Shaytan have learned of our plan," the Queen explained, making Kesi jump. "They are making attempts to secure the portal over the Barrier, although they have yet to find the right timing. They will soon enough." The Queen paused. "I know what kind of panic this must bring, but do not doubt your magic. You are more powerful than you know."

Kesi looked down at her feet, swallowing fear. "Am I?"

"You must believe in yourself to move on," the Queen explained. "All of Jinn City believes in you, Kesi. You will find out why soon enough. All you need is a little self-faith; it is the most powerful magic anyone can possess."

"I understand, Mother," Kesi replied, her voice wavering. "If I see any Shaytan, I won't hesitate to fight."

"Good," the Queen sounded proud. "Goodbye, Kesi."

"Goodbye, Mother," Kesi pocketed her phone once the line went dead. Her head was swarming with the information she had just been given. The Shaytan were coming, Kesi was sure of that. Her Queen hadn't said it directly, but Kesi knew that was what she meant.

'*Where do you buy self- faith?*' Kesi thought to herself, mulling over the Queen's advice. Taking a deep breath, Kesi composed herself and walked back over to her friends, who were all chatting amongst themselves.

"Well?" Ben asked once she re-joined them. "What did she say?"

Kesi waved them off. "It was just my little sister. She wanted to say hi."

"Aww, that's so sweet," Aasma smiled at Kesi. "Your sister sounds very nice."

"She is," Kesi replied, also smiling. She wasn't so sure what else to say about someone who didn't really exist. Every lie she told felt like another mark against her newly awarded Jinnhood.

"I can't wait for you to see downtown!" Aasma squealed in delight. "It's so pretty there, especially at night."

"You better bring your camera," Kharim joked, elbowing his sister playfully. "They say it's supposed to be a clear night on Friday."

"Unlike today," Kesi rolled her eyes, motioning towards the window behind them.

"I know, it's so gloomy," Roman commented. "I wish it would just rain already."

Ben pulled out her own red-and-black cased phone and checked the screen. "We should probably get to class."

Kesi loved Chemistry, she really did, but with the class being at the end of the day, she found it hard to focus on the information given to her and kept thinking about the practice ahead of her. Kesi thought that the boys were warming up to her- today would be her third practice and it was becoming clear that even those like Owen were beginning to value her at least a little bit. She just didn't understand why it was so hard for them to understand that a girl was on their team in the first place. Kesi knew that deep down human society would never make sense to her no matter how much time she spent in their world.

You should know better than to try a boys' sport, Owen's almost animal-like voice still rang clear in her head. At first, she was afraid, especially since he had her pinned to the ground and she was a little short on magic, but then she became angry. What right did he have to tell her what to do? He didn't even know her!

It was the same thing with Becky, Alexis, Ruby, and all the others who had already picked her out from the rest. They all acted like they knew her, but none of them took the time of day to talk to her civilly. If she were in Jinn City, things would have been different. Not only would they not think of her as different, but she would have enough magic to show them why they should all leave her alone.

'*But I'm not in Jinn City*,' Kesi reminded herself bitterly as Dr. Denney let her students out of class. Kesi felt an elbow softly jab at her side and she looked over to see blonde Dimitri smiling at her as they all walked through the hallways. Kesi smiled back, not exactly knowing what to say. She knew that he could see how deep in thought she had been.

Returning to the present, Kesi laughed and talked with her friends until they had to part ways to go to the locker rooms in the Health Wing.

"Will you wait for me?" Kesi grinned at ever-blushing Roman as they made their way across the sky bridge.

"Yeah, of course," he answered, offering her a smile.

"When is our first game?" Kesi asked him happily, trotting down the hall.

"Not until Homecoming," Roman answered. "Which is in a few weeks."

Kesi turned to him then, smiling wide, and jokingly said, "Will you be my Homecoming date, Roman?"

She laughed as Roman blushed harder and his mouth poured out stuttering words that Kesi couldn't understand. He furrowed his brow at her laughter, frustrated, before joining her. It seemed he was catching onto her playful teasing.

"You're just… not nice," he mumbled as they approached the girls' locker room. "I'll wait for you."

"Thanks, Roomie," Kesi threw him a wink before ducking inside the doorway and out of his sight. Kesi found her way to her locker and changed quickly, hoping to avoid Becky or anyone else that might cause trouble. She shut her locker and slipped out of the locker room, spinning around to make sure that Becky wasn't standing behind her, waiting to pounce. After what Becky had said to Roman the other day, Kesi wasn't so sure that she would be able to keep her temper under control. Thankfully, there was no one to be seen, but the chatter and giggling of the other girls in the room reminded Kesi that she wasn't alone. Keeping this in mind, she quickly slipped out of the locker room and grinned when she saw Roman standing there, looking down at his cleats.

"Hey," Kesi said, catching his attention. He smiled when they made eye contact, his white teeth flashing happily.

As the two started to walk to the stairwell, Kesi heard a series of boys laughing behind them. Kesi turned as Nico and Taylor ran past them, snickering as they looked at Roman and Kesi. They both wore gray shorts and green t-shirts with *Waterford Soccer* printed across the front in white letters.

"Is she good in bed?" Taylor called, and Kesi looked over to see Roman blushing. Was he talking to them? Kesi spun around to see Taylor's retreating back, the meaning of his words hitting her like a monstrous rainfall. Human slang hadn't exactly caught up with her yet, but this time she wished revelation had stayed far away.

"Better than you!" Kesi barked back, picking up her pace to run after the two boys. Before she could get very far, Roman's strong arm wrapped around her waist and pulled her back towards him. Kesi, clumsy as ever, tripped over her own feet as, with no choice, she yielded to the pressure of Roman's arm, falling back into him. In order to steady her, Roman tightened his grip more securely around her waist and braced her against his chest.

Kesi looked up to see Roman staring after Taylor and Nico, anger burning in his green eyes. The sight startled Kesi enough for her to stop fighting his grip. Roman responded by releasing her.

"Roman-" Kesi started, turning to face him fully.

"It's Becky," Roman growled, not looking her in the eye. "Remember what she said on Monday?"

Do you think they've done it *yet?* It was the comment that had lured Kesi from the depths of the locker room to listen to the scene outside it. Kesi scowled at the memory of Becky's sharp words before realizing what Roman was getting at.

"You think she's telling people that we…?" She let her sentence hang in the air, unwilling to finish it. The idea was just too much for Kesi to think about. She knew what Becky had implied and she found it ridiculous. Her and Roman? Kesi couldn't imagine the two of them being together, much less the two of them being… *together.* She didn't even know if her body worked the same way or looked the same way in human form. She didn't know much about how those things worked, especially for genies. Once she came of age when she turned twenty years old, it was custom for her older peers to teach her, but Kesi was still far from that stage. Even though Elder Iamar's spell had taught her about the workings of human bodies and relationships, no one had ever told her how it worked for a genie. In fact, it didn't even matter to Kesi, not until now. Now it seemed like every other person was talking about it or doing it themselves.

'*They care so much about those kinds of things,*' Kesi mused to herself as she watched Roman cautiously, his breathing calming slowly and the anger slipping from his features. In a way she was glad that he was angry. It showed that he felt the same way that she did. It showed that he was upset with how much things like this mattered. But mostly, she was angry at Becky. Kesi could tolerate Becky's taunts against her, but Roman? That drew a line. Still, that wasn't what Roman needed to hear.

"A lot of people don't like her, Roman," Kesi reassured. "It'll only be people like Nico and Taylor who are too stupid to think otherwise that will believe her."

"You don't... you don't understand...," Roman still couldn't meet her eyes. "People have been waiting for something like this to happen, ever since...ever since Sophia. Everyone has been waiting for me to fall into some kind of bad habit. They'll turn *this* into something awful. I've been trying so hard to not do anything remotely out of line of who I was before. But now..."

Kesi shook her head, not believing what she was hearing. No matter what, if Roman made any sort of bad decision, it would be his choice, and no one could blame that on the death of his sister. The fact that Roman continued to move away from whatever "bad habits" people expected him to start despite his mourning was something he should be given credit for. Instead, it was viewed as something that wouldn't last very long, so much so that Roman even doubted it himself.

"You have to prove them wrong," she told him. "Especially if they're trying to make you seem like someone you're not. You have to do what they don't expect and challenge who they're portraying you as."

"I...I can't *challenge* them," Roman met her eyes finally, the fear and sadness in the sea of green making Kesi swallow down guilt. She wished she knew how to help him. She'd never been in this position before. She was only now beginning to process emotions without a Jinn City buffer. There was no way she would be able to help Roman with his own emotions, and it tore a deep gash into her heart. Lights flickered, and Kesi wasn't sure whose emotions they were corresponding to. Kesi took a deep breath.

"Well, that's what they expect," Kesi replied. "Besides, remember what I said about no one believing Becky? There's a lot of good people here that know you better than she does...that know me better than she does. It seems like something out of character for us, anyway, so why would anyone think that it's true?"

Roman stared at her for a few moments while the anxiety dimmed from his eyes, replaced by chuckling as he took in her words.

"What?" Kesi asked as she laughed along with him. She gave him a confused look as he wiped the darker emotions from his face.

"Nothing. It's nothing," Roman smiled and nodded towards the stairwell. "Shall we?"

Kesi decided that she was alright with not understanding Roman for the moment. After all, she assumed that there were many things that he didn't understand about her. "Let's go."

Kesi really liked the team captain, Ian Burrows. He was kind and considerate, and Kesi could tell that he loved every single boy on the team like a brother. Even to the chatty freshman and people like Owen. It reminded Kesi of her relationship with mostly everyone around her age and younger in Jinn City. They weren't classified as siblings, but they were still family. Ian himself reminded Kesi of Ra'id, except with darker skin and brown hair.

Ian was right about one thing. He was being hard on her. He really put Kesi's skills to the test during practices in methods that often left her exhausted by the time she got home. Kesi was proud of herself for making it hard on Ian too, as her energy wasn't easy to diminish.

"Why do you do this to me?" Kesi rolled her eyes playfully at the senior while she dodged several of the older kids on the team. Ian had instructed Kesi to play against them in a one-against-five manner.

"If you're not outstanding, they won't let you play in games," Ian called back as Kesi slipped under Roman's arms.

"You gave her that one, Roman!" Ian was laughing, prompting Roman and Kesi to do the same.

"Alright, that's enough," Ian said as Kesi made it to the end zone. Keeping the ball in one hand, Kesi followed Ian and the others to where Mr. Murray was coaching the rest of the team. When Mr.

Murray spotted them approaching, he yelled at the other football players to stop their exercises and waved the whole team off.

"See you tomorrow, boys! And Kesi!" Kesi giggled at his last statement, jogging over to grab her water bottle from the grass before heading out.

She didn't ask Roman to wait for her this time, but he still did it anyway, which made Kesi almost giddy. She'd never been able to have a sort of unspoken communication with someone before, and it was exciting to know how easily she was fitting into this world.

'*Maybe Mother was right*,' Kesi thought, smiling to herself. '*Maybe I really am meant to be here, to do great things.*'

Kesi could only hope so, because whether the Queen was right or not, here was where she was.

CHAPTER TWENTY-TWO

DANVILLE, VIRGINIA

Kesi

KESI WAS WRONG. She *was* close to getting used to waking up early, although she wasn't sure that waking up and immediately wanting to jump out of bed was humanly possible. Or genie-ly possible.

Speaking of genies, she hadn't heard any more from Queen Ena and the Elders. Kesi wasn't sure if that was because the Shaytan weren't making any progress or if Queen Ena and the Elders were too afraid to contact her in case the Shaytan overheard, especially since they practically had one foot in the portal already. The anxiety was eating away at her brain, and if Kesi wasn't distracting herself with schoolwork or sports, her friends would catch her in a far-off state, daydreaming the many disastrous possibilities. Which were a lot of things, naturally, when the world was at stake. Her overactive imagination was having a field day.

"Earth to Kesi?" Kesi snapped her gaze to Kharim at the sound of his voice.

"Huh? What?" Kesi said to him, still shaking her mind out of its foggy state. It was the beginning of morning break, and Kesi and her friends were lounging on the couch, enjoying themselves. Everyone was there except for Ben, who Aasma said had stayed behind after Health to talk to Coach Ridley.

"I just asked you what you had next," Kharim laughed at her. "Man, what were you thinking about?"

"Uh… Football," Kesi lied. "I really want to play in a real game."

"With the progress that you're having with Ian, I'd say that you will," Roman told her, making her grin.

"You really think so?" She was ecstatic about the very idea, considering that the first game was the Homecoming one and so many of the students would be there. With what she knew about the human world so far, she knew that it would stun everyone just to see a girl playing on the field, much less a girl playing *well*.

"Sure, I mean-" Roman started before Ben exploded on the scene, looking beyond angry. She held a thin bundle of papers in her hand as she leaned over Roman, who had to crane is neck to look behind and up at her.

"Bad news, guys," Ben announced, waving the paper in her hands. "Very, very bad news. Ruby and Alexis wrote an article for Waterford's Newspaper."

"What does it say?" Kesi questioned, picking up on Ben's sense of urgency. The dark-haired girl quickly handed the paper to her.

"You won't like it, girl," Ben shook her head. "I saw some by the desk back there and as soon as I saw the front page…" She let the sentence drop.

Kesi looked down at the paper in her hands and unrolled it, revealing the front page of the newspaper. At the top in big, bold print read *Waterford Academy School Newspaper,* and in smaller print under it: *August addition.*

Kesi glanced down the page and nearly threw up in her mouth at the sight of a picture of herself, smiling wide, as she turned around to look at someone in the Kasper House dining hall.

"When was this taken?" she asked no one in particular. "I never... I never wanted this to be taken. Who... what?"

"It gets worse," Ben droned, prompting Kesi to look further down the page. The title beside the picture read *Exchange Student from the Middle East Already a Victim to Bullying at Waterford*.

Outrage poured through Kesi when she saw the two names printed under the title. *Written by Ruby Willow and edited by Alexis Folley*. Kesi thought about ripping the paper to shreds before her eye caught onto the first sentence.

On Friday of last week, Waterford welcomed its first exchange student from the Middle East, the Egyptian Kesi Haddad. Kesi is in sophomore year and is being hosted by Roman Lovett of the same grade. Alexis and I had the opportunity to interview her on her second day of school. Kesi was a delightful source of information for us and really opened our eyes to how to better battle Islamophobia, racism, and other phobias and false ideals imbedded in our society.

When asked about battling the stereotypes regarding the Middle East, Kesi became agitated and told us, "I am not a victim." Kesi does not want the people of her country and region to be seen as victims of crimes. Kesi wants us all to be reminded that even when people live almost entirely across the world, they are still human and deserve respect.

Kesi also admitted to us that, even by her second day of school, she had noticed that she had been labeled as an outsider by her peers. She hopes to change this by showing her classmates who she is by tearing down the stereotypes surrounding the Middle East and its people.

Kesi also feels strongly about issues on gender identity, especially the education of such. "I judge people on their character," she had told us when discussing the topic of gay rights. Kesi feels as if there should be more education on gender and sexual identity, not just in the Middle East but around the world as well.

Kesi assured us that we would be hearing more of her voice soon, and we hope to have the opportunity to write about her in our next issue.

-Ruby Willow & Alexis Folley

"None of this is true!" Kesi yelled, startling several students around her. "Okay, I mean some people have said things about me being from the Middle East and I *do* care about those issues but... I never said *any* of this!" She tried to take deep breaths, but she felt panicked. Never had someone stolen her voice in this way. "Are they really so stupid to think that they could just twist my words like that? This is crazy! No one I've ever met has ever acted like this!"

The anger humming through her veins was suffocating, pulling her brain in every which direction. Kesi felt like her privacy had been violated. The words that Ruby and Alexis had used weren't really hers. They weren't hers at all. They were all Ruby and Alexis' ideas bundled up in flippant comments that didn't even show how hard Kesi's life was here.

'Is this how Roman feels when he said that he feels like other people are just waiting for him to fall into bad habits?' Kesi thought. *'Everyone is creating this false idea of Roman in their heads when it's the farthest thing from the truth. He's stronger than they know. He's been fighting so much harder than they know...'* It was awful, awful, and Kesi felt as if she were going to tear the world apart because of it.

The lights in the library flickered as her magic spiked with her emotions, affecting the electricity around her and ripping Kesi out of her angry rant. Looking around at the now-stable lights and the expressions of confusion on the faces around her, Kesi took a deep breath. She needed to get herself under control. She was lucky that she didn't have all her magic, or she would have started a fire or some other disaster.

"Whoa," Aasma mumbled, glancing to the ceiling before turning back to Kesi. "I know, it's not right. It's the farthest thing from right. But luckily no one reads the school newspaper except for Ruby and Alexis' friends. Everyone else knows how they normally don't write the truth… So, you have that." She reached over and touched Kesi's arm gently. "Don't worry, we'll get this all sorted out."

"How?" Kesi looked back down at the paper in her hands before shoving it away from her. She didn't care that nobody read the paper. It was still out there, and it was still untrue. She bit her bottom lip. Aasma's words echoed those that she told Roman yesterday about Becky. She really had to work on her comforting skills if she wanted to get any closer to anyone. "It's already out there."

"Not if there's no more prints to give out," Roman's voice made her look up.

"What?" Kesi asked, furrowing her brow at him. She couldn't see what he was getting at. He was reading the article in his hands, his expression both angry and calm. It was an odd mixture, but Kesi could tell he was thinking of something good.

"Fighting fire with water, Kesi," Roman answered, looking up at her. "These words aren't spoken, they're written, so the only way to make them shut up is to…"

"Get rid of the words," Kesi's grin returned in full force. "Get rid of the copies."

"You're brilliant, Roman!" Ben shook the black-haired boy's shoulders playfully. "We'll just take all the copies from the news stand!"

Kesi looked over her shoulder at the librarian's desk, where the dark-haired librarian sat behind his computer as always.

"Do you think he'll notice if we just take them?" Kesi muttered to her friends.

"I'll distract him," Aasma offered. "I need help making a video for French anyway, maybe he can help me out. Just wait until I get situated up there, I guess."

Kesi had to hold back giggles as Aasma took her tablet and walked over to the librarian, glancing over her shoulder awkwardly. When Kharim waved her on and hissed at her to keep moving, she stuck her tongue out at him, but did as he asked. Once it became clear that Aasma was starting a conversation with the man, Kesi grabbed her messenger bag and motioned for the others to follow her.

Kesi glanced over at Aasma as they approached the news stand embedded in the wall next to the desk, but quickly reminded herself to avert her gaze. With Ben and Dimitri to her right and Kharim and Roman to her left, they created a sort of wall to block them from the librarian's sight. Kesi giggled out loud at the funny secrecy and seriousness of it all.

Roman chuckled along with her, grabbing a stack of Waterford newspapers from the middle row. Kesi quickly opened her bag and let him shove them inside while Dimitri reached up and gave Roman a few magazines to fill the empty slot with. Roman did as Dimitri motioned before repeating the same for the other sections.

Kesi's bag was full to the brim of Waterford Newspapers by the time the five teens scampered away, laughing the whole way.

"You guys are so bad at this!" Aasma whispered as she came up from behind. "I could hear you guys laughing a mile away! Thank the heavens he didn't notice. Did you get them all?"

Kesi held up her stuffed bag. "Every last one. I'm going to burn these when I get home."

"I'll help," Roman added, making Kesi smile. "I'm glad we did that."

"Me too," Kesi replied. "Now people can't even see the front page as they walk past."

"Are you just going to carry those around all day?" Ben asked. "You can't fit anything else in your bag."

Kesi looked down at her bag. "We could divide them?" She looked up at all her friends, who nodded in return.

Kesi and Roman soon headed off to Spanish, each with one-sixth of the newspapers they had taken. Kesi couldn't stop laughing at the whole scenario, glad that they had done something about the horrible situation and made it into something hilarious.

"What do you think they'll say when they see all of them gone?" Roman mumbled to Kesi as they opened the Spanish room door.

"They'll probably think that it was so popular that they ran out," Kesi replied. "But that's ok. We don't need them to know that they were taken. It was only so that no one would be able to see it. It's a sort of empowerment even if only we know it."

"That's the best kind," Roman agreed as they took their seats.

Kesi decided to ignore Becky's snickering and whispering all throughout Spanish class, however, she could see that it worried Roman. She reached over and gave his arm a squeeze when it became clear that he was physically jumping every time he caught wind of Becky's clipped voice, which oddly seemed to make him relax a bit. Even during lunch, Kesi could tell that he was still thinking about what Taylor had said the day before. She didn't know how to help him, so once they were alone in the hallway after class she asked, "Health?"

Roman shook his head, "No, PE."

Kesi could feel her face brighten. "Oh! Good!"

Roman laughed at her, making Kesi's worries calm a little bit. At least he wasn't so anxious that he couldn't find the will to laugh. "I don't get you sometimes. But yeah, we have PE. I'll wait for you outside the locker room... If you want."

Kesi smiled at him. "Of course, I would, Roomie. I don't know where else to go anyhow."

Roman smiled and ducked his head, showing her the spots of

red that were creeping up his neck. She almost giggled at his reaction. He really needed to learn how to control that flustered nature of his.

It turned out that the PE class met in the Trophy Hall - the long hallway that connected the gyms and was adorned with glass on one side and a canvas of golden trophies on the other.

"Wow," Kesi exclaimed as she walked in by Roman's side, admiring the way that the light caught on the trophies. Several students were milling around the hall in their own clusters, orbiting an unseen mass like planets around a star. Kesi found the analogy amusing, especially since some of the groups seemed to be battling attention from their peers, wanting to be stars while acting like planets. Kesi was glad that she could see through the whole metaphor.

"Look," Roman motioned over to brown-haired Asher, who was sitting by himself on a wooden bench in the hall.

"Hey Asher!" Kesi smiled, walking over to the other boy.

"Hi, Kesi," Asher looked up at her and smiled before dropping it when he said, "The Waterford School Newspaper came out today."

Roman snorted as he came up behind her and Kesi elbowed him swiftly before replying. "Oh really? I haven't seen it around."

"It's on the shelves by the desk in the library," Asher explained. "I'm sure you saw it, even if no one buys it. It just leaves more copies hanging around all month before they're replaced by the next issue."

Kesi shook her head, trying to contain her laughter as mirth threatened to spill out into her expression. "I just walked by there. I didn't see it."

Asher looked confused. "I swear I saw it… Never mind. It's not important, I guess. Maybe someone complained and took it down. Ruby and Alexis' article was ridiculous."

"Knowing them, I'm sure it was," Kesi grinned before jumping at the sound of excited shrieking. Kesi turned to the doorway that she had just exited to enter the hall and had to resist an eye roll upon seeing Alexis and Ruby's cheery faces.

"Guess what, Waterford?" Alexis announced. "The Waterford School Newspaper is all sold out! Mr. Brown said that it must have happened so fast that he didn't even see it happen!"

"And it's all thanks to Alexis and me," Ruby said proudly. "We wrote the article on the front page."

Kesi leaned in close to Roman and whispered. "I told you."

Roman chuckled. "Never said I doubted you."

Kesi grinned at him as Alexis and Ruby skipped into the center of the Hall, chattering about what they perceived as an achievement. All the while, Kesi was glad that at least one person took her seriously, even if that person was as reserved as Roman.

"How could it have sold out?" Asher's voice was bewildered. "It wasn't... even that good."

"I wouldn't be surprised if you were right and they actually just took the copies down," Roman said to him. Kesi could tell he was being careful not to give anything away. "No one probably had the heart to tell them, though."

Asher thought about it for a moment. "I guess that makes sense."

Roman turned back to Kesi, smiling wide. Kesi smiled back, knowing that the secret of why Waterford's School Newspaper had vanished would stay between Kesi and her friends.

"Alright!" Coach Ridley's voice was booming. "Are we all here?"

A chorus of "*yeses*" answered her, but the coach was busy counting people herself. "Okay, let's go to the Green Gym. We're playing dodgeball!"

Roman and Asher groaned as the clumps of students moved in unison towards the large, open double doors at the end of the hall.

"What's wrong with dodgeball?" Kesi questioned as the three of them started to migrate into the gym.

"It's *awful*," Asher pouted, rolling his eyes. Kesi turned to Roman expectantly, wanting a second opinion.

"It's not that bad," Roman reassured. "It's just that it's the game we've played every other PE class ever since freshman year," he explained. "It gets boring, especially when you play three games in a row."

"Oh," Kesi replied, trying to digest the information he had given her. "Well… I'll try and make it interesting."

"You always do," Roman grinned at her, a gesture that Kesi returned gratefully.

The Green Gym was huge. '*Almost as big as a football field*,' Kesi thought to herself as she walked in. The ceiling stretched far above her, showing metal popes of pieces jutting out. '*I wonder if it's as high as the ceiling in the High* Palace.' The floor was smooth and gleamed in a way that Kesi knew that wood shouldn't. '*It's so shiny! What did they do to it?*'

Kesi was so busy marveling at the room that Roman had to grab her elbow and guide her where they were supposed to be. All the students were lined up along a thick black line that split the gym in half. Coach Ridley was directing students to different ends of the room with her finger, diving the class into two groups on opposite ends of the gym.

After a second, Kesi realized that the coach was dividing them into two teams. Once she made that connection she shouted. "We should go boys versus girls!"

Coach Ridley laughed at her comment as she pointed for another girl to move to the far side of the room. "That wouldn't be very fair, would it?"

Kesi furrowed her brow at the teacher, confused. '*How can that not be fair?*' Kesi thought. '*There's about an equal number of boys and girls in the room…*'

Kesi contemplated if she should say anything or not, tugging on the edges of her athletic shorts that she had brought for PE that day in her sports bag. The coach didn't seem to notice her expression as she threw her thumb over her shoulder, indicating that Kesi should go to the far side of the room. Kesi tossed Roman a grin before she ran off, eager to join her new teammates.

"Hey!" Kesi was nearly there when Asher's voice echoed after her. She turned to see him trudging towards her.

"You're on our team?" she said excitedly, grinning when Asher nodded.

"How are you so *fast*?" Asher was already out of breath. Kesi only had time to laugh at him before Coach Ridley yelled out. "Okay, go!"

Kesi turned quickly to see the coach emptying a bag of soft-looking orange balls out onto the floor, and almost as soon as the first one touched the floor, one of Kesi's taller opponents swooped in to grab it. He hurled it at a boy running to grab another ball. It missed its target by mere inches, landing on the floor with a *smack*!

"Whoa," Kesi breathed, adrenaline starting to race through her veins.

Asher groaned. "This is why I hate this game. Matt is so competitive."

"I'll get him out," Kesi replied, grinning at Asher's expression of disbelief. "No really, just watch me!"

Kesi ran forward and grabbed the ball that the tall boy, Matt, she assumed, had thrown before searching for the same boy in the crowd on the other end of the gym. When she found him, she grinned and sucked back, waiting for him to try and hit another student. Once the boy moved forward to grab another ball, Kesi shot to the line dividing the two teams, her tennis shoes practically gliding on the floor. She pulled her arm back and threw the ball as hard as she could, sending it flying across the gym. It hit the boy's arm, not only slamming against his skin, but also knocking the ball he was about to throw out of his hand.

"You're out, Matt!" Coach Ridley called, laughing at Matt's shocked expression. He turned and looked around for his attacker, mostly glaring at the other boys, as if accusing them.

"Hey, over here!" Kesi put one hand on her hip and waved at him cheerily, catching his attention. Once Matt figured out what was going on, he looked furious, making Kesi laugh at his reaction. "It's just a game."

Grumbling, Matt went to stand against the far wall by Coach Ridley, leaving Kesi grinning.

"Go Kesi!" she heard Asher yell, and she cheekily blew a kiss at him from across the gym, making several students chuckle.

"Kesi watch out!" Asher yelped and Kesi turned to see Roman chucking a ball with all his might towards her. Kesi ducked out of the way just in time, hearing the wind brush by as the ball almost collided with her head.

"Nice try, Roomie!" Kesi called over to Roman, who was rolling his eyes playfully, grinning.

Kesi bounced on her heels as she watched him smile. She could get used to this.

CHAPTER TWENTY-THREE

DANVILLE, VIRGINIA

Roman

WHEN ROMAN READ the article that Ruby and Alexis had written, he couldn't believe what he had seen. The two girls had taken their handful of meager conversations with Kesi and turned them into outright lies. He'd been present every time the two girls had approached Kesi, and none of the statements in the article aligned with anything she personally believed. They had taken Kesi's words and twisted them into the story they wanted and depicted her in a completely different light. He couldn't tell from the article or the reactions of the two during PE if they knew what they had done was wrong, or if they were just too stupid to think anything of it. Regardless, Roman was glad that Alexis and Ruby hated the idea of him enough not to interview him and twist his words into some sort of feministic article about his sister. He also sincerely doubted that it would be the last time they approached Kesi like that.

"I'll wait for you outside the locker room," he told Kesi as the exited the trophy hall. "We got let out early, so we have a lot of time before class."

Kesi grinned. "Awesome!"

Roman, excited about the opportunity to spend more free time with Kesi, tried to change as quickly as possible in order to meet her in the hall. He was in such a rush that he didn't even pause to say goodbye to Asher, something he normally would have done. His haste was in vain though, for when Kesi finally emerged, almost the entire PE class was finished changing and crowding the long hallway, just as excited about the long break.

Still worried about the newspaper article and how it was making Kesi feel, Roman kept throwing glances at her as they made their way down the hall. "Are you feeling alright?" he finally asked. He had almost lost her in the crowd a few times due to her inability to weave through the openings left between students. If she wasn't moving gracefully down the hall, then she was almost hurling herself into others, stumbling as she tried to regain her balance. It reminded Roman of the way a baby learned to walk. There were times of agility and times of clumsiness. It was as if Kesi had was still getting used to walking on her own two feet.

"Why wouldn't I be?" Kesi replied, puzzled. They broke away from the congested hallway and into more open air. "We defeated a couple of villains, *and* my team won two and a half dodgeball games. I'd say that it's a good day."

They began to walk towards the library, eager to officially start their afternoon break. Roman laughed at her. "I guess so," he said. "You're such an optimist. I don't even know why I was worried."

"No, I'm a realist," Kesi corrected. "I see the truth in the situation. And the truth is that there's nothing to be upset about enough to let it get in the way of my day!" She poked him in the chest playfully. "I think you're just pessimistic."

"A lot of people say that," Roman grumbled, recalling his friends' similar words on the first day of school. He knew that already his outlook was changing. All it took was Kesi talking him through all the things that could go *right* to get him to see things differently. No one had ever done something like that for him since Sophia.

Once Roman started to see the similarities between Kesi and Sophia, he couldn't stop his mind from finding more. At first it scared Roman, as if he were afraid that she would send him spiraling into the depths of happy memories that were tarnished and depressing. But Kesi didn't make him sad. It was almost calming in a sense to connect the dots between the two girls. For the first time Roman felt as if Sophia were keeping true to her promise, sending good things his way and staying by his side even though she was in the grave.

"Are you ready for the party thing tomorrow?" Kesi asked him, and continued when he nodded, "I'm so excited! I really want to see downtown."

"There's a lot of cool stuff there," Roman told her as they climbed the grand staircase, "There's a lot of restaurants and ice cream parlors and shops." Roman paused. "My favorite is Blue's. It's a really cool ice cream place. There's also Joey and Bianca, an Italian place." Roman started to grin as Kesi's eyes went wide at the word *Italian*.

"*Pizza!*" Roman almost expected her to drool as the word bounced out of her mouth.

"The best kind," Roman laughed. "It's where we got our pizza for our last party. They make the best pizza in Danville."

"*Mmm*," Kesi hummed happily, obviously remembering her first time trying pizza. "I can believe it."

"But I think we're just going to have ice cream at Blue's," Roman continued as they made their way to where the rest of their friends were sitting. "You'll like it."

"Because it's called Blue's?" Kesi questioned, making Roman smile. That was part of the reason.

"Yeah, and also because it has ice cream much better than the stuff in my freezer," Roman replied. "There's like… thirty flavors. I think that's in their slogan or something."

"*No way*," Kesi cheered. "That many flavors *exist?*"

"Some of them are kind of random," Roman answered as they sat down next to Ben, the twins, and Dimitri. Ben gave him an odd look before he said, "We're talking about Blue's."

"Ah!" Ben clasped her hands together happily. "I *love* Blue's! But Roman is right, there are some kind of strange flavors, or at least the names of them…"

"*Firecracker?*" Sophia's voice echoed in his mind as he remembered one of the last times that they had gone to Blue's before she got sick. "*That's new.*"

It had been a warm August Saturday night, and the whole Lovett family had decided to eat dinner at Joey and Bianca before heading to Blue's to celebrate their last Saturday before school started.

"*To our senior and our freshman!*" His mother had said earlier over dinner, holding up her glass of wine as if to toast to her children. Sophia held up her own glass of soda and added, "*May our teachers be sick and our subs be lazy!*"

The boy working behind the counter laughed at Roman's sister. He was one of Sophia's classmates and recognized her once she walked in. He often worked in Blue's on the weekends, but Roman was only half-sure that his name was something like Josh. "*Yeah, we replaced Summer Breeze with it,*" he said. "*Mrs. Blue said that it wasn't selling as well as she thought it would, or something.*"

"*Oh, I remember that one,*" Sophia had replied, leaning up against the cold glass protecting the ice cream underneath. "*Remember, Romey? Sounded like an air freshener.*" She giggled, eyes sparkling. She turned back to the boy behind the counter.

"Right, Roman?" Ben's voice shook him out of his daydream. As he jolted himself back into the living world, he noticed that the light seemed to dim and then brighten suddenly, but that might have just been his imagination. He quickly brought himself back to the present so not to lose any more of what Ben was saying.

"Wha-," Roman stuttered, unsure of what Ben had just asked him. After seeing her expectant expression, Roman decided to say, "R-right. Right."

Ben just clucked her tongue. "*Chico*, you need to get your head examined," she told him. "You would forget your head if it wasn't attached to your shoulders."

"I think that describes *you* better, Kesi," Kharim laughed over at her. "Didn't you almost forget your bag in Chemistry yesterday? Or was that the day before?"

"I did?" She paused to think about it. "Ok... maybe I did. I don't remember doing that, but I probably did," Kesi rolled her eyes, making everyone else laugh. Kesi soon broke out into giggles as well, happiness erupting onto her face. Roman found her especially easy on the eyes in these moments, but each time that thought wormed its way into his mind he locked it away. He still didn't feel like it was right to go chasing after girls only a year after his sister's death, even if he wasn't particularly the chasing type. It just felt wrong somehow. Roman wasn't quite sure if he wasn't ready to have feeling for someone or if he was scared, but he decided it was best to play it safe and try and push back any emotion that might be developing. It was better for both of them that way. Roman was sure of it.

"Try not to lose your head, you only have one class left," Aasma told the blonde before she started grinning again.

"And then it's Friday!" Kesi replied excitedly before backtracking. "Or, erm, then it's football, then it's nighttime, *then* it's Friday."

"Have you heard any word about being able to play in games?" Dimitri asked quietly, his words almost lost in the chatter of the library.

Kesi picked up on them, though, and answered, "No. I think Mr. Murray is waiting until I really start to help the team so he can go to the principal and explain how important I am, or something," she shrugged. "We still have time."

"I'll come to every game if you get on the team!" Aasma cheered, and Dimitri nodded his head in agreement.

"Me too, girl!" Ben added. "And I'll make those big ass signs with really embarrassing pictures and words on them! For both you and Roman."

Roman groaned at her comment. "Please don't."

"I'll yell at everyone to watch you," Kharim teased. "What's your number again?"

"Seven," Kesi replied. "I'm number sixteen."

"Thanks," Roman grumbled. "Nice to know you're on my side."

Kesi laughed and put a hand on his shoulder. "No problem, Roomie. I always got your back."

"Hmm… why is that not reassuring?" Roman joked, making Kesi feign offence. She gasped dramatically and placed a hand over her heart, as if she were mortally wounded.

"Ouch, Roomie, I thought we were closer than that," she giggled, unable to control herself.

'*We are*,' Roman thought, but decided just to grin at her instead. She turned back to talk to the others, but Roman fell a little behind. He didn't know why it seemed so awkward to say those words, but he hoped that it was just another one of the things that Kesi would give him the courage to say.

CHAPTER TWENTY-FOUR

DANVILLE, VIRGINIA

Kesi

KESI HAD HER last class, plowed through football practice, and slept like a log last night. Now it was Friday, the day of the long-awaited party downtown. Kesi could hardly contain her excitement in the car on the way to school, much less during her classes. Art was a nightmare, Mr. Bratton's squinty gaze making her feel self-conscious about her still life drawing even more than before. Roman tried to help her for a few minutes, but soon gave up. It was no use- Kesi's artistic ability, or lack thereof, was hopelessly unsalvageable.

Thankfully Math was much better. Math, with its numbers and logic, requiring no elegant pencil movements or creative brush strokes, was something she was good at. It was also hilarious since Kesi, as well as her friends, were all entertained by the battle of wits and wills going on between her and Mrs. Pendergrass. The more the teacher, or Mrs. P, as Kesi liked to call her, tried to fight with her, the more frustrated the woman got. Mrs. P should, by now, know better than to try and pick on her, in Kesi's opinion. If Kesi were her, she would have understood that the student just wasn't going to have any of it, which was true of course. She wasn't going to be bullied by some low-life adult who had a serious detention-giving addiction.

Their lunch came in the middle of Math, releasing Mrs. Pendergrass' students temporarily from her clutches. Kesi, Roman, Ben, and Dimitri filed through the school to the front of Fiore Hall to walk across the street to the Kasper House. Once the front doors were around the corner, Kesi heard a series of yelps and groans from her fellow classmates as they exited the building.

"What's going on?" Kesi asked her friends, who all shrugged in response.

"Oh no," Ben sighed as they came around the corner. "It's raining."

"Raining?" Kesi echoed, almost not understanding the term. She trotted ahead to stand beside Ben in the hall, blinking at the sight of tiny, clear droplets of water attaching themselves to the glass of the doors and walls. Curtains of rain crashed against the pavement, sparking small raindrops to bounce back into the air before settling on the ground. The sight was both foreign and enchanting. She'd only ever heard rain from inside a house the night that Roman had played her a song on his guitar. Kesi had never seen it up close or had to walk through it before. She considered asking if it hurt when it touched skin, but she soon dismissed the idea. Surely it rained in Egypt too - it would be too out of character.

"Can we skip lunch?" Dimitri suggested quietly, but Roman shook his head.

"I'm starving, and it's only across the street," Roman replied. "Come on."

Kesi let her friends move ahead of her as she found her way through the glass doors, the sound of the rain fall sounding like a thousand Djinn Field flowers whispering at once. Ben yelped once she made it outside, covering her dark hair from the rain, yelling, "Run, *chicos*, run!" as she sprinted across the street.

Kesi stepped out from under the rounded awning of Waterford's building, about to do the same as Ben, before feeling a steady stream of droplets collide with her skull, each with their own *plop!*

Startled, Kesi slammed her hands over her head quickly and looked up to find the source of the strange feeling. She was rewarded with a cascade of droplets falling across her face. She giggled and ducked her head away to shield her eyes. Holding a palm out in front of her, Kesi watched as the lukewarm water hit her skin and rolled off, marveling at the way the water sailed through the air. The scene was beautiful and oddly symbolic in a way. Even if the human realm didn't take care of its inhabitants like hers did, it did take good care of itself.

"Come on, Kesi!" Roman's voice made her look up, noticing her friends already at the entrance to the Kasper House. Kesi grinned over at them and ran across the street swiftly, slipping into the doorway that Roman made sure was held open for her.

"Don't see rain much?" Roman asked, chuckling.

Kesi smiled up at him. "Y-yeah… it's uh… been a while."

The four of them made their way to the dining hall. The large room was made up of white walls made of some type of stone, hardwood floors and big, glassy windows. It was split into four parts: two on the edges for seating, and two in the middle for food. The seating areas were crowded with tables and chairs as students chatted with one another. The food area was adorned with long metal self-serving stations holding all sorts of types of food, in both hot and cold varieties.

Kesi and her friends normally sat in the section closest to the entrance of the dining hall. Their usual table was far enough away from the doors that they weren't caught up in the crowds of people pouring into the food area, but they were close enough so that they were able to leave swiftly. Kesi made her way through the lines and piled her plate with rice, chicken, and vegetables before heading back towards their table. While she approached, Kesi waved to her friends with her free hand. It was in that precise moment that she felt her feet leave the ground and her body was hurled forward. Her plate was sent flying into the air and she crashed onto the ground, almost completely on her face. She felt rice sprinkle down into her hair and her chicken and vegetables bounce off her skin.

Groaning, she lifted her head off the ground and shook the food out of her hair. As she gingerly pushed herself up and turned her body over, Kesi heard a now-familiar snicker from behind. Turning, she leveled her blue-eyed glare on the girl sitting in the chair closest to her and met Becky's jade green eyes.

"Oops," Becky laughed, flipping a lock of curly brown hair over her shoulder. "Did I trip you? I'm so sorry, must not have seen you there."

Fury enveloped Kesi, causing her mind to race with the chant of, '*She did* not *just trip me, she did* not.' Kesi ground her teeth as Becky laughed again, clearly amused by her anger. Her laugh bounced off the walls of Kesi's head, and her temper flared in a way that it had never flared before. Becky's whole table seemed to be laughing hysterically, some clutching their sides as if it were hard to breathe. Kesi was sure that if it hadn't been such a physical attack, and had those people not been laughing so hard, she probably wouldn't have surged forward so furiously with plans of strangling the girl running through her mind.

"Kesi!" She heard Ben's voice cry out as she nearly reached Becky's now-terrified face before a strong arm looped its way around her waist, holding her back. Kesi struggled in the grip, still reaching for Becky's face.

"Let me go!" she screamed at her well-intending assailant. The lights in the room were going crazy, but Kesi couldn't have cared less. Plates flew off tables and crashed to the floor, but Kesi barely heard the sound. "Let me go!"

"Not until you calm down," Roman mumbled softly against her ear, careful not to let anyone else eavesdrop.

"Whoa, Beck," Nico's laugh made Kesi snap her attention to the dark-haired boy, who was sitting across from Becky. "Looks like she's going to kill you."

"I'm sure it wouldn't be the first time she's killed someone," Taylor's tone was vicious, and his expression was dark and full of humor. "You know, being from the Middle East and all."

"What does that even *mean*?!" Kesi screamed at him, startling the boy. She could feel everyone's eyes on her, but she didn't care. '*I don't care. I've had enough. I don't understand how humans like them can't seem to control their words. Do they not have any sense of morality? Or pride?*'

"You people are crazy!" she yelled. "All you care about is what you hear and what you see...you don't really know anything! But you act like you do, and that doesn't make *any sense*!"

Kesi turned to Becky. "And *you*!" She struggled again against Roman, who only grunted and continued to hold her tight. "You attack people for what they can't change... or for having feelings... or because they've lost loved ones. Do your little lovers know that you teased a boy about the loss of his sister?" Becky's face was scared in fear as the other students in the room started to whisper feverishly around her, casting the brunette glances of distain. "That is *disgusting*!" Kesi was almost shrieking in fury as she tried to push Roman's arm away from her waist. One of the lights popped and sent sparks flying to the screaming students below. "You are *disgusting*!"

"Miss Oakley!" The strong voice made everyone in the room jump, and Kesi turned to see a tall, gray-haired man standing in the mouth of the room. He had a wiry frame and was wearing a plaid shirt and dark-colored pants, looking very professional and put-together. Kesi stopped struggling against Roman, but didn't let go of her anger, not sure if the adult would understand what had been going on.

Becky's eyes went wide, and she suddenly buried her face in her palms, the sound of forced sobbing echoing in the room. Kesi only rolled her eyes at her, scoffing. '*Does she* really *think that's going to work?*' Kesi looked over to the man again, and from the expression on his face Kesi guessed that he also knew Becky was faking her reaction.

"D-d-did you hear what she *said* to me?" Becky cried. "S-s-she is a *bully*, Principal Alves!"

"Principal Alves?" Kesi questioned quietly, not exactly so sure who she was talking to. She blinked at the man in disbelief. Of course, of all the people who had to walk in on the situation, it had to be the principal.

The man crossed his arms over his chest as he approached Becky and Kesi, who was still trapped against Roman, with an air of authority that would have frightened Kesi if she hadn't been able to feel the warmth of her magic beneath her skin.

"Yes, I heard what she said," he explained. "And I also heard and saw what the rest of you…" He pinned his gaze on Becky, then Nico, and then Taylor. "…did. Becky, come to my office after you finish eating and I'll talk to the rest of you somewhere throughout the day."

Becky made a noise that resembled something that Kesi thought a dying animal might make as she turned back to her salad, poking at the contents. Nico and Taylor looked beyond terrified, Nico adorning a cherry-red face and Taylor not daring to meet anyone's eyes.

"T-thank you," Kesi blurted before the man had the chance to walk away. Her face started to heat up as she realized what she had done. '*What was I thinking, trying to attack Becky? I mean… she definitely deserved it… but that's just not me.*' Her face burned in embarrassment at her own behavior, at what had almost just happened, and at the un-payable debt she now owed Roman for stopping her. '*What if I had gotten expelled or suspended? How would I protect Roman? Mother said that the Shaytan are close. That might have killed him. You're so stupid, Kesi. Is that what a Jinn would have done?*' she scolded herself, promising never to let anything like this happen again, "Thank you, Principal Alves."

Principal Alves turned to her, plastering on a wide smile, completely different than the angry expression he had on moments before. "It was no problem, Kesi."

Kesi nodded before asking nervously. "Am I... going to have to come to your office too?"

The principal glanced over a solemn-looking Becky and her friends before moving closer, forcing Roman and Kesi to inch back. When they were far enough away from the others that they wouldn't be overheard he replied, "Just between the... three of us." He glanced up at Roman and flashed him a quick smile. "I'm willing to let your actions go. From what I saw it was very... provoked." He paused for a moment, thinking over his next words as Kesi let out a long-held sigh of relief. "I suggest keeping that from Becky and the others, of course. They may be upset that only they are going to be punished..." He trailed of, obviously not sure what to say next.

"Thank you, Principal Alves," Kesi replied hurriedly. "I can't thank you enough. And this won't happen again. I swear. I'm just... still adjusting. It's different here. *I'm* different here, to everyone else."

The principal smiled at her gently before softening his tone and saying, "I'm sorry that all of this happened." He sighed, quickly looking over at Becky before returning his gaze to Kesi. "To be quite honest, we- the school board and I- were expecting this to happen sooner." The principal looked up at her with sad eyes. "We've been on our toes since you arrived. It was only a matter of time, I suppose."

"Is it.... because I'm from the Middle East?" Kesi asked sadly, finally relaxing her tense limbs as she realized that he was one of the civil humans she had the pleasure of meeting. She was coming to understand the way that most humans at Waterford worked now. For some reason, her being "from" the Middle East was a huge problem or important note in one way or another. Kesi only wished that she knew why it all mattered so much. It made no sense to her.

Principal Alves could only nod. "Unfortunately, we cannot stop the media and other influences from touching our student body, although I will do everything I can to ensure that this does not happen again." He paused for a moment. "Is there any way that I could make it up to you, Kesi?"

Unsure if she was actually supposed to think of something, Kesi debated with herself for a moment. *'He seems genuine, but I don't know if I should really ask for something. I feel like I should be punished, but maybe...'* her face split into a grin as an idea rushed to the surface.

"There is one thing...," she blurted, unable to stop herself. "Coach Murray let me join the football team because of how fast I am and how much I love to play, but he's not so sure if I'll be allowed to play in an actual game. Would it be possible for you to let me do that...?" She gave him as charming of a smile as she could muster, wishing with all her might that he would agree.

Principal Alves laughed, throwing his head back in mirth. Kesi's happiness almost extinguished itself as she was sure that he was laughing *at* her.

Wiping tears from his eyes, the principal answered. "You certainly know how to negotiate, Kesi." He thought for a moment. "I suppose if I can pardon you for almost attacking another classmate, I can let you play football."

Kesi's smile grew wider than she had ever felt it grow before, and she started to jump up and down like a child, cheering. "Thank you, thank you, thank you!"

The principal laughed again. "Stay safe, Kesi, I'll check in soon to see how you're doing." He turned back to Becky and, resuming his stance of near-terrifying authority, he told the brunette, "Let's go, Miss Oakley, shall we? Your friends should be nice enough to clear your place for you."

As the principal disappeared through the hall doors, towing a sulking Becky along with him, excitement started to bubble up inside Kesi. She turned to Roman who was still standing behind her like a silent guardian and she was about to exclaim her happiness when she froze. The look in his eyes was so intense and so uncommon that Kesi was unsure for a moment what it was. A memory flashed before her eyes of that same look on Roman's face when Taylor and Nico yelled at him in the Health Wing. He was angry. But this time his anger wasn't directed at Taylor or Nico or even Becky. He wasn't even looking at her, but Kesi knew that he wanted to. Her happiness fizzled when she realized who Roman was angry with.

'Me. Roman's really angry... with me,' her inner voice choked on the words.

"I'm sorry," she said quietly, her voice sounding pathetic and weak even in her own ears.

"You can't do that crap, Kesi," Roman still wasn't looking at her, but his tone was dark. "All that talk about how fighting and arguing doesn't get you anywhere-"

"Are you calling me a hypocrite?" Kesi wasn't sure if she should feel hurt, ashamed, or angry, although in that moment her brain decided to make her feel a mixture of all three. "I was *defending* myself."

"By calling her disgusting? That's something that she would do," Roman's voice was quiet. Kesi opened her mouth to respond, but nothing more than a guilt-ridden squeak slipped out. She gulped as if trying to swallow down the memories of what had just happened.

'What have I done?' Kesi thought, tearing her eyes away from Roman's face. 'Calling a person disgusting... that is something that Becky would do.' Her stomach lurched at the thought of being anything like that girl, although she knew that it was already too late. She had done exactly the same thing that Becky Oakley, school bully, would have done. 'What happened to staying above it all, to putting the mission first? To putting Roman first? What have I done?' Now Roman was angry, and she just might have ruined everything.

Kesi felt a burning sensation behind her eyes and soon felt

wetness trail down her cheeks. She almost looked up to see if the rain had caused a hole in the roof above her, but as soon as she touched the water on her face, she knew that it had come from her own eyes.

"Kesi…," Roman's image before her turned blurry as tears overtook her vision. "Wait, I… I didn't mean to…"

"I'm fine," Kesi replied, sniffing and wiping her eyes quickly, blinking back new tears. This was a new sensation, and Kesi didn't like it at all. Water burned as it escaped her eyes, and she felt as if her throat were closing. "I'm fine."

"No, Kesi-" Roman started, but Kesi cut him off, averting her eyes from him. His gaze was too intense for her right now.

"You know… I'm not really that hungry. I'm just going to head back to class," she tossed him a half-hearted smile before moving to pick up the pieces of her glass plate that had shattered on the floor. Roman mimicked her actions, grabbing any piece of food or part of her plate within reach.

"I'll go back with you," he offered. Kesi still wasn't looking at him, but she could feel his eyes on her, searching her worriedly. She had never cried in front of him before, much less because of words *he* had said. She couldn't blame him for being flustered about it. It startled Kesi, too. She couldn't remember the last time that she had cried. She didn't think she ever *had* cried before. Nothing this bad had happened to her. Nothing as bad as her first week of school had ever happened before. All her life, the emotional buffer Jinn City provided had protected her from things like this. Without it, she had no idea what to do with all these feelings.

The first day, Taylor and Nico had interrogated her about her religion and her looks. The second day, Ruby and Alexis had spoken to her about being an outsider and had made her feel as if she should look at herself that way, even if she hadn't before. They had made her feel like she was expected to feel out of place, and it made her start to pay attention to things that didn't matter back in her old realm. Looks. Beliefs. She didn't even want to think about how she was tackled by Owen Green during her first football practice. On her third day, Ruby and Alexis had tracked her down, demanding that she care about things she hardly knew about. Things that she never thought about because in her realm they didn't matter. On her fourth day, Alexis and Ruby published that horrifically untrue article about her and her beliefs, portraying her as someone that she didn't even know how to be. They had taken her words and twisted the into a false article that fit what they believed in.

And then today, Becky had tripped her, insulted her, and laughed at her pain and humiliation. Taylor had made awful comments about her, and their whole group had laughed until they couldn't breathe while everyone else just watched. All of this on top of her repulsive reaction to it made Kesi feel horrible. The more she thought about it, the harder it was to keep the tears from falling. Kesi bit her bottom lip in the hopes of stopping it from wobbling and initiating her to break down sobbing.

"No, it's fine," Kesi found it hard to choke out the words. Was this how all humans were when they cried? It felt as if a huge weight was trying to crush Kesi flat, pressing down on her chest. She quickly grabbed the items from Roman's hands. "I'll be fine."

"Kesi, wait, I…," Roman started, but she didn't let him finish his sentence before she ran off, dumping her broken plate and dirty food in a trash can she passed before practically sprinting out of the Kasper House, leaving Roman behind.

Kesi ducked into the first bathroom that she found, slamming a stall door shut behind her, giving herself some privacy. She leaned against one wall, trying to calm her labored breathing. She didn't like this feeling that came with the crying. She felt as if her body were crumbling into pieces. Giving up on trying to hold herself together, Kesi closed her eyes and allowed the tears to fall. They fell for the stress of the week, the comments made by those who couldn't care less about her, and the words of the people she couldn't care less about. For the first time, Kesi really allowed herself to miss home.

She missed the warm, comforting air and all her friends that she loved. She missed watching the sunset over the Ghul and the stars from the roof of her camp. She missed going to the marketplace and visiting Kefira. She missed walking through the streets of the City with Fatima or Shakila or whoever she had run into that day. She missed having to save Ra'id from Divya. She missed the way that Jinn City took care of her, made sure that no one felt fury, or sadness, or desperation. The homesickness, guilt, and sadness only made more tears fall as Kesi sank to the bathroom floor, feeling defeated and alone, letting herself become completely undone.

CHAPTER TWENTY-FIVE

DANVILLE, VIRGINIA

Roman

CHEMISTRY, AS ALWAYS, was full and energetic. Dr. Denney's sound effects were just as strange as she wrote, and the habit she had of pausing class to draw one cartoon character or another on the board was in full swing. However, as engaging as the class was, Roman couldn't will himself to concentrate. His gaze kept flickering over to Kesi. He was surprised that she'd still sat beside him, after what he'd said. He knew that it was only a few words, but he'd implied that what Kesi said was just as bad as everything that Becky had ever done. Implied that she was the same person as, or similar to, Becky. '*And I don't believe that. I don't believe that at all.*'

After everything that had happened that week with Ruby, Alexis, Owen, Taylor, and Nico, Becky and her gang of friends, he should have at least stood by her side. He should have at least waited for her to recover from what had happened before telling her that she could have handled the situation better. '*I know that she was only trying to defend herself, but she could have gotten in a lot of trouble,*' he thought to himself. He had only reacted badly because he was worried about her and upset at how close she came to getting into serious trouble. *'Alves could've expelled or suspended her. I don't know what I'd do if she had to leave. I haven't had enough time with her. I haven't...'*

His thoughts were cut off as Kesi adjusted herself in her seat. He was surreptitiously starting at her between his fingers, his head resting in his hand.

Kesi's mouth was turned down in a soft frown that Roman had never seen on her face before, and she looked paler. *'Are her eyes red? God... seeing her cry...,'* he thought, his chest tightening uncomfortably. It killed him to see her break down like that. It made him want to rip his own heart out and stomp on it. Sophia would have been so disappointed in him. She always told him to stay kind. *'She doesn't deserve to feel like this,'* his mind continued, *'Not after everything Becky put her through... put us through... since Kesi got here. She's allowed to be angry. And stand up for herself.'* He glanced at Kesi again, his breathing becoming more difficult as he thought about how she almost got expelled. If Kesi had only stood up for herself in a less public place, she wouldn't have put herself at risk. That was what he wanted to say in Kasper House. He just wanted to remind her to be careful. *'Should have told her that, Lovett,'* Roman thought bitterly. *'Stupid. Why did you have to put it like that?'*

Roman cast another glance at the blonde sitting next to him. She had come back into Algebra with her head lowered, and when Ben leaned forward to rub her back affectionately and mumble in her ear Roman had heard Kesi sniffling and gasping for breath. When he had leaned forward to apologize to her, Ben had caught his eye and shook her head seriously at him. Her reaction made him sit back in his seat instead of apologizing, which he was now regretting. Kesi hadn't spoken to him for the rest of the class and was now sitting silently next to him for Chemistry. She hadn't said a word to him at all, and he worried that he'd hurt her in a way that they couldn't come back from. It scared him senseless to think that she couldn't trust him anymore because of a few stupid and careless words.

After Dr. Denney told them that they could head to their next class, Roman heard Ben mumble something to Aasma before swooping to Kesi's side and guiding her out of the classroom. Ben's actions only made Roman feel more terrible. Kesi must have told her something, said something about how the whole sequence of events made her feel. Roman wasn't blind- Ben was keeping Kesi away from him.

"You alright, man?" Kharim put a hand on Roman's shoulder as they exited the classroom, letting Ben and Kesi move farther ahead.

"Is she?" Roman motioned towards Kesi, making Kharim sigh.

"I don't know," he admitted. "She didn't talk to me. Did you say that you're sorry?"

"Ben is giving her time to cool off," Aasma replied. "She's still… I don't know. Ben said that she told her that she hasn't cried in a long time and it kind of freaked her out that she cried in the first place."

"Does she hate me?" Roman questioned, the words tumbling out of his mouth. Kharim and Dimitri both snorted, clearly amused by Roman's statement. Aasma only looked at him sympathetically.

"You're over thinking it," Aasma assured him. "I don't think she's as upset with you as she is with herself."

"What do you mean?" Roman asked, not feeling any better. He didn't want his words to make Kesi feel bad about herself.

"I mean, she knows what she did," Aasma explained. "And she's not proud of it. Just let her deal with that first."

Ben and Kesi didn't come to the library for break, and Roman only saw Kesi again when she returned from wherever Ben had dragged her to before Ben had to leave for Dance class. Kesi took a seat on the other side of Aasma, away from Roman, for their free block. Roman couldn't stop staring at her, waiting for her to look up at him and smile, or at least give him some sort of sign that she was ready to talk again. Roman wanted nothing more than to apologize, but he just didn't know when or how.

"S-should I wait for you?" Roman asked as he trotted after her like a lost puppy as she made her way to the Health and Fitness Wing to change for football practice.

"I uh...," she didn't bother to finish her sentence, ducking her head away the more that Roman looked at her.

"I'm sorry," Roman felt as if the words had been pent up inside him for a thousand years. "I'm so, so, so sorry. I didn't mean what I said."

"I know," Kesi replied, still not turning to meet his eyes as they made their way to the locker room hallway.

'*You're killing me, Kesi,*' Roman wanted to tell her. '*Please, please look at me.*'

"You don't have anything to be sorry for," she added after a bit of silence. "So, I... don't have anything to forgive you for."

"Can you still forgive me anyway?" Roman replied quietly. "I don't like to see you upset."

"Well, I don't like to see you angry at me," Kesi retorted, finally spinning around to face him as they approached the girls' locker room. "So, *I'm* sorry for being a complete idiot and not thinking straight. If I could go back and fix it I would, but I can't, so I'll just take your advice next time and not try to rip out Becky's throat."

Roman just blinked at her for a few seconds, bewildered at her words. How could she think that she was the one who needed to apologize? She was clearly confident in that idea, though, since her eyes and face were free of tears and her blue gaze was determined as she looked at him.

"For the love of... Can you stop looking at me like that?" Her face formed a scowl. "I wish you'd just hit me."

"What?" Roman snapped out of his shocked silence at her words. "Hit you?"

"Yeah," Kesi replied, placing both hands on his chest and pushing him backwards. "Hit me. Punch me. Isn't that what people do when they're mad?"

"Why?" Roman looked at her, confused beyond belief, as she

pushed him again. Angry tears started to form in her eyes as she replied with, "Because… I'm an idiot. A-a-and I need a good punch in the face."

"I'm not going to hit you," Roman told her, shaking his head the more she tried to push him.

"Why, because I'm a *girl*?" Kesi huffed, pushing him harder. "Or is it because I'm from the *Middle East*? Because I'm a *victim*? Why, Roman, why? Just *hit me*, Roman!"

Roman grabbed her wrists before she could push him again, causing her tear-filled gaze to look up at him. He understood now, or at least he understood the best he possibly could. She felt like, because she had almost physically hurt someone else, she deserved to be hit, punched, whatever she was trying to make him do. It didn't help that everyone was treating her different because of who she was or who people saw her as, making her feel like she deserved it more.

"I'm not going to hit you," Roman said seriously, looking her in the eye. "Not because you're a girl, or because you're from the Middle East, or because people think that you're a victim, but because you're my friend and I care… about you. I'm not going to hit you because I don't *want* to hit *you*, Kesi."

The blonde blinked at him for a few moments before sighing, letting her forehead crash into his chest. "I'm an idiot."

"Kind of," Roman chuckled, releasing the girl's wrists and wrapping his arms around her in a brief hug. "We should get changed."

"You'll wait for me, right?" Kesi looked up at him with wide eyes, making Roman laugh more.

"Of course, why not, Roomie," he told her, making her smile. Roman had to resist sighing in relief. He was glad to see that he hadn't hurt her so bad after all. Aasma was right- it was more of Kesi going against herself than Kesi hating him, and he was glad. As long as she didn't hate him, Roman could help her get through high school and Becky Oakley. And Roman wanted nothing more than to help her.

CHAPTER TWENTY-SIX

DANVILLE, VIRGINIA

Kesi

KESI HAD KNOWN what stereotypes, bullying, and teasing were long before she came to the human world thanks to Elder Iamar. Still, it was so… odd to experience it herself. Like with all things- city lights, humans, Roman- it was different once Kesi saw it, or rather, felt it, firsthand.

She was glad that she and Roman started talking again, it was hard to ignore him when he was looking at her like he wouldn't be able to live with himself if he even sensed that she was about to cry again. Crying, another thing she had experienced firsthand earlier that day, was something that she planned never to do again if she could help it. Fighting with Roman was also on that same list.

One other thing to put on that list: becoming the way that Nico, Taylor, and Becky wanted her to be. That girl would be violent, easily disturbed, and disliked. Kesi didn't want to be that girl. She didn't want to be the kind of girl that Alexis and Ruby wanted her to be either. She didn't want to search for victims of crimes or injustices and force them to comply with her own plans, she didn't want to spout her opinions on things she didn't understand, and she didn't want to manipulate other people so she came out looking like the hero. She didn't want to be that girl either. She couldn't. She wouldn't.

Kesi knew that she needed to remind herself who she was before she got lost in the mess of the human world. She wasn't Kesi Haddad, not really, she was Kesi the Genie. Kesi the Jinn Savior sent to this world by an all-powerful Jinn goddess who believed in her with every fiber of her magical being. Now Kesi just had to believe in herself too, in genie and in human form. These people wouldn't break her, especially not with the Chosen One and a couple of level-headed humans on her side.

The bathroom mirror was showing Kesi the nervous look she had on her face, and she sighed. Dressed in a baby blue t-shirt and jeans, makeup done, and hair brushed and hanging down her back and sides, Kesi was ready for the night's adventure. She only had a few minutes before Emma would be driving her and Roman downtown to meet Ben and the others, but she wasn't ready to go downstairs yet. Downtown Danville was completely foreign to her, having never been there before, so she didn't know what to expect. It was sending nervous and excited butterflies through her stomach. She had felt much better earlier after practice, where she'd excitedly told Coach Murray that Mr. Alves was going to let her play in real games. Ian was trying to go harder on her because she'd be playing when it counted, but she had been too giddy to let exhaustion set in, not even at the end of practice.

A knock on her door drew Kesi's attention, and she turned to see Roman poking his head through it, looking around the space for her. Kesi giggled, making Roman look over at her and smile, taking her reaction as an invitation to enter.

"You ready?" he asked, leaning against the wall and shoving his hands into his pockets as he smiled at her from across the room.

Kesi glanced at the mirror before turning back to him. "Yeah," she replied. "Are you?"

"Am I ever?" he chuckled. "Come on, let's go."

Kesi followed Roman downstairs and to the garage, where Emma was waiting for them in the car. Kesi recognized some of the first streets that they drove down from the path to school, but they soon veered off to travel along another road framed by small, brightly-colored houses before emptying out to a large square, larger than even the marketplace back in Jinn City.

Old-looking brick buildings stood edge to edge, the only thing marking them as different being the color of the bricks and the different signs above the doors. A small road separated the buildings from the green area at the center, decorated with a few trees and cobblestone paths. As Emma drove around this area, Kesi spotted a marble fountain in the center, the water flowing from a decorative, tower-like structure.

"Here we are!" Emma said excitedly as they pulled up to a little blue building on the left side of the green area. It stood apart from the rest of the buildings by being separated with roads and sidewalks on both sides. The sidewalk crossed over a lovely bridge that overlooked a waterfall and a charming little stream. The building itself was painted light blue with an awning spreading from one edge to the other, colored in a striped pattern of navy and white. Above the awning, the words *Blue's Ice Cream* were placed on the wall in fancy, white letters. There were two pairs of doors at opposite ends of the building. The pair on the left had the words *enter* painted on the glass in white, and the pair on the right had the white word *exit*. A few white metal tables and chairs were scattered in between the two sets of doors directly in front of the building. That was where Ben, Dimitri, and the twins sat waiting when they pulled up.

"Do you have the money I gave you?" Emma asked Roman as he opened the car door. Roman nodded and smiled at his mother, giving her a, "Bye, Mom!" before darting out the door.

"Thanks for taking us, Emma!" Kesi grinned at the red-haired woman before copying Roman, sliding out of the door that he had left open. Kesi closed it softly before Emma pulled the car away.

"Kesi!" Aasma's voice drew her attention to where they were sitting. Kesi turned and smiled at them, trotting over to join them.

"Did you two kiss and make up?" Kharim asked, making his sister elbow him in the side. "Ow! I was just asking!"

"Yeah, we're fine," Kesi answered, smiling at the twins and then at Ben. Ben had been especially worried about her.

"Finally," Ben rolled her eyes and laughed. "It only took you forever."

"T-that's... just not true. It was like... two hours," Roman mumbled, and even without looking at him Kesi could tell that he was blushing.

"Can we get ice cream?" Kesi asked, almost whining. Her friends responded by laughing and quickly guided her inside, taking Kesi into a white tile-floored room with stacks of candy on the wall to Kesi's left and a long counter holding up glass at an angle right in front of her. Kesi ran up to the glass, looking down at the two rows of colorful ice cream spanning all the way down the counter.

"Oh! This is so cool!" Kesi exclaimed, her fingertips now cold to the touch. She'd never seen so much ice cream before! Kesi observed the stickers on the glass, two for each section of ice cream. "Fire-cracker," she read aloud, looking back at the ice cream below her. "Which one is that?"

Roman appeared at her side and pointed to the tub of red-colored ice cream right underneath her. "That one."

"Oh," Kesi replied. "Oh! What's that blue stuff?"

Roman laughed at her child-like curiosity. "That's superman ice cream. It's good."

"I want superman, then," Kesi replied, grinning at Roman.

"I got you, girl," Ben smiled at her before turning to the boy behind the counter. "Hey! Can we have a medium superman ice cream in a cup, please?"

"No cone?" Kharim asked, looking skeptical. Ben turned to him seriously and said, "She's not ready yet. Did you see how she was last week with the ice cream at Roman's? A cone would be too much."

"Thanks, I guess?" Kesi wasn't so sure if Ben was insulting her or looking out for her.

The boy behind the counter held out a clear plastic cup for Kesi to take. She felt the coldness of the ice cream through the cup as she took it from the boy. Ignoring the sounds of her friends ordering, Kesi grabbed a plastic spoon, scooped some of the delicious treat onto it, and shoved it into her mouth. Her tongue was still surprised by the cold texture of the treat, however, that did not stop the flavor explosion going on in her mouth. The superman ice cream was sweet, and tasted like... '*Honey, berries, and something* else," she decided, although she couldn't identify the last ingredient. She rolled the taste easily through her mouth and hummed her approval. Roman, who was paying her more and more attention, noticed her reaction as he received his light green ice cream and laughed. Kesi smiled back cheekily. She had to give it to these humans. For all their faults, they really did know how to make good food. '*I have to take some ice cream back to Jinn City. It'll be great on those hot days.*'

The six of them sat outside in the white chairs provided enjoying the warm evening air. The temperature reminded Kesi of home. She gobbled up her treat quickly before throwing the cup in a nearby trash can. Kesi waited impatiently for the others to finish, all her friends besides Aasma trying to chomp down on the waffle cones that were holding their ice cream.

Once they were all finished, Aasma grinned and started to unzip the small bag hanging around her waist. "Now it's time for pictures!"

"Yes!" Ben pumped one fist into the air. "I'm ready to be a model, Aasma!"

Aasma and Kesi giggled at the girl's reaction. Kesi watched

Aasma pull a digital camera out from her bag, swinging the strap attached to the device around her neck. Aasma took Kesi's hand and guided her across the street carefully, looking both ways to avoid any cars. Kesi glanced behind her to see the rest of her friends following them, talking happily.

Aasma directed Kesi to the fountain. "Sit down and kind of lean back on your palms...," Kesi slowly did what Aasma commanded of her, making Aasma grin. "Good. Now look away from me, like towards the street... you got it! Great!" Aasma laughed as Kesi did as she was told. Kesi heard a series of clicking sounds before Aasma continued. "Now... um... How about you lay down and put your head in Roman's lap."

"What?" Kesi snapped her head around to the giggling girl. "Oh, come on, stop trying to get us together."

"Just do it!" Aasma laughed, pointing Roman over to where Kesi sat on the cool edge of the marble fountain. Roman did as Aasma suggested, sitting down next to Kesi and awkwardly shuffling his feet on the cobblestone under the soles of his shoes. Kesi giggled and flopped down on her back, resting her head carefully in his lap.

"Hi," Kesi grinned up at him, making him roll his eyes playfully.

"Hi, Kesi," he replied, looking down at her and breaking into a smile.

Click-click-click. "Aw, you guys are so cute!" Aasma squealed, skidding over to sit next to them as Kesi raised herself into an upright position. "Come on, guys!" she called. "Group photo!"

Kharim, Ben, and Dimitri laughed and joined the three of them on the fountain's edge. Aasma raised her camera high, positioning it so that they would all end up in the photo once she took it. Kesi grinned at the lenses, feeling Roman slip his arm around her shoulders before the camera *click-click*ed again. They all laughed as Aasma brought down the camera and showed them the picture of the six of them smiling wide at the camera, even catching Roman mid-laugh.

Kesi admired the way that his eyes shone in that picture- it was nice to see pure happiness in his eyes.

"That's going in the family photo album," Kesi joked before Aasma put her camera away.

"What... what is your family like, anyway?" Kharim asked. "You haven't talked a ton about them."

Kesi paused, unsure of how to answer. She bit her lip and looked away, not wanting to reveal her lie. "I... don't even know how to explain them, that's all."

"What about your dad?" Aasma leaned forward, interested, making it impossible for Kesi to avoid her gaze. "What is he like?"

Kesi looked around at her eager friends, frantically trying to collect her thoughts. '*What* is *my father like?*' It was a stupid question to ask, of course. The name on her documents that was listed as her father didn't link back to anyone- Azeem Haddad, Bonnie Haddad, Yasmeen and Panya, none of them really existed. Still, Kesi had to answer Aasma's question in some way, any other way than with the truth. Kesi thought about her real home back in Jinn City and recalled all the people that she saw as family. If she were to pick out one, who would be her father?

Ra'id's face appeared in her mind and Kesi smiled, finding her answer. "He's...well, he's a dad, he's responsible. He can be serious when he needs to be; he takes his work seriously, of course, but he also knows how to have fun. He's a family guy- he plays sports with me and... my younger sister a lot. That's how I know how to play football and stuff."

"And your mother?" Dimitri questioned quietly. This one was easy. After all, who had she been calling "Mother" all her life?

"She's... very motherly. Your stereotypical parent, I guess," Kesi answered. "She's a go-with-the-flow kind of person. I don't think I've ever seen her angry or scared. You guys would like her."

"What about your sisters?" Even Roman sounded interested now. Kesi realized how little she had talked about her own family in that moment. She'd mentioned them enough to pipe her friends' interests, but not enough to let them know anything about her or them.

Kesi thought for a moment. She knew lots of girls in Jinn City, but who did she know well enough to describe for her friends, much less remember that they were who she was based her mythical sisters on?

Kesi snorted when an idea came to her, laughing at herself. '*So now I'm missing Divya? I really am in a different world.*'

"Well, my older sister, Panya, is such a kiss up at times, especially to my parents. A lot of people think she's this perfect girl, but I know better," Kesi said, thinking back to her last encounter with Divya - how Divya had bowed to her and called her the Jinn Savior like everyone else. "Still, she has her kind moments, I guess."

"What about your other sister?" Ben asked, looking at her with wide eyes.

Kesi chuckled, remembering little Fatima back in Jinn City, wondering briefly what she was doing now. Was she playing games in the Ghul, or was she already asleep by now? "F- Yasmeen… she's a lot like me. Except clumsier. Maybe it's a…a nine-year-old thing," Kesi ended with a shrug.

"Or a Haddad family thing," Roman nudged his shoulder with hers playfully.

"I am *not* clumsy!" Kesi retorted, shoving Roman slightly. She felt heat rise to her cheeks as her friends began to laugh at her. "Hey-!"

An almost snake-like hiss screamed from above, attracting attention from everyone in the square. Kesi's head whipped around to see a dark figure on top of one of the old buildings, eyes glowing a murky purple in the dim streetlight. The creature had night black skin that looked leathery in the glow of downtown. Pieces of black metal covered its shoulders like sharp pads or armor and continued to climb but its head like a poorly constructed helmet. It moved, pacing from one edge of the roof to the other, swinging its head around like a wild animal as it observed the terrified humans below. When it turned, Kesi could see glimpse of more dark metal patches embedded in its skin, jutting out like thorns on its back.

Black magic had deformed the creature's figure, making it less than a genie. Kesi knew what it was from myth and legend, but only when it hissed again, flashing purple-black fangs, did she snap into action.

"*Run!*" Kesi screamed at her friends, joining the chorus of terror-ridden cries rising all around them. "*Run!*"

Kesi grabbed Roman's shirt and pulled him to his feet, prompting the others to do the same. Kesi pushed Roman forward as he started to run for his life as well, and only seeing that they were obeying her command did Kesi start to sprint as well, making sure to keep behind the rest. Kesi turned to look back at the Shaytan as the creature jumped off the roof and landed on the sidewalk underneath him with a *boom*. Kesi narrowed her gaze at the creature, her heart racing as she knew what she had to do.

'*Self-faith, self-faith,*' Kesi's brain repeated as she branched off from the rest of her friends, ducking into the first alley she saw. She glanced quickly around the corner to make sure that her friends were still running before she pressed her back against the wall, taking as deep of breaths as she could manage.

Kesi grabbed the necklace at her throat, rubbing the pendant furiously. She sighed in relief as she felt the cold, magical mist wrap around her ankles. '*At least the spell worked,*' she thought. She didn't even want to ponder what she would do if Queen Ena's spell decided not to function in the human realm. Once the mist disappeared, Kesi looked down at her genie form and grinned. Her glittery skin, blue hair, clothing, and magic were all back in full force. Her veins were humming with energy. It had been a long time since she'd felt like this.

"That's better," Kesi muttered, squaring her shoulders. After being without all her magic for so long, to finally have it back was euphoric. Somehow, she felt as if it were even more powerful now in a world that normally lacked magic. She felt like water -untouchable and dangerous.

Kesi propelled her body straight up into the air, looking down on the square beneath her. The wind rushed past her face and she allowed herself a small smile. It felt good to fly again.

'*Focus,*' she told herself, concentrating at the scene below. The Shaytan was now running after a human couple who were screaming bloody murder as they caught sight of its shiny black claws.

"Hey!" Kesi shouted at it, catching its attention. The Shaytan stopped and cocked its head at her like a very dangerous dog. Kesi summoned a ball of blue-white light to her fingertips before throwing it at the creature in the same way that she had thrown a dodgeball at Matt during PE. The creature hissed once the ball hit him square in the chest, sending him fumbling into the street. A car skidded to the side once the Shaytan was in its headlights, almost causing an accident. The Shaytan regained balance and looked up at Kesi, hissing with anger flashing in its eyes. It then started to run towards her, baring its dark fangs. Kesi sucked back from her position in the air before diving downwards at full speed and colliding with the leathery chest of the creature, pushing them both against a brick wall of a shop. Before the dust had settled, the Shaytan grabbed Kesi by the shoulders and spun her around, throwing her against the wall. Kesi grunted at the impact, trying not to cry out in pain as the broken bricks dug into her skin.

The Shaytan chuckled a raspy, almost painful chuckle that caused Kesi to cringe. Then, to Kesi's surprise, it started to speak in the same hard-to-hear voice. "So... you're Ena's Chosen," it growled. "Can't say I'm impressed."

"You can talk?" Kesi squeaked, knowing how pathetic she must have sounded.

The Shaytan... did it roll its eyes? "Not a very bright one, are you?" it croaked before gripping her shoulders again and flinging her across the square.

Kesi yelped as she flew through the air, unable to regain enough balance to stabilize herself. Instead, Kesi somersaulted once her palms hit the ground to lessen the impact and to get her on her feet again. She spun around just in time to see the Shaytan propelling himself in the air towards her, not flying exactly, but defiantly throwing himself at her.

"Oh Jinn, this is gonna hurt," Kesi cursed before the Shaytan collided with her, knocking her to the ground on her back with such force that Kesi swore she could feel her bones vibrating. Luckily, Kesi had been practicing getting tackled all week during football and she was able to reel herself back to the present. However, being tackled by a human was nothing like being mowed down by a Shaytan, and she had to brace herself against the pain coursing through her. Grinding her teeth together, Kesi resisted the urge to wince in front of such a sinister creature.

Kesi forced herself to breathe as the Shaytan's claws started to slice into her arms. If she wanted to survive this, she needed to think fast. The Shaytan had her slammed against the grassy ground of the square as it reveled in its own power. It hissed down at her, letting strings of black drool fall onto her face.

'He's got my arms pinned...,' Kesi thought, 'But... he forgot one thing.'

As the idea came to her, she grinned, startling and confusing the creature. It slackened its grip a bit, allowing Kesi to move. In one swift movement, Kesi folded in on herself, placing her bare feet on the Shaytan's chest and vaulted the creature away with one kick. It was so magic-fueled and powerful that she sent it crashing into the fountain several yards away while she scrambled to her feet.

Kesi stood quickly, rubbing her arms that now had tiny, bleeding punctures around them. She straightened her spine and pushed her hair out of her face. Her fingers came away with little streaks of blood. Her bottom lip was bleeding even more than her arms. Swallowing the taste of her own blood, Kesi took a deep, steadying breath in then held out her right hand. Concentrating hard, she focused all her magic on her outstretched fingers, imagining a sword fading into existence. Kesi could feel her magic flowing through her. She could feel it when her magic granted her wish and conjured a sword for her, the heaviness of the weapon like a friend in her hand. Mentally directing the river of her power to pour out into the hilt of the sword and fusing it with her magic, Kesi thought, '*It may not be a bow... but this will work nicely.*' Then she grinned at herself as she continued, '*Plus, a sword is pretty badass.*'

The Shaytan stood from the fountain then, and quickly realized what Kesi was trying to do with the now half-glowing sword. A purple-black spike of metal appeared in his hands and he threw it at Kesi. It collided with the weapon in her hands, with spun out of her grasp. Once it left her fingertips, the sword dissolved into thin air, no longer having any magic to keep it in the human realm.

"Crap," Kesi mumbled to herself. She turned and glared at the creature, who was readying another spike to throw as it stood to its full height. Observing it closely, Kesi found that it was blinking rapidly as if trying to get the world to come to focus. Kesi smiled, '*All that portal jumping and fighting made you tired, didn't it?*'

Feverishly, the creature finally threw its spike her way, but Kesi simply jumped out of the way. She found herself underneath the branches of a tree and decided to make them work to her advantage. She climbed up the trunk and tucked herself into the leaves as the Shaytan recovered from its magic using. From there, Kesi flung herself at the Shaytan again, knocking it backwards onto the street. She summoned another ball of light and slammed it into the creature's face, making it yell in pain. Angrily, the Shaytan grabbed Kesi's throat and pulled her upwards, slamming her against a brick wall. Kesi gasped in pain as her oxygen was cut off from her lungs.

The Shaytan chuckled at her for a few moments as she clawed at its grip on her throat, searching desperately for air.

"Stupid Jinn," the Shaytan's figure started to become fuzzy in Kesi's vision as he taunted her. "You don't know that you will lose. The Shaytan will kill the Chosen One, flood the human world, and drain it for our own good. You have already lost."

Kesi's arms went limp at her sides as dark spots started to cloud her vision, blocking out the Shaytan's purple-black fanged grin. With her last amount of energy, Kesi conjured a knife to her fingertips.

"Maybe," Kesi croaked, redirecting the flow of her magic. The Shaytan looked down as the weapon in her hand began to glow, but it was the one who was too late. She tossed the creature a wink. "But not today."

Kesi smiled at the Shaytan as she shoved the magic-infused weapon into its chest. Its purple-black eyes went wide, and its mouth opened to give one final cry. As its strength dwindled, Kesi felt the pressure ease around her throat, and was able to gasp for breath as her feet hit the ground. Still, she didn't dare let her guard down enough to release her weapon.

After a few seconds, Kesi's eyes were objected to a horrific sight as the Shaytan started to disintegrate. Black ash-like particles swarmed around her, but she was too shocked to do anything except stare in horror and amazement as its face started to break apart. The ash settled on the sidewalk, leaving no trace of the creature's body. Glancing down, Kesi caught the sight of her knife, which had changed had summoned it. Its light was dimmed and the whole object was tinged in a purple-black color, like the creature it had just killed. She blinked for a few moments, not understanding what had happened.

"My magic absorbed the black magic," Kesi said to herself, suppressing a hysterical impulse to laugh. The knife must have worked in the same way that the barrier spell in her realm did. Shaytan were made of up black magic and nothing else, meaning the genie it had once been no longer existed in the flesh. Light magic, if used in the right way, could overtake something as evil as that, absorbing and nullifying the darkness. When Kesi had used her knife to take the Shaytan's magic away, there was nothing left but the ashes of the genie that had died so long ago inside of it.

Desperate to get rid of the knife, Kesi used her magic to heat the blade in her hand. It didn't take long. Soon it had been completely melted and reduced to bluish-white ash.

Kesi looked beyond the pile of dust at her feet to see several police cards, lights flashing, stationed on the other side of the square. A large group of men and women in police uniforms stood by them, all with their gazes and guns pointed directly at Kesi. After a few tense moments, the police must have determined that Kesi wasn't planning on rushing towards them, and they lowered their weapons.

Kesi glanced over to where she had left her friends and spotted five heads poking out from the edge of a large window. She nearly collapsed in relief when she saw Roman's wide green eyes, frightened but safe.

Kesi turned back to the police as the tallest of them all approached her, putting away his gun completely. He had tan skin, dark eyes, and graying brown hair. He wasn't ashamed to look scared at the sight of Kesi, however, she could sense that he had been much more terrified of the Shaytan she had slain.

"Who are you?" the officer called out to her.

Kesi had to resist the urge to say her own name. At first thought, what else was she supposed to say? But then she remembered Elder Ashraf's words: *To mend into both duties you must lead two separate lives.*

'*Okay*,' Kesi thought, '*Separate lives... the genie and the human...*'

"Genie," Kesi blurted, not having any other ideas. Mentally slapping herself, Kesi thought, '*Points for creativity, Kesi! Duh, you're a genie!*'

"Genie…" The man repeated before pausing. "Should we be afraid of you?"

"You should be afraid of that," Kesi pointed a finger at the black ashes at her feet. "I'm here to fight them, not you. I'm here to protect you and your people. That's all. I swear."

Figuring it was best not to say any more, Kesi vaulted herself up into the air, disappearing from the square. She landed in a dark parking lot behind a building and quickly thought of her human form as she rubbed her pendant. Her bare feet hit the pavement, and she felt the mist surround her again. When the mist disappeared, Kesi gave herself a once-over to make sure that she was really back to Kesi Haddad. She touched her bottom lip gingerly, expecting her finger to come back coated in blood.

'*How would I explain this to my friends?*' she worried, but when she brought her finger before her eyes, there was nothing there. She blinked in confusion. Queen Ena didn't say anything about injuries transferring between forms, but Kesi supposed that it would be easier on all of them if they didn't.

"One less thing to worry about," Kesi sighed to herself before making her way back to her friends. She slipped through downtown Danville, shifting through the crowds of people who either desperately wanted to see what had happened, or desperately wanted to get away from the square as fast as possible. The people were everywhere, filling spaces between the two sides of the square and making the grassy area look like a popular festival.

Kesi shoved her way to where she had last seen her friends, spotting yellow police tape surrounding the pile of black-and-white ashes that she and the Shaytan had left. She heard police officers yelling at citizens to return to their cars and drive home, as well as a few directing traffic out of the square. Downtown Danville was now a crime scene.

"Kesi!" she turned when she heard Ben's frantic voice somewhere in the crowd. She spotted Roman fighting his way through the people to get to her, Ben hurrying feverishly behind. Kesi couldn't see the twins or Dimitri amongst all the people, but she had no doubt that they were close behind.

'*Oh, right…,*' Kesi cringed when she remembered how she'd disappeared from their sides in the midst of the chaos. Judging by the expressions on Roman and Ben's faces, she was afraid that they wouldn't be very happy with her, maybe even angry with her.

"Where have you been?" Roman exclaimed, grabbing her by the shoulders softly to get a better look at her. His eyes were cloudy with anxiety. "Are you alright?"

Kesi spotted the others appear behind him, all wearing the same look on their faces.

"I'm fine," Kesi told them, taking Roman's hands off her carefully. "I uh… I just tripped back there, and I didn't want to slow you guys down, so I just…I just ducked into another shop when it started to get really bad."

"*Kesi,*" Roman protested, his tone telling Kesi that he clearly aggravated by her actions. Kesi met his gaze shyly. "You can't just… just run off like that, you should have told us, you should have… Just, don't do that again, alright? Next time just ask for help I…," Roman ducked his head away and mumbled softly. "I don't know what I'd do if I got hurt."

"But I didn't," Kesi reassured, putting a hand on his arm. "That… Genie person showed up."

"You saw her too?" Aasma's voice was ecstatic. Kesi looked over to her and saw excitement clear across her face. "She was amazing! I can't believe that Danville has its very own superhero!"

"She was pretty cool," Kharim agreed, hovering over his sister protectively. "But what was that thing she was fighting? Can we talk about that?"

"Evil, let's leave it at that," Kesi replied. She didn't want to speak about her other persona any longer than she had to.

"She… she looked kind of familiar," Roman mused, a lost look on his face. Kesi almost stopped breathing. *'Was Queen Ena wrong about how long I would have before Roman found out the truth?'* she looked over at him, but his face gave her no clear signs that he thought Genie and Kesi were the same. She almost sighed in relief, *'I can't wait to share everything with him, but it's just not safe. I still have time. What he doesn't know can't hurt him, even if that means I have to lie all the time.'*

"What are you talking about, *chico*?" Ben laughed. "I've never seen her before in my life."

Roman thought for a moment. "I guess so. Maybe she was in, like, a textbook about genies or something. Or a comic book. I don't know"

"Benita!" a familiar voice yelled across the crowd. The six teens turned to see the tall police officer that had talked to Kesi as Genie earlier find his way towards them.

"Uncle Ernesto!" Ben giggled, racing up to hug him before talking in a rhythmic tongue that Kesi only half-recognized.

"She speaks Spanish?" Kesi looked at Roman, who nodded.

"Her whole family is fluent," he replied before they both turned back to Ben and the police officer.

"He's my dad's older brother," Ben explained, looking at the rest of them. "He's the sheriff."

"Oh!" Kesi exclaimed, studying the man closely. He did look a lot like Ben- same face shape, same skin tone, same eye color, "Hi, uh…"

"Ernest is fine," the man chuckled. "What are you kids doing out here? You need to get home."

"We were having a party," Ben explained. "Before that evil thing showed up."

Ernest glanced back through the crowd where Kesi could see police lights still flashing. "I probably shouldn't leave but… do you kids need a ride home?"

Ben nodded. "Our parents are probably worried. Is it too much trouble?"

The sheriff shook his head. "None of you live far from here, do you?" He looked at the six of them, politely waiting for their replies.

"No, I don't think so, Sheriff," Roman replied respectfully. "Kesi and I live about five minutes away... If you just want to get us away from all of this, you can drop everyone else off at our house."

Ernest smiled at the teens. "Alright, you six come with me. I'll take you home."

"*Gracias*, Uncle Ernesto," Ben smiled at her uncle before he started to lead them through the crowd to the cluster of police cars stationed a little way down the street.

"I'm sorry that the party was ruined," Roman mumbled into Kesi's ear as they trailed behind the sheriff and the others. Kesi turned and smiled at him.

"What are you talking about? That was awesome," she said. "Of all the things that I thought that I would see here, I didn't think I would see *that*."

Roman chuckled at her but seemed to be at a loss for words. They continued to move through the crowd in silence.

When they reached the bank of cars, the sheriff opened his cruiser's back door so that Kesi and her friends could climb in. Ben took the front passenger seat next to her uncle, giving the rest of them more room. Roman went in first, eager to get out of such a crowded and public setting. Kharim and Aasma entered next, leaving Kesi alone for a few heartbeats. She looked over her shoulder to the Shaytan's ashes and smiled to herself with pride.

'*Queen Ena was right... a little self-confidence and faith went a long way,*' Kesi thought, seeing how it was true. She wouldn't have been able to defeat the Shaytan if she didn't believe she had the strength to do it. And she also knew that she wouldn't have believed she had the strength to do it if she hadn't wanted to protect Roman so fiercely.

Kesi ducked into the police car and situated herself before looking over at Roman. He was staring out of the window with an expression that she couldn't make out. She knew that this first attack wouldn't be the last. Until all the Shaytan were defeated, Kesi doubted that they would stop venturing into the human world, hunting Roman down. She knew now that she would be ready. She had to be, not just because Roman was the Chosen One and Kesi was the Jinn Savior, but because she was starting to understand that she was feeling things for Roman that went far beyond a professional relationship. She wasn't sure what those feelings meant for what they even pointed towards, but she knew that because of those feelings, she couldn't let Roman slip through her fingers.

Kesi turned and looked out the window, watching the houses and cars whizz by. It reminded Kesi of her first night here, and she slipped into a daydream thinking about everything that had happened since. She had come so far since then. Things mattered now that she didn't think would matter, and this mission she had been sent on had become more personal than she had ever imagined.

'*I'll protect you, Roman,*' Kesi thought, as if she could speak to him with her mind. '*Nothing bad will happen to you with me around. I'm the Jinn Savior, I'll watch over you until the time is right for you to save the world. Then you'll be the one protecting me.*'

And for the first time, with a smile on her face and the glow of the streetlights painting her skin, Kesi actually believed that. She really was the Jinn Savior now, and Kesi was sure that there would be turning back now.

End of Book One

Jinn Book Two:
Case of Destiny

Written by Katica Howard

CHAPTER ONE

DANVILLE, VIRGINIA

Roman

DESPITE THE COOL darkness of his room, Roman just couldn't get to sleep. He lay on his back and stared at his ceiling for minutes upon minutes until he started to grow restless in waiting for his brain to doze off. He tossed and turned, his mind switching back and forth between thoughts of the danger that Kesi put herself in tonight by separating from the group and the fight between Genie, with her mysterious identity, and... what did Kesi call it? A Shaytan? Kesi.... Kesi... Kesi. She could have been hurt badly tonight. What was she thinking? She said that she had fell and didn't want to endanger anyone else by making the group wait for her. Roman still wished that she would have called out for his help.

Roman groaned and placed a hand over his eyes, giving up sleep. Kesi told him a week ago that she was a "nervous sleeper." He wondered how she was doing on her sleep. When she said she fell... did she hurt herself? Why didn't he check for that? God, he was so stupid. He should have made sure that she didn't injure herself. Once he realized that she was missing from the group after the Shaytan attacked, he was scared to pieces. He couldn't believe his luck that he had found her unharmed. The possibilities of all that could have happened to Kesi made Roman's heart climb to a panicky beating that he lost control of.

In that moment, Roman heard the sound of his sink and shower bursting to life erupt from his bathroom several feet away. Roman sat up in his bed, throwing the covers off himself and inching closer to try to peek into his bathroom. He nearly screamed when the lamp attached to the top of his loft flickered on by itself.

"What... who-?" Roman stuttered to himself, throwing glances around the empty room while pressing his back up against the wall and keeping an eye on his now-glowing lamp. "What just... what just happened?"

Silence met Roman and he sat on his bed, shocked, for several moment before there was a soft knock at his door.

"Roman?" Kesi's voice made Roman sigh in relief. "Are you ok? I heard you yelling and..."

Roman tossed another look around his room, unsure of what he was even looking for. A Shaytan? The thought sent his already skittish heart racing. What if there was another Shaytan in his room?

"N-no," Roman said in response to Kesi, his breathing rough. "No, I don't know what's happening. Help."

At those words, Kesi burst into his room as if searching for the source of his panic. It didn't take the girl long to notice the sound coming from the bathroom. Roman held his breath as she disappeared through the bathroom doorway to investigate. Roman dug his hands into the sheets around him, frozen in place until he heard Kesi turn off the sink and shower. Once Kesi emerged from the bathroom, Roman let some of the tension escape his shoulders and he relaxed slightly.

"What happened?" she asked as she walked over to look at him from the ground where she stood.

"T-the water and the light just... turned...on...," Roman

replied, straightening himself against the wall, which put the most distance between Kesi and himself. He took one look around his room again, searching for anything that Kesi might have missed, before meeting Kesi's wide eyes. Except that he didn't meet them exactly, since Kesi wasn't looking at his face. At first, Roman was confused as to what Kesi was looking at and why she looked so shocked. When Roman remembered that he was wearing nothing but underwear and that he was giving Kesi virtually a full view of his torso from where he sat, he felt an ocean of heat crash up against his face.

"I...uh...," He couldn't find the right words to say. He couldn't even move. All he could do was stare at Kesi's brilliant blue eyes while she stared back at him.

After what seemed like an eternity, Kesi turned away and cleared her throat, crossing her arms over her chest protectively. Snapping out of his own gaze, Roman found that Kesi's outfit wasn't exactly a full coverage either- a blue tank top and gray shorts covered much but not all, but it was better than what Roman had on.

"They just turned on?" Kesi asked, clearly trying to recover from the awkward situation at hand. Roman covered his stomach with his covers, wanting to disappear into his mattress.

"Yeah," Roman replied, finding just as hard to look at Kesi as it was for Kesi to look at him. "I just... couldn't get sleep and then my shower and sink turned on and then not soon after that so did my lamp."

"Ok, well...," Kesi ran a hand down her face. "Maybe it was just an electrical fluke. Or... or maybe some magic from the Shaytan thing is still left over in the atmosphere... or whatever. I don't know, lots of weird things are happening tonight." She snuck a bashful glance at Roman, making him blush more. "You ok?"

Roman nodded, looking between her and the wall behind her, too embarrassed to meet her gaze on full. Her eyes were too intense in that moment.

"Ok, well," Kesi rocked back and forth on her heels. "I'm going to go, I guess. Night Roomie."

"Night," Roman replied as she moved to leave the room. Once she escaped his sight, Roman leaned forward and flicked his lamp off.

"Roomie?" Roman could barely see her figure in the doorway of his room from over the top of his loft as her voice called out to him from the newly made darkness.

"Yeah?" He asked, echoing her cry from the dark.

"You've been holding out on me, Roomie. You should take your shirt off more often," Kesi muttered her words quiet but still rang like bells in Roman's ears. Once the words had left Kesi's mouth, Roman was mortified to the point where he buried his flushed face into his pillows before she had even closed the door.

'*That did not just happen,*' Roman's head screamed, his eyes wide despite the fact that there was nothing to see in his night-cloaked room. '*She did not just... that did not just happen. There is no way that just happened. She did not just flirt with me. God, I hate her.*'

Click. Roman glanced up as a blinding light filled his vision to see that his lamp had turned n again, all on its own. At first, Roman started to panic again, fear- ridden heat rising from his chest, but then he remembered Kesi's almost-sound explanations. Electrical fluke or... leftover magic. The Shaytan was dead.

Growling at the lamp, Roman twisted the switch at the end of the funnel-shaped light to turn it off again. Whether it was an electrical fluke or leftover magic from an evil genie, it was sure growing annoying.

ACKNOWLEDGEMENTS

I have so many people to thank for getting this off the ground that I don't even know where to begin. I wrote this novel when I was fourteen years old, and it was the first story I'd ever finished, so naturally I wanted to eventually see it in print. It's been many years since I started this journey and there were many times where I didn't believe that it would ever be published, but the people I'm about to thank helped me push through so I could get to this point.

First, I would like to thank my family, who always encouraged me to write and never told me that I was a terrible writer (which I probably was when I first started). They've always believed that I could do this, even after they've watched me abandon multiple projects, lose my passion, and lose my mind over the years.

It's one thing to have your family be there for you but getting praise from other adults and friends in your life really spurs your confidence as well. I also want to thank all the English teachers I've had over the years (which is probably the closest thing I've ever had to a "professional" writer in my life) who have complimented me, pushed me to be a better writer, and to read the writings of others more carefully for guidance. My friends have also been a similar source of encouragement for me. They're always willing to read my writing when I ask, and even though I tell them it's okay to make some less-than-kind notes, they always make sure to let me know that my talent isn't all in my head. So, thank you, you all know who you are.

I would also like to thank my editor, Brittany Campbell. She was the first person who really taught me how to write creatively, how to tweak my stories and how to make them better. Before I started working with Brittany on this project, I had no real idea of how a random, outside person who I had never explained the plot to would perceive my book. She really helped me make it readable and the story would not be as great as it is now without her help.

Lastly, I also like to thank Mrs. Sunderhaft, a family friend, who started me on my writing journey. From my early childhood, she always encouraged me to write and helped me develop my writing style. No matter how I felt about my writing or how strong my desire was to publish a book, Mrs. Sunderhaft was and is one of my strongest supporters, and I could not have gotten to this point without her. I cannot thank her enough and I sincerely hope that she fully understands the influence she's had on me as a writer and as a person.

www.ingramcontent.com/pod-product-compliance
Lightning Source LLC
Chambersburg PA
CBHW030417180626
46812CB00005B/2048